SHROUD OF EXILE

Moira Kane

To all the people in the real Port O'Henry, tethered to that murky bay. This story is for you.

Chapter 1

Gator Bait

Cady

I KNEW WHAT I was supposed to do if I was kidnapped. Jerk my arms down like *this* to break zip ties. Pull the inside release on the trunk if there was one. And if there wasn't one, I knew how to punch out the back brake light and signal for help.

What most of those online self-defense videos don't teach is how to handle being kidnapped when you're *freaking out because you've just been kidnapped.*

Adrenaline zinged up my legs, urging me to run. Run where, exactly? I was in the trunk of someone's car! Or at least that was where I thought I was. The surface beneath me bumped up and down, jostling my body in the cramped, dark space. My eyes were covered with thick fabric, hands firmly cinched behind my back.

Breath rushed between my lips. I felt like a cornered animal. Panic. There was too much panic to think straight.

Focus, Cady. Focus or you're going to get serial killed.

Gravel crunched and clanged against metal beneath me. Definitely in the trunk of a car. If we were driving on a dirt road it didn't tell me much about my whereabouts. Plenty of the older roads in Port O'Henry were unpaved. Private driveways, too.

Oh, lord. What if I was heading to one of those secluded houses way out on the edge of town? They were surrounded by acres of property and seven-foot privacy walls. No one would hear me scream.

Speaking of screaming—"Hey! Someone help me! Help!" The cry came out shrill. I yelled again but it was like one of those nightmares where I couldn't squeeze my voice out of my throat. More clanging covered any noise I made. I heard the buzz of a radio turned up too loud.

No, no, no. This wasn't happening to me.

I struggled against the ties on my wrists, but they were so tight my forearms ached. My shoulders were pinned behind my neck and every little wiggle hurt.

The sudden jolt as the movement stopped was so ominous and horrifying that vomit threatened at the back of my mouth. How did I get here?

Really, what was the last thing I could remember before waking in this trunk?

Cool air whooshed into the cramped space, and I seized my opportunity. My scream was cut short as a hand clamped my mouth shut. Another slapped tape over my lips. The cry I choked on was so loud it buzzed in my throat. Blood seeped between my teeth and pooled on my tongue.

I couldn't see. I couldn't speak. I couldn't move as more hands gripped my arms and hoisted me from the car, depositing me roughly onto uneven ground. Gritty sand brushed my cheek. Muggy air hung heavily around me, the scent of swamp and earth.

The bayou. They'd taken me to Barbeaux Bayou.

The panic that was already a fluttering bird in my insides became more vicious and painful. It pecked at my heart until I was sure it would seize up and stop pumping. A deep reptilian hiss sounded, and I knew what I would see before the blindfold was ripped from my eyes—alligators.

Two massive alligators were perched halfway on the shore of Paxton River. Water lapped against their scales, their tails thrashing as they hissed at each other again. I wasn't normally afraid of alligators. They weren't aggressive unless provoked. You avoided them and they would avoid you.

But I'd heard whispers of man eaters from the time I was a little girl. As I grew, I learned the rest of the story: there were alligators accustomed to the taste of human flesh because someone was feeding it to them. It seemed I had discovered that someone.

The only real knowledge I had of crime came from watching detective shows with my grandparents. Not particularly accurate but I was pretty sure of one thing; if they took the blindfold off, they didn't intend for me to live.

There was no word for the dread in my stomach. Fear became all-consuming and the world tilted around me.

"Dale Barlow," a man clipped from behind me. His voice was unfamiliar, the accent indistinguishable from any other East Texan.

I winced when he ripped the tape off my mouth, taking skin with it. "W-what?"

"You're his secretary."

"N-no—" I had to swallow back more bile. "I'm his book-keeper."

"Same thing." This voice was different, Hispanic but also unfamiliar.

"I only tracked his business expenses." Was mister Barlow doing something illegal and somehow involved me? "I'm not even a real bookkeeper," I blurted, "I'm just good with num-bers. It was a favor to my Nana. The job, I mean. It was—"

"Do I look like I care about your sob story?" The first man spat. He paced closer, long shadow looming over me. "Barlow stole a shit ton of money from us. I want to know where it is."

"I don't know!" I screamed it.

The second man was prodding the alligators with a long stick. As he did, he tossed a piece of raw chicken high in the air. One alligator caught it with a snap. "They're hungry tonight, chica."

Holy shit, no!

"Please!" Tears spilled down my cheeks. I'd always imagined I would be strong in this kind of moment, glaring defiantly at the men who dared assault me. Nope, I was just a blubbering mess. It would be embarrassing if not for the whole about-to-die thing. "I don't know anything about missing money. Please!"

"Miguel is going to jog your memory." The binds behind my hand suddenly popped away. Before I could react, I was yanked forward, knees dragging across gritty earth because I just had to wear shorts in October. An iron grip shackled my forearm, forcing my hand toward the waiting mouth of an alligator.

"Wait!" I sobbed, "please wait. I have copies!"

"Copies?" Miguel halted, my arm throbbing in his hold.

"Of his business records. I have all the paperwork he left when he died. Surely, it's in there somewhere!"

"I don't give a fuck about paperwork." He twisted my arm closer and the joint at my elbow popped painfully. "What I want is the money he owed us for what was on the boats."

"B-boats?" As far as I knew, Barlow only had one boat. Three if you counted kayaks but somehow, I didn't think he was ferrying criminal amounts of cash on those.

Suddenly I flew backwards into the sand, a foot connecting with my gut. I gasped but it did nothing to inflate my flattened lungs. My chest pounded and the air still wasn't coming. Was a piece of my rib stabbing into my organs?

Miguel and his accomplice were arguing. I couldn't understand what they were saying over the hammering in my skull.

Above me the stars seemed too bright, waving and blinking. The moon was watery as it melted into the black silk sky. I never did take time to stargaze. In a town like Port O'Henry light pollution was non-existent, the moon and stars showy and vibrant. Now I would never have the chance to see them again.

With a gasp I was finally breathing, though every inhale hurt. Somehow, I was still peripherally aware that I was a mere ten feet from two alligators that were ready to eat me.

I glanced at the man I thought was Miguel. With the headlights shining into my eyes and his face turned toward the blackness of the bayou I couldn't make him out, only the shadowy silhouette of a well-built figure. He threw his hands up in the air and shouted something to his partner, reaching into his waistband and pulling out—a gun.

Pleas tumbled from my mouth. I wasn't sure what I was saying. But I didn't want to die, *God I don't want to die!*

A rustle sounded from a copse of bald cypress at the river's edge, something heavy moving fast through the tangled understory. Miguel's attention snapped up and he squinted into the bayou foliage. From my vantage point on the ground, I could see the moment his eyes recognized whatever was coming toward us. They rounded into whites and his mouth dropped open in horror. I'd never seen a grown man so battered by terror before.

"What the fuck?"

The whisper of branches ceased, and a preternatural hush fell over the bayou. Miguel and his partner froze, the alligators stilled, even the crickets went quiet. Goosebumps shivered up the nape of my neck as the pressure dropped like an impending storm hung over us.

Then all at once chaos erupted. The alligators started hissing madly and Miguel's partner quit chanting, "Shoot the bitch," as he pivoted toward the hulking form that was pounding the sand in its thundering approach. With a splash the reptiles retreated into the water, just in time for Miguel to let out a gurgled scream.

I was still prone on the ground, clutching my chest and trying to follow the carnage in my peripherals. Liquid smattered across my neck and chest. Miguel made another sound, more like a frightened dog than a person. Then there were animal noises—distorted, vicious snarls—and the first man took off running. A gargantuan shape was chasing him. Fast. Faster than anything should move on two legs.

I forced myself up, ignoring the pain stabbing through my side. I wasn't going to stay here and get eaten. The outline of a person crossed over the headlights and only then did I notice the return of that unnatural silence.

"You shouldn't be here," a thick voice sliced the tension holding me captive and I screamed. "*You shouldn't be here*," the newcomer repeated more urgently, his words rasping and steeped in unwarranted rage.

My eyes fluttered up to him. A tight, square jaw. Shaggy, shoulder length hair tangled at his nape. Copper eyes burned into me, glowing oddly with the reflection of the moon. A northeastern wind howled through the bayou, catching his unkempt hair and making him appear otherworldly. Like some fallen angel dropping from the heavens to tear my attackers to pieces. Not malevolent but definitely vengeful.

There was a faint familiarity, but my brain was too frayed to place it. I was even more baffled when I looked down and saw the gore outlining his chest. No shirt, no shoes. Just a tattered pair of Levi's.

"Go!" He snarled. "You don't belong here."

"I was kidnapped!"

He stomped toward me, and my panic soared. I stumbled to me feet, shuffling for the gravel road as fast as my wobbly legs would go.

"Get gone!" He shouted, lunging at me. "Before it's too late."

I blundered blindly away from the murky riverbank. The moon was full, but the bayou wore a pall of black. The car! Why didn't I climb into the car? I could have driven straight to the Sheriff and avoided the risk of more alligators or snakes lying out on the road.

There was also the risk of Miguel and his friend coming back for me. I was unclear if they were dead or if that bayou-mad stranger had only knocked them around. *Right, because he just punched two armed men into submission.* They weren't about to wander out of the bayou sporting black eyes.

What was someone doing out here in the middle of the night with no clothes? Forget about the alligators and snakes, the *mosquitoes* could kill you.

Can't think about that, I told myself. *Just get gone. Do as he said and get out of here.*

I ran until I couldn't run anymore, and then I kept running. The early October air was cool, and my lungs burned. Every inhale stretched the bruising on my ribs, and I feared I would pass out from the pain before I ever made it off the bayou. My legs had gone from aching, to trembling, and now numbness. Stiffly I threw one in front of the other, urging them to keep going now that my adrenaline was ebbing.

There were many roads into the bayou, some of them so remote and narrow that they didn't have official names. Just numbers on a map. I knew most roads in and out of everywhere in this town, but even I found myself lost on the unending gravel. How many predators were out here watching me grow weaker with every step?

I didn't care. Didn't stop.

When the streetlights on Ames Avenue finally appeared, I sobbed. There were three houses visible as the asphalt road merged with a half a dozen unpaved bayou back roads. Tourists had left for the summer and the fall crowd was small. Even in the middle of tourist season, I might not knock for help in this part of town.

Port O'Henry had a drug problem. There wasn't much else for people to do when jobs were seasonal and every few years a hurricane left half the town in financial ruin. The problem was growing though, and there was a good chance my late boss was involved. Anyone could be involved.

I couldn't trust strangers right now. There was only one sure place to go.

Ames led to Columbus. Columbus led to aptly named Beach Place which led to Main Street. I stuck to the jagged shoulder, limping and tripping. There were holes forming in my sandals from rocks grinding into the plastic soles but at least they had Velcro to keep them secured to my ankles. Every few feet I glanced over my shoulder, terrified someone would be on my tail. I felt *hunted* and it wasn't my kidnappers I was worried about.

It was *that man.* If he even was a man and not some bayou spirit made corporeal by the full moon.

Nana warned me never to venture too far into the bayou. I assumed it was to keep me from doing something dumb like drinking with my friends and stumbling into alligator turf.

"There are ghosts out on the bayou." Nana said it playfully, but there was that tone in her voice, that chiding one like I was being scolded for something I hadn't done yet. "Ghosts and beasts that take girls like you and leave nothing but bones."

I would have rolled my eyes at the warning if it wasn't one repeated by all the town elders. There was always talk of howling deep in the trees. Shadows that moved too quick to be ordinary predators. Locals sometimes teased tourists with tales of chupacabras and vampires—there *were* missing goats and slaughtered hens from time to time—but there was more truth to it than they openly admitted to outsiders.

A shiver sent my legs buckling and I collapsed. I was in the parking lot of the Sheriff's department. Only two lamps lit the spot where the sole SUV was parked. More desperate sobs had me coughing and dragging myself off the ground. With shaking hands, I pushed open the door and walked up to the stale brown information desk.

Shawna was the front desk clerk during the day, and I knew her well enough. Nana and Shawna were friends, and I would have given anything to see a familiar face just then.

"Please!" was the single word I choked on when I saw the empty desk and the mostly dark building.

It *was* a familiar face that stumbled around the corner, coffee cup in hand and gun belt nowhere to be seen, but it wasn't one that provided any relief. "What the fuck is goin' on?"

Ricky Holt—now Deputy Holt—squinted at my disheveled appearance and slurped from his disposable cup.

"Ricky!" I gasped, collapsing to my knees. "Help me."

"Cady?" He paled, his throat bobbing. "What are you doing here?"

"I've been kidnapped."

Chapter 2

Fatal Condition

Eli

S WEAT COVERED EVERY INCH of my body, my shirt clinging to my back. In my irritation I almost ripped the damn thing off. It wouldn't be that out of the ordinary for someone to see a man traipsing through town shirtless, even this time of year. But I wasn't interested in doing anything that would draw attention to myself. Especially not at this hour.

I slipped through the shadows with ease, my muscles flexing as I loped down Columbus. My destination was two miles east, adjacent to *Rocky's Dock*, and I would make it quicker if I followed the road. A smarter man would have gone home and fetched his truck, but I wasn't the smartest Barbeaux.

And I needed answers. *Now.*

A scent tickled my nose, and I froze. Every muscle in my body went rigid. *Her.* She was here—or had been. Was she still out here? Highly likely. Wherever she was going, it would take her a long time to get there from the bayou.

Damn. It was only then I realized I'd been doing exactly what I was trying to avoid. *Hunting her.* The faster route to the boat ramp would have been to go south and take Perry Street. Columbus went toward the town center.

Columbus also went towards her, apparently.

The effort it took to turn myself south and break my course was almost more than I had in me. It didn't make any sense. The moon was dipping down out of sight, a silver coin on the horizon. For hours my brothers and I ran, fighting and hunting and sating our predatory hunger. I should be spent, the monster in me dormant as he rested.

A full moon run was like good sex and a Thanksgiving meal. The after effect was a delicious exhaustion that made me feel almost human for a few short hours. That was under normal circumstances. Right now, I felt about as far from human as I could be without wearing fur.

If I got where I was going quickly, I could catch the woman responsible unawares. Madame Celine was more inclined to give me answers if she didn't have time to gain leverage over me.

Celine wasn't evil, necessarily. Most witches weren't. But they were cunning, and they didn't hesitate to take advantage of weakness. Whatever weakness of mine she'd found was splintering my insides like thin glass.

I snarled as I came around the back of *Shells and Shards*. The tiny shop sold all manner of tourist junk in the front; seashells and crystals and poorly made jewelry. In the back was where most people lost their money.

To say that Celine was good was an understatement.

The trick to convincing someone you were a genuine fortune teller was to *be* a genuine fortune teller. Celine never gave anyone the full truth, but she infused just enough of it to leave customers walking out with a sense of wonder and an empty feeling in their wallet.

The old witch lived in Port O'Henry for as long as my family had. From what I gleaned, she was older than us. When it came to witches, old was always more dangerous. They had decades—maybe centuries—to hone their craft. Saul considered her an ally because our father did. That didn't mean he trusted her, but they had the same goals. Keep the secrets of Barbeaux Bayou.

Celine didn't live on the bayou anymore, but she visited regularly to restore herself. A witch was like a battery, recharged by certain places, items, or ingredients.

The bayou was a well of magic. Probably why my family was attracted to it all those years ago. It certainly wasn't because it was a homesteader's heaven.

Farming in the sandy soil was an uphill battle. Livestock were always breaking legs, bitten by snakes, or infested with some parasite or disease. The weather worked against us, ruthlessly tearing down structures and washing away whole herds of cattle. That was before we had the technology to track storm systems and judge the impending damage.

But my father was faithfully rooted in the bayou, even when we lost everything and started over with nothing but the splintered scraps of our destroyed home. When he died my brothers and I gave up the homesteading life, turning toward modern trades to make our living.

I knew it was already too late when I twisted the handle on the back door to Celine's shop and found it open. The cloying scent of incense poured out of the shrouded room and beeswax candles twinkled on an alter adorned with anthropomorphic statues.

"I've been expecting you, Elijah."

Instantly my hackles were up. I whirled to where the hag stood beside her alter, teeth bared. "What did you do to me?"

"Why do you assume I've done anything to you?"

My boots nearly broke holes in the laminate floor of the aging mobile home as I stomped over to her. "I'm not playing your games, witch. You know why I'm here."

Celine was unfazed, dark eyes welling with a wicked sort of amusement. Her posture was tired and hunched, her small frame seeming fragile as I loomed. Ashen hair draped over her red floral robe and made her more matronly than evil. I was smart enough not to trust her appearance. A witch could make you see what she wanted you to see.

"I know only that I was expecting company at an hour most people would consider rude. Would you like tea?" She turned her back and scooted barefoot into a narrow kitchen. Celine was the only living thing that dared turn her back on a creature like me.

"No, I don't want tea," I growled, feeling that rising irritation shift into a force much deadlier. There was already blood on my hands tonight and it would be easy to paint them again. "I want answers. What do you have to do with the girl?"

Celine paused, the kettle in her hands hovering over a red teacup. "It's about a girl, is it?"

"You know what this is about!"

"Now, Elijah. You're just as bad as those gullible tourists." She raised a superior brow, then turning back to her tea she clarified, "I am not all seeing. God gives me a hint, a sliver of what is to come. I cannot tell you how to change it or whether you should. I cannot see what vexes you."

"But you cast curses. Remove the one you've put on me."

She smirked. "Why should I?"

I was not a violent man, not without cause. But there was violence breeding under my skin, withering roots come back to life after feasting on fresh blood. Something more was growing there too, something ugly and agitated. A beast that made the world bend to his rule. My hand was around the old woman's throat in an instant, fingers digging in just enough to remind her of my strength.

"And here I thought we were friends," she wheezed.

Suddenly my hand was burning, a heat so unbearable I leapt back with a cry. Celine's eyes seared into me, their color a hellish red.

"I will pardon your tactless behavior once. I know it's hard for a man with your *condition*," she sneered, "to control himself when the moon is full. But if those hands come near me again, it will be the last time."

In a battle of strength, I was sure I could win. If she had a moment to concentrate on magic like what she'd just used...I wasn't too sure.

"Now drink the damn tea." Celine all but slapped the cup into my hand.

Feeling guilty, I took a sip. A cool clarity washed over me, and I belatedly realized how foolish it was to accept anything from a witch. But I saw how irrational I was being, wound dangerously tight. I should be the picture of peace and calm now.

"That's better, isn't it?"

"What's wrong with me?" I rubbed my jaw and took another sip of tea. It was too hot and more bitter than what I had the taste for, but I *did* feel better. At least a little.

"What are you willing to pay for that answer?"

"Celine," I warned.

"Don't take that tone with me, *loup garoux*. It's three in the damn morning and you broke into my home with malicious intent. You owe me for that alone." She lifted a finger to silence my protest before it could begin. "And even my friends pay the price for my gifts. Magic always has a price."

I considered, that itching agitation tingling under my skin. "Name your price."

The answer came immediately. "Blood."

I set the cup of tea down onto the kitchen table with a clack. "Never."

"Then you will never get your answers."

"Fuck!" I wanted to strangle her again.

I couldn't live like this. Madness was a family trait I'd long avoided. We were famous for it, even if no one knew the true story. My great grandfather was responsible for over one hundred deaths and if it wasn't for his son, my grandfather, there would have been many more. There was only one way to stop a werewolf lost to madness.

If this wasn't a curse, I needed Saul to kill me. I didn't want to harm anyone that didn't deserve it. Worse, I didn't want to expose my brothers. The world had changed since we were young. Stories about monsters were passed with video evidence and immediately shared across the globe.

The stakes were much, much higher if I made a mistake.

"What do you need blood for?"

Celine looked at me like I was stupid. "Magic."

"What kind of magic, damn woman?"

"I haven't decided yet. Blood from your kind is powerful. I might save it until I know exactly what to do with it." Her brow creased. "All I know is that I need it."

I shoved my hand in her direction. "Don't make me regret this. You're not invincible."

"That you know of." Celine's eyes had taken on that evil red tinge again. I forced myself to breathe slowly through my nostrils. Those eyes triggered a fight-or-flight response, and my kind never chose flight. Celine twisted to fetch a sharp knife and a copper bowl. She reached for my hand, knife outstretched.

"Uh-uh." I snatched the knife from her. "You cut me, and my meaner half will retaliate."

The blade parted the flesh of my middle finger like a boat on still water. I squeezed my finger and let three droplets collect in the bowl before pulling my hand away and sucking on the wounded finger.

"That's not enough."

"That's what you'll get. Take it or leave it." I wasn't in a position to bargain but I also wasn't interested in making a powerful witch even more powerful.

Celine's lips thinned. After a quiet moment she came to a decision. I didn't see what she did with my blood as she hurried into the deep pantry in her kitchen. I didn't want to. That bitter cup of tea became my sole focus as I waited longer than I thought I was capable.

Finally, Celine reappeared, her irises a soft brown. The deep lines on her face were more pronounced and she looked weary. Her magic was strong, but it didn't keep her from feeling the weight of age the way my "condition," as she called it, did for me. I wasn't sure the clock was ticking for me at all, which was a depressing thought. Only a mate would age me and that was never meant to be.

Wordlessly she steered me to the round table where she did client readings. Wafts of old incense and stale perfume filled my lungs as I was pushed into the overstuffed chair. She settled primly in her throne across from me and placed both hands palm up on the table.

I didn't immediately move, and she sighed, snatching my hands into hers. A hot prickling travelled up my arms and my instinct was to recoil from the magic. Instead, I forced myself to be still, gritting my teeth to keep from growling. Her silence became an entity of its own and I almost slashed out at it with a curse when her eyes flew open.

"If you continue on this hunt the bayou will run red." Celine released my hands and rubbed hers together gingerly. "If the girl remains alone in the dark, she will die."

I sucked in a breath so sharp it wounded me.

Finally, she finished with, "When the hunter's moon rises and falls, both of you will choose."

The buzz of magic died and Celine didn't say anything else. "That's it?"

"Three hints for three drops."

Rage reignited in my spine. It pressed at my skin. I needed to set the beast loose.

Celine's murmured comment ripped my attention back to the present. "The next full moon is the hunter's moon."

"I know." I stood and turned for the door.

"Such savage manners, you Barbeaux boys." Before I could twist the knob she said, "Consider, Elijah, that you have encountered kismet, not a curse."

I wrenched the door open and rushed out into the salty autumn air. My body was consumed by agony as I held back the demon under my skin. I raced to the sanctuary of the bayou, only releasing myself when I breached the perimeter of my home. Then I dropped, fingers burying into the sandy soil as my body ripped apart and I became another shadow in the night.

Chapter 3
Small Town Legal
Cady

I LOCKED THE FRONT door with shaking hands. Whether they were shaking with rage or fear, I couldn't say. One party. One party almost nine years ago and a guy couldn't forget a rejection.

Maybe it wasn't fair to believe *that* was the reason Ricky Holt was skeptical of my story, but I couldn't fathom any other explanation. I was *kidnapped*, dragged from the office at my dead boss's house, and knocked unconscious. There was even a goose egg on my head! Not to mention the scraped knees and bruises blooming all over my arms, ribs, and shoulders.

I rubbed my tired face and wondered if I should go to the clinic and be checked for a concussion, only to realize I couldn't because Holt *took my keys.* If I died in my sleep tonight, I would haunt him.

And come Monday I was filing a complaint with the Sheriff.

When I dragged my weary body into the Sheriff's department at almost three in the morning, I expected an earnest response. Instead, it took Deputy Holt almost ten minutes just to get me seated. Then he fussed over his coffee like I wasn't even there. When I finally snapped and told him to take my statement he froze like a deer in the headlights.

Even after hearing my story in its entirety, he didn't believe me. There was a lengthy inspection of my abdomen but he claimed not to see any damage. The bruises on my wrists and raw skin from where the duct tape ripped my face? Invisible.

He checked out the bump on my head and mumbled something about clumsy drunks. It only devolved from there.

"You had anything to drink tonight?"

"No, Ricky. I haven't. I was working."

"Deputy Holt," he corrected. "Last I heard, your boss is dead."

"And his estate is a mess. No one has been able to reach his son and I'm still responsible for getting his business finances in order." I crossed my arms then winced. Was it possible I had a broken rib? Now that the adrenaline ebbed my whole chest throbbed, and breathing was painful.

"Isn't Dustin in South Africa?"

No one knew where Dustin, Dale Barlow's only son, was currently. He hadn't spoken to his father in almost three years. I wouldn't be surprised if he was dodging calls. Despite his opulent lifestyle, Mister Barlow had accrued significant personal debt. His business was going to end the year in the red if the *Stop N' Shop* continued performing as it was. Off season was hard on all businesses in Port O'henry but I was coming to realize Barlow wasn't a very good businessman.

I sighed deeply, wincing again. "Shouldn't you be taking photographs? For evidence? And recording this conversation too?" Admittedly my knowledge of law enforcement also came from television, but it seemed wrong that Ricky—*Deputy Holt*—was perched on his desk without even a notepad.

"Listen sweetheart," Holt stood. "You show up here in the middle of the night with this wild story about being kidnapped and you can't tell me where exactly you were, who took you, or how you got away." He lowered his voice and said, "You can't file a report because you regret what you did when the booze wears off."

I stiffened. So, we weren't talking current events anymore.

"I had *one*—" I snapped the sentence off. This was a game I didn't need to play. Not after tonight. "If you're not going to take me seriously then I'll come back when your boss is here and talk to him instead."

That got his attention. "Don't make a scene, Cady." He picked up the radio from his desk. "I'll send someone to the Barlow residence to look for signs of a disturbance. As for the rest, I can't do much with one first name, no plate numbers, and no location."

Ricky stepped away, mumbling something into his radio. When he returned, he ruined any reassurance he'd given me by demanding my keys.

"My—what?" I fished around in my pocket and realized I did have my keys on me. Of course, I did. My jeep was still parked in the empty spot at the back of Barlow's home, unless my kidnappers moved it. Before I could react, Holt snatched the keys from me and tucked them into the front pocket of his shirt.

"Is that even legal?" I demanded.

"Small town legal. You want a ride home or are you walking?" Oh, there was definitely a sneer in that question.

I was probably an idiot because by the time Holt dropped me at the end of the driveway to my grandparents' home, I was too livid to ask him to come inside with me. Or maybe I wasn't an idiot because what would a man like Ricky assume if I asked him up? Never mind he was a deputy and I wanted him to verify the kidnappers hadn't come to my house to recapture their escaped victim.

Every window in the house was locked—silly since the house was on stilts and someone would have to come up the stairs and over the gate to get to the only accessible windows. The front door was bolted, and I put a chair in the way for good measure. If someone was truly determined it wouldn't keep them out, but it would make enough noise to alert me.

Papa kept a metal baseball bat next to the shoe rack by the front door. I carried it over my shoulder as I searched both bedrooms and their respective closets. I also checked the linen closet and pantry even though both were too small to hide a person. Hell, I was spooked enough to check behind the glass door for the shower.

Whoever took me tonight, they weren't in the house.

As I settled onto the sofa—I was too scared to go to bed and the sun would be up in a few hours anyway—I replayed everything I could remember.

Walking to the jeep. Looking over my shoulder because it was dark, and I was nervous being out there alone after Barlow died.

Leaning across the driver's seat to put paperwork on the passenger side.

Careless. It was so careless to stand there in the dark with my back to everything.

That's when they grabbed me. There was pain and then suddenly I was bound in someone's trunk.

Miguel and his accomplice. The bayou. The alligators. Oh God, they were going to feed me to alligators!

More pain as I took a blow to the ribs.

Screaming.

Blood.

I could smell the tang of it.

And then then he appeared in the beam of the headlights, chest glistening red.

I started at the last part, as if even the memory of his eyes on me somehow drew his attention my way.

He killed them. I hadn't seen the bodies, but I knew they were dead.

He saved me.

Who was he?

There were people who lived on the bayou. Most of them came from the earliest families that settled in Port O'Henry. I hadn't imagined any of them to be particularly altruistic. I didn't think they would be wandering around half-naked in the middle of the night either. Folks who lived out there should know better than anyone what you could run into.

A shiver raked down my bruised body and I winced. I didn't know if I would ever stop trembling. Someone kidnapped me. Planned to kill me over missing money I'd never seen or heard of.

Maybe Holt was an idiot or maybe he knew something he didn't want to admit. The trouble with drug trouble was that it was contagious, and it was insidious. I heard gossip, whispers of corruption among politicians in Port Tortuga. There was no reason to believe the Sheriff's office here in Port O'Henry wasn't plagued with the same corruption.

Worse, I *didn't* have evidence, other than bruises.

And an eyewitness.

A man without a name. With barely a face for me to recall.

Still, when I closed my eyes to the blooming sunrise, finally subdued by exhaustion, his murky features were all I saw.

Chapter 4

Chance Encounter

Cady

"I NEED TO BUY a gun." I leaned on the glass counter at *Uncle's Tackle Plus,* trying to look calm as I eyed the two dozen firearms beneath my forearms.

This was Texas. Everyone owned a gun, and it was easy to buy one. But for some reason I was afraid I would be interrogated and kicked to the curb.

Afraid was a word I used to describe myself often after that night.

Four days had passed since I ran from the bayou with hell on my heels. Four days and I hadn't slept, could barely eat. This was my first time leaving the house. I was determined to get to the bottom of this Barlow money mystery. If the Sheriff wasn't going to look into it—he'd made it crystal clear that he wasn't—I would just have to do it myself.

"You okay, Katydid?" A year later and that nickname was still drenched in sadness. Fred Cheney, the owner of *Uncle's,* was one of Papa's longtime fishing buddies and the only other person who called me that. One of hundreds of bitter reminders that my grandparents were gone for good.

"I've been better." I rubbed the back of my neck. "I'm having a rough week."

Fred removed his baseball hat and used it to scratch the bald top of his head. "Rough enough that you need a gun?" He lowered his voice, propping an elbow on the glass and cupping his mouth. "You in some kind of trouble?"

"I'm just—" The bell above the door jingled and I nearly leapt from my skin.

I twisted over my shoulder to see a burly, bearded man stomp toward the tackle aisle. He was the typical duck-hunter-redneck type we saw around these parts during the fall, filthy Carhartt shirt and all.

Two more men followed him in. One was wheezing with laughter, the other waving his hands excitedly, a devil-may-care grin brightening his face. They were big guys—well-built and crazy tall—and I wondered if they were roughnecks from one of the offshore rigs beyond the bay. Shrimpers was a possibility too, but I knew most of the locals, at least in appearance, and these guys were only vaguely familiar.

"All I'm saying is, if the bear is pretty enough, I think Saul could get a little—" The last man stopped dead in his tracks, his attention fusing to me like a hot brand.

He was all muscle and tan skin, his dark hair long enough to be tied back in a lazy knot at his nape. As a general rule I found man buns feminine, especially when paired with too tight jeans and whatever overpriced t-shirt wealthy tourists wore. There was nothing about this man that could be called feminine.

He pinned me with eyes like plates of polished copper and I was frozen in place, captivated as if he was a wild animal that unexpectedly crossed my path. Unease mingled with awe. His expression was fierce, crisp jaw tense, and he held unnaturally still. If someone could look gorgeous and deadly simultaneously, that was him.

I sucked in a breath. Suddenly I was back on the bayou, staring at copper eyes tinted with moonlight moments before I ran for my life.

"Hey bush cricket! Surprised to see you here." Brandon startled me out of my daze, wrapping an arm around my shoulders.

"Hey, Brandon." I gave him a halfhearted hug, craning my neck to see past him at that familiar stranger. When I finally managed a glance, the man was gone.

"What's up? You seem spooked." Fred's son frowned at me. He was the older brother I never had, and I feared if I told him what was going on he might approach my bayou savior. I wasn't interested in getting anyone else involved in this. Not until I knew how deep I was in. I'd lost enough this year.

"It's just been a long week. I haven't been sleeping well." I forced a smile for him.

"I'm sorry to hear about Mister Barlow. This town won't be the same without him."

Right. Mister Barlow. Such a local treasure, that asshole.

I nodded sadly.

I peered over my shoulder again. "Who was that?" I asked quietly, gesturing toward the door with my chin.

"That's just the Barbeaux boys." Brandon said with a scornful hitch. "Bunch'a bayou rednecks."

That was the Barbeaux boys? Surely, I'd seen them before today. They were rugged but more attractive than I expected from some fifth-generation bayou homesteaders. Well, *he* was anyway. I'd heard just about every nasty rumor about them and while I didn't believe most of them, I had a healthy respect for distance. Not because I was superstitious like my grandparents but because the realistic rumors usually carried the most truth.

People out on the bayou had hardly any sources of income, but plenty of *alternative* opportunity. Lots of discreet places to hide drugs and the boats on which they were smuggled. I was painfully intimate with addiction, and I avoided anyone that watered the roots of that poisonous tree.

I didn't get that vibe from them. Murderous rampage? Definitely. But dealing drugs? No, I couldn't see it.

What I could see was a Barbeaux standing in the headlights of my kidnappers' car, blood dripping down his bare skin.

That man *literally* went on a murderous rampage four nights ago and before he noticed me, he was laughing as if nothing happened. Seemed like the Barbeaux family was as crazy as people believed.

I shuddered and turned my attention back to my task. *Get a gun. Protect myself. Find out who wants this money.*

After some deliberation I walked out of *Uncle's* with the weight of a Sig Sauer P238 in my bag. Brandon paved the way for the perfect explanation without worrying anyone enough to get them curious.

"She's been working all alone at the Barlow house, Daddy. Of course, she's nervous. The days are getting shorter, and everyone knows no one is living out there this time of year. What if someone breaks in?"

"Sweetheart, why didn't you say somethin'?" Fred's expression turned sympathetic.

"I didn't want y'all to worry about me."

"Now he won't have to." Brandon winked. "Just make sure you get yourself to the range. A gun is useless if you can't use it."

He was right. I had never fired a gun, much less held one. But if I was going to defend myself, I needed to learn and fast.

The hairs on the back of my neck raised in a wave just before I reached the jeep out front. I froze, clutching the bag with the unloaded gun as if it could save me. There were eyes one me. I felt them plain as the autumn sun on my skin. My head moved on a swivel, scanning the rows of trucks. Half a dozen men, mostly duck hunters, were loading bags and coolers into their truck beds. None of them paid me any mind.

I was about to chalk it up to paranoia when I glimpsed a rusty green ford pulling out of the parking lot. He was there in the front seat, eyes burning into me so intensely that sparks ignited along my skin.

"Who are you?" I shouted, knowing he couldn't answer me but hoping he would acknowledge me somehow.

No such luck. The truck peeled out onto the road, picking up speed and breaking the twenty-five miles per hour limit. I watched the taillights disappear and promised, "I'm going to find you."

Chapter 5

Knight in Tarnished Armor

Cady

THE AROMA OF HOMEMADE chocolate chunk cookies was oozing from my kitchen, and it wasn't even a little comforting. More than once I'd talked myself out of it—shutting off the oven, hiding my car keys—but if I wanted to know what was going on, this was the best start.

The Sheriff was useless as all-git-out. After dropping in Monday to retrieve my keys and make a complaint, I was given a lecture about inebriated driving and wasting the time of law enforcement. It seemed Ricky got to him first and convinced him not to help me. Which was fine. I didn't trust him anyway.

If I wanted my answers, I was going to have to brave the unknown.

And there was a twisted curiosity that had me shifting into drive and following handwritten instructions to a no-name road in the middle of the bayou. I almost died out there so obviously the smart thing to do was go back.

"What am I doing?" I whispered shrilly when asphalt ended where a poorly kept gravel road began.

The Tupperware of cookies bounced on the front seat when I went over a nasty pothole, and I snapped my hand out to catch it. Crumbled cookies wouldn't do.

The county did their best to manage the roads since there were public recreation areas in the eastern half of the bayou but heavy rain, especially when hurricane season blew in, led to frequent flooding. More than one road washed out during the last tropical storm and with my luck, it would be the one I was instructed to take.

It took some detective work to find the address I needed. Seemed like folks living on the bayou didn't want to be found. People knew only the most basic information about the Barbeaux family. Plenty of them didn't have good things to say. If I was to give credence to the rumors, they were criminals, poachers, and, "downright strange and unfriendly."

Eventually I ended up on the phone with a woman who worked for the library with an extravagant lie about mixed up mail. It helped that my last name was Barber, so the mistake wasn't out of the question. Thankfully, Miss Margaret Stokes, librarian, was older than dirt and not that astute.

"You can just bring it to the post office."

"I know but it's stamped as urgent. It looks important." I worked to make my voice extra sweet and helpful. "Besides, it's the neighborly thing to do."

"Oh, bless you! I can find you an address, but you be careful, sugar. Normal people don't live on the bayou. There's Indian graves out there. It's not right." Miss Stokes was as superstitious as the worst of them. She also followed Deputy Holt's model of "small town legal," because I was sure the library was not supposed to give out personal contact information.

There were three living Barbeaux brothers and three different addresses for them. I assumed they all lived together since, from my memory, I'd never seen one in town without the other two. Now that I knew who they were, more little blips of encounters kept popping into my head. I'd driven by them dozens of times at the *Stop N' Shop*, the gas and grocery combo that Barlow owned. At least once I saw them loading their boat at *Rocky's*. Never close enough to say hello. Not that they were the chit-chatting type anyway.

Another jarring bump had my teeth clacking. My cell service dropped to one bar, and I was praying something fierce that I didn't get a flat tire out here. A Jeep was a good vehicle for this type of terrain, but I was overdue for some new tires. This was only the first address on the list—Elijah Barbeaux. By the end of the day, I might be hiking through the bayou with my thumb out.

Just when I was beginning to think I'd gone the wrong way and would spend my last living days wandering the bayou with the ghosts, a house appeared. It was on stilts, as most houses were in Port O'Henry, but it was more rugged in appearance than the colorful vacation homes along the beach. The salty bay air was unkind to buildings and this one didn't have any-one concerned with aesthetic.

The design was similar to my grandparents' home. Enough square footage for two or three modest bedrooms upstairs, utility room downstairs. A deck stretched way out past the front door, perfect for watching the sunrise over the bay. The simple structure looked at home among the tangled backdrop of opportunistic foliage.

The looming steel garage behind the house was out of place in comparison. Definitely room for multiple boats in there. Offshore boats based on the height of the roof. My impression of people living this far off the beaten path was that they were making do. Inheriting ramshackle houses and carving out a rough living raising livestock. Seemed like the Barbeaux brothers weren't doing so poor after all.

I squinted at my surroundings as I climbed out of my jeep, realizing I didn't see any evidence of animals.

There was an old Ford truck parked beside the staircase to the porch, blue and not the tired green I saw yesterday. The typical bayside rust had eaten at the exterior, but it was superficial damage.

The grounds around the house were clear, wild grass and weeds trimmed neatly. Firewood was stacked in a tidy pile against one wall of the utility room. Weird since I couldn't imagine anyone having a fireplace here. There were a few weeks of cold between December and January before the temperatures climbed to sweat fest again.

Past the shadow of the porch, I noticed potted tomato plants that were finishing off for the season. It was homey in a rural kind of way.

Yes, homey was what I hoped for when visiting a murderer on his private property, miles from cell service. My pulse kicked up and I almost dove back into the car and turned tail. This was such a bad idea.

"Out of my damn mind," I whispered, gripping the container and shuffling towards the staircase.

Relying on anyone else to look out for me was just as stupid. The Sheriff's department didn't believe my story and there was no one I could involve without putting them at risk. Dale Barlow was up to no good and by hiring me to sort through his financials, he marked me. I couldn't wash away that mark until I knew what I was dealing with.

"Can I help you?"

I shrieked, whirling so hard my knees threatened to buckle. Why did I leave my gun in the car? Rookie mistake. *He* was between me and my purse and probably ready to murder me for witnessing what he did. Even if I didn't *see* anything.

The fear on the drive was manageable. There was only a one in three chance this would be him. Now he was standing in front of my jeep, and I was going to collapse at his feet.

"Hi!" I said too cheerfully, almost hysterical. "Are you Elijah Barbeaux?"

"Who wants to know?" Elijah stood taller than ever, a tackle box in his hand. His rust-colored shirt was dusty, and a sweat/mud combo was smeared across his forehead.

I stared longer than was polite, mouth agape and hands trembling. There was a strange, paralyzing place between fear, gratitude, and attraction, and I'd found myself stranded in it.

He really was *so damn* tall. At two inches below average height, every man was tall to me, but even I could see he was gargantuan. Miles stretched between his mountainous shoulders. I didn't know what he did for a living, but he probably did it well.

His dark hair was salt mussed and tied back to reveal a stern face. Days of stubble lined his jaw, making the hard set even more pronounced. I'd seen him before and somehow this felt like our first meeting. The line of his nose wasn't quite straight, the slope of his forehead shadowing his eyes and making him look mean, but there was also a sleek, attractive quality to him. A compelling force that made me want to orbit him like a moon.

I'd seen him but I'd never looked into those eyes. Those deep, intense eyes. They were the eyes of someone that *could* do terrible things, not the eyes of someone that *wanted* to do terrible things.

"I'm cookies—Cady!" I stammered. "I meant to say, 'I'm Cady and I baked you some cookies.'"

He scowled. Or scowled harder because he was already scowling. "Cookies?"

"Yes!" I stepped as close as I dared and held out the Tupperware, my cheeks flushing as it visibly shook in my grasp. "They're chocolate chunk. My Nana's recipe. I made two dozen because one dozen is a serving size, in my opinion, and I thought you might like two servings."

Elijah eyed up the Tupperware skeptically. "How did you find me out here?"

"I lied to a librarian, and she gave me your address. It's small town legal, don't worry."

"Why?"

Tears skimmed over my bottom lids. This was getting awkward fast. "You saved my life."

It was just a whisper, but he reacted all the same. His jaw locked tight, and I was pretty sure this was the part where he killed me because I was the last witness to his crime.

"Don't know what you're talkin' 'bout." His East Texas drawl got thicker as he mumbled. Then he turned his back to me and tramped away, disappearing behind a patch of bald cypress.

I hovered there, Tupperware still outstretched, with tears burning my nose. This was not how I expected this to go. Not at all.

He walked away from me.

Well, he tried to. I wasn't going to let him get far.

There was purpose in my step as I power-walked to catch up with his long stride. Through the trees I saw a plush stretch of shore, where the bayou met the bay. If I wasn't in such a hurry, I would have stopped to admire the view. Out here there were no power lines or new stick-built houses with obnoxious pink paint to block the view of the bay. Only green water and blue, blue Texas sky. Elijah had a private beach and boat launch, and I was damn envious.

My grandparents' house was only two blocks from the beach, and it was nice to see the waves from the front porch. But come tourist season I would be putting up plastic poles all around my yard to keep jerks in seventy-thousand-dollar trucks from using it as a parking lot. Crowds of people would wade into the waves, blaring country music and leaving enough plastic waste to kill an entire reef.

Out here it was quiet. Tranquil.

A bay boat was tied to a disintegrating dock that didn't necessarily look safe to walk on, much less hitch a boat to. Elijah had one hand on the steering wheel, expression surprised as I hurried over with my Tupperware tucked under my arm.

"Hey!" I shouted as he pulled the rope loose at the bow of the boat. He rushed to untie the second one at the stern and I moved onto the dock. "You're lying!"

The motor of the boat roared to life, drowning out my curse as he started to steer away from the beach. I did what any insane woman would do and jumped into his boat, landing clumsily, and wincing at the force on my injured ribs.

"What the hell are you doing?" Elijah stalled the motor, but the boat was snared by the tide, drifting far enough from the dock that I didn't stand a chance of climbing back onto it without getting wet and maybe nibbled by a stray alligator.

Sweet. Now I was trapped on a boat with a hot bayou serial killer who looked very unhappy about having company.

"I'm getting answers!" I snapped, glowering so he didn't think I was terrified. "I was kidnapped five days ago and no one in this damn town will help me. You were there that night."

"I told you, I don't know—"

I yanked my shirt up, not because I thought flashing my tits would get him talking but because I wanted him to see the boot shaped bruise spanning half my torso. "You saw something." I swallowed the emotion that was still lingering in a lump at the back of my throat. "I need to know what you saw."

The way Elijah Barbeaux moved shouldn't have been possible for a man his size. His shoulders and neck were unnaturally rigid when he prowled across the boat. His advance felt distinctly predatory, eyes glittering with menace, and my instincts told me to run. There was no escaping now, so I forced myself to freeze, waiting to see if he would strike.

He was so close I could see every fine black hair on his cleft chin. But when his hand skated over the bruise on my rib it was such a tender touch that I shivered. His fingers were rough and warm, erasing the pain with delicate strokes. After he was satisfied with his survey of that one, he took my right arm, turning it gently to look at the black handprint from where Miguel almost wrenched my hand off to feed it to a gator.

If looks could kill, the one he was wearing would have stopped my heart. One hundred percent murderous rage bled from his eyes, his nostrils exhaling violence. I had zero doubt that Elijah killed the men on the bayou that night and that he would kill them a second time over if given the chance. Tears surfaced again, quietly leaking from the corners of my eyes as he studied every tiny mark the incident left on my skin. My fear faded and for the first time since that night, I felt safe.

Floating in the bay with no escape while a killer put his hands on me.

Elijah blinked, taking a step back with none of that earlier grace. Whatever trance he'd been in was broken. The brightness washed from his irises, and he crossed his arms like he needed to trap his wandering hands.

"I'm sorry about your bruises, but I can't help you." That was all he said before kicking the motor up and edging the boat back to the dock. He gestured for me to get out and I obeyed, but not before dropping the Tupperware of cookies onto one of the bench seats.

"Rain is coming. You better leave before the roads flood."

The boat motor roared, and he turned toward the bay before I could say another word, vanishing into the water and leaving me more confused than ever. I glanced up at the sky. Barely a cloud in sight.

Well. So much for my questions. I trudged back to the jeep, feeling embarrassed and off kilter. What in the world had I expected? Did I really think he would be any help?

Or was some reckless part of me just extremely curious about him?

Gravel hissed under tires as I backed out a little too fast, eager to be free from this uncomfortable experience. I was almost back onto the paved road when an enormous dark cloud blew out of nowhere, bringing with it a typical autumn downpour. According to my weather app there shouldn't be anything but wind.

And Elijah Barbeaux became that much more intriguing.

B EING ALONE HAD ME on edge. I sat in the front seat of my jeep, keys still in the ignition. The rain was letting up. Maybe I could go back the way I came. Even Elijah Barbeaux would be better company than none. A second visit to his property in one day was probably pushing my luck. That man was occupying more of my mind than he should be, given my current circumstances.

The last drops of rain left rivulets on my windshield as I stepped onto the wet driveway, grimacing at the textured humidity that made my clothes cling to my skin. With a click of the fob over my shoulder I locked the jeep and let my feet carry me where I was aching to go.

For the first time since I was eighteen, I was considering leaving Port O'Henry. I spent yesterday morning in the Sheriff's office and the outcome was not good. He didn't believe me. I shouldn't have been shocked but somehow, I was. This town wasn't what it used to be. Or maybe I'd never seen it unfiltered by childhood before.

I found my way to the pier. There were perks to living two blocks from the beach and this was my favorite. A quiet place to clear my head. Didn't matter who was out fishing or if the beach was filled with people playing God awful country music. At the end of the pier the earnest rush of waves would silence all of it until it was just me and the bay.

The wooden structure severed the tide, sending water rippling down both sides of it to give the beach an oval shape.

It wasn't much as far as beaches went. Some years they filled it with sand dredged from the canal that connected

Cadalina bay—my namesake—to the intracoastal waterway. Then the wrath of tropical storms and the ever-present tide would drag it back out into the bay and sooner or later it returned to its rugged state. Hemmed with grass that bit into you with sticker burs, littered with crushed shells, and loaded with trash that even the locals didn't care to clean up.

If I was an outsider looking in, there wouldn't be much appeal to Port O'Henry. Too far from where La Salle landed to be famous and nearly an hour from the nearest grocery store. The most sightseeing you could do without a boat was on the pier or the jetty and both had seen better days. Boards groaned threateningly under my sneakers, and I wondered how long it would be before someone went right through them. Salty wind crusted everything in rust and rapidly stole the color from even the brightest colored homes. Being adjacent to the bayou meant summers were humid as hell and the clouds of mosquitos were so thick you breathed more of them than air.

But I wasn't an outsider. To me this place was heaven on earth. The town was rustic, and the people were too but it was all I'd ever known. All I thought I would ever know after I gave up my scholarship and stayed to help take care of Nana when she got sick. There were problems in a town straddling the edge of nowhere—drugs, theft, vandalism—but even so, I never felt unsafe here. Neighbors took care of each other. It was just what you do.

The spiral started when my neighbors stopped being neighbors. When wealthy families started buying up properties for hundreds of thousands more than what locals paid for it, life in Port O'Henry changed rapidly. Fishing was one of the only pastimes in town, but it wasn't long before massive, gated communities and strip malls started popping up just outside of the town limits. I was standing on a rotten hunk of wood, surrounded by fish guts and beer cans, but I could drive thirty minutes north and get a three hundred dollar chemical peel.

Corpus Christi, Galveston, and the like were too expensive and too crowded, so people started coming here. Then they told their friends and suddenly doctors, and lawyers were building three thousand square foot homes a mere hundred feet away from the beach.

What appeal they saw here? Well, I didn't really know. Those people showed up half the year with their golf carts and their massive boats and their extended families and made the economy come alive. But they left like the tide. This time of year, Port O'Henry was a ghost town. Only the snowbirds messed around with autumn on the bay. To them the humid chill probably felt tropical.

A fish caught my eye, sea trout hooked on a tangled line that someone left wrapped around a pillar. It wriggled helplessly and my chest hurt because I felt a kindred struggle. That was life for people in Port O'Henry. We were hooked. We could never leave, even if we wanted to.

I considered the cost of a plane ticket to Seattle every hour, but I knew I wouldn't buy it.

A gull swooped from the end of the pier, snatching at the hooked fish with an open beak. I swallowed, suddenly feeling ill at the comparison. The gull dove again, and I swatted at it, giving the fish a short reprieve as I flicked open my pocketknife, gripped it between my teeth, and swung myself through an opening in the guardrail.

The water wasn't too deep at the end of the pier, maybe three and a half feet, but it was cold enough to take my breath away. I waded through the surf, sneakers squishing into the sand, and prayed I didn't step on a stingray. They were more common in the shallower parts of the bay as the weather cooled, probably seeking warmer waters.

The fish panicked when I gripped the stray line, swimming furiously away. I carefully reeled it in, catching it between palm and fingers like Papa taught me and slipping the hook from its mouth. The trout thrashed toward freedom, and I released it, watching it vanish under the surface with tearful eyes. I used my pocketknife to cut the stray line and then I stood there as high tide came at me one frigid wave at a time.

Every crash of salty water was cathartic, drawing fresh tears down my face. There was no one to witness me crumble, adding my own salt spray to the bay. I wasn't just crying over the terror of the previous days. I cried for my grandparents, for the future I never got, and for everything that slipped through my grasps like that trout returning to the Gulf.

In one year, my entire life turned upside down. In one night, everything I thought I knew was gone. I believed the ground beneath me was solid only to realize I was standing in quicksand. Sinking like a log in the bayou, struggling to keep my head above water.

I slogged back to my house an hour later, sneakers squelching. Doing my rounds with the baseball bat—why wasn't I using the gun?—was harder in wet clothes. Someone hiding in my closet would hear me coming.

My grandparents' home—I guess it was legally my home now, but it would always be theirs too—was modest. Seventeen hundred square feet plus the utility room tucked beneath the stilted house. The largest room was the kitchen, per Nana's request. No one loved to cook as much as Nana. Second to the kitchen was the living room. Technically, they were kind of the same space, the kitchen island and the bar lined with stools being the only separation between the two. Nana and Papa loved entertaining company.

The bedrooms were small and sparsely decorated. Nana never saw the point in decorating a room where she spent more time with her eyes closed than open. Later, when she was constantly tucked under the sheets as she fought with cancer, she would lament that, wishing for more color and life. I did my best to accommodate, hanging family pictures with kitschy frames made from painted seashells. There was only so much I could do to brighten the world of a dying woman.

Papa built the house with the intention of retiring here, spending the rest of his days boating and fishing and acquiring those leathery wrinkles Gulf Coast men always wore with pride. He and Nana had only one daughter, born when they were newlyweds out of high school. They sent her to college and managed to retire early with decent savings.

But they hadn't expected their only daughter to show up on their porch with a two-year-old girl, three years after she dropped out of college. I was a shock to my grandparents—they hadn't even known my mother was pregnant—but they took me in all the same.

In the end that decent savings wasn't enough to float two people plus a toddler. Papa took work where he could, odd jobs and whatever else he could scrape up in a town as small as Port O'Henry. His smile was apologetic every time I came home from a shift at the fishing center after school or spent my Saturday weeding gardens for extra cash, but I never regretted it. I was proud to help where I could, to remove some of the burden on their shoulders. I saved every penny I earned for college, not once splurging on any of the frivolous things a high school girl might want.

My rigid pride seemed silly now. I should have indulged in a pair of jeans that wasn't from Jo Beth's thrift shop or paid for a haircut instead of taking kitchen scissors to my curls every six months. I would never get to go back and experience those things. What was all that hard work for when my grandparents were gone, my money depleted, and my life on the line?

Not today, Satan. Nana always said that when she was having a bad day and it started to turn her sour. If that woman could see sunshine through the storms she weathered, then I could too.

After stripping off my drenched jeans I shuffled through the tower of mail accumulating on the kitchen island, pausing every time Papa's name appeared. The hardest part about grief was that it was never really over. Every time a name popped up, a memory, or a favorite photo you were dragged right back in. I wasn't sure if it ever got easier.

I was about to chuck the whole pile when a postcard caught my eye.

"Shells and Shards," it read across the front in a glittering gold font. Below it said, *"The answers you need."*

Goosebumps rose along my arms. I didn't believe in palm readings and whatever other hokey stuff Madame Celine did. I'd never stepped foot in the crystal boutique that was crammed next to the parking lot of *Rocky's Docks*. It was overpriced tourist junk as far as I was concerned. But these were unusual circumstances and so far, no one had been particularly helpful.

I clutched the postcard so hard that my hands began to shake. I did need answers. Really badly.

The keys jingled as I slipped them off the hook on the wall and trotted down the stairs to the driveway. I couldn't help but give myself a short, humorless laugh.

I guess desperate times called for desperate measures.

Chapter 6

Violent Tendencies

Eli

"**W**HAT'S WRONG WITH YOU?"

"All your many years and you still haven't learned any manners." I grinned up at my big brother.

Saul shoved my shoulder as he settled on the dock beside me. "I'm the oldest. I don't need manners to get you to do what I want."

"Keep telling yourself that." I'd been cradling a worn out Tupperware of cookies when Saul approached. I did my best to hide it behind my back. I had no intention of offering him food that came in contact with her bare hands, and I knew it would only add to his suspicion.

"You're quiet."

Funny, I hadn't thought I was being quiet. In fact, I thought I was doing a decent job pretending nothing was bothering me. When you knew each other as long as my brothers and I did, it was hard to miss these things.

I stared out at the water. The wind had calmed after the storm this afternoon, a gentle breath that rocked waves into the old dock. A groan and creak accompanied each receding swell, warning that the dock probably wouldn't withstand another tropical storm or worse.

"I made a mistake." I ground my teeth with the admission. "Actually, I don't think it was a mistake. I would do it again if I had to." I remembered the mottled skin on her delicate rib cage and my fists clenched. *I would do it again just to cause them pain.*

Saul stiffened. "What kind of mistake, Elijah?"

"I was just protecting what's mine."

We were no strangers to violence. My brothers and I had less blood on our hands than most Barbeauxs. Less than our father and his father. It didn't make us innocent, but we were determined to break the vicious cycle of death and misery, vowing to ourselves as we buried our father that we wouldn't make his choices. We wouldn't be mindless killers.

And we weren't mindless when we patrolled the bayou year after year, disappearing thugs and thieves that thought they would find sanctuary here. *In our home.* The bayou and the town that surrounded it belonged to us. The territorial beast inside me had a strong claim over this land and he had an even stronger opinion about what business people got up to while they were here.

I knew exactly what I was doing when I set the beast loose on the bayou that night. Moonlight glistened in pools of crimson, a sacrifice to the force that ruled our lives. Not mindless killing at all. I saw what they were going to do to *her*, and I made a calculated move.

Violence was necessary to maintain order.

That was how it used to be, anyway. It wouldn't be obvious to locals that it was our retreat from duty that contributed to the increase in crime. I saw it, though. Night after night I heard the roar of engines on back roads, gunshots through the trees. Sometimes, like that night I found *her*, I was out there. Watching. Stalking. Planning my kill.

I wasn't supposed to. After what happened with our cousin Jacques, Saul forbade it. Claimed we were too exposed, and it wasn't our place dole out justice. That was why his face was turning a pretty shade of red as he grasped what I just admitted.

"Dammit!" Saul stood, stomping his boot, and tossing out several curses in French. "What could possibly justify—"

"Someone innocent was going to get hurt!" I stood too. "She was going to get hurt because she got tangled up in a mess that *we* made."

"It's not our mess anymore. Jacques's gone, Barlow is dead, and nothing ties us to any of it."

"Doesn't mean we can just walk away."

"That's exactly what it means!" Saul paced, the worn wood threatening to give under his weight. "You're supposed to stay out of it, Eli. Innocent people will always get hurt. That's the way of the world."

"I couldn't stay out of that." I squeezed my eyes shut and breathed deeply, willing myself to calm. I hadn't been calm since the moment I heard her jagged scream puncture the night. Not much disturbed me, but *that*? That sound, the scent of her fear collecting in the air? It played in my head over and over until I felt sick.

I had the strangest feeling that if I let her die out there, felt the loss of someone precious like her, a part of my soul would wither too.

That night was supposed to be about freedom. When the moon was full, and I was just another shadow. A hunter made of smoke and starlight, whispering between trees. If I wanted to, I could snap my jaws around any number of creatures, catching them completely unaware. Some of the wildlife had learned of our presence and how to avoid it. Most were still dumbstruck when a beast that shouldn't be within a thousand miles of them appeared from the darkness like the devil himself.

That was how I appeared to those bastards the other night, too. I knew the look in their eyes, the horror when an animal sees death barreling at him. Such a delicious, tantalizing terror. Part of me wanted to kill them just for the sport of it. To show men that believed themselves to be the top of the food chain that they were mere rats.

Years of careful practice gave me control over that depraved part. Allowing it to rule me would only lead to the madness our family was so famous for. Murderers and devils, roaming the French countryside and spilling blood as we pleased. That was our legacy, and I wanted no part of it.

It was her that snapped my conviction in two. If she was a drug dealer or some other waste of space begging for mercy from the monsters they helped make, I could have walked away.

But Cady wasn't a monster.

Cady. She had a name and now it was wedged in my brain as the taste of chocolate lingered on my tongue. That combination had my mouthwatering and not because I wanted more cookies.

So trusting, driving into the bayou to deliver a box of cookies to a man she knew committed murder. So, so naive.

"If the girl remains alone in the dark, she will die."

Was I going to kill her? Was that what this sensation was weaving under my skin?

I'd chosen prey before. Followed them for days, even weeks. But they always deserved it. When the moon rose plump and white, they knew what was coming for them.

Cady was blind to it all. She didn't even know why she was out there on the bayou that night. People like her needed to be protected, not hunted.

"You need to lay low." Saul ground out, his silver eyes burning. "Did she see you?" He looked down at the poorly concealed cookies like they were a loaded gun. "Is this her?"

"No." The lie came as easy as breathing. I expected my brother to call me on it. Saul knew my tells. Either he didn't catch my dishonesty, or he didn't care to point it out.

Instead, he stood there, hand gesturing to the cookies and waiting for an explanation. I didn't go into town much. We'd long since removed ourselves from the local community as it became too obvious that we weren't aging the way we ought to.

I shrugged. "I made a friend."

"Unmake one. We can't get mixed up in this town. Not anymore."

Saul scored a rough hand through his beard. It reached all the way down to his collarbones. Generally, my brother's stress level could be read by how poorly he was grooming his beard. Maybe I should be the one asking him what was wrong.

"You heard from Isaac?"

"Nope." I reclined onto my back, propping my hands under my head. "He'll turn up. Just out chasing a different kind of prey."

He sighed. It was a heavy sound that carried all the weight of his years. "He's not supposed to do that."

"A man needs female company."

Saul gave me a disbelieving look. "I don't."

"Maybe you do," I teased. "Might take that tension out of your neck."

"Elijah?"

"Saul?"

"Just be careful."

"Always."

Then he left without even a muttered goodbye and my mind—or the beast that ruled half my mind—immediately jumped back to the same loop I'd been stuck on since this morning.

Cady.

Chapter 7

Death Omens

Cady

*S*HELLS AND *S*HARDS WAS a dumpy tourist trap. Madame Celine clearly worked hard to disguise it and I'd seen enough expensive SUVs parked out here to know her work paid off.

The shop and parlor were set up in a double wide trailer, teetering on the edge of the most popular boat ramp in Port O'Henry. Queen palms swayed happily in the October wind and a handful of evergreen shrubs were planted in front of the trailer to hide the bricks holding it off the ground.

The most offensive part was the giant red sign, advertising psychic readings, complete with glitter and flashing lights. It was a scam, and I was not a fan of scammers. There weren't a lot of ways to earn money in Port O'Henry but that didn't justify dishonesty.

Okay, so what the hell are you doing here, girlfriend?

With a reproachful sigh I pried the door open. Inside, Celine's shop was exactly what I envisioned. Huge, expensive crystals decorated dark wood shelves along the front window. Their glittering forms blocked out most of the light, making the whole space dim. It added to the mysterious allure that the decor was obviously going for. Incense thickened the air. Candles shimmered among overpriced jewelry and gaudy blouses.

Fake candles, I noted with increasing skepticism. Bored wives wasted money in shops like this all over Port O'Henry while their husbands were out fishing.

"You can roll your eyes. You wouldn't be the first."

I jumped at the sudden raspy words. I'd been so fixated on the interior that I hadn't noticed the door to the back room opening. A petite elderly woman stood in the doorway, leathery skin tinted from years of sunshine reflecting off the bay. Her silver hair draped to her waist, almost covering a t-shirt that read, "Talk to me when Mercury isn't in retrograde."

"Not what you expected, eh?"

I flushed. I *had* expected some Gypsy costume with jingling golden jewelry and crystal pendants.

Madame Celine stepped closer, a wizened hand outstretched. My gaze flicked to warm brown eyes, sparkling with mirth. "It's my day off. Usually, I am a little more inspiring." She took my hand and squeezed it too firmly for how frail she appeared.

"I'm sorry, I didn't realize you were closed."

"I left the door open for you." She winked. "You can call me Celine."

"You knew I was coming?"

"I knew I was expecting an important visitor today. Now, do you want your free reading or not?" Celine didn't wait for me to respond. She vanished through a doorway behind the cash register, firelight flickering on the walls inside.

I inhaled and followed her in because why the hell not? This room was lit with real candles, beeswax by the smell. Crystals and animal figurines decorated overcrowded bookshelves. No, not animals, I realized, but anthropomorphic depictions. There was a woman halfway between human and tiger and a man with a wolf's head. For some reason my attention snagged on that one and goosebumps tickled my upper arms.

I tore my focus to the middle of the room, where two sage green chairs flanked a small round table. It was plain and free of decor.

"No crystal ball?"

"Those are bullshit."

I snorted. "What kind to readings do you do, then? Isn't a palm reading on par with a crystal ball?"

"Have a seat and we'll see." Celine settled into one of the chairs and exhaled loudly.

"Did you really know I was coming?"

"Yes." The answer was short and confident.

"How?"

Celine laughed. "God alone knows. He saw fit to give me this gift. I do not question it."

"I don't usually do this," I gestured around the room," sort of thing."

"But you're desperate." Celine held up a hand. "Uh-uh. Don't bother asking. Those are not the kind of answers I promise." She stretched her arms across the table. "Now give me your hands."

I obeyed, reaching hands across the table and gingerly laying them over Celine's. Warmth bloomed where our skin met, and I felt distinctly aware of the contact.

Celine sucked in a breath. "It's been a hard year for you. Lots of loss." She closed her eyes and exhaled again. "Pain. Fear."

I almost agreed in earnest, but I held my tongue. This year *was* terrible. I lost my grandparents just months apart, lost my boss, my job. This kidnapping was only the icing on a rotten cake. Then again, hadn't everyone experienced pain and loss? Was it too far of a stretch for Celine to guess that and wait for affirmation?

As if reading my thoughts, Celine smirked. "Clever, Cady. You are clever."

Well, that was impressive. I hadn't introduced myself. This was a small town, and it was possible she'd known my grandparents. Papa knew just about everyone.

"Let me be more specific. You've been asking questions about the Barbeaux family."

"I have." I nodded, though Celine couldn't see with her eyes closed.

"Why the curiosity?"

I had a sudden, strange feeling of being compelled. Without thinking I began spilling the whole story.

"I was kidnapped. No one believes me. They drove me out to the bayou and threatened to kill me over some money Dale Barlow was supposed to have. Elijah Barbeaux saved my life that night and I had to ask him if he knew who kidnapped me and if they would come back. I don't think they will because I think he killed them, and I really need to know why."

Celine opened her eyes with a start. Apparently, she wasn't all knowing. "Why he did it? That's your most pressing concern?"

"I also need to know that someone else isn't going to try to feed me to alligators." I chewed my lip. "But yes, I need to know why. Why was he there? Why did he help me?" *Why can't I stop thinking about him?* "There's just this nagging feeling like I'm missing something."

The fortune teller was thoughtfully quiet. She glanced down at my palms, lashes fluttering down. "I can't tell you why." She sucked in another breath and shuddered. "I can tell you to tread very carefully."

Duh.

"And I can tell you that Elijah Barbeaux is a dangerous man. He may be easy on the eyes but never let yourself believe that he is docile." Heat burned up my arms and I almost jerked my hands away. "Even so, you need him. Without him you will be lost."

"Lost?"

"Eternally lost."

"I—thanks for your time. I should go." This time I did jerk my hands away, rising quickly.

My head felt light, and I wanted to run as far from here as I could get. This was stupid. A stupid distraction from the very real danger I was in.

"One more thing, Cady." Celine stood. "Eli needs you too. He just doesn't know it yet."

I nodded awkwardly and hurried back to the front door. My attention caught on a shelf decorated with old photographs and my steps faltered. I approached with quaking breath, somehow knowing what I would see. There on the middle shelf was a dusty picture of three men, posed in front of a barn.

The tallest sported a thick beard and a scowl, looking every bit the small-town farmer that he was. Standing to his right were two smiling young men, one lean and handsome, his smile dashed with mischief. The other was nearly identical to the first, except he was broader, his features more prominent, his figure thicker. His smile was much sweeter, all crinkled eyes and easy charm.

That smile was foreign to me, but there was no denying who this was.

"I'm somewhat of a history buff," Celine said from behind me. "Most of these photographs are from the old Barbeaux homestead, before the hurricane of '53."

"As in 1953?"

"Of course."

I raised my cell phone and snapped a picture, not believing the conclusion my mind jumped to but not knowing what other possibility there was. Elijah Barbeaux and his brothers were in that photograph, looking as young and healthy as they did two days ago.

I waved at Celine, trying to swallow my heart back into my chest as I hurried out to the parking lot.

MY HANDS WERE STILL shaking as I wandered away from Madame Celine's shop and followed the boardwalk at *Rocky's Dock.* This time of day the boat launch was seeing the last busy hour as early season duck hunters were coming in for the evening. Heavy duty trucks with long boat trailers were parked in rows along the gravel parking lot, adjacent to the water. More were lined up and idling near the concrete ramps that led into the Cadalina canal, waiting to haul boats out of the water. The sun wouldn't set for an hour, but the foamy waves were already golden brown as daylight came to a close.

Just past *Rocky's* was a series of boat storage units on the edge of the water. Further down the road was the cheapest motel in town—and the entire Gulf of Mexico, probably—and a country bar that I wouldn't go into if someone paid me. The patrons were a combination of people I knew and chose not to associate with and people from out of town that thought every small town girl was desperate for the attention of city slickers.

It was a shame because the area was beautiful in that special Port O'Henry way. Everything reeked of diesel and fish but even the putrid smell was nostalgic to me. The bar had a broad boardwalk that connected the surrounding waterside businesses and eventually led to a short pier. During low tide the water retreated enough for a fluffy beach to stretch out under the pier. It wasn't any cleaner than the main beach and I'd cut my foot on stray hooks more than once.

What I liked about it was that it was mine. Every once in a while, a motel guest would come out at the right time of day and discover it, but most often, it was one last secret about Port O'Henry that I didn't have to share with the swelling tourist population.

I let out a watery sigh, covering my face with my hands and clenching my teeth. I wanted more days of strolling secret beaches under pink sherbet sunsets. More days to fish and swim and live my life. How was I supposed to do that now?

Even without being kidnapped I was months away from destitution and the job prospects in Port O'Henry were worse than ever. Property taxes were through the roof, and I could scarcely afford to run the AC in the summer. For all the vitriol I was gathering for Barlow—God rest his wicked soul—the job he gave me was a life raft.

My grandparents left me the house and for that I was grateful, but their income was depleted when they passed. They were constantly being cheated by their health insurance and cancer treatment wasn't cheap. At seventy-three Papa was still taking odd jobs to keep the lights on.

I doubted myself most during those days. How would our lives have looked if I hadn't abandoned my scholarship and gone to school in Chicago instead of staying? I probably wasn't going to pay the bills writing poetry, but a degree would have opened so many doors for me. A practical job with practical income.

Then Nana might have died while I was almost fifteen hundred miles away. She would have spent long days alone in a dim bedroom, contemplating her own mortality. The heartbreak of that would have been ten times worse than sitting at her bedside and holding her cool hand as she took her last breaths.

I shook the thought away. I didn't leave Port O'Henry then and I wouldn't leave it now. Cowards ran from their troubles, and I wasn't raised to be a coward.

A shadow passed in my peripherals, and I whirled on the boardwalk, hoping I was about to run into a happy hour fisherman. I could handle a little harassment. I couldn't handle being clubbed over the head and dropped into the canal. Or tossed into another trunk.

Not planning to repeat that experience.

There was no one behind me. Music leaked through the back doors of the bar and the scent of garbage wafted toward me. It was only then that I realized how stupid I was, walking alone on the boardwalk near sunset. I wanted to believe that someone wouldn't attack me in a public setting like this but there definitely weren't security cameras, except those along the entryway to the boat storage, and most people who were out in this area had already been drinking for some time.

I reached for the strap of my purse to remind myself I wasn't helpless anymore.

Gun? Check.

I scurried back along the boardwalk toward the gravel lot where I'd left the jeep, suddenly feeling watched. I was almost back where I started when the name of a steel building caught my attention.

Lone Star Boat Storage.

I knew from monthly bills that this was where Barlow kept his boat. The fancy houses in *Pelican Bay* were nice to look at but they didn't have room to store an offshore vessel like the one he owned. Still riding my wave of stupid choices, I ducked around the corner of the main building and started down the narrow dock that separated the individual storage sheds. The boats suspended over the churning water could probably cover my cost of living for a year, so I was a little surprised there wasn't more security.

The sound of waves sloshing against the concrete wall was loud enough to drown out any other noise. That prickle on the nape of my neck was still tingling and I knew that this was a terrible idea. It was also the perfect time to investigate a boat that I wasn't technically supposed to be messing with.

The men that took me mentioned boats and money. They'd probably already searched Barlow's boat. There was one camera at the start of the dock, and I knew during peak season they had an attendant in the main office. The hum of trucks had died down as I passed through the parking lot, and I realized that just about *everyone* was gone now.

Just me and the boats. And the ghost I swore I could feel at my back.

I peered over my shoulder every few steps, making sure I wasn't being stalked by a hooded figure.

Nope, still alone.

I didn't know which unit was Barlow's. I wasn't even certain what kind of boat he owned. What I did know was the name, *Dewy Pearl*, given to honor his first wife and the mother of his son. I peeked into every unit, skimming the sides of boats and murmuring names. It wasn't until I got to the final unit and saw an empty space that my stomach sank. Somehow, I knew this was Barlow's space.

His boat was gone.

I stood there longer than I should have, watching the water wash in and out of the concrete ramp where the boat could be lowered into the water. If there was money on that boat, someone already had it. Did that mean they would leave me alone?

No, it probably meant they would kill me because I knew they were looking for it.

But the men who took me are dead.

Yeah, and the thought that I couldn't get out of my head lately was, *what if whoever they worked for thinks I killed them?* I already had a target on my head for being the closest person to Barlow's finances. Now gangster thought I whacked his guys—*too much TV, Cady girl*—and coming after me in retribution.

Damn, I really had no idea what to do next. I wanted to believe that this nightmare ended that night on the bayou when Elijah Barbeaux ended those men. But I knew better. I could feel myself being hunted.

A scuff on the dock had me whirling. The sun was lingering on the very edge of the horizon, thin rays reaching out but not quite making it to me. When I saw a shadow zip behind a storage shed this time, I knew I wasn't seeing things. Someone else was out here.

My heart hammered behind my ribs and for a breathless moment I was paralyzed. Fresh fear coated my skin in cold sweat, and I trembled. But was I trembling because I was afraid or because I was *pissed as hell* at whoever thought they could wreck my life?

Tucking one hand in my purse, ready to draw my gun, I shuffled back down the dock, hurrying after my stalker like the dumb blonde in a horror movie. Blondie wasn't strapped though.

Wow, was my confidence going to get me killed. I hadn't even loaded the damn thing.

The huge silhouette of a man passed between the office and the storage buildings, turning toward the bar. His long legs carried him quickly and I picked up speed, jogging on the slippery wood and praying I didn't fall into the water in the dark.

I made it to the boardwalk when I saw the last hint of light glinting off copper irises and my heart stuttered. Elijah Barbeaux was watching me from the edge of a shadow. My shock stole my reaction and by the time I had my feet moving again he was gone. I lost him at the same moment I lost my courage, realizing I was well and truly alone out here now. Country music still blasted out of the concrete building ahead of me and light spilled out onto the boardwalk as a woman burst outside in a frantic shuffle.

Her blonde hair streaked behind her as she made her way toward my secret beach. She stopped when someone snagged her attention, another bar patron stepping out the back door. I caught a glimpse of his profile and I blinked.

What the hell?

It was Elijah again, wearing completely different clothes. His hair was slicked back too expertly to have been done in the last thirty seconds.

"Mister Barbeaux?" I called hesitantly, wanting to call him out for following me but not understanding how I could have seen him moments ago.

The man looked over his shoulder and it wasn't Elijah. But it also was. Leaner with a more angular face. His eyes were greener, and his dark hair was cropped short on the sides. I remembered the third Barbeaux brother from the photograph. I'd seen him at *Uncle's* too.

What were the odds that they were both here?

What were the odds that I was losing my mind?

Not wanting an awkward confrontation, I opted for option B, "Cady is going bonkers," and ran back to my jeep as fast as my short legs would carry me.

Two weeks ago, I was bored out of my mind, daydreaming of a job at some big city publishing company. Now every day was loaded with more excitement than my poor brain could manage.

Nana always warned me to be careful what I wished for. "Ask and God delivers," she would say.

I wondered if it was too late to make a return on this particular delivery.

Chapter 8

Fever Dream

Cady

"**C**ADY."

Sweat collected between my breasts. The fabric of my shirt clung to my tacky skin. I shifted on the couch, failing to find a good position. Deep in my chest I felt a tug.

"Cady."

Why was it so hot? I'd been keeping the AC down—the energy bill was already expensive and now I was jobless—but even so this was unbearable. October was not supposed to be this warm.

"*Cady.*"

I sat up, rubbing my slick forehead. Impulsively I headed for the front door, twisting the deadbolt, and throwing it open. Brined air rushed through my hair, cooling my nose, and drawing out an audible sigh.

But that wasn't why I was out here.

Overhead the stars were pinpricks of light on a black velvet canvas. The moon was a waning gibbous and it lit up the distant waves of the bay, trailing a silver path all the way to my driveway. That was how I spotted a set of tawny eyes watching me from the bottom of the porch.

Some inborn animal part of me immediately kicked into flight. There was a predator watching me and the urge to run made my legs quake. Yet the urge to gravitate toward those oddly familiar eyes had me walking to the railing and leaning over, ignoring the voice of self-preservation. Whatever—whoever—was down there would still have to climb the stairs and get over the waist-high gate. It would give me plenty of time to retreat inside.

My gaze focused on the shadows, and I gasped. *He was here.* Elijah Barbeaux was standing at the foot of my stairs. In the dark he was otherworldly. *More.*

A savage smile spread his lips. The saltwater breeze swished through his dark hair and took the breath from my lungs as it did.

"Cady," he purred, "Come here."

I almost did. I almost unlocked the gate and raced down the stairs with reckless abandon. Then I remembered that this man was a murderer.

Was he even here? Or was this some strange fever dream? His truck wasn't within sight of the house and there was no way he walked this far from the bayou. It would take half the night.

I blinked, startled that I was standing at the top of the stairs. When did I—

"Cady."

Elijah was just on the other side of the gate, bending over to scent the sweat on my skin. He was so close I could feel his breath. The sweet and smoky fragrance of campfire clung to him, mingling with a zest like bald cypress after hours in the sun, as if he was so much a part of the bayou that it lived in his blood, permeated his pores.

As he studied me, hands inches from me, flexing like they were just waiting for permission to touch, I saw it. The man from that photograph and the man in front of me were the same. They had to be. He was just too intense. Too different.

"Who are you?" I whispered hoarsely.

"Who?" His nose traced a line from my collarbone to my ear. "Or what?"

I shuddered and it wasn't out of fear. "What are you?"

He nipped my earlobe. "I think you know."

"Elijah."

"Eli."

"Eli," it rolled sensuously off my tongue, and he made a dark, satisfied sound.

His mouth swept a bead of sweat from my neck, lacing my insides with an electric thrill. My resistance snapped like an overstretched rubber band, and I arched forward, hips bumping into the gate, an infuriating separation between bodies. Those massive hands finally made contact with my skin, running up my arms to cup my shoulders, and my body ignited. I reached across the gate and fisted his shirt, trying to drag him closer.

His salacious expression melted into tender affection, eyes glinting with surprised delight, and he leaned into my eager hands, bringing my chest flush against his. "I've waited so long for you. You're more beautiful than I ever could have imagined."

I wanted to tell him that I didn't understand but I couldn't form words. My lips were too busy nibbling at his throat, tasting that smoky sweetness. I was delirious with desire, a sudden burning need oozing through my veins and gathering in my belly, then lower and lower until I was rubbing my thighs together.

Movement was limited and awkward because of the gate between us but it didn't stop Eli's wending hands from slipping beneath my shirt, circling sensitive flesh on his languid journey down. At the same time his mouth skimmed over my collarbone and my knees went weak.

It wasn't *where* he was touching me so much as it was the fact that *he* was doing the touching. Eli Barbeaux occupied nearly one hundred percent of my waking thoughts. He was becoming an obsession. There was probably some psychology to that, a hero worship complex that wasn't going to serve me well when I woke up from this fantasy.

That's what it had to be—my stressed brain conjuring some vision to cope—because this was not the Eli that chased me off his property. This Eli was purring at the barest caress, tasting me like I was his favorite food. I couldn't reconcile the two versions of him.

His fingertips thrummed with magic, spelling me with a ravenous appetite that only he could fulfill. "What are you doing to me?"

"Only what you've been doing to me for days, darlin'." It didn't really matter what he said, those throaty words alone could bring me to climax.

The night air was cool, but my skin was scalding as his thumbs traced over my hips. He was the only cure for the fever that consumed me. It wouldn't break until Eli was *inside me*. Right now, if he asked me to walk off the end of the jetty into the waves I would, as long as he didn't take his hands off me.

As if reading my mind his fingers dipped under my cotton shorts, my lack of panties eliciting a delicious groan from him. This was a dream so there was no harm in indulging, right?

I opened my legs in invitation. He continued to tease just above my curls. I squeezed his wrist and begged him, "Touch me."

His fingers darted between my legs, finding me slick and swollen. "Like this?"

"*More*. Inside me." I shook with need, afraid I would collapse before he could get rid of this ache.

His mouth hovered over mine, but he didn't kiss me, only breathed against me. "Whatever you want, darlin', you can have it."

"I need you to touch me. *Please*." I had this sudden fear that I might die if he didn't stop teasing.

Eli Barbeaux saved my life for a second time as he pressed his middle finger deep inside me. When I didn't protest, he added a second, pumping a slow rhythm. I rocked my hips desperately, grinding into the heel of his palm and panting each breath. I burned hotter and hotter until it seemed fire was collecting between my legs.

Eli bit down on the side of my neck harder than a lover should and that edge of pain unlaced my tension in a flowing ribbon of pleasure. I moaned as an endless climax crashed through me, loud enough that the entire block probably heard. He didn't silence me, didn't say anything as those burnished irises were devoured by his pupils.

My hands were digging into his shoulders, and I was pretty sure that was the only reason I was still upright. Eli waited until my muscles stopped clenching before dragging his hand out of my shorts and leaning away with a wicked smile.

"Eli?" It was meant to be a question, but it came out as a pouty noise I'd never known myself to make. He'd barely scratched the surface of my craving for him and now he was retreating. I needed to keep tasting him, to let his lips seal with mine. My core fluttered with aftershocks, achingly hollow, desperate to be full of him. I tightened my grip on his shirt, trying to draw him back to me, but he gently removed my hands, kissing the knuckles on each one with a chuckle.

His voice was full of grit when he promised, "I'll be back when the moon is full, if I can stay away that long."

I wrapped a hand around my throat, mostly to stop the tingling from where his teeth marked my skin. The full moon? I had so many questions I didn't even know where to begin. But in an instant, he was gone, running—yes, running like a track star in Levi's—into the darkness. If this was a dream, why was he leaving? And why was I suddenly so cold?

I was beginning to think the rumors about the bayou weren't all that absurd anymore.

I was also starting to wonder if Eli Barbeaux was more dangerous than the people who wanted Barlow's money. Maybe it wasn't them I needed to worry about.

Chapter 9

Sleepwalker

Eli

I COULDN'T BELIEVE I was here again. The moon was bright, the stars were out, and I was sprinting toward Celine's shop, barefoot. She wouldn't have answers for me. Not without a price. But I was growing desperate, and I wasn't ready to go to my brother with this. Saul was a good sounding board when it came to practical problems. This problem was not practical.

The whole situation was foreign. My mind was becoming a strobe light of deviant images and bestial chaos.

It wasn't uncommon for me to sleepwalk. When there were two consciousnesses inside of you, one civilized and one feral, there was bound to be some overlap. Even when I didn't take the form of the beast, I would often have *urges*. Usually, those urges kept me safely in the bayou. Like the need for a midnight patrol of my property or the desire to chase a small creature.

Never in my many years had I left the bayou. It wasn't safe. My instinct was always to stay within my territory.

Unless I was hunting bigger prey.

Dread made my stomach dip in time with the distant rush of low tide. Why was I hunting Cady? The echo of her screams were still burned into my soul, and I felt no thrill when I recalled them.

In my brief glimpses of memory from tonight, thrill was all I felt. That zing of adrenaline when I was on the trail of something small and delicious.

Delicious indeed. Cheeks flushed, hair mussed by the wind, eyes hooded with sleep as she looked out over her deck. Those tiny cotton shorts revealing tanned legs. The beads of sweat cooling on her skin as I inhaled the peachy scent of her.

How did I get close enough to smell her? It was all a blur. Her scent was coating me, drugging my animal half into a stupor. I was going to have some serious explaining to do. Especially if she called the cops. Poor woman was already spooked enough after what happened to her and now I was...fuck, what the hell was I even doing there?

I cursed the dozing beast inside me.

It was bad when she ambushed me today. I used all my willpower to let her off that boat. The voice in my head—the voice of the beast—wanted me to drive her out into the bay and stay there. She was safe from collecting anymore bruises if we were on the water. There shouldn't be any marks on her perfect skin, but the ones left by me. Out on the bay she couldn't escape me. She was always running, like a little mouse darting away. Sooner or later, I was going to catch her for good.

I wasn't surprised when I twisted the handle on Celine's back door and found it unlocked. Nor was I surprised to find her sitting at her table, dressed in a black satin robe and pouring a cup of tea from a jade green tea pot.

"I hope you're not going to make a habit of this, Elijah. A woman my age needs her beauty sleep."

"Am I going to kill her?"

"Kill who?"

I slammed my hands on the table and snarled. I knew the face Celine saw at that moment was barely human. "No more games! Am I going to kill her? Am I the reason she dies?" I ripped my hands from the table and started pacing frantically. "I was at her house tonight. Not *this* me."

For once Celine dropped the facade, her face crinkling in alarm. "Did she know you were there?"

Fur shivered up my arms and I bared my teeth in an animal grin. "I made sure of it." I had the sudden vulgar desire to smell my fingers. Memories zipped in and out of my mind in fractured pieces. *Her eyes wide with shock, my hands enveloping her soft flesh, my teeth on her skin.*

Her crying out before I fled.

The color drained from Celine's cheeks. "What did you do?"

It wasn't me that answered. "Took what's mine." I clapped a hand over my face and moaned, "Lord help me, I can't remember."

Those little flecks of memory kept dripping in, painting a hazy but decipherable picture. Damn, I was definitely not trying to kill her. For the first time since I was a young man, I blushed.

Celine cackled. She laughed so hard her tea sloshed over the side of the cup as she tried to set it down. "Elijah Barbeaux, do you mean to tell me that an old coot like you can't tell the difference between aggression and attraction?" She wiped beneath her eyes, sobering a little as she did. "You're sure she knew you were there?"

My face still felt hot when I confirmed, "I was impossible to miss."

"Interesting."

"I hate that sly tone, woman. What did you mean about attraction?" Cady was beautiful, I'd noticed.

I'd noticed the freckles that splashed across her nose and down her neck, painting her arms and shoulders in the same delicate constellations. I'd noticed the way her loose curls were a touch too brown to be red. Looking into her eyes was like watching the evening sky over the bay, a deep dusk colored blue that made you feel settled.

Those were all superficial. What was it about her that burrowed so deeply into my grey matter?

"Oh, hell." My bloodline was old and the hunger for death was always a looming threat. I assumed I wanted to eat her in a more literal sense.

The smile on Celine's face was downright evil. "You're not going to kill her, idiot."

I dropped into the chair across from her with a sigh. "But she's still going to die."

"Everyone dies." She poured a second cup of tea and pushed it my way.

"The last time I was here you made it sound like she would die *soon*."

"Would you care if it wasn't your fault?"

My growl was so violent it surprised me. "*Yes*."

"Interesting indeed."

"Stop saying that."

Celine scoffed. "Quit acting so much like that older brother of yours and lighten up, Eli. She could die. Or she could live. If only she had someone to shield her from the threat she will be blind to..."

I gulped my tea, wincing when it burned my throat. "I'm not supposed to interact with outsiders anymore. S'too dangerous."

"You should make an exception for this one. Seems like your other half already has."

"Why?" Even as I questioned her, I knew Celine was right. I wasn't going to stay away from Cady. If the beast wasn't planning to kill her then I wasn't even going to *try* to stay away from her. What was the point when I was sleepwalking up her porch at one in the morning?

"Your kind is so bull headed sometimes." She rolled her eyes. "Because you've bonded with her, Elijah."

"Impossible." I shook my head too vehemently. "Barbeauxs' don't get bonds. Not since the first one."

The magic that made us what we were was built on a bond. A reckless, foolish bond that ended with one lover dead and the other a raving monster with nothing to stop him. No one knew the true story of the Beast of Gévaudan except for those of us descended from him. A tragedy that would haunt our blood until our kind ceased to exist.

My great grandmother crafted the original spell to bind herself to my great grandfather, believing that the threat of her life ending with his was enough to stop her family from separating them. To guarantee they kept their promise, she made him strong. Gave him the ferocity and instincts of a wolf by twining two souls into one body.

But magic always had a price and in the end they both paid it. And every generation after them, right down to my brothers and me.

"Who told you that?" Celine looked pleased, as if she was in on a secret that I didn't know.

Even as I went to deny it again, I knew she was right. That deeply primal part of me knew the same way I knew when a storm was blowing in before the clouds appeared.

"What does that mean?" The question made me feel like a sheepish boy, especially when Celine laughed.

"You're much too old for the birds and bees talk, Elijah."

"But bonds take two people. She and I haven't...bonded." Not that I was going to say no if she wanted to.

"And you may never 'bond.'"

I swallowed, suddenly feeling ill. "What happens to this then?" I gestured vaguely at my chest, as if that explained my compulsion to be near her.

"Madness, I suppose."

Madness.

I never cared much for family history. My father would wax on about *the old ways* and how much he hated the changing world, and it bored me to tears. Now I wished I paid more attention, took mental note during those rare moments of honesty where he exposed the depth of what we were. Saul was the only one with answers anymore and I was still skirting around him like a teenager avoiding the authoritarian parent.

My only real option was trial by fire, and I wasn't too keen on the stakes.

Win and I would get the girl. Lose and I became what I loathed.

I WASN'T FINISHED WITH Celine, not even close, but she was finished with me. She left me wandering the poorly lit streets of Port O'Henry, mind whirring with unanswered questions.

Eventually two sleepless nights—couldn't risk sleepwalking to Cady's house again—gave me a plan. If Saul asked, I was sleuthing. He told me to stay out of it but this whole missing money situation had Jacques written all over it. We needed to know if he was back in Texas.

And if Cady asked? Well, I was just being a good neighbor. I was still figuring that part out when I parked my truck on a patch of gravel near Barlow's property and hopped out.

Crickets chirped cheerfully in the grass. The wind whistled along to their tune, cool but still humid from the autumn rain. I rubbed the back of my neck for the third time in ten minutes. A light was on in the shop house on the corner of the Barlow residence. Beside it a luxury RV was cast in shifting shadows as someone moved around in front of the window.

If it was a different part of town, I would have suspected burglary. Or whoever Barlow had been wrapped up with coming to collect what they were owed. But even when these oversized vacation homes were left empty, the properties weren't unsecured. From here I could see the blinking red lights of at least three security cameras.

In fact, Barlow's was the only house on the street without one of those fancy doorbell cameras and a top-notch security system. That alone was an admission of guilt.

The man had problems. Drinking and gambling and occasional womanizing were the least of them. Men like Dale Barlow got themselves in deep one way or another. Some people were just like that.

The worst part about them was that they dragged everyone around them down too. Poor Cady was just too innocent to realize what she was getting herself into. Using her to keep his business books was probably part of his cover. She was one of the few honest people left in the world. Someone like her could manage the *Stop N' Shop* finances and make it look like Barlow was a successful businessman.

Technically he had been a successful businessman. His success just hadn't come from selling overpriced sunglasses and cold beer to tourists.

Now the question was, who did Barlow do successful business with? Once upon a time my brothers and I were intimately acquainted with his darker deeds. Not something I wanted to associate myself with back then and it certainly wasn't something I would turn back to again, even if I found myself as desperate as before.

Plenty of regular folks made a living in regular ways. Saul was so fixated on avoiding life outside the bayou that he let our bastard cousin manipulate him into all his schemes. Our troubles would be much, much bigger if we got wrapped up with law enforcement. Saul didn't see it that way.

That was the struggle with my brother. His past had formed thick blinders around his vision. He couldn't see much of what was going on unless it was smacking him in the face.

Isaac and I still looked to Saul to lead us. He was the firstborn and to our kind, that held significance. Not only that, but he also spent the most time with our father. He was entrenched in the old ways, and we were raised to believe we were meant to follow them.

Maybe that was why Saul was so unbending. He never really left that life behind.

I did. No use remembering things that didn't do you any good. I was coming to realize there was still a chance for happiness. We'd done so much wrong, but the beauty of a long life was that we could do so much right too.

I had no intention of telling my brothers that. Not yet. First, I needed to find out if Barlow ended up back in business with the undesirables of the Barbeaux clan. Then I could talk to Saul.

Never about Cady though. Only after I followed this thing to its end.

This thing. Isaac would tease me for being unromantic. I didn't really have a word for it. It wasn't a *bond* if both of us didn't accept it. But somehow, I was still *bonded*. Didn't really seem fair. Didn't really make sense, either. Only because Saul wouldn't tell us anything about bonds except that, "They don't happen for direct descendants." Something about family curses and soiled bloodlines.

I wasn't sure I believed in curses. Ironic, given my condition. But the original werewolf wasn't cursed. We were born out of love, a desperate sort of love that made people do stupid things.

Stupid things like linger in the shadows for a chance to talk to the woman I couldn't get out of my head.

I looked between the shop house and the red jeep parked at the end of the driveway. The sky was already bathed in purple light. Soon it would be dark, and Cady was out here alone again.

Now that I was trying to figure out how to approach this situation, I realized what a terrible idea it was to be here. I didn't have much experience with this, especially not recently.

But the scent of her was woven into my lungs, lacing every breath with an intoxicant that dulled my logical mind and dissolved my inhibitions. I wanted this woman more than I wanted to breathe and however long it took, no matter what she asked of me, I would do it to make her mine.

Chapter 10

Nosferatu

Cady

I BROKE THE LAW once before. Well, a series of times within one weekend. Sixteen years old, getting plastered with my friends during a summer camping trip. I thoroughly regretted it then and I prayed I wouldn't regret it nearly as much now.

Stealing paperwork and personal items from a dead man was a lot worse than stealing a bottle of gin from Nana's closet and mixing it with fruit punch until I hurled.

The hurling might still happen before the night was over.

Bile crept up the back of my throat. I hadn't intended to be here this long. Until tonight I wasn't brave enough to come back. Though I couldn't remember what happened that night, not clearly, I knew I wasn't safe here. My survival instincts were blaring the flight alarm at full volume.

But I had to know what was going on. Otherwise, I had no idea if someone else would come to me believing I knew about this missing money.

I did all my work for Barlow in the shop house at the back of the property. Originally it was designed to be a guest home but half of it had been converted into an office. The bathroom still doubled as a laundry room and there was a single bedroom furnished for guests. Every few weeks Barlow would ask me to work from home because there were guests in the house.

Before, I never questioned it. Now I was suspicious of everything that went on under this roof.

That was why I searched the place.

I wasn't the first person with the same idea, unfortunately. The door to the shop house was ajar when I arrived, indicating that someone had departed with little concern about what was left in here. Papers from the filing cabinets were strewn everywhere. Stuffing from the cushions curled under my feet as I shuffled around the narrow space, and the mattress was off kilter on the bed frame.

Another point deducted from the Sheriff's trustworthiness because supposedly he sent deputies to "investigate." Unless it was the deputies—specifically Ricky Holt—that were responsible for this mess. That wouldn't shock me at this point. Most of Port O'Henry was on my suspect list.

In my own search I found little more than a sealed safe in the desk drawer, some pills I assumed were illicit because they were stashed in a plastic baggy in the guest room nightstand, and a lot of condoms. More condoms than a portly widower over fifty should have, as far as I was concerned.

It was lodged in my head that I was looking for off the books money or anything about boats. Barlow only had one boat. *Had* being the operative word because it was missing. It was an offshore boat, fancier than most fishing boats but not in yacht territory. Plenty of room to hide money.

But the boat was gone so it didn't matter.

With arms full of filing boxes, I hurried out the door, this time loading everything into my trunk and occasionally turning to make sure no one was at my back. I took all the paperwork that was left, not bothering to check if it was directly related to finances or not. There had to be information hidden in this disordered mess.

The driveway was bathed in shadows as I stepped out into the evening with a final collection of stray papers. I hadn't anticipated sunset coming so early—we were only a week into October—and now I was panicking. I could almost hear Nana saying, "They have an app for that now."

Speaking of apps. I fumbled to slip my phone from the back pocket of my jeans with my free hand, hoping to scare the dark away with the flashlight app.

That distraction was my downfall. A shadow passed the jeep, coming at me fast. The kidnappers were back. Or whatever mobsters Barlow owed money to were here to collect and I was the only one with kneecaps to break.

Suddenly I remembered the weight in my purse and dropped everything. Papers scattered at my feet, immediately catching in the wind as I released them. I fought with the zipper of my purse, frantically pulling at the cheap metal. The shadow moved closer still, obviously a man now. A big man.

I finally yanked my gun free and pointed it wildly into the dark.

"Don't come any—"

A huge hand flew into view. It gripped the slide of the gun and pushed it back so hard that I stumbled. A second hand came to my waist, whirling me around until my back slammed into a man's chest. The first hand finished disarming me by wrenching the gun out of my grip and holding it high over my head.

I was about to scream when my attacker said, "Guns are much more effective if you load 'em, darlin'," in a deep drawl.

My body betrayed me with a delighted shiver. That gravelly voice filled my dreams, soothing away the nightmares as I replayed every lurid detail of our encounter on my porch.

I shoved away and was surprised when the arm around me relaxed. I twisted, heart pounding, and found I wasn't mistaken. He was the last person I expected to meet at the foot of Barlow's porch and that was probably foolish of me. Eli Barbeaux was popping up in all sorts of strange places lately.

My thighs clenched together involuntarily. "Mister Barbeaux?"

His mouth hitched up in a half smile, crinkling the skin around his eyes and revealing an almost-dimple. "Eli."

"Eli," I echoed, feeling a sense of DeJa'Vu and swallowing down the buzz of nerves that wanted to reenact last night.

Then I remembered myself and scurried as far away as I could get. The porch for the shop house was small and the door swung out. I wasn't sure if I could open it and get inside while he was standing this close.

My mind started conjuring images of him from the first night we met. Blood on his face.

Vampire. Vampires lived eternal lives, right? And killing people wasn't out of the question either. My neck tingled where his mouth had been the night before and I started to panic even harder. That *wasn't* a dream. When I looked in the mirror this morning, I found the faintest outline of teeth marks on my skin.

Vampires are not real, Cady. You have PTSD. This man is a crazy, hot bayou murderer and your brain is just trying to make it make sense.

"Give me back my gun."

Eli made a show of pulling back the slide again, double checking the thing was unloaded before handing it over with the muzzle pointed down. I snatched it away from him and gripped it so hard my fingers hurt.

"Trigger."

"Huh?" I risked a glance away from him to look down where my finger was curled over the trigger.

"Your finger is on the trigger and your safety is off."

"Okay?" It wasn't meant to be a question, but I didn't know what he was getting at.

"You've never used one of those, have you?"

"I haven't shot anyone, no."

"Have you shot *anything*?" When I just stared dumbly, he asked, "Range target? Soda cans? Nothing?"

I shook my head.

"Dammit, woman, you're going to accidentally shoot yourself. Assuming you ever load that thing."

"I'm not going to shoot myself." Self-consciously I removed my finger from the trigger and stuffed the gun back into my purse. If he was going to attack me there was no use keeping the gun out. He was right about loading it, but I hadn't found the guts to do it yet. Because, *yes*, I was afraid I would shoot myself.

"What are you doing here?"

Eli bent to scoop up a Tupperware he'd dropped in the altercation. *My* Tupperware. "Just thought I should return this."

"In the middle of the night?"

He checked an invisible watch on his wrist. "S'only just the end of the workday, miss."

"But how did you know I would be here?" Without meaning to I thumbed along my neck where his teeth had been the night before. He didn't seem like the Eli that I saw last night, half-wild and with an appetite for more than chocolate chunk cookies.

Every time I encountered Eli Barbeaux, he had a different personality.

"Process of elimination. You weren't home."

"So, you know where I live." I studied his face, waiting for him to admit that he'd been on my porch last night with his hand down my pants. He kept eye contact, a mischievous smile creasing his eyes, and my cheeks started to burn.

"You know where I live," he countered.

Friction expanded between us the longer I stared, a tangled web of fear and illicit thrill. His expression gave away nothing and again I felt the sensation of being watched by an eager predator.

"You ate the cookies? If that wasn't you on the bayou those weren't for you."

Eli's rumbling laughter was unexpectedly soothing. "A man only has so much self-control." That was an innuendo, I just knew it.

"I need to ask you something."

I had a dozen questions for him, but I asked the one that seemed most important. And no, it wasn't, "Did you give me the best orgasm of my life while standing on my porch at one in the morning or was that some other Eli?"

Instead, I asked, "Who are you?"

Not missing a beat, he extended a hand for me to shake. "Elijah Barbeaux. My friends call me Eli."

I didn't shake his hand.

"*What* are you?" It wasn't crazy to ask. He was the one that suggested the question.

This time there was a moment of hesitation, so brief it was little more than a blink, but I saw it. "There are a lot of malicious rumors out there about my family."

It was true that there were plenty of rumors about the Barbeaux boys and what they got up to on the bayou: cooking meth, illegally hunting and fishing, even witchcraft. But that wasn't what I was referring to.

I whipped out my phone and showed him the picture I took at Celine's. "This is you and your brothers. How do you explain that?"

His lips spread in a slow, indulgent smile. "It's not called Barbeaux Bayou for nothin', darlin'."

That crossed my mind. I knew a big portion of Port O'Henry used to be the Barbeaux homestead. It even occurred to me that Elijah, Saul, and Isaac were family names. But it wasn't just a resemblance I saw in that photograph. The three men were the *same*, right down to Saul's shaggy beard and the way Eli smiled.

"You were at my house last night."

"I sleepwalk."

I choked on an incredulous laugh. He was seriously trying to pass that as sleepwalking?

"I ate garlic bread for lunch." Dammit, I shouldn't have watched that vampire movie marathon alone. This was getting out of hand. I was absolutely positive that I was having some kind of stress psychosis episode.

And I was absolutely positive that something very strange was going on with Eli Barbeaux.

"Tuna salad sandwich." Eli pointed to himself.

"What?"

"That's what I had for lunch, since we're sharing."

I edged closer to the shop house door. If I could just catch it with my foot—yes! I rushed into the safety of the doorway and clicked the light on.

"You don't have permission to enter."

Eli nearly startled a scream from me when he pushed past me, strolling into the shop house and looking around with an impressed nod. "Nice place. A little stuffy. Not sure I like how you redecorated."

He dropped into an office chair and propped his feet on the desk. "Pretty sure that trick only works if it's your own home." With a grin, Eli scratched his chin. "Oh, and if I'm actually a *vampire*."

"You're making fun of me." I collapsed into the chair across from the desk and dropped my head on my arms. "I've had a really shitty week, mister, and the last thing I need is to be eaten by a vampire."

"I think the scientific term is 'exsanguinated.'"

I peeked up from over my forearm. "You know a lot about vampires for someone that isn't a one."

"I watch a lot of television." He bared his teeth. "Don't look so surprised. Somehow, I find the time between victims."

"Shit!" I bolted out of the chair and ran back onto the driveway. "No, no, no!" In my tussle with Eli, I completely forgot the papers now scattered down the street.

I was on all fours, scrabbling to grab whatever I could see in the faded light.

I was only peripherally aware of Eli until he appeared beside me, a handful of papers extended in a peace offering. I was the one who needed to make peace. First, I showed up at his house and climbed onto his boat, then I accused him of being a vampire like a total lunatic.

"You must think I'm so crazy." I gave a halfhearted laugh and added the papers to a box in the front seat of the jeep. "I'm so embarrassed. I'm really not like this."

"I think you're scared. Makes people desperate."

Those words made me feel oddly vulnerable, and I had to blink tears away. "And what exactly is it that I'm scared of?"

"Vampires, apparently."

"I was kidnapped last week. My boss was hiding money from some mobsters or something and now they believe I know where it is." I shut the door to the jeep and crossed my arms. "But I think you already know that because you were there that night."

Eli leaned forward, that generous smile still plastered across his face. It was a terribly disarming smile, handsome with just the right amount of masculine appeal, and it was throwing me off. Plus, the man was huge and having to look up to him put me at a disadvantage.

"Can't say I recall." It was a blatant lie, and he didn't bother trying to hide that.

"You should know I've gone to the police." I walked around the hood of the jeep, keys in hand. "Technically the Sheriff."

Eli followed behind me, unperturbed by my admission. "They find your kidnappers? You don't look kidnapped to me."

"Yes, that's what they said too." I jammed the key in the door and twisted until the lock clicked up. "I'm glad you enjoyed the cookies, mister Barbeaux, and I don't mean to be rude but if you're not going to tell me what I need to know then I'll find my answers elsewhere."

I was proud of how composed I was, given the circumstances. That careful composer crumbled when Eli dropped a hand on my shoulder, grip firm but gentle. "What kind of answers are you looking for?"

"Why?" My voice broke and I didn't dare turn around to let him see me on the verge of hysteria. "I need to know why me. Who thinks I've got this money? Are they going to come back for me?" I expertly swiped a tear from under my eye and yanked the driver's side open. Eli stepped back before I could clip him with the door.

"I'm in danger and no one will help me."

"I can help you." He was so earnest it made me skeptical.

"You can?"

"Sure can." Eli shaped his hand into a finger gun. "I'm going to teach you how to shoot."

"Why would you do that?"

"Because I'm a man with a conscience and I can't bear the thought of you shooting yourself in the foot." He moved in, towering over me as I shrunk back against the open door. "Don't worry, I'm a professional. I teach shooting lessons for cash during the busy season."

"I don't know if you heard that part, but my boss is dead. I can't pay for shooting lessons."

He waggled the Tupperware he still had in his hands. "I want more cookies. I have a sweet tooth and I've got this craving I can't seem to satisfy."

Eli was close enough that I could smell the sunscreen and sweat on his skin. I wasn't sure if it was giving me a tachycardia episode or butterflies in my stomach. The man scared me. How could he not after our first encounter?

He could deny it all he wanted. My memory was lucid.

Eli Barbeaux standing under the full moon, headlights shining in his strange eyes. Drops of blood flecked his bare chest and neck. Beautiful and lethal.

But he was the reason I wasn't alligator food. Plus, a psychic told me that he was going to keep me from becoming "eternally lost." Dumb was better than dead, right?

"Yes, I think I do need shooting lessons. Do you teach at that range in Tortuga?"

"Private lessons are at my place." Something wicked gleamed in his eyes, but it wasn't the kind of wicked that kidnapped women and scattered their body parts in the bayou. It was the kind that wooed them into heavy petting on the porch in the middle of the night.

That didn't stop me from asking, "Are you luring me out to the bayou to kill me?"

Eli laughed, a big booming sound that made me jump. "I'm really not."

"When you say it like that, you kind of sound like you'd been considering it..."

"I'll follow you home and make sure you get in safely."

Eli did as he promised, hopping in his muddy Ford and tailing me home. His headlights illuminated beneath the house where the shadows often had me running for the stairs. Nothing there but the laundry room and Papa's two-person sailboat tonight.

I started unloading my boxes of paperwork. There were four which meant four trips up the stairs. I was in good shape and the boxes weren't that heavy but there was no way my short arms could fit more than one at a time.

That was fine because some hunky stranger climbed out of his truck and carried them for me. I stood with keys in hand, blinking at the sight. Eli dropped the remaining three boxes at my feet before tousling his hair like a TV lifeguard or something equally sexy.

"Tomorrow after lunch. I'll be expecting you."

Before I could conjure a single word, he was peeling out of the driveway and vanishing down the dark road, leaving me wondering what exactly was going on with that mercurial man.

Chapter 11

Trigger Happy

Cady

"**Y**OU'RE NERVOUS."

"Not at all." I lifted my chin as I loaded the magazine with the practice ammo I picked up that morning.

Truth be told I *was* nervous. All night I tossed and turned on my couch, thinking of every way this could go wrong. I couldn't forget the scary stories I'd been told about the bayou when I was a little girl. Especially not with Barbeaux men appearing all over town—including my porch—with sixteen different personalities. Something was fishy on Barbeaux Bayou and it sure as shit wasn't old bait.

Another thought kept teasing its way in, distracting me from my feigned bravado.

Without him you will be lost.

I hadn't quite figured out how Madame Celine knew about my encounter with Eli but there had to be an explanation. She wasn't *really* psychic. And yet those words sent chills up my arms each time I recalled them. I couldn't get past this feeling that I was missing an important piece of this puzzle.

Some vague death prophecy from a psychic and a series of strange encounters with Eli Barbeaux was all I had to go on right now. I needed to be in action. Sitting at home waiting for someone to come kidnap me again—or worse—was driving me mad.

So here I was, back on Eli's property. We were standing in an open field behind his garage, staring at an arrangement of aluminum cans and animal shaped steel targets. A sturdy wood table was set before us, every type of gun imaginable laid out neatly. Eli had more guns than the entire Sheriff's department and I had to wonder what he used them for. I was certain he didn't usually take students for lessons on his private range.

Someone was using this range a lot, though. The ground beneath my feet was so littered with bullet casings that they clinked as I shifted my weight.

Bald cypress, cabbage palm, and a bunch of brushy bayou plants formed a barrier around this side of the property, like even the flora was working to hide the Barbeaux family from prying eyes.

"S'ok," he drawled from a little too close to my right. Eli was either unaware of how much space he took up or he didn't care about getting in my bubble. "Everyone's nervous the first time. I'll be gentle."

My eyebrows shot up. "Do you flirt with all of your students?"

"Just the old ladies. Makes 'em giggle." Eli winked at me, taking the magazine from my hands, and shifting it. "If you press down with your thumb like this, it doesn't pinch you."

I nodded, trying not to sweat when he was this close to me. October or not, it was hot. Seventy-five and sunny was fall weather in east Texas. By noon the sun was high enough to reflect off the water, magnifying the heat.

Mostly it was Eli. There was this dominating aura radiating off him, so potent and heavy that it felt alive, a presence with extruding claws that sank into my skin. It was in the way he looked at me too, those bright eyes glittering with a secret smile. This was a game to him, and I agreed to play without knowing all the rules.

"Two important gun safety rules." He took the loaded gun from my hand and held it sideways so I could see his pointer finger along the barrel. "Finger off the trigger unless you're actively shooting. And don't ever aim this thing at anything you don't want to shoot dead."

We went on like that, Eli talking me through the safety before arranging my hands and preparing me to shoot. Callouses scraped over my knuckles and I had to steel myself from jerking back. I was intimately aware of how those callouses felt on the most sensitive parts of my body. The way he moved was confident and easy and it made me act the opposite.

"We're going to shoot right here?"

"What's wrong with here?"

"What if a bullet ricochets and hits us?"

Eli laughed, pressing his ear protection muffs over his ears and motioning for me to do the same. "Darlin', you watch too much TV. Those targets are hundreds of feet away."

I inhaled for courage and said, "I'm not going to report you to the police, if that's what you're worried about."

Then I fired. If I hit something, it was so far from target it didn't leave a mark.

Quietly Eli shifted my footing, pushing on my bare thigh with a big palm and making my lower belly flutter in anticipation of something that was definitely not happening. Not again, anyway. Damn, why did I wear shorts for this? Sweat collected on the back of my neck and I gulped in a breath. This had to be an intimidation tactic.

"Private shooting lessons are perfectly legal," he stated calmly.

"I'm talking about what happened on the bayou." I felt like I was shouting with my ears covered but at least it got my point across.

"Less talking, more shooting."

"What would it take to get an honest answer out of you?"

"Hit a target." A slow smile curved his lips and the belly fluttering increased. "Every time you hit one, I'll answer a question. But every time you miss one, you answer one of mine."

I glanced over my shoulder at him. "What could you possibly want to know about me?"

"Deal," he said without waiting for me to agree. "Now shoot something, miss Cady."

I didn't. Good heavens did I try. Every time I readjusted my grip, shifted my footing, or changed the target I was aiming at, I grew more determined. And every time I missed, Eli seemed a little more excited. Wasn't he supposed to be teaching me to *hit* the target?

We went through two magazines of practice ammo and just as many questions. Eli started out innocent enough, asking about how I take my coffee and my favorite movie, but by the end he was getting very personal. I couldn't figure out his angle.

"What's your boyfriend's name?"

"Don't have one."

"What are you doing living alone in that house?"

I scowled at him, lowering the gun to rest my arms. Guns were heavy. "Do you have any kind of boundaries?"

"Not your turn for a question, darlin'." He wasn't smiling anymore but even with such steely features his expression was warm and open, like that aloof version of him was never there. "But you don't have to tell me anything you don't want to."

He was giving me an out from an uncomfortable conversation but for some reason I blurted, "It's my grandparents' house. They both died last year and left it to me. I grew up in that house."

"I'm sorry to hear that."

There was an awkward pause. I came here to force Eli's hand and make him admit the truth. Instead, I was telling him my life story and becoming that much more vulnerable. Somehow, I didn't feel as frightened as before. The longer I was around him the more dulled my caution became. Maybe that was the point of the flirting and the subtle touching.

Eli lightened the conversation after that, talking about cowboy movies and sometimes skipping a question even when I hit nothing.

By the end of my third magazine, I felt like I was on the strangest first date. And if I was being honest, I was having fun. For the first time since *that night*, I stopped thinking about what happened to me. The deep drawl of his voice dragged me to the present. Once I even caught myself laughing.

I was enjoying myself so much that Eli took me by surprise with his next question. "What are you planning to do with all that paperwork?"

"I'm finishing some bookkeeping stuff."

"Uh-uh, darlin'." He took the gun from me and removed the magazine, double checking it was fully unloaded before setting it down. "You're supposed to give honest answers. I saw the title to a boat."

This was my chance. "Yeah, about that boat. As it turns out, it's missing. Oh, and you know what's strange?" I smiled coyly at him. "I saw you and your brother at the dock where it was stored just after it went missing."

Eli didn't even blink. "The one by that bayside bar? You didn't see my brother disappearing boats. You saw him chasing tail."

I pulled my ear protection off and faced him. "And what did I see *you* doing?"

He did the same, making such direct eye contact that I was mesmerized. "Did you see me?"

His question fed my swelling doubt. At this point I wasn't sure if anything I experienced was real. With trembling words and burning cheeks I said, "I saw you on my porch at one in the morning."

His voice was a low vibration, and it was only then that I realized how close he was, breath skimming my skin, chest brushing mine. A knuckle grazed my chin and he asked, "what did you see me doing?"

Unraveling me in the very best way. "You know what you were doing."

A subtle step shifted him away from me, uncertainty flickering across his face. He hid it with one of those roguish smiles, believing that I didn't see it. But I did. Eli wasn't as good at masking himself as he thought.

"I was—"

"Elijah Barbeaux if you try to tell me you were sleepwalking with your hand down my pants, I will sandpaper you!"

He chuckled darkly, running his thumb along my jaw. "You are a little spitfire, aren't you?"

The flush from my cheeks spread down my neck. My pulse drummed madly under my skin. I glanced up at the sky, hoping to see storm clouds to explain the crackling electrically between us. It was more than tension, more than desire—I was *bewitched*, so utterly captivated by his perfect, rugged face. By those unnatural copper eyes and the way they seemed to glow.

"What are you hiding?" I whispered.

He licked his lips. "Absolutely nothing, darlin'."

"My life is on the line, and no one believes me."

"I believe you."

"Because you were there."

I pushed through my heated thoughts and backed out of his reach. Taking a deep breath, I focused on loading the magazine like he showed me. I slid it into the gun, adjusted my stance, and fired each bullet in quick succession. The last one hit a goose shaped target with a loud clang.

I dropped the gun, fixing my meanest look on Eli. We locked eyes, this time in a silent battle of wills. Eli was stubborn and strangely disarming and I was tired. I was *so* tired, and I wanted this to be over. How could it ever end if I didn't have answers?

Answers that he was keeping from me.

"What do you know about the money Dale Barlow stole and the men that are looking for it?" I demanded, finally getting a question of my own after hitting that stupid target.

Every muscle in Eli's body tightened and he sounded like thunder when he said, "only thing I know about Dale Barlow is that he's dead, and he's not the only one."

I was wasting my time. That was as close as Eli would get to sharing his side of the story. I guess I couldn't blame him. I wouldn't want to admit my crimes to a complete stranger either. He was going in circles with his vague responses.

No matter which angle I approached him, I always ended up finding my way into this ruthless tension, waiting to see what he would do next. Clearly, he wasn't the solution to my problem. So why did I feel like I needed to be here?

Maybe I would go home, find a job, and return to my normal, mediocre life. No one would come to leave a horse head in my bed in the middle of the night. I would be safe and undisturbed. The first time was also the last time.

But I would never stop looking over my shoulder. The perceived threat would always be there.

Eli broke the staring contest—which felt more like he was declaring himself the victor and not like capitulation. "Want to come in for a beer?"

When I didn't respond he tucked his hands in his pockets, more antsy than casual. "I get it. You're still suspicious of me. I'd be suspicious of me too. Whole situation is just crazy." For some reason that made his smile stretch a mile wide. "So damn crazy."

"Definitely crazy." I bit my lip and added, "I'll take a beer but only if you have something better than Bud Light."

Eli

Don't be too eager, I reminded myself, hands still in my pockets to keep myself from touching her again. She liked it—I could tell she liked it—but it was too forward.

"Darlin', I don't drink anything you can buy at the *Stop 'N Shop*." I rushed to tidy up the worktable, not wanting to give her time to change her mind. I tossed empty boxes of practice ammo away and arranged my guns back where they belonged in the locker bolted to the floor in the garage. The finishing touch was loading Cady's gun and handing it back to her. No point in an empty firearm.

I waved her over to the porch steps and she followed. Thankfully my place was relatively clean. I hadn't expected her to come up. She was skittish and I was bordering on brash.

Nerves had me throwing the door open and stomping inside, hoping I sounded calm as I offered, "I'll get glasses, make yourself at home."

"This is..." She made a half-circle past the entryway, eyes wide.

"Not what you expected?"

Cady smiled at me from where she stood in the living room, temporarily forgetting whatever pretense she had for being here. "Not at all."

"I might look like a hick, but I've got some taste."

My chest felt a little too inflated as I watched her take in the beautifully polished Douglas fir floors, the exposed rafters, vaulted ceiling, and the new granite top kitchen island. Isaac and I replaced the cabinets last year, adding to the log cabin feel. My furniture was meant for comfort and not visual appeal, but the forest green flannel and chestnut leather did match the dark woods that made up the open living room.

"Did you do this yourself?"

"My brothers and I did. Isaac is the brains. I just wait for him to tell me where to swing my hammer." I cracked open a Belgian stout and poured each of us a half glass. I wasn't about to get her drunk before she drove home in the dark. That was assuming she stayed another hour and let the sun set on our day together.

She accepted her glass and settled politely on the edge of a recliner. "How big is your family? Seems like the original family would be pretty extensive."

"We aren't really the original family. Otherwise, this whole town should be called Barbeaux." Partially true.

We owned the biggest portion of land by far but the O'Henry homestead was much more lucrative back in the day. Homesteading on the bayou wasn't easy work. When Tom O'Henry sold his land in parcels more than a hundred years earlier it made sense to name the town after him. The Barbeaux family kept to themselves. It was a necessity when you were shapeshifting beasts at the mercy of the lunar cycle.

"But to answer your question, it's just me and my brothers." *And my psychopath cousin but hopefully he's a wolf rug on some rich asshole's hearth.*

"Are you the oldest?"

"Middle. Nine years younger than Saul, seven minutes older than Isaac."

Cady drew shapes in the condensation of her glass, her eyes narrowing almost imperceptibly. "Right, I forgot y'all were twins."

"We're not identical, in appearance or personality." My feet thumped on the coffee table as I dropped onto the couch. I studied Cady, sipping her beer, waiting.

"Thanks for teaching me to shoot, by the way. Hopefully I never have to use that skill." More sipping, more fidgeting with the glass.

"Why don't you go ahead and say what's on your mind? Neither of us likes to waste our breath beating around the bush."

She looked me in the eyes, a bold move if she knew who—*what*—I was. "I haven't decided what your motives are yet."

"Isn't that for me to decide?"

"I guess so." Her lips perched on the glass, and she took a micro sip. Was she pretending to drink? Guess I hadn't gained as much trust as I thought. "Why don't you just tell me then?"

"Tell you?"

"Why you're doing this." She made a finger gun and pointed it at my chest.

"I haven't done my job well if that's how you're going to handle a firearm."

Cady set her beer glass down and stood. "You haven't killed me, and you haven't asked about the money, so I don't think you're looking for it. It feels like you're toying with me and I'm all out of patience for games. What do you want, Eli?"

My movement was breathtakingly fast. Literally. Cady gasped as my hand cupped her chin, thumb tracing her bottom lip.

Shit. *Out of control.* This was too much. But she was so delicious when she was all fired up and I wanted a taste so badly.

Moonlight burned in my eyes, the bane of the Barbeaux line coming alive in my blood. She wouldn't know what she was seeing but I was damn sure Cady recognized the change in me.

And maybe she didn't care. She was fixated on my hand, leaning into my touch with shallow breaths. Desire cinched tight in the space between us. It wasn't just me craving her.

"I think I've been pretty clear about what I want," I purred, my voice throaty and dark.

That spark of need instantly faded. It was like her entire body turned to ice, freezing me out as she backpedaled toward the door.

"Thank you for your time, Mister Barbeaux." There was a razor sharp edge to her polite words. "If you'll excuse me, I need to go find whoever might try to kill me next."

I hurled myself to the front door as it slammed, gripping the knob but not daring to twist it. By the crunch of gravel, it sounded like she was running. If I saw her running the beast wouldn't be able to resist chasing.

Cady's jeep was disappearing down my unpaved driveway before I allowed myself to step onto the porch. Dammit. Now that I was thinking with my upstairs brain, I realized just how I must have come across.

Timing, I told the wretched beast inside me. *Women care about timing.*

And that was when they hadn't potentially witnessed you shifting shapes and dispatching two men with your claws. Cady believed someone was going to show up at her door and demand that money at gunpoint any second.

She was probably right to believe that.

I was so obsessed with this new bond that I hadn't considered how serious her situation was. Add Jacques to the mix and this was one dynamite keg we did not need exploding in Port O'Henry.

Time to change tactics. I was going to find out exactly what was going on, and I would keep her safe in the process. No one would lay a finger on Cady without feeling my wrath.

Chapter 12

Boundaries

Cady

I DREAMED OF ELI and not because I was having bayou nightmares. The phantom press of his fingers on my jaw left me tossing and turning. Such a simple touch became incendiary fuel for my uninhibited brain in the early hours of the morning.

I almost kissed him in his living room yesterday. Every part of me down to my cells was urging me to give in and do exactly what he wanted. Hero worship and a great smile could do terrible things to a woman in crisis. Eli Barbeaux was the man equivalent of comfort food.

And I was dying to sink my teeth in.

Lightning flashed into the living room. A devouring roar of thunder followed, rattling the windowpanes and startling me from a vision of using much more than my teeth on Eli. Sweat dotted my neck and back, causing me to shiver in the unexpectedly cool air.

Autumn was temperamental in Texas, never sure if the cold was coming to stay or just sweeping in for a stormy afternoon. It was hard to know what to wear when the temperature could change forty degrees overnight.

The skies were an ominous grey. Clouds tumbled over each other in rhythm with the surging waves below. I could see the bay churning behind my neighbors' three-story home, making the neighborhood feel like it was adrift in the ocean. It was eight AM, and it was barely bright enough to see the water. A good day to stay in and start sifting through papers. Otherwise,

I might be tempted to drive back down to the bayou and find some excuse to see Eli again.

My obsession with him was completely inexplicable. At best he was dangerous. But it wasn't at his best that I last saw him.

Anger heated my chest, rising to my cheeks to ward off the chill in the air. The gall of that man, pretending to care about my predicament only to use it as an opportunity to get laid. Some people had no morals. That was what I'd always heard of the Barbeaux brothers. Foolish not to believe it just because they had a charming veneer.

I was letting myself get worked up again. This bothered me more than it should. One too many stressors during the worst week of my life. If I became anymore overwhelmed, I would have a nervous breakdown.

I rose from the couch—where I'd slept every night since my abduction, as if seeing someone coming through the front window would save me—and slipped into a pair of fuzzy leopard print slippers. Halfway to the kitchen there was a thump on the front door.

I scrambled backwards, hitting the coffee table, and falling to the floor where I kept the baseball bat. Belatedly I thought of the gun in my purse, but I was already at the door, bat raised, arm outstretched to unlock the deadbolt.

In my mind I could hear Eli scolding me for leaving the gun loaded but inaccessible. Was I seriously going to die with him as my last thought?

Panic clawed at my insides, and I flung the door open wildly, swinging the bat out and hoping I didn't accidentally pummel my mailman. My bruised rib exploded with a fresh wave of pain, and I staggered as I swung.

Eli easily caught the bat before it hit him, wrapping his hand around the thick end, and yanking it from my grasp. He rested it on the floor against the doorframe as he passed me to kick his boots off on the welcome mat.

"You expecting someone, darlin'?"

Not at all. His presence was so *unexpected* that I didn't immediately respond. A soaked and sorry looking Eli sauntered into my kitchen like he lived here, and I just stood there, clutching my throbbing side.

"Where's your gun?" He dropped a plastic bag on the counter, drying his hair with a hand towel from the stove.

I didn't answer him, couldn't while he was standing in my kitchen like he owned the place. Water droplets clung to the tousled ends of his dark hair and glistened in the stubble that was almost a beard today. The damp fabric of his shirt clung to his biceps, outlined the muscles of his chest, and molded to his narrow waist. He might as well not be wearing a shirt for all I could see.

I swallowed dryly, trying to get my brain back online. "I knew you would say that." I shut the front door and scowled. "What are you doing in my house?"

He gestured at the rain smattered bag like the answer was obvious. "Bringing you breakfast."

"If you think showing up with food is going to—"

Eli palmed the air to cut me off. "And an apology."

I scooted into the kitchen on my leopard printed feet, staring at him expectantly.

His lashes sealed together, and he inhaled slowly. "Darlin', if you want me to say anything coherent, you're going to need to put something else on."

Too late I remember the white tank top I was wearing. Cold air teased at my breasts, making them press through the fabric in a lewd display. I covered my chest with one arm and rushed to grab a discarded sweatshirt from the couch. As I did, I realized just how messy I'd allowed my space to become.

In another life I would have been embarrassed for Eli to see it. The unfolded laundry piled on the recliner, the half-emptied dishwasher still open. At least two apples were molding in the fruit bowl and the package for a microwave lasagna was on the floor next to the trash can where I missed and couldn't be bothered to try again.

Even worse was my appearance. Hair unbrushed, teeth in the same state. The cotton shorts I was wearing had a hole in the crotch and yes, my tits were one hundred percent visible through my tank top.

What did it matter if Eli judged me? Someone tried to *feed me to alligators*. Kind of changed a woman's priorities.

"Better?" I spread my arms out to show off the frumpy University of Texas sweatshirt, wincing when my rib protested.

Eli frowned. "What's wrong with you?"

"You're the one that waltzed into my house uninvited. What's wrong with you?"

He ignored me, lifting my arm and the sweatshirt he insisted I put on to examine the bruise on my chest. It was a gross green color now, the damage on the surface almost healed. Beneath the skin was the problem and a day of target practice exacerbated it. His guttural noise startled me, and I pushed his hand away.

"Your ribs are bruised." And he looked furious at me for that, like I'd kicked myself in the lungs.

"I've noticed." I was not being the gracious host my grandparents raised me to be.

"You don't need to be swinging baseball bats and throwing yourself around. Ribs take forever to heal." Eli reached for my sweater again and I swatted him.

"You have no boundaries."

His gaze briefly wandered to my exposed legs, proving my point. "You hungry?"

I skirted around him and hopped onto the kitchen counter, perching on the edge so I was eye level with him. This was my home, and I had no intention of being intimidated by him.

Was I crazy? I think maybe we both were. Like attracted like and that was probably why Eli was in my kitchen at eight in the morning. What happened to me stirred some reckless, angry thing inside of me and it was steering my life. A man like Eli seemed to have his own internal monster and the two creatures were locked onto each other.

But that didn't mean I was going to sleep with him as payment for favors, or for any other reason. Priority numero uno was staying alive. Eli was distracting me from that.

"Well?"

"Already fired up this morning, I see." Eli reached into the plastic bag and offered me a foil wrapped burrito, some of his usual levity returning. "Still warm. Maybe a little damp but rainwater never killed anyone."

"Flash floods kill people every year."

"I'm not going to argue with you. The way you're looking at me is scary."

I took a huge bite of breakfast burrito and mumbled, "You should be scared."

The burrito was from Jody's—one of the few businesses left in Port O'Henry that was owned by locals—and it was exactly how I liked it. All bacon, eggs, and cheese. Zero vegetables.

"I realize how I came across yesterday." Eli rubbed the back of his neck, and I relished the discomfort on his face. The tables had turned. "I didn't mean it the way it sounded."

I waved my burrito around, accidentally spilling eggs on the counter. "How did you mean it?"

"I'm not myself around you." His gaze traveled to the lights over the sink, searching for the words and studiously avoiding me. "I haven't been thinking straight."

That dangerous sizzle heated the air around me and I longed for the snapping cold from moments earlier. I wasn't myself around him either. My inhibitions were becoming untethered and I was helplessly drifting toward him.

Another bite of burrito saved me from admitting any of that.

"You are—you're beautiful. I can't stop thinking about you." He made a throaty noise, staring me down with simmering eyes. "But I had my priorities mixed up yesterday."

His admission made me clammy, my heart pummeling my aching ribs furiously. I knew what he was describing because I felt the same. Even as I lay awake in fear every night, my wayward mind was wandering to him. Wondering about him, desperate to know his secrets. To know him.

But no matter what he did that night on the bayou, whether it was for me or for selfish reasons, I couldn't trust him. I asked for his help, and he denied me. He *lied*. I had little tolerance for liars.

I swallowed tightly and asked, "Did you get any of those mini cinnamon rolls?"

Eli had this bright look to his face when he smiled, like he knew something I didn't. Secrets danced in his eyes, and I wanted to fish until I caught all of them. But he was good at evasion. He had this way of saying things without really saying them. His relief came in an easy laugh, and he pulled a Styrofoam package from the bottom of the bag.

Maybe it should have been awkward to have Eli standing in my kitchen, silently eating takeout breakfast, and watching me inhale cinnamon rolls after confessing that he was obsessed with me. Instead it was comfortable. Oddly normal. Years ago, I used to do things like this. I had friends, a life outside of Nana's illness.

Now, it was just me.

Me and the local bayou murderer.

Eli's eyes flitted between my mouth as I licked frosting from my fingers to the pile of papers I'd left scattered on the coffee table. "What's your plan?"

"Reading." I shrugged, not sure if I was going to tell him the rest.

"You really think you're going to find missing money in all this?" He gestured to the overflowing boxes of paperwork.

"Probably not," I sighed, "but I think I'll find clues."

He moved into the living room, plunking down on the couch. "Suppose you spend the next seventy-two hours reading through useless business records and don't find anything. What then?" His arms stretched out across the back of the couch, and I noticed the way they flexed beneath his damp shirt. "Do you know if anyone else is looking for this money?"

I planted my palms on the counter, pinning him with a hard stare. "Do I know the men that kidnapped me are dead? They could show up any minute and finish what they started." Saying that out loud made my breakfast burrito try to climb back up my throat. I swallowed, unwilling to give into the fear any longer.

Silence sucked the air from the room. Eli's eyes gleamed like briny jetty stones in the late afternoon light, so much intensity searing into me. He knew what I was really asking, and I knew the answer he wasn't going to give me.

My kidnappers were dead. *Why* they were dead was the truth I needed. Hard to believe that Eli walked up on two men and killed them for what they did to me. I was a complete stranger to him. Most likely the rumors about the Barbeaux boys were true. There was something out there that they didn't want people to see, and they were willing to kill to keep their secrets.

"You're safe here, darlin'." Eli breathed life back into the living room with his quiet promise.

Prickling heat gathered behind my eyes and I glanced at the laundry pile in an attempt to compose myself. "I don't think I am. Thanks for breakfast. You can see yourself out."

I came around the kitchen counter to the laundry, grabbing a pair of jeans and a sweater. I froze halfway to my bedroom when Eli murmured, "You were screaming."

Those barely contained tears were suddenly all over my face. "I remember," I whispered, knowing he probably couldn't hear me.

"You were screaming and I—" His voice dropped to a frightening depth, and he stopped himself. Clearing his throat, he finished with, "I hear your voice every time I close my eyes. I couldn't let them hurt you."

I pivoted then because I had to see his face, unable to read the emotion in his words. His features were caught in a tangle of agony and fury. Somehow it made him look *other*, the fury so deep it was inhuman, a dark creature trying to overtake his body and do terrible, violent things. Hairs rose along my nape and my skin pebbled with goosebumps. A different kind of tension charged the air now and when I saw that eerie glow coming from his eyes I shivered.

There were secrets swirling in those molten copper eyes, secrets I instinctively knew were not meant for someone like me. Eli terrified me but not because I really believed he would hurt me. It was because his presence had me questioning my entire reality. I knew, deep in my most primal brain, that he was not like me. He was not *normal*. Even if it seemed so silly to my logical mind, I knew.

And by the way he was watching me—calculated, ravenous—he knew that I knew.

I took a step closer anyway. Two steps. He rose from the couch with that too fluid movement, meeting me halfway but this time not touching. Not invading my space. Just looming over me with an aura of death clinging to him. That part didn't scare me. As twisted as it was, that part relieved me. Made me want to move closer. To step into that aura and be protected by it.

"I couldn't let them hurt you," he repeated softly.

"Why did you lie to me?"

"This isn't just about me. Whatever happens with me hurts my brothers too. You understand?"

I nodded, jaw clenched too tight with emotion to speak. He didn't say anything else, so I scurried to my room to sit on the edge of the bed and sob until the tears ran out. Even with the door closed I could feel his presence, out of place among the familiarity of my childhood home. The scent of him seemed to carry down the hall, overpowering the smell of stale breakfast burrito and minty toothpaste.

I reentered ten minutes later with clean teeth and my untamed curls pulled into a decent bun. Eli was scanning a handful of papers from the box labeled "miscellaneous," but he looked up when he saw me.

"I can't trust you." I crossed my arms. "I understand why you lied but I can't trust a liar."

"Fair enough."

"I appreciate what you did." It felt like it wasn't enough—the man *saved my life*—but I was wary of letting him believe I owed him for his choice.

"But?"

"I'm not clear on why you're here. Not just in my house but everywhere. I've lived here all my life and only seen you a dozen times. Now every time I turn around, you're there. On my porch. In my house."

"I could say the same to you, darlin'."

For some reason that made me blush. I did hunt down his address and invade his space first. "I'm not interested in dying over this money. If that's why you're here, just say so."

Eli shifted, studying me quietly. He was so still sometimes. It was uncanny. "I don't care about the money. This is personal for me, too."

I hadn't really thought about that. The chances of anyone connecting Eli to the men that kidnapped me seemed astronomical, but maybe I was wrong. I had no idea where I was on the bayou that night. What if we were a thousand feet from his property and *that* was why he was out there?

An image of a murderous Eli stomping down his porch steps, gun in hand, as he followed the sound of my screaming made me shudder. But...

I didn't hear gunshots.

So many questions still lingered on my tongue but even if he would answer them, I wasn't sure I wanted to hear it now. I felt too raw.

"So that's why you're here then. To make sure no one comes after you and your brothers."

"And to make sure you don't get yourself killed."

Another "why" perched on my lips but I clamped down on it. Eli had been very clear about that one particular thing, and I didn't need to hear him say it again. He still thought he was going to get laid. Not happening. There was no use getting attached to a man with a reputation like his.

I knew better than anyone that secrets only led to heartache.

With a sigh I moved back into the kitchen and asked, "How do you take your coffee?"

"Cream. Lots of sugar." Every word out of his mouth sounded like innuendo and it was doing things to me that were not helping my concentration.

"So, what, are you just going to follow me around like a bodyguard?" I handed him a mug, trying to ignore the electric shock when our fingers touched.

"Sure, that works."

"Not that I'm ungrateful for the help but, don't you have anything better to do?" How did Barbeauxs pay their bills? I knew the rumors, but I was much more interested in the truth.

"I don't work during the off season." He shrugged when I raised my eyebrows. "Perks of working for yourself. During peak season I charter a fishing vessel and teach city slickers how to shoot. Sometimes my brother puts me to work on one of his construction projects. Otherwise, I do what I want when I want."

"That must be nice. I'll be lucky if I can get a job running the cash register at the *Stop N' Shop* now that my boss is dead." In other words, *I'm broke and I can't pay for your help.* "To be clear, I'm not sleeping with you in exchange for protection."

"Darlin', when I get you in my bed it's going to be because you begged for me."

"*When?*" I challenged. "You're very sure of yourself."

"I know what I want and I'm a patient man."

I sipped my too hot coffee, burning my throat. "You're missing my point."

He sipped his too, licking milk foam from his upper lip. "I'm not here to coerce you. I'm only here to protect what's *mine.*" I gaped at him, pretty sure I got his meaning. Before I could give him a piece of my mind he said with a smirk, "My brothers and my bayou."

"Right." I gulped more coffee. "So, you're going to help me find whoever Barlow was hiding money from?" *With no strings attached, please.*

"I'll do my best."

I lowered myself onto the chair across from him. "And you're going to tell me the full truth?"

Eli didn't bat an eye. "There are some truths that aren't mine to tell."

I considered him, replaying his words. I should be wary of him. I should kick him out of my house. I should also pack my bags and leave Port O'Henry for good. But I'd already decided I wasn't going to do any of that.

"Fine, at least tell me this; did you know the men that kidnapped me? Did you have anything to do with their plans?"

He had the decency to look offended. "It was the first and last time I saw them." Coffee mug in one big hand, he tipped his chin up. "I haven't always been a good man, Cady, but I would never purposefully hurt someone innocent."

Never purposefully hurt someone *innocent.* I filed that phrasing away for later. Obviously, he would hurt someone guilty.

"Should I be scared of you?" Eli had already proven himself a liar and there was no reason to believe his answer.

But when he plainly said "never," I heard the truth of it.

"Okay."

"Okay?"

"I need you, Eli." I coughed, quickly correcting myself. "I need your help."

Chapter 13

Near Miss

Eli

F OR SOMEONE THAT DIDN'T trust me, Cady was very trusting. She was letting me in on her little investigation, sharing all her thoughts in a disorganized stream over her cooling cup of coffee. I had to admit I was impressed by how much information she'd gathered.

"Where did you learn to search public records?"

"Google." Cady shrugged. "Anyway, I was only confirming things I overheard working for Barlow. The *Stop N' Shops* were in the red during slow season and he wanted to get in on the development boom."

It was that answer that inspired the story I used to explain why I knew Barlow. Sooner or later, she would find out I knew him, and it was best to get it out in the open. Lying to her made me feel dirty, my tongue coated in the wrongness of it, but I knew her faith in me would be shattered if I admitted the truth now. And I wouldn't incriminate my brothers.

It was an easy story to craft, laced with truth. Isaac did his own real estate development, and it wasn't uncommon for him to enlist Saul and I to do some of the heavy lifting. His investing genius and obsession with regaining Barbeaux territory—more like owning all of Port O'Henry—was the reason we were able to cut ties with Barlow and his smuggling schemes.

After Saul chased Jacques off, anyway. Jacques introduced us to Barlow and the thugs he tangled with. He was never content to tuck away on the bayou and live the simple life.

My cousin inherited the worst of our traits. Power hungry and half-feral, Jacques became a liability. That made it sound cold, our removal of him from the family too clinical.

It wasn't. Saul was haunted by his choice to exile Jacques. We were raised together, bound by blood. No different than brothers. Forcing him out of Texas was for the good of all of us. Not just the Barbeaux family, but our kind. Werewolves already lived a precarious existence, teetering on the edge of discovery as technology became ever present. Every move we made had to be calculated.

Unfortunately, being a man led by animal instincts didn't make precision easy. It was in our nature to be bold. We craved domination and violence, some of us more than others. That was in the best case scenario, living quiet and isolated the way my brothers and I did. What Jacques was trying to do would have led to death and destruction.

Werewolves were dissimilar to our animal relatives in most ways. We didn't operate well in a pack unless it was built like a family unit. The alpha hierarchy that most werewolves tried to create was purely human. Man wanting to stand on the shoulders of his kneeling brethren and call himself king.

It was true that as the first of the first—firstborn son from the first line of werewolves—that Saul had unique gifts. He had true dominance, sway over all our kind. A very dangerous gift in the wrong hands, as proved by our forefathers. Saul never had the inclinations that Jacques did, preferring to keep to himself. Sometimes I thought even Isaac and me was too much company for him.

"So, you down for a little small town legal?"

I blinked, realizing I had been so fixated on getting my story straight that I missed the last half of what Cady said. "Small town legal?"

"You know, when you break the law, but no one cares because it's a small town and you can get away with anything if the Sheriff likes you." She frowned. "Or you bribe him."

"Sure, I'll break the law for you, darlin'." I set my coffee mug on the table with a wink. "Who do I need to kill?"

Cady paled. Right, that was probably too soon.

"I meant trespassing. Did you drive here or do another one of those crazy sprints?"

"I took my truck."

"Perfect. You drive."

"You always this bossy?"

Cady collected our coffee mugs and set them in the sink. Then she tugged a denim jacket over her pale blue sweater and curled her lips. "You don't like being told what to do?"

I infused my words with all my desire as I told her, "I'm usually the one giving orders."

Her blush said she understood my meaning loud and clear.

Despite my teasing, I did as she asked, glad to have gained some control in this situation. Having her riding shotgun in my truck, one leg tucked against her chest as her arm dangled over her knee, was making me sentimental. Until today my brothers were the only two people to ever fill that seat.

It sounded much lonelier when I thought about it like that.

Port O'Henry was divided into four quarters. The first was mostly industrial, businesses that lined the canal to the intracoastal waterway and out into the bay. There were boat mechanics and gear shops, big waterside warehouses where shrimpers brought in their catch for the day. All the boat launches and fishing centers were in that part of town. It was accessible from the main road which made it busy even during the slow season.

The second quarter was south of that, closer to where the bay met the shore in a beautiful display of sand and sunrises. That was where the development boom had taken its toll on the locals. Where Barlow and his ilk built their four-story monster homes complete with tropical paint and tiki torches. The neighborhood known as *Pelican Bay*. It wasn't technically a gated community—there were no gates—but the four-foot wall that surrounded the development, as well as the residents-only pool sent a clear message.

It made the other two quarters of Port O'Henry look lower than a gopher hole. Cady's neighborhood wasn't as bad, that third quarter that was still close enough to beach and bay to have property value. The view from her front porch was spectacular and unfortunately, a lot of newcomers agreed. The houses were old and though plenty were in good shape, they didn't match the breezy island getaway feel that the tourist crowd was going for. Every day another was torn down, replaced with some stick-built shit that wouldn't withstand a tropical sneeze much less a tropical storm. Sooner or later folks like Cady would be priced out of there too.

That left the last quarter, where we were headed now. Old Port O'Henry, as the locals called it. Technically I lived in old Port O'Henry, the area encompassing the bayou. It was where the last of the homesteaders and farmers lived, their houses ramshackle and weathered. Most of them were barely scraping by. The humidity from the bayou made the heat unbearable and access to the bay was sparse.

My brothers and I were lucky with our private beaches. The sand was mostly clean, and the plants were to a minimum. Most waterfront property in this part of town was covered in mean, stubborn plants. Not to mention ticks, mosquitoes, snakes, and the occasional gator.

Every year more properties back here were foreclosed on, only to be snatched up by hopeful developers. Crumbling buildings and acres of dry grass were walled off with chain-link and barbed wire, as if anyone cared to trespass. There was an old boat launch with a handful of concrete buildings that withstood *the storm*—the famous hurricane that wiped out most of the town in 1953—and teenagers would mess around there from time to time. Otherwise, no one cared about this part of Port O'Henry, except where they thought they could make a buck.

It was why Barlow bought the old Cray Homestead and the ancient stone house that still sat in the middle of it. Figured one day someone would want property out here bad enough to settle for bayou adjacent land. It wouldn't surprise me if Isaac owned some of those properties too.

His acquisition of land surrounding the bayou had nothing to do with wealth and everything to do with his territorial tendencies.

We weren't more than a minute from Cady's house when she turned to me with a serious expression. "Do you remember where it was?"

"The Cray Homestead?"

"Where they took me out on the bayou."

My hands tightened on the steering wheel, slowing as I turned north. "Not going to happen."

Her blue eyes were beseeching as she leaned on the center console. "I just want to know what happened."

"You know what happened." It was a challenge to keep the growl out of my voice. "No need to revisit that."

She blinked softly at me and that was all it took to realize I was in deep trouble with this one. Somehow, I managed to hold my ground. "The answer is no, darlin'. I'm not taking you there."

"Fine," she sighed. "What did you do with the, um, evidence?"

I didn't want to have this conversation with her, but I was trying to be as honest as I could. "Gators were hungry." It was impossible to look at her when I said it. I didn't want to see how I horrified her. "I took the car to the boat launch in old Port O'Henry."

Cady was quiet for a painful moment before murmuring, "That was smart." In my peripherals I saw her scratching at a thread on a frayed hole in her jeans. "Almost like you know what you're doing."

"I watch a lot of late-night television." I gave her my most innocent smile. "Don't believe the rumors you hear about us Barbeauxs." *Even though plenty of the worst ones are true.*

The rest of the drive was silent but there was no awkwardness or tension. Cady was relaxed, unperturbed by the beast beside her. She didn't know the full truth, but she knew enough for any sane person to flee.

She would have to be crazy if she was going to survive the Barbeaux clan.

There was no fencing around the old Cray Homestead. There wasn't much need. The house had no valuables in it, evidenced by the state of the property when the Cray family finally sold it and left Port O'Henry for good. The first step to developing it would be to tear down whatever ramshackle structures were left.

The first step ought to be fixing the driveway. My teeth clacked together as the truck bounced. White stone reflected golden in the October afternoon, a ghost of what this place used to be hovering on the horizon. I stopped the truck there, not wanting to risk whatever debris the last tropical storm left to puncture tires.

Cady climbed down before I even took the keys out, speed walking toward the house. That woman was a trigger-happy lunatic sometimes.

A wrinkle of distaste lifted my nose as I scented the air. Someone had been out here, though not that recently. Rain had washed away most of the smoke scent, but it did nothing for the carrion smell. Some poor critter probably died in the old barn. The three walled structured looked like a good place to croak.

"I had a friend that snuck into the Cray house in high school," Cady said breathlessly, lifting her foot over a scraggly shrub and almost tripping when it snagged the tip of her sneaker. I caught her elbow, steadying her and guiding her to the left. The gravel drive was nonexistent now. We might as well take the straightest path.

"She said everything in the house was still in place. Plates on the table, cups of unfinished coffee. Newspaper was laid out like they were in the middle of breakfast and just vanished".

"Judah Cray had a heart attack when he was in his fifties. S'why the family sold the property. Ma Cray wanted nothing to do with it after that. She probably didn't even come back to pack."

Cady stopped walking, staring at me suspiciously. "How would you know? This house has been empty for as long as I've been alive."

Shit. "My family has been here for generations. You think I'm not familiar with the history?"

"That's a reasonable explanation," She said flatly, trudging closer to the house.

I wasn't clear on what Cady expected to find here—doubtful that Barlow was stashing money in a rat den like this—but I knew what I was looking for. If someone searched this place before us, they would have left a scent trail. I wasn't a bloodhound ready to follow a bunch of gangsters back to their headquarters, but I would file it away. Sooner or later, someone would surface, probably looking for Cady, and I would know who I was dealing with.

Except Cady was the ultimate distraction and it took far too long for me to realize the smell of smoke wasn't from some stray campfire left by drinking teenagers. The Cray house was a one-story home, not built on stilts like the more modern houses in this area. Stone walls closed in the small living space and those stones were probably the only reason the whole house wasn't reduced to ash right now.

Black streaks licked up the sides of the shattered windows where smoke and fire had made an attempt to climb out onto the overgrown property. A perimeter of soot surrounded the entire left side of the house, the crumbled door burned away, leaving a gaping hole like a sickly wound.

Death clung to the air wafting from inside, putrid and stale, and I knew immediately we weren't dealing with a dead raccoon. Even in a state of decay, the smell was obviously human.

"What the hell happened?" Cady covered her nose and mouth with her forearm. "Can you smell that?" She was walking ahead of me, barreling straight for the door without caution.

"Cady, stop!"

I lost my mind when she screamed. I was vaguely aware of lifting her up and out of the house. Otherwise, I was in attack mode. Body rigid, muscles prepared to pounce. I came to with my nose in the air and a body at my feet. My fingers were splayed, claws extended, and I prayed that was the only part of me that visibly shifted. In the dim light of the half-burned structure, it might be hard to see my hands but there would be no mistaking an eight-foot, furry monster.

"That's a person," Cady whispered from behind me.

I inhaled deeply, scenting for other trespassers. Any signs of them were muddied by the stink of rot. Even tapping into all my senses, I detected nothing. It was Cady's fear that made me feral, the same way it had that first night on the bayou. Being around her was going to prove dangerous if I didn't rein it in.

I pivoted away from the corpse at my feet, prowling back to Cady and crowding her until she took a step back. When I kept moving, she held her ground, placing shaking hands on my chest and staring up at me with watery eyes.

"Go wait in the truck." It was a command, and it didn't land well.

"I'm not going to hide in the truck like a scared girl."

"I'm not suggesting that," I said evenly. Surprising because I was not feeling even at all. My world was off its axis, tilting me wildly in Cady's direction. I cupped the sides of her neck, rubbing a thumb along the corner of her jaw. Her hands fisted in my shirt, and she stopped shaking. "I'm telling you to wait in the truck so you don't have to see this. It's not cowardly, darlin'."

Her eyes darted from my face to the house. There was no way she could see anything past my shoulders, but the whites of her eyes expanded anyway. Fear was still spilling from her pores, clouding my vision, and making my bones ache with the need to change.

"Who is that?" Her chest inflated rapidly, breaths coming in small bursts.

"I need you to calm down."

"Calm down? Are you serious?" She let go of my shirt and rubbed her palms together. "How can I calm down? There's a dead body ten feet from us."

"Cady," I growled, barely clinging to my humanity as her hysteria increased. "Whoever it is, they're already dead. Take a deep breath."

"I can't."

"Yes, you can. In and out, darlin'. Slow and steady."

My attempt to calm her wasn't working, probably because I wasn't calm myself. The beast in me was agitated, ready to free itself from my skin and destroy whatever threat had Cady in a tailspin. Problem was that you couldn't claw anxiety to death and her panic was going to increase tenfold if I went beast mode in front of her.

"There's a body in there." She was gasping for air now. "That was almost me. They tried to kill me."

I squeezed my arms around her, too tight, but it wasn't just for comfort. With her face pressed to my chest Cady wouldn't see the fur rippling along my arms or the snout trying to protrude from my face. I buried my nose in her hair, inhaling deeply. Three breaths later and my muscles slackened. My chest vibrated with contentment and Cady jolted at the low sound.

"It wasn't you," I murmured, soothing her shoulder with my thumbs. "You're safe."

She stepped out of my hold, and I let her go, watching her eyes swirl with confusion. There was a loaded moment where I could see more questions dangling in the space between us. Her instincts were good. Most people sensed there was something not quite right with the Barbeaux family, averting their gazes and flinching away when we got too close, but their logical minds wanted to explain it away with human assumptions. We were unfriendly and unprincipled bayou hicks.

Cady saw beyond those presumptions. What she would do with her suspicions was yet to be seen. I swallowed thickly, hoping there wouldn't always be such heavy accusation when she looked at me.

She exhaled, grounding herself. "Okay, what do we do? We can't call the Sheriff. If he's not involved in this, his deputies are." I was surprised by how quickly she found her head. "This has to be related, right?"

"I don't believe in coincidence."

"We need to find out who that is. Don't touch anything though." She was already heading back inside, shoulders back and chin high.

Damn, this was not the time to be turned on, but I was into this confidence.

"Almost like you know what you're doing." I echoed her earlier words.

Cady squinted at me over her shoulder. "Touché"

All levity dispersed as we stepped back into the house. Unlike the outer walls, the floors and fixtures were wood. There was a yawning black hole in the middle of the kitchen where tables and chairs had burned down into the floor. By the shape of it that seemed to be where the fire started. Gasoline evaporated quickly but I could almost scent a lingering stink of fuel.

It wasn't the rot and burn that had my stomach twisting into knots. This was familiar. Not the house and the poor bastard on the floor, but the scene. I knew someone that used fire as their favorite way to rid themselves of evidence.

This had Jacques's name written all over it. If he was back in Port O'Henry we had trouble. Saul and Isaac needed to know about it immediately.

I dropped my hand to Cady's lower back, prepared to catch her if the floor gave way where she stepped. She didn't remove my hand, so I took liberties, sliding along to her hip and losing my focus again. Maybe agreeing to help her wasn't such a good idea.

But if I hadn't, she would be here alone.

"I guess we can thank that unexpected storm for this." She gestured to the intact side of the house. Everything was coated in a layer of ash and the decrepit furniture had been tossed just like at Barlow's house but otherwise it was in surprisingly good shape.

They didn't build houses sturdy like this anymore. The Crays were one of the only families not devastated by the hurricane of '53 and it was probably because this house was made of stronger stuff.

"Someone was definitely trying to hide this." Cady cleared her throat. "Him. Sorry, whoever you were."

She crouched to examine the corpse, her eyes watering, and I did the same. Even as she wiped tears from her cheek, she examined him. I didn't know much about Cady, but I doubted she understood what she was looking at.

I did and it made my heart pound. Someone had slashed this man's throat and it wasn't with a weapon. Claw marks were carved deep into his crusted flesh and through it, right down to the bone. This was a killing done by my kind.

The body was a sickly grey color, the insides rotten but the flesh still holding some of its original form. There were characteristics to the face that looked memorable, but I couldn't place them. Cady whipped out her phone. I was about to scold her for taking a picture when I realized she was flipping through them. She paused on one, finger hovering over the bright screen, and held it up for me to see.

"Please tell me I'm crazy."

"You're crazy," I muttered, taking the phone, and staring at the picture of Dale Barlow and his son. It was old, taken six or seven years earlier, but I saw what Cady did. I recognized that face too. He was the one that met my brothers and I when we made midnight deliveries.

"But not that crazy." I handed it back to her. "Shit, that's him."

"I don't understand. He's supposed to be in South Africa doing charity work."

"Dustin Barlow doing charity?" I snorted. "Who told you that?"

"His daddy." She lifted back onto her heels, shifting her gaze away as if studying the blackened interior of the kitchen. Sunlight poured in through the shattered windows, illuminating the sheen of moisture on her face. I wasn't sure if she was crying, or the smell was that unbearable. "How did you know him?"

"I told you my brothers and I did work for Barlow. Dustin liked to come by the work sites when he was in town, drink a couple'a beers with the guys." It was true, but the work sites hadn't been developments. And usually he was doing heroin, not drinking Bud Light.

"I guess this explains why he hasn't dealt with the estate." She let out a pent up breath. "He and Mister Barlow were supposed to be estranged."

"They were sometimes, from what I gathered. But Dustin liked to gamble even more than his daddy and he was always getting himself into trouble."

Cady stared at me. "I can't believe I didn't know any of this."

"I kind of can't believe it either. Barlow had more vices than you could poke a stick at."

"I think it's safe to say there's no money here. And unless whoever—" she covered her mouth, choking back whatever emotion that was riding her. "Unless whoever *did this* left a business card lying around, there's not much for us here."

"Best to get gone before anyone else shows up." I was already propelling her back into the fresh air, my mind racing as I considered what I was going to tell Saul.

"Wait, don't you think we should check the barn?"

I kept pushing her until we were far enough from Dustin's body that the smell wasn't making me taste bile. "You're not going to find anything. Not in the house or the barn. Whoever was here was thorough. They just thought more of the house would burn before the rain came."

I tapped my fingers on my hip, my instincts telling me something wasn't right here. I said I didn't believe in coincidence, and I meant it. Maybe this was about missing money or maybe the missing money just happened to come up in a scheme of a different kind. Barlow was always skimming, that was nothing new. Whoever caught him stealing hadn't anticipated his sudden death.

I kept thinking about those men bringing Cady out to the bayou. Crime on the bayou was common but right on the edge of *my* territory? It didn't happen. Even thugs and drug dealers knew to steer clear of Barbeaux property. Too many of them went missing out there to take the risk.

And the Cray homestead bordered the bayou, along Saul's land. Sooner or later the scent of death would have carried his way and he would have discovered this body. A body that was a blatant werewolf kill. Even if the house had burned with Dustin in it, the claw marks went down to the bone. Saul would know what he was looking at same as I did.

Warning whispered up my nape, that preternatural intuition telling me that I was on the right path.

This was Jacques and he wasn't quietly going about business as usual in Port O'Henry, trying to get rich by exploiting the worst of folks out here. This was Jacques prodding at our defenses, waiting to see how much damage he could do before we noticed.

I glanced at Cady, the soft arch of her brow disturbed by a frown. She'd said something and I was obviously not listening. I couldn't hear her over the pounding in my ears.

Jacques wanted to get some payback for being chased off Barbeaux territory? Fine. We could take him and whatever filthy mutts he'd obviously taken up with. But I didn't just have to worry about my brothers and me now. Of all the times to bond, to *finally* find a mate, it had to be now.

Cady was a firecracker, but she was fragile compared to us. And my cousin had his savage gaze locked on her.

The worst part was that I couldn't tell her. Not yet. She would believe me. I was sure of it. Problem was that I knew without a doubt it would send her running from me and right into harm's way. Her trust in me was already threadbare. I wasn't going to make it worse by admitting that this was my fault.

Fucking coward.

Maybe, but the alternative didn't keep Cady by my side, under my protection. I couldn't risk it.

"We need to regroup." I told her, walking back to the truck and expecting her to follow.

She did, though that scowl still hung low over her eyes. "What about Dustin's body?"

"You said it yourself. Sheriff is in on this. You can't risk calling him and getting this pinned on you."

She climbed into the front seat, her eyes sad. "So, we're just going to leave him there? It doesn't matter what he did. He doesn't deserve that."

"When this is over, I'll make sure he gets a proper burial."

Cady looked at me with a newfound respect. "Thank you."

"Back to your place, or you want to go get lunch?"

"I'm not going to eat again until next week." She covered her mouth and made a gagging sound.

I silently agreed, rolling down the windows and letting the salty air whip away some of the lingering stink. Even as we pulled up on Cady's driveway the stench of death still stung my nose, like it was following us, coming closer, and there was nothing I could do to avoid it.

Chapter 14

Two Lies and a Truth

Eli

THE CLOYING SCENT OF rot and smoke still clung to my clothes as I climbed into the truck. A storm retreated out over the water, breathing frigid breath across the bay. Mist collected around the lights on Cady's porch, adding a sense of foreboding to the early evening. The sun hadn't set yet, but the clouds turned everything a dusky shade of blue. I needed to get home and catch Saul before he went on his nightly walkabout.

Once again, I found myself noticing how abnormal that was—my brother spending his night roaming the bayou on four legs instead of sleeping. Our life appeared strange and otherworldly when I was looking at it through the lens of Cady's world. More so, it was erratic. Unhealthy, bordering on unhinged. Saul's behavior was raising red flags that I should have seen months ago—maybe years ago.

I rolled the window down, hoping to cleanse my lungs and my head with the cool salt air, only to smell *more* smoke. Fresh smoke. Instinct rose inside me like the tide, calling me down the street and away from the bayou. I drove slowly, following the chemical laden fumes of a burning house. That had to be what it was, the combination of wood, paint, and the many plastic items inside a home rising in a sickly haze.

My breath came short and shallow as I neared the edge of *Pelican Bay*. I knew what I would see before the flashing lights of a firetruck came into view. Flames hissed as firefighters fought to quench the blaze. At this point all they could do was put it out, so it didn't spread to the surrounding homes. Barlow's house was toast. Quite literally.

Whoever started this fire wasn't destroying evidence. From what Cady said, they already had the Sheriff in their pocket. No need to hide what they were up to when law enforcement was turning a blind eye. No, this wasn't about covering anything up. This was a message meant for my brothers and me. Just as Dustin Barlow's body was a message.

Someone was leaving a trail. A blazing, gory trail, that led back to what we did for Barlow out on the bay all those years ago. The list of people who knew how low we stooped was short. The list of people who knew and wanted to bleed us slowly was even shorter. This was my cousin's work. It had to be.

I didn't know what his ultimate goal was, but I needed to find out fast. Jacques was playing with fire, and we were the ones who would get burned.

S AUL WAS ON HIS boat when I pulled my truck up his gravel driveway. The boat trailer was tucked under his tiny, stilted house, a yellow overhead light giving his complexion an unhealthy glow. His head was down, concentrating on tying off a fishing rig. But the waves were four feet, at least, not to mention the sun was setting. No way was he planning to fish right now, which meant he was trying to control himself.

I felt like I was waking up for the first time in decades, like I'd been sleep walking through life and hadn't seen what was really happening around me. Not with myself or my brothers.

Was it any wonder Jacques was back in Texas, and we hadn't noticed? There could be a pack on our doorstep, and we were just...existing.

I dropped onto my brother's boat without greeting. "It's him, Saul."

Saul glanced up from the tackle box and grimaced. "Isaac?"

"No. Isaac is fine." I hoped he was fine, anyway.

Lately, I only saw him during the full moon and only on four legs. Once or twice for a supply run in town, if it was slow season and there weren't enough women from out-of-town for him to seduce.

Shit, we were all losing it. Was this what happened to werewolves that couldn't bond? A bond was supposed to be an anchor, channeling our magic and our lifeline, and tying it off, making us mortal. Otherwise, we were doomed to live on forever.

Unless someone managed to kill us.

There was hope though because *we could* bond. Cady was proof. I knew that if I told Saul, when this was so fresh, he would deny it. Actually, denial was the best case scenario. Talk of bonds incensed my brother, maybe because he genuinely believed he would never have one.

I'd always thought he didn't care about bonding, believing it to be a chain that would steal away his freedom. My bond with Cady felt like a literal chain, pulling taut every time we were apart. I only had vague memories of discussing bonds with my father. It was a matter of family history, and I detested that subject.

Life without it—a life as long as mine—was tedious. Boring and petty and maddening. That was why I was suddenly so worried about Saul. At least Isaac and I delved into the outside world. Isolation wasn't good for Saul—for any of us.

I felt like a frayed rope, too taut for too long, when Cady stumbled into my path. Maybe because all this time that rope was stretched across Port O'Henry, tied to a woman that I needed but never knew.

Now I was learning the bond could be more than desire. I was coming to crave her reserved smile and the way her dark eyebrows pinched together when I said something too forward. The single laugh I edged out of her made me feel lighter.

"Have you heard from him? I'll believe he's fine when I see him." I'd almost forgotten we were talking about Isaac

"Saul, are you listening?" I shut the tacklebox, eliciting a growl from him. "Jacques is in Port O'Henry again."

"There are a lot of people doing a lot of malicious things in Port O'Henry, Elijah. No reason to believe it's Jacques."

"Why are you so unwilling to believe that he's back?" I snapped.

Saul's words were icy as the autumn wind. "Because he's dead."

The quiet lasted for so long that Saul went back to his knot, assuming the conversation was over. As if he hadn't just admitted to killing his own blood. When did he become this man?

"You killed him." It wasn't meant to sound so accusatory, but I couldn't back down. It wasn't just that Jacques was blood. The implications for Saul were huge. After everything he'd seen...he couldn't take much more violence.

"I didn't have a choice. "

"Of course, you had a choice! Jesus, Saul. "

"He was building a pack. It was only a matter of time before he picked up the old ways." Saul closed his eyes, shutting out the memories that haunted him. "You haven't seen a pack in action. There's no controlling it. Even I wouldn't be able to keep their instincts at bay."

Saul was adamant that we weren't a pack and that we didn't build one. My brothers and I had separate homes and territories on the bayou because Saul wanted to make sure we had plenty of time apart.

Werewolves weren't animals. We could look like them and we had instincts like them but at our core we were beings of magic, a dark magic that was easily twisted. Too much concentrated in one place and the very worst of it caught like wildfire, spreading to every pack member and making them mad with blood lust.

Or so Saul claimed. He was right that I'd never seen it. I was too young to remember our life before settling on the bayou. I wasn't haunted by memories of death as Saul was. Sometimes I wondered if those memories skewed his judgment.

"One life to save hundreds. I did the math, Eli."

I sank onto the bench seat behind the boat's wheel and rubbed my face. "Why didn't you tell me?"

"You know why."

"It's not your job to protect us anymore."

Saul's expression grew fierce. "It will always be my job to protect you."

He would never be a true alpha, despite his birthright, and he would never call us a pack. But he carried the weight all the same. Saul, Isaac, and I were bound by blood and time.

That was why Saul risked his sanity to kill Jacques. It was messed up, but I understood. Packs were bound by nothing but an antiquated hierarchy. There was no loyalty or safety. Survival of the fittest became law.

Werewolves were always at risk of becoming unbalanced. Sway too far toward our baser selves and we went feral. A danger to innocents and to our own kind.

Jacques was born feral. Or maybe heartless. He was the product of the darkest seed in the Barbeaux line. The ones that lost their way and followed in the footsteps of the infamous beast.

I peered at my brother, who was studying his tackle box in a perfunctory fashion, void of the emotion from moments earlier.

No, something was there. Something cold and dangerous. Maybe *this* was the explanation for why he'd been distancing himself.

Jacques.

Saul killed family and even if he was the worst of our family, it didn't change what we were to each other. Was this what would finally push Saul over the edge?

I shook my head. He wasn't there yet. Edging close but my brother still had time. There was hope for all of us. Finding Cady made me believe that.

Thinking of her shot me back to the present and I stood, pacing the length of the boat, and asking, "If it's not Jacques then what the hell is going on?"

"What does it matter to you?"

"Someone is trying to get our attention." I told him about the Cray homestead, Barlow's son, and the fire tonight at Barlow's house.

Saul assessed me with eyes like the sunrise reflecting from the pier. They seared through me, looking right at my soul. My brother knew I was lying, omitting an important detail that tied the whole story together. He just didn't know why.

"Remind me again why you were at the Cray homestead."

I rubbed my chin, leaving the silence for too long to come up with a decent excuse.

"This about that bookkeeper?" He closed his tackle box and set it gently in a compartment under the seat next to mine. Those slow, careful movements raised the hair on the back of my neck. Saul was a predator pretending to be docile.

"This is close to home. Too close." I pushed off the seat and walked to the bow of the boat, pretending to watch the waves move through the trees on the edge of Saul's property. "My instinct says something strange is going on and it all leads back to us and what we did."

"Yeah," Saul said, suspicion hanging heavy on his words. "Mine too." I didn't respond so he added, "You should have let her die. Not your place to decide who lives."

I pressed my fist to my mouth, biting down on my knuckles so I didn't whip around and rage at my brother. Even the thought of Cady dead had the place in my chest where I felt the ever-present buzz of the bond snapping painfully. I didn't know her well and I couldn't claim I loved her, but I saw my future in that woman. Bonds happened for a reason and whatever reason it was, I wouldn't question it.

"You can trust me, brother."

As much as I hated to admit it, I wasn't sure I could. Saul kept what he did to Jacques a secret for nearly a decade. What else was he hiding?

There wasn't anything Saul wouldn't do to keep the family secret. At some point Cady was going to be let in on that secret. I would complete our bond and then it would be done. Saul wouldn't dare touch her if she was my mate. If anything happened to her it was a death sentence for me. A beast would go mad from a broken bond, my ancestors proved that.

My parents weren't bonded, just two people that married for convenience. It was why my father so easily moved on with his life when my mother died. If she was his mate, he would have lost himself upon her passing.

I glanced at Saul in my peripherals, considering for the first time that he was lying about more than what happened with Jacques. What if he knew we could bond but convinced us it was impossible to spare us the risk of madness? To spare himself from having to put us down if we did go mad?

An ache formed in my chest as I watched him, patient, almost pleading for my trust. The problem with trust was that it had to go both ways. I was lying to my brother but only because instinctively I knew he was doing the same. There wasn't honesty between us, not for a while, and I wasn't ready to give away my secret.

The only thing Saul cared about as much as the family secret was freedom. He couldn't bear to give it up. Couldn't take it if he wasn't under the open sky and free to roam the wild.

For me that freedom had warped, the monotony of it twisting into a collar around my neck. It chafed and choked until I was numbing myself just to survive the days. Then I saw Cady, those blue eyes too keen as they noticed all my hollow places, and I felt everything again. The longing for *more*, for a real life, a normal life. A life with an inevitable end, after many happy days with a woman that made my world bloom like springtime.

I couldn't let Saul threaten my chance at that life. I couldn't let anyone. And as I murmured a quick goodbye to my brother, leaving him hanging on those last beseeching words, I knew what I had to do.

Chapter 15

Up in Smoke

Cady

"BARLOW'S HOUSE BURNED DOWN!" I shouted, flinging the door open and waving Eli inside.

At the same time, he said, "I gotta tell you something you're not going to like," handing me a plastic bag full of groceries so he could slip off his boots. "But apparently you already know."

"Know what?" The bag distracted me, and I peeked inside, mouth watering when I saw bacon—the good kind, not the cheap-y microwaveable stuff from *Stop N' Shop*. "Breakfast again? What are you apologizing for now?"

"I can tell by the look on your face that you were up all night researching and you had nothing to eat but coffee." He took the bag from me and headed into the kitchen, making himself at home as he opened cabinets and drawers. "Besides, it's almost eleven. This is brunch."

That was a surprisingly accurate assessment. "Wrong. I had a frozen waffle at three AM."

The smile he gave me was easygoing and carried far too much fondness for someone that hadn't known me but a handful of weeks. I mentally swatted at the butterflies in my stomach, reminding myself to stay focused.

This was a mutually beneficial arrangement, and I wasn't going to fall for him because he brought me bacon. Or because his smile stopped my heart. Or because of the way his shoulders filled out his shirt.

"You got milk?"

"Huh?"

Eli didn't bother repeating himself, instead yanking open the fridge and digging around until he found half a dozen eggs and a gallon of milk.

"Darlin', you got something alive in your fridge and it's not because it's farm fresh."

"Cut a girl a break. I've been preoccupied." I passed him at the stove, pulling two mugs out of the cabinet and asking "Coffee?" Eli nodded and I fixed up his coffee with enough sugar to make my teeth hurt.

"So, you know about Barlow's house?" He wrapped his fingers around the mug as I handed it to him, grazing my hand with a sensual caress.

He was persistent, I would give him that.

"How do you know about it?" I hopped onto the edge of the counter, powering up my laptop.

"I smelled the smoke on my way home the other night. Drove over there and saw it."

"I heard the sirens just after you left. Why do you think they waited so long?"

He cracked three eggs into a pan and tore open the package of bacon. "What do you mean?"

"Whoever tried to burn the Cray house burned Barlow's too. That's a given. So why didn't they burn it when they broke in and tossed it?"

Eli had his back to me, but I felt that reticence drawing over him.

"Eli? What aren't you telling me?"

He stilled, his broad shoulders tensed. "I went back to the Cray homestead this morning."

I waited, fingers tight around my mug. I wasn't going to beg and prod for honesty. He told me from the start that there were things he couldn't tell me—*wouldn't* tell me. He could keep his secrets, but he had to realize that they might be the reason I sent him packing and finished this on my own.

"Dustin's body was gone, and the rest of the house was torched. Everything inside is ashes."

My hands started shaking and I thought back to the gruesome scene, scouring every detail in my mind. If someone had been there watching, I wouldn't have noticed. The sight of the body and horror of knowing who it was consumed my focus.

Eli held a plate of bacon and eggs under my nose, but my stomach was too twisted to feel hungry. "I have two bedrooms."

The two topics collided, shattering into a bewildered mess. "Bedrooms?"

His face was lined with unspoken worry and seeing the dent in his unwavering confidence made my throat feel like it was closing. "You could stay with me until it's safe."

Safe? Would it ever be safe again?

"I—wait, do you think we're being followed?"

"I don't know what to think, except that maybe this is more complicated than stolen drug money."

I finally accepted the breakfast plate, breaking into laughter as I did. "You just asked me to move in with you. Most men ask a woman on at least one date first."

Eli bit down on a piece of bacon. "I'm not like most men."

"That's true. How do you know your house is safer than mine? Maybe they're following *you.*"

"Anyone wants to come mess around on the bayou they have to deal with me *and* my brothers. I like those odds." I could tell he was choosing his words carefully. "I'm not worried about my safety, Cady."

"I am!" Was he oblivious or careless? "Eli, these are people that didn't bat an eye about *feeding me to an alligator.* Don't you think you should be taking this a little more seriously?"

"I am serious." He dropped my plate next to me on the kitchen island and slipped his hand up my calf, cupping the back of my knee and tugging me until only the pressure of his hand kept me from falling into him. "No one fucks with the Barbeaux family and lives to talk about it."

I couldn't tell if this was hyperbole or an admission. He made it sound like they were some bayou mafia. For all I knew, they were. It would certainly do the rumors justice.

I wobbled on my perch, leaning toward his delicious, smoky chest, and parting my lips to whisper, "Who are you really?"

"You know who I am." There were always layers to what Eli said, another meaning buried under his simple statements.

My next question was interrupted by a forkful of eggs sliding into my mouth. Eli watched me chew, my mouth watering at the taste of bacon grease and cheese. He fed me another bite, transfixed by my lips, and I found it hard to swallow. This was the most intimate experience I'd ever had, and he was hardly touching me.

Carefully, he pushed me back up onto the granite, setting the fork down and returning to his own breakfast as if he hadn't just set me on fire.

"Eat. Your hunger is distracting."

We didn't talk through breakfast, other than the "thank you" I moaned through a mouthful of bacon. There was a lot I needed to tell him about what I uncovered last night but it seemed wrong to interrupt this moment of peace. My mind was constantly occupied with unraveling this mystery and I wanted a break.

For a heartbeat I let myself fantasize about the life I could live when this was over. I would spend my mornings writing on the beach as the tide came in. Walking with friends to the jetty and back like I used to. Going out for pastries and coffee at Jody's with a man—maybe even Eli. I hadn't been on a date in four years.

Maybe a life like that didn't exist in this town. Most of my friends moved away years ago. The ones that didn't fell on the kind of hard times that made them difficult to associate with.

Port O'Henry was full of bright, beautiful houses. Big boats and shiny cars and all the wealth anyone could dream of.

But that glamour came and went like the tide, receding with the tourists and leaving the town desolate and dead. There was no opportunity here. No room to grow.

I felt that lack of growth acutely, like I was a houseplant spilling out over my pot. My roots were planted here but I was desperately reaching out for something beyond the known. Maybe this kidnapping was a sign from God. I should have immediately packed my bags, sold the house, and headed for anywhere that wasn't here.

What would I do when I figured out who wanted this money? Finding it and giving it to them was just as much a guarantee of death as being kidnapped again and admitting I didn't have it.

A sadness as deep as the gulf opened in my belly. Port O'Henry was my home. All my memories resided here. This house was built by my grandfather, one of the only real pieces I had left of the man that raised me. But I felt the jaws of this unseen monster snapping shut and if I didn't make the right move, I was going to be devoured.

"Cady?"

My attention snapped to Eli as he held out the pot of coffee, eyes carving into me in that too seeing way of his.

"Sorry, zoned out."

"Did you sleep at all last night?" He added another splash of coffee and cream to my mug.

I forked a bite of eggs instead of answering.

"You can't keep going like that." He scolded. "You'll lose your mind before you find anything useful."

"I can't sleep." I admitted to the last slice of bacon on my plate. "I'm either having nightmares or waking every time a mosquito flaps it's wings."

Eli opened his mouth to respond but stopped before any noise came out. He hovered there in conflict for several long seconds before swallowing his last bite of breakfast and whatever words he meant to say.

I filled in the silence before it could get tense. "Did you know there have been six fires in Port O'Henry in the last five months? A dozen in the county since February of last year. They're calling him The Gulf Coast Arsonist." I slurped my coffee. "Not very imaginative."

Those worry lines deepened around Eli's eyes and I still had this feeling like he was holding back. "You think it's the same person that hit Barlow and the Cray house?"

"How could it not be? The news articles I dug up said police claim there's no pattern besides gasoline being used as the accelerant, but that's not true. They could be too useless to see it, or they're paid not to make connections."

I finished my breakfast and pushed the plate aside, bringing my laptop close and scrolling to the parts of the article I highlighted. Eli took full advantage, crowding against me to better see the screen. I didn't stop him, either.

"Look at the buildings that were burned. Three very nice beach houses, all owned by local businessmen. The rest are industrial buildings, one of which was a suspected meth lab. Someone is using fire to destroy evidence."

Eli scanned the words, brows pinched. "So, what's this connection you found?"

"They owned the industrial buildings!" I almost shouted it, my previously contained excitement spilling out. "Barlow owned two of the warehouses. I didn't find it immediately because he owned them through an LLC I'd never heard of."

"And whoever lived in those other two beach houses owned the rest?"

"Or invested in the companies that owned them. Guess what else?"

Eli rubbed his jaw. "They're all dead."

I grinned, then realized that made me look like an insane person and tried for somber. "Yes. Barlow had a heart attack, no debating that. He had a heart problem for years. And if I knew I was hiding money from someone that would burn my house down and drag me out to the bayou for gator bait, I would have a heart attack too."

He nodded at me, returning to the article, and scrolling. "The other two were burned alive. Shit."

"They probably died of smoke inhalation, if it's any consolation." It wasn't that I felt nothing about these strangers being murderer by the same people responsible—at least distantly—for my kidnapping. It was that they knew what they were getting themselves into, what they were drawing the unwitting people around them into, and well, you got what you paid for.

"The thing is," I pushed Eli's hand out of the way and pulled up the document of property searches, "*we* know this isn't an arsonist. This is probably gang related. Drugs or something worse. And we know these properties are connected."

"Right." He stepped away from me to lean against the stove, arms crossed. "Now, explain how this helps us."

I opened my mouth. Closed it. "Fuck!"

Eli waited while I rubbed my face before saying my worst thoughts out loud. "Even if you find a name, an address, and a social security number, it doesn't change anything. They think you've got this money, they'll come looking for you. If you have it, they want it."

"But I don't have it! I don't know how much money it was or why Barlow was hiding it!"

"I know, darlin', I know." He put a hand up like he was calming a wild animal. I was all coffee and no sleep, and I felt like a wild animal. "Which is why I suggested an alternate plan. I know you want answers. But at what cost?"

"What's the cost if I don't find them? This doesn't end until I end it."

"It could end with me ending it and you don't have to lift a finger." He mumbled it and I wasn't sure he wanted me to hear. When I shot him a questioning look, he strolled into the

living room and dropped a box of files onto the coffee table.
"I guess it's paperwork then."

I RIFLED THROUGH SOME of the boxes I took from Barlow's
office before the fire but there were years of financial
records, personal paperwork, and other crap and the task
seemed daunting. Even with Eli sprawled on the couch next
to me—with his feet resting in my lap because the dude had
no concept of personal space—it was still daunting.

Clearly, he was giving up on Plan A, which was find out who
wants this money and...do something about it. Okay, it was a
shitty, half-cocked idea with no real planning. It was fueled
by a vengeful fury that had me plotting to find whatever drug
lord sent his goons after me and make him pay. I wasn't going
to bind him and feed him to alligators piece by piece so I'm
not sure what kind of payback or justice I would get.

I had a feeling that Eli would do that or worse if I asked him
to. My eyes wandered away from the 2016 tax return in my
hands to study him in my peripherals. The weirdest part of
this whole situation was that I wasn't afraid of him anymore.
In fact, my fear came swelling back when he left and didn't
dissipate until he returned. His presence was a reassurance I
hadn't realized I needed.

Either trauma did strange things to your dating standards, or
I just discovered my type was bayou mad man with shoulders
wider than a double wide and a penchant for homicide.

Part of why I hadn't been on a date in so long was because
I knew it was a wasted effort. Modern men were impatient,

untrustworthy, or both. They couldn't be bothered to earn my trust and if they could, that determination died as soon as they realized they weren't getting anything out of me. People came and went as quickly as the tide, and I wasn't giving myself to someone that would be gone by morning.

I switched my focus back to reading, shoving those un-wanted memories into the darkest hole in my brain. A healthy person would deal with them, go to therapy or something, but I was never one for talking about my feelings. It didn't change anything.

Minutes dragged on into hours and before I knew it, we were setting paperwork aside for lunch. I use the word "lunch" loosely because all I had left in my kitchen was peanut butter and jelly. Poor Eli was going to starve. He didn't complain though, just licked grape jelly from his fingers and got back to work.

It took most of the day to get through the first three boxes of papers. We were probably being too thorough, but I didn't want to risk missing the only clue that would tell me where to go next. Multiple times Eli suggested we stop for the day and get dinner, but I couldn't eat until this was done.

"You can leave." I said through a yawn. He was collapsed in the recliner across from me now, eyes rimmed with red. "I won't hold it against you."

He fixed me with a simmering look. "Darlin' I'm just getting started."

Lord help me, this man would wear me down if he kept doing that smolder-y thing. "It's probably going to be another all-nighter and I'll be grumpy if we get through these and find nothing. You don't have to subject yourself to that."

"You're cute when you're grumpy."

I raised a letter from a car insurance company in front of my face to hide my smile. "Don't say I didn't warn you."

My late boss was a hoarder. There were hundreds of saved letters and bank statements from accounts that didn't exist anymore. He even had a few crumpled credit card offers. I couldn't fathom why he kept any of this, other than he was too lazy to organize and purge. Nana always told me it was wrong to speak ill of the dead, but I was beginning to despise Dale Barlow.

My eyes blurred across the paper in my hand, and I blinked. A yawn made my jaw click and I blinked again. I peered over the top of the paper and saw Eli's head propped against his shoulder, eyes closed.

"Lightweight," I mumbled as I slumped against a throw pillow and lost the fight with sleep.

Chapter 16

The Beast on Barbeaux Bayou

Cady

"SHOOT THE BITCH!" THE chant echoed around me, and I flinched, unable to see the source of the sound from my prone position.

Blood mingled with the taste of bayou air on my tongue. I was sprawled on my back, breathless and stunned. Above me the stars were alight, making the blackness that was swallowing me up seem even more fathomless. A shape moved in the shadows, hulking and animal, carrying itself on two legs.

It sprang.

Blood sprayed.

I tried to scream but my voice was trapped in the walls of my throat.

I was still on my back, muscles frozen in paralysis.

Then it was standing over me. An otherworldly creature, russet eyes glinting dangerously in the moonlight. Red dripped onto my chin as he opened his maw, tasing the breath that left my lungs in stuttered puffs.

The head of a wolf sat atop the brawny, overgrown figure of a man, and he was pinning me into the sand.

His presence seemed to devour the time, freezing us both as the stars moved and shifted, the moon dropping to rest on the horizon. Movement returned to me in a sudden burst, and I slipped from beneath the monster, rising to my feet and running like I'd never run before.

Trees blurred past me, gravel dug into my bare feet, and thorned vines reached for me. There were spirits on the bayou, turning the flora into moving things that would wrap their arms around me and shackle me for eternity. Over my shoulder the creature pursued, it's eyes shining madly.

I turned my attention back to the road and skidded to a stop.

Impossible.

He was in front of me now, lips raised to reveal a row of deadly teeth, clawed hands outstretched as he grabbed for me. I knew no matter how fast or far I ran, I would never escape him. The beast wanted me, and he *would* have me.

This wasn't how it was supposed to end. *He* was meant to be here. To save me.

"Eli!" I screamed, tumbling from the couch, and hitting the coffee table on my way down.

A shadow passed over me and I screamed again, scrambling backward into the side table, and toppling a lamp as my shoulder smashed into it.

Eli leapt over the couch, rushing to the front door, and flinging it open with his gun drawn. He disappeared for only half a second before he was storming through the house, searching every corner where night had settled darkly.

I tried to speak, to explain that it was only a nightmare, but my tongue was glued to the roof of my mouth. Frantic breath rattled my chest, and I squeezed my eyes shut, only to reopen them when I saw the wolf-man coming right for me.

Warm hands gripped my upper arms. "What is it, Cady?"

I looked up into Eli's face, seeking something familiar. Instead, I saw someone different. The shape of his face was the same, his features unchanged. But there was wrongness there, his eyes too bright, expression too sharp. A muscle twitched in his jaw. The tendons in his neck danced as he moved his lips. I couldn't hear what he was saying.

Arms came around me and I dropped my forehead to his chest, shivering. All at once the sound rushed back into the room and I inhaled deeply.

"Wolf." It was barely a whisper on my lips, the only word I could form.

"What?" Eli jerked back, hitting the coffee table as he rose to his feet.

"There was a—a wolf on the bayou. I couldn't get away from it." Why was I telling him this?

The color drained from his face, and he rubbed the back of his neck.

"Just a nightmare," I said, mostly to myself.

"Yeah. Bad dream." This time he rolled his shoulders, jaw tight like he was uncomfortable. Then Eli vanished from the living room, and I heard the deadbolt twisting open.

I pushed off the floor and hurried around the couch. "Where are you going?" I didn't want him to leave. Fear pulsed in my blood, and I couldn't bear the thought of being alone.

"Just jumpy. Gonna go walk."

I nodded, lip trembling. Wind whipped through the front door as he stood in the doorway, his back to me. His shoulders were up to his ears and even though I couldn't see his face, I sensed that wrongness was still shrouding him like smoke.

Could I really blame him for leaving? I was screaming his name in the middle of the night, and not because I was having a good time.

"I'm sorry," I murmured.

He turned so fast I startled, wrapping an arm around me, and holding me steady. "S'ok, darlin'. You didn't do anything wrong."

"Are you coming back?"

"Just need to make sure no one is wandering around out there." He didn't give a real answer. More secrets buried under careful words.

I blinked at him, bowing my head even though I didn't understand. There was a strange aura around him, his muscles jumping with every second he was still. A feeling niggled at me, but I didn't know what my instincts were trying to tell me.

All I knew was that I wanted Eli close and that scared me more than the nightmare.

"S'ok, darlin'." He repeated, kissing my temple, and turning for the door. "You're safe here."

We locked gazes and I suddenly felt so exposed, like he saw me down to the rawest core. I didn't like it, which was why I let him go.

I stared at the front door long after Eli was gone, my fingers pressed to my freshly kissed temple, as I tried to figure out exactly what was happening to me.

The floor was firmly under my feet and yet, I was falling, fast and reckless.

Eli

I fumbled with the lock on Cady's utility room downstairs. My fingers shook as I undid my belt and ripped my jeans off. There was barely time to brace myself before I was slamming onto my knees, my body breaking apart to reveal *him*.

The beast.

Wolf, she'd called him, but this version of me was not the sleek, graceful hunter I became on the full moon. That was the embodiment of the animal I shared my soul with, the animal whose strength was borrowed to create the very first werewolf and with it an unbreakable bond.

This was the monster, the creature of legends that devoured villagers and haunted the countryside. The beast was the result of forbidden magic, the lethal consequence of power unchecked. He had the body of a man but the features of a wolf, a true wolf-man incarnate. I had to hunch to keep from hitting my head on the low ceiling as I paced the concrete floor.

The beast was strong, but he wasn't particularly clever. With enough effort he could figure out the lock and let himself out the door. With enough impatience he would break the window and claw his way out.

It was dangerous when the beast showed himself. I didn't always shift, sometimes taking on only his heightened senses. The night I climbed Cady's porch it wasn't really me. It was him—the monster inside me. The reason my brothers and I were supposed to hide ourselves away from others.

It wasn't only to protect our secret.

It was to protect them from our secret too.

Now I was mentally fighting, failing to control the impulsive creature that had one subject on his mind: Cady.

That was why I shut myself in here, fearing the worst from him. Overhead the floor creaked as Cady moved around the living room. Restless, pacing. So close but still out of my reach.

Below, I did the same, stuffing my snout into every crack and pushing at the door. Hopefully Cady didn't notice the gouges in the frame. I didn't have an explanation that wouldn't horrify.

Internally, I cursed. She was having nightmares about me and somehow the beast took that as a compliment.

Wolf. That word on her lips was a summoning spell, drawing him up through my skin until he nearly ripped free.

Again, I cursed the animal, hating that I was so out of control. Cady was scared and instead of comforting her, I ran. Seemed like I was running from her as much as I was running to her.

An unbidden growl filled the room and I tried to cut it off before Cady heard. I didn't have to run from her. Right now, I could be up there, taking a sip of those perfect lips. Tasting her.

Shit.

I kissed her.

I ran from her.

I was a monster and somehow, I would have to reveal that to her.

But she was dreaming of me *like this* and that didn't bode well. I hoped she hadn't seen me that night, that I would have time to ease her into this.

Fear did strange things to memory, and it was possible she was only just remembering my presence. A pang hit me in the chest, and I paced the small room faster. Cady was going to flee as quick as she could when she found out what I was.

How could she not? Even now I wasn't really sure what was keeping her here, in Port O'Henry.

Maybe my brother was right about bonds. They were the source of endless agony, a match on a dynamite stick of crazy. Each hour I spent with Cady made me more attached, more desperate. I would do just about anything to earn her affection.

That was starting to scare me, seeing as part of me was a vicious brute who thought a nighttime chase on the bayou was romantic. The full moon was fast approaching. I wasn't confident I could keep myself from her then.

I *knew* I couldn't.

Which meant I had less than two weeks to win Cady's heart or get her as far away from me as she would go.

I T TOOK THE BETTER half of the night to calm myself after my unexpected shift. When I was finally settled enough to think straight I did exactly what I said I would and walked the property. Unsatisfied, I walked further, peering under every house, and making certain we weren't being watched.

Even as I found no evidence of intrusion, I felt the weight of eyes on me. Paranoia crept up my spine to tingle at my neck and I was exhausted by the time I let myself back into Cady's house. I pocketed the key she left for me under the mat, not trusting the promise of safety a small town like Port O'Henry was supposed to offer.

Cady was asleep on the couch, curled around her baseball bat. It would be useless against the type of people after her, but nothing would happen to her while I was here anyway. I sat on the edge of the cushion, carefully slipping the bat out of her death grip.

There was a collection of papers scattered around her, some on the floor and some littering the coffee table. Resting on top of a manila folder was a leather-bound journal, the chestnut color worn and the threads fraying where fingers had pried it open hundreds of times. A diary. Confidential and not meant for my eyes.

I scooped it up, flipping through the pages fast enough that I couldn't read the words. It was possible this wasn't her diary, filled with her most private thoughts. For all I knew, it was tucked in Barlow's stuff. That was how I justified opening it for a second time, scanning the first page, then the second.

The words contained on the pages were personal, but they weren't journal entries. This was poetry.

I shouldn't have been surprised by the lyrical verses or the evocative way she made the mundane seem enchanting. Cady was more multifaceted than I suspected anyone gave her credit for.

I didn't care about poetry, never had an appreciation for art. Not unless old cowboy movies counted as art. But the way she painted the world, noticed every intricate detail of the sunset and the sea and the way they came together, made my chest buzz.

Fingers itching, I turned to the last entry. The title "bayou stranger" was scratched hastily across the top of the page. My throat clamped tight on the breath trying to leave it and I reread the words until my vision blurred.

Whiskey bright eyes drink me down
and I'm love-drunk dizzy,
a honey tide rising until I drown,
pushing and pulling me in like the moon,
Amber seas swallow me whole
and I'm ravenous for more,
a frothing wave spilling across the bay,
coming to rest on his golden shore.

My pulse raced, the sudden need to shake her awake and tell her everything nearly shattering my will.

Tell her, just tell her, and let her see how right this could be. I needed her to understand, to know that what she was feeling was real. That she could trust me. That whether I wanted to be or not, I was beholden to her for infinity.

Not yet. I couldn't yet. There were too many consequences. Once I opened that door, I could never close it again.

I slid onto the couch beside her, inching toward her until I could feel her breath on my neck. My insides still burned with the beast, and this was the only way to keep myself steady. Being away from her splintered me apart. The further the distance grew, the more I crumbled until any semblance of self-control evaporated.

Auburn curls tumbled over her shoulder, the color matching her freckles. I watched her mouth twitch, chest rising gently, and ran my thumb along her bottom lip.

"What did you see that night, darlin'?"

Blue eyes flicked open, and her hand yanked on my arm. Confusion wrinkled at her brow when she realized the bat was gone, my forearm in its place.

"Eli?" She was looking at me, not really seeing me. Sleep glazed her sight and shadows carved deep craters under her eyes. The exhaustion weighing on her was heavy and I wanted to ease some of that burden. "You came back."

"I'm not going anywhere." I tucked hair behind her ear. I couldn't help myself. "Get some rest."

Her head was already lowering back onto a navy throw pillow, eyes shuttered. She shifted, rolling over and snuggling her back into my chest with a sigh. I was desperate to run my hands under her shirt and enjoy the silky texture of her sun kissed skin. My lungs filled with the scent of her, and I was drowning in the need to touch her.

Touching her would be that much sweeter when she was desperate for me, though. I could enjoy a little delayed gratification.

I exhaled, wrapping my arm around her in the most chaste way I could manage with our bodies pressed together. The air was cool, but I was too hot, my blood still burning with the beast. But as I lay there with my neck kinked on a too-soft throw pillow, long legs cramped as they curled to fit on the couch, I felt the creature settle in me. The only thing he—*we*—wanted more than to claim Cady was to protect her.

Let this new threat come. He would see what kind of terror waited for him if he touched what was mine.

Chapter 17

Progress

Eli

MY SLEEP WAS LIGHT and disturbed, caught in that twilight state as the beast simmered near the surface of my skin.

I was used to it. When the full moon was nearing or the busy season had me on edge, the beast would come alive, waiting for his chance at freedom. Watching for whatever threat left me agitated.

Last night he was awake for a different reason, peering out of my cracked eyelids to check the surroundings, on alert for any risk to the woman in my arms. Unlike me, Cady never stirred. Maybe because instinctively she knew there was no place in the world safer than my embrace.

Fine rays of light were beginning to stretch through the blinds, the first hints of sunrise reflecting off the bay, and exhaustion was finally taking hold. My lids were heavy, body limp as I lay stiffly on Cady's couch.

Fingers ghosted through my hair, the tickle of a dream stirring me as I imagined Cady was combing the hair from my face, whispering my name. "What have you done to me, Eli Barbeaux?"

Water rushed through my ears, and I startled awake, leaping to my feet to scan the living room. Light poured through the windows, sunlight now brightening the crystalline sky. Not even a wisp of clouds shadowed the bay. Autumn was giving her very best.

Down the hall the water heater groaned, and my attention was drawn to the bathroom door. The door was cracked enough for me to see steam dancing across the mirror. I wanted to pretend it was left open in invitation. Picturing Cady slick and soapy made my blood pump dangerously fast.

Her freckled skin painted with bubbles. The way my hands would slip over her under the water. Pressing her against the tile wall and taking her like she belonged to me.

My feet took two steps before I caught myself, forcing them to turn into the kitchen and prep a pot of coffee. With one hand I cracked eggs onto a hot pan, using the other to fill out the grocery list Cady kept on her fridge.

I smiled to myself then, noticing all the ways she had already surrendered. I knew the way she liked her bacon cooked and how she took her coffee. When I showed up on her porch, she let me in. The scent of her clung to my shirt from where she pressed into me as she slept.

What have you done to me, Eli Barbeaux?

Hope fluttered gently in my chest and my smile widened.

"I didn't realize you liked eggs so much." Cady surprised me as she walked into the kitchen, still toweling off her hair. Even shadowed by sleepless nights, her eyes were vibrant. Such a dark shade of blue, reminding me of the foamy waves during a winter storm.

My gaze fell to her lips, and I swallowed.

Control yourself.

Noticing where my attention wandered, she ducked her head, turning to the fridge and pulling out milk and jam. The only sounds in the kitchen were the sizzling eggs and the stretch of tension pulling tauter with every minute.

"I finished the last box last night while you were gone," Cady said, handing me a cup of coffee as I plated eggs. "At first I thought it was useless." She slid onto a bar stool propped against the countertop and picked up her fork. "But I realized I was looking way too hard."

"So, you found something?" If there wasn't anything in this paperwork, then we were at a dead end, and I could take things into my own hands.

Her eyes danced. "Addresses."

Ten minutes later I was staring at scribbled addresses on sticky notes that had long since lost their sticky. "Darlin', these could be anything."

"They could." She tapped on her phone screen. "But I googled them. These are clubs. Look." She handed me the phone. "They don't even have business pages. If I was going to meet a bunch of drug dealers and take their money, I would go to a seedy club like that."

I couldn't hold back my grin. "Would you?"

"Don't look at me like that." Cady planted hands on her hips, stubbornness steeling her features and turning her into an unstoppable force. "This is all I've got! Are you coming or not?"

I could feel myself smacking headfirst into that dead end I was hoping for, but I didn't say anything. She needed to feel like there was a solution. What harm was there in indulging her one more time?

One more time. Then I was going to figure out how to convince her to stay with me until this was over. And how to explain her presence to Saul and Isaac. And find whoever was using my cousin's calling card and put a stop to it.

Damn, even thinking about it made me tired.

"I'll be there," I told her. "But not until tonight." I glanced out over the bay, where the water shone like glass. "There's something else we need to do right now."

C ADY PROPPED HER ARM on the center console of my truck, drumming her fingers impatiently. "I still don't understand why you can't just tell me."

"I thought women liked surprises."

"I thought men were smart enough not to generalize about women." She craned her neck to look out the window as we left the main road. "Why are we on the bayou?"

"Don't panic, darlin'. I just need to stop by my place first."

She *was* panicking, at least a little, and I started to second guess myself. This needed to happen while there was still time. I had to hope she forgave me once there was no going back.

I waited until the dust settled around the truck before shoving the door open and beckoning for Cady to follow me up the porch. Nothing was disturbed when we stepped into my dark entryway but somehow, I could tell Saul had been here. I wanted to think he was here to clear the air after our last conversation but that would require my big brother to have the emotional intelligence to realize he needed to. No, he was irritated that Isaac wasn't the only one wandering off the bayou and he was either planning to confront me or snooping.

Saul could betray a lot of trust without remorse if he believed it was to look out for us. Maybe it was time Saul and I had a real heart to heart. Usually those ended as more fist-to-face, but I would chock that up to the emotional intelligence thing.

Cady wandered around the living room while I rushed to pack a cooler, flitting from the sailboat painting over the fireplace to the family portraits that dotted the bookshelf. I didn't have many pictures of my brothers and I, so the few we did take were special. Isaac always accused me of being too sentimental.

After Cady confronted me with our very first homestead photograph—the one Celine kept on her wall as a taunt, no doubt—I did some redecorating, tucking away the obviously dated images until the time was right to tell her the whole truth.

What she looked at now was modern enough, mostly pictures of Saul and me out on the boat with Isaac as the photographer. Even so, I could feel the curiosity radiating off her. If it was a general curiosity about me, I would be flattered, but her eyes narrowed in a speculative study.

Was I going to tell her before the full moon and risk it all? Suddenly, I felt like there was a vise grip over my lungs. Today might be my only chance.

"Isaac took most of those," I said across the living room, hoping to distract her from whatever line of thought she was chasing. "He went through a disposable camera phase. I have dozens of envelopes full of fish pictures in a closet somewhere."

"He's not bad. Got your good side in every picture."

I bared my teeth smugly. "All my sides are good." Her cheeks pinked and she ducked my gaze. So, she agreed.

"What's with the cooler?"

I dropped the lid on the mini cooler and hefted it off the counter. Until this morning I had no plans and so my options weren't fantastic. I was also out of ice and had to throw a bag of frozen corn in there instead. Hopefully the cool weather would keep the food from getting too warm.

"Just something I need to take care of. Trust me."

Her eyes narrowed subtly but she didn't argue. No more tension in her shoulders, no aura of wariness seeping off her.

She dipped her chin and followed me out of the house and down the little path that led to the dock.

My property backed up to the bay. Lush river soil carried through the bayou from years of flooding made a soft little beach to launch the boat from. Now that hurricane season was almost over, I'd taken to leaving my boat tied out on the dock. Made the next part of my plan easier.

Questions were about to come tumbling out of Cady's mouth, so I squelched them by asking, "You know how to drive a boat?"

She crossed her arms. "I'm downright insulted. I'll get you from here to Cadalina island with my eyes closed."

"I just need you to get her off the dock and onto the trailer. Storm is coming through tonight." Mostly true. There was a chance of rain after midnight.

Cady nodded, no more questions. She climbed gracefully onto the boat, not noticing me slip the cooler onto the stern before I started undoing the first rope.

"Go ahead and get your trailer ready. I'll need to turn it around." She called before kicking up the motor. The nose of the boat was pointed out toward the bay.

I didn't answer, instead unlacing the other rope from the cleat and pushing the boat away from the wood with my foot. Before Cady could get too far out, I jumped in next to her. She gasped, jerking to a stop too quickly and almost sending me toppling backwards into the water.

I strode over and took the wheel, nudging her out of the way. "I thought you said you knew how to drive."

"What are you doing?" Eyes rounded, her head bobbled between me and the dock that was quickly disappearing as I powered out into the bay. "Have I just been kidnapped for a second time in three weeks?" There was a surprising dose of humor in her voice, the corner of her lip curling.

"I'm not kidnapping you," I bellowed over the wind and the motor. "This is a date."

Chapter 18

Ruthless

Cady

WAVES SHIMMERED LIKE QUICKSILVER under the boat. The only wind out on the bay was the air whipping past us. Eli took us out and around the intracoastal waterway, navigating between the many tiny sand bars that surrounded Cadalina island. He was taking his time, slowing to point out the shiny white tops of cabbagehead jellyfish and the vanishing fin of a small bull shark.

I could have objected when he tricked me onto his boat but there was nothing left for me to do this morning, so what was the harm in a little detour? I wasn't going to call it a *date*. He hadn't asked me. That meant it didn't count.

But as I sat with my legs curled to my chest, watching droplets of water fly off the side of the boat and sparkle in the pure autumn sun, I couldn't hold back a small smile. There was a change in the air between Eli and me, a softening that had my walls lower than maybe they ought to be.

He could see it, too. Every time I caught his eyes, they were bright with this knowing look.

Was it so wrong to let myself develop feelings for Eli? Yes, there were some red flags, but I could sense his walls coming down too, truths I'd been waiting for coming closer to the surface.

My eyes caught sight of a blue-grey fin and I squealed, pointing, and jabbering some excited nonsense that Eli managed to interpret as, "Stop the boat!"

Another fin popped up in the water right beside it, then both dolphins surfaced with a whooshing spray. I'd seen dolphins all my life and the awe of such graceful, intelligent creatures never wore off. In a month or two the bay would be crowded with them, dozens and dozens of dolphins coming to warmer waters to birth their calves.

These two were curious, circling the boat and curving out of the water. Their skin shimmered in the early afternoon sun. I leaned over the boat, waggling my fingers with a splash. I knew they weren't dogs that were going to come up to be pet but a girl could dream.

"Eli," I whisper shouted. "Come see!"

He had one hand casually draped across the wheel, relaxed smile crinkling his eyes in that way I was coming to like so much, but he shook his head. "Don't think that's such a good idea."

"The boat isn't going to drive itself away and crash into a sandbar. Get over here!"

His crinkly smile faltered. He shoved his hands in the pockets of his jeans and eased a little closer to me, leaning far over to glance down. The dolphins were right up against the boat now, their little round snouts peeking from the water just two feet from my hand.

"Are you sacred of dolphins or something?" I teased, grabbing his forearm, and hauling him toward me.

He dropped onto the bench seat next to me, spine stiff and straight. "Animals and I—we don't really get along."

"What are you—" I yanked my hand from the water and jumped back as a spray of terrified chittering noises erupted from beside me. Those two fins that had been playfully circling moments ago were quavering as they sunk below the surface, leaving triangular ripples behind them.

I stared after them with a palm pressed to my chest, heart thundering with momentary adrenaline. Eli was watching me with a guarded expression, guilt making his mouth droop.

"That was...strange." At this point I shouldn't be surprised. Everything was strange when Eli was around.

"Animals don't like me," he repeated, returning to his spot behind the wheel and starting the motor back up. Then he changed the subject, pointing the boat toward Cadalina island. "Let's go walk the airstrip."

"Sure, I haven't done that in ages."

Cadalina island was the largest of several small islands that enclosed Cadalina bay. At its widest it was three miles across, but it narrowed from one end to the other. That long, narrow stretch was what drew the U.S. Air Force here in the late seventies, utilizing it to train pilots. Before that it was a homestead. Word was the government drove the family off the land without compensation. Locals were still bitter about it.

Eventually the winds of time shaped and changed the island and the Air Force abandoned their airstrip. There was a lighthouse on the far side of the island too, somehow still standing after decades of hurricanes and tropical storms, but it had long since been out of use and closed to visitors.

Personally, I loved Cadalina for the beach. On the bay side of the island there was a swampy, grassy shore and shallow alcoves perfect for lounging during hot summer days. On the other side, where the crashing waters of the Gulf Coast battered the island, there was fluffy, white sand. If the winds had been particularly strong the sand would be piled in high dunes. Though they were often home to rattlesnakes and ornery crabs, I still spent hours rolling down those dunes with my friends when I was a girl.

During this time of year, at the tail end of hurricane season when those frigid last breaths of nor'easters were blowing in, the beach was full of treasure. Papa and I would spend hours combing the shore, finding everything from old TVs to whole coconuts. Hurricanes carried all kinds of stuff across the Gulf.

I hadn't pictured Eli as someone that would enjoy the island. There was so much open sky. For some reason I imagined that bothered him, the openness of the ocean compared to the quiet shelter of the thick bayou canopy. Yet here he was, out on the bay with the unfiltered sun washing over him, and he was smiling.

Smiling at *me*.

For the rest of the trip, I kept my focus ahead, watching the island zip toward us through the water. When Eli angled the boat against the shore, I kicked off my sandals and hopped out barefoot, taking hold of a rope with a small steel anchor on the end. It was tied to the bow of the boat, and I used it to guide the boat further up onto the beach. At the same time Eli punched the motor just enough to push us partway onto the sand. When he was satisfied it wouldn't float out with the tide, he shut everything off and joined me on the shore, that small red cooler tucked under his arm.

We only walked ten or so feet before Eli plunked down in the sand. Far off to the left I could see the airstrip, the cracked concrete and overgrown grass making it desolate as ever.

"You want a beer?" He lifted a plastic bag of frozen corn out of the cooler and rifled around the contents underneath.

"Is that lunch?" I lowered myself beside him, wiggling my toes into the warm earth.

Eli feigned offense. "You think I'm going to feed you freezer food on a date?" He cracked the lid off a glass bottle and handed it to me. "Lunch is hot dogs."

I laughed at the package of uncooked dogs in his hand. "You are—you're so different from anyone I've ever met."

"You like it that way."

I nodded. It was all I could manage, not sure where the conversation would go if I admitted it out loud.

He was about to open a second beer when I held out the one in my hand. "You can have mine. I don't really drink."

Eli accepted the beer back, taking a drink and chuckling when he asked, "Is that why you pretended to drink the last one I gave you?"

"Awkward, right?" I nibbled at my lip. Then before I could overthink, I blurted, "My mom was an addict. Or maybe I should say is, but I don't know if you can live through 27 years of heroin abuse, and I haven't heard from her since I was knee-high."

"That's why you lived with your grandparents."

"She dropped me on their doorstep before I was old enough to speak a full sentence and never looked back." I lifted a handful of sand, watching the grains slip between my fingers and form a hill beneath. "I drank a few times when I was a teenager. Got plastered with my friends on stolen gin and thoroughly regretted it. Went to a party with some older boys and had a beer. Ricky Holt had like ten and he tried to force me into the backseat of his truck."

"Ricky Holt," Eli repeated coolly. Like he was remembering it for later use.

"I realized how easy it was to get out of control. To let the alcohol numb me. So, I don't drink anymore. Not worth the risk."

"You're a smart woman, Cady. Not a lot of people see the world like you." He shifted closer. "Tell me more."

"More?"

"About you."

"What do you want to know?"

"Why poetry?" He went back to the cooler and pulled out a can of root beer, handing it to me with a wink.

I knew why I wrote poetry, why it was so vital to my existence, but I hadn't talked about it in years. Hadn't shared my work with anyone since the scholarship application when I was eighteen. It didn't seem right to even call myself a poet when I just had a collection of scribbled poems in old journals.

Then I remembered the most recent addition to my journal and the color drained from my face. "Wait, how did you know I wrote poetry?"

"Saw your book."

I gaped at him, too horrified to look away. "Did you read it?" I wasn't sure if I meant the entire book or the page about him. Either way it was personal, almost more of a diary than a portfolio.

For once he looked remorseful for his absolute lack of boundaries. "Only a few pages." That sheepish expression morphed into something warmer. "You have a way with words."

"It's just how I see things." I couldn't decide if I was mad at him or proud that he liked what he saw. There no was use hiding anything from him. "I look at stuff and I just...I have to get the words out." Embarrassment flushed up my neck. "I don't sound very poetic at all, do I?"

"You don't have to." He shrugged, tearing open the package of hotdogs and handing me one.

I wrinkled my nose as I accepted it and took a bite. "Weirdest first date ever."

"This isn't the first. Fifth, at least."

"You're seriously going to count the day we found a corpse as a date?"

"I got halfway to first base on that date."

I laughed again, almost tumbling back into the sand. It was so *wrong* and yet, Eli made it feel right. He was twisted and dark, but in this carefree way that made my heart lighter.

I finished my hotdog, staring out over the bay. High tide was coming, and that typical autumn wind was beginning to pick back up, sending shuddering ripples toward the shore. Eli swigged his beer, biting into an apple. Apples and hotdogs. It was all he brought on this hilariously impromptu picnic. I would never pin him down. He was too enigmatic.

"Eli," I swirled my finger over the top of my root beer can. "I need to ask you something."

"Anything." But there were still some truths he wouldn't give me.

"You—" I choked on the words. "You saved my life. You're here, doing all this," I waved a hand in front of him like that could do justice to all that he'd done for me in the past few weeks. "What's in it for you, really?"

His answer was immediate. "This."

I swallowed nervously. "Cold hotdogs and warm beer?"

"*With you*, Cady."

I forced myself to look at him. He leaned back on his elbows, thick arms flexing with the weight of his body. A few wispy clouds had rolled in, their shade making it almost cool enough to shiver, but he looked comfortable in a pair of well-loved jeans and a T-shirt.

The shirt was white, highlighting his perfectly tanned skin. The front of his dark hair was tied back in a loose knot, the back blowing freely over his neck. I liked when he wore his hair like that, even though it revealed the full force of his face.

Defined jaw, angular cheek bones—not sharp, just enough to give him a hard edge. Those edges were softened by his unusually colored eyes. Warm honey, oozing sweetness and mirth.

They weren't so mirthful now. He was staring me down with all that Barbeaux intensity and I started to shake. He wasn't letting me hide this time, allowing a swift and merciful change of subject. I was pinned in place, swallowed up by the unchecked emotion in his expression.

This wasn't a man trying to scratch an itch and be on his way. There was too much depth, too many things he didn't have to put words to for me to feel them.

I'd never had real feelings for someone before. Never nurtured infatuation beyond that fuzzy butterfly stage. It was pointless. Everyone left or moved on. Seemed so cynical when I thought it now, but it was true. Or it had been.

Eli though? He was as deeply rooted as the oldest trees on that bayou.

He wasn't going anywhere. Not if I wasn't.

I don't know how I gleaned all of that from one look. Maybe it wasn't just the look but his actions too. Over the past three weeks he was the only solid ground I had to stand on and he seemed glad just to hold me steady.

"What if... " My throat bobbed. "What if I don't know how to be *this*?"

He stretched out onto his back, one hand tucked behind his head, the other inches from me. "S'ok, darlin'. I can wait."

Slowly, I unfolded myself, reclining beside him. Our knuckles brushed, my fingers caressing the backs of his. I slid them between his, our fingertips touching as our hands entwined. Eli didn't say anything about the contact, didn't try to direct the intimacy in one direction or another. This was what I could give, and he accepted it with that easy confidence.

He had all the reason in the world to be confident, knowing I was already ensnared. That I was captivated with his otherness, and I had already surrendered to my burgeoning feelings, even if I hadn't acted on them yet.

"That one looks like a canoe." I pointed to a thin, milky cloud as it passed over the sun.

"Log."

"Fish." I pointed to another.

"Leaf." He argued.

"Mushroom."

"Dick."

I sat up, scandalized hand pressed to my chest. "Unbelievable."

His chuckle was deep, the most melodious sound.

I loosed my fingers from his, standing to stretch. Time was moving strangely today, seeming to slip by and trickle unhurriedly all at once. It was past lunchtime, long past noon, and sooner rather than later we would need to go back, if only to get a break from the sun. My skin was turning that pink color, a warning that I was on the cusp of a burn.

Not yet. Just a little longer pretending like there wasn't a shit show waiting for us back home.

"When I was a girl, my Papa would drop my friends and I on this side of the island and challenge us to race to the other side. We couldn't take the trail, had to run up and over the dunes."

Eli stood too, lips spreading languidly. Somehow his eyes seemed brighter, grin more wolfish than playful. "And you won every time."

"How did you know?"

"You're ruthless. You pretend you're not, but I see it."

Like attracts like.

"I haven't felt particularly ruthless lately." Sadness pooled in my legs as I realized what was truly stolen from me. Not just my sense of safety but my boldness. Eli was right. Before, I was so sure of myself. Of my choice to stay through my grandmother's illness, of the life I had in front of me. It wasn't wildly adventurous or audacious, but it was mine and I stood proudly in it.

Now I second-guessed everything. The last person I had left that I could truly count on, trust wholeheartedly, was gone. When death snarled in her face she crumbled. How could I trust her to be strong after that? How could I trust her perception of the world when it was built on this lie? A false belief that she was unbending. What happened on the bayou bared me to myself for the first time and I saw how weak I was under all that ego.

That was why I was so hesitant to let Eli pursue me. I didn't want to rely on him. People weren't reliable and I was the ultimate proof of that now. A reflection of the woman I never wanted to become.

"Stop it." Eli was suddenly nose to nose with me, his voice harsh.

"Stop what?"

"Giving in." He took my chin between finger and thumb, lifting it high. "We all have fear. Every single person on this earth has something that makes them weak."

"You're not afraid of anything."

"Darlin', there are things that terrify me like you wouldn't believe." I licked my lips, waiting for him to continue. "And I have weaknesses that would bring me to my knees." The pad of his finger traced my cheekbone. "But you can't give in. You lost one round in a fight. Doesn't mean it's over. Doesn't mean you're done."

Blood rushed to my cheeks, following the trail of his finger. I didn't know what to say and he didn't really give me a chance to respond. The color of his eyes intensified, the grin on his face spreading wider until he almost felt like someone else. No, someone *more*.

The same, but different.

Eli, but not.

The one guttural word he said next shot adrenaline into my thighs and had me whirling like the devil himself was on my heel. "Run."

Sand slid under my bare feet, sucking down my momentum. The first glance I risked over my shoulder was a mistake. Eli stood there on the beach, just stood, and followed my journey across the dunes with hungry excitement. Energy pulsed from him, some primal power that whispered along my spine, filling my senses with urgency until my mind repeated nothing but that one word.

Run.

Run. Run. Run.

I didn't see when he moved, couldn't hear his silent feet as they left the shore, but I knew he was coming. I could feel him as if he was a raging storm right overhead, seconds from raining down on me.

And even though a tiny lick of fear burned in my chest, I wanted to feel the full potency of him crashing into me.

I was halfway up a large dune, the loud rush of the tide just on the other side. Wind roared in my ears, fighting against me, and slowing my pace. I pushed back, gritting my teeth and urging my legs on and on. Powered through the burn. Climbed. Feet kicking almost vertically.

I reached the top and twisted to look behind me. Eli was right there, diving for me. His arms were a cage around me as we rolled down the other side of the dune, sand spraying the air around us. I closed my eyes with a squeal, squeezing Eli for dear life. His back hit the beach first and he grunted when I smashed into him.

I was on top of him, my legs straddling his hips, forearms propped on his ribs. A breathless chuckle bounced me, and I couldn't help but join with my own laughter. Then the expression on his face darkened, gaze flicking to my lips only a breath from his.

I was going to kiss him. How could I resist when he was staring at me like I hung the moon—no, like I *was* the moon. I was the moon, and he was the tide. We'd been doing this dance for days and days, rising and swelling around each other. Gravitating endlessly toward one another.

I lowered my head only to find myself flying away from Eli, crashing into the sand with a gasp. Seconds later I heard the snap of canine teeth and the rising pitch of two dogs, barking viciously. Eli was in a crouched position, swatting at the two animals as they tried to attack us.

They were Labradors, usually so docile and dopey, but these two dogs, sleek black and crusted with salt water, were going in for the kill. I'd never seen anything like it. The noises they made weren't warning barks, they were panicked and savage.

"I'm so sorry, they've never—" their owner ran up, an older man in a teal windbreaker and a baseball cap. Just as he stooped to yank one of the dogs by the collar it turned tail, yelping loudly. The other followed, diving into the surf and swimming out into the water. "What the hell? Banjo! Maya!"

My eyes followed the stranger rushing into the waves after his dogs, but my focus was on the man in front of me. I had a hand on his back, and I felt more than heard the distinctly animal noise that came from him. A soundless vibration that made the earth quake beneath us. His muscles swelled and bunched under his damp shirt, like they were doubling in size.

What are you? The question echoed in my head over and over again. It was absolute madness to even consider but I could see two black dots on the horizon, dogs so frightened they would risk drowning rather than face Eli.

I thought about the dolphins zipping away from the boat when Eli approached.

What are you?

He was watching me warily, waiting for me to pose the question out loud. When I didn't, he laced his fingers with mine, drawing me up close to his side and murmuring, "Think that's enough fun for one day."

We drove back to shore in tense silence, all the closeness we built in the last hours evaporating in the late afternoon sun. Soon enough the bayou came into view, and we were planting feet back on land.

But even as my toes hit the shore, I still felt like I was floating out to sea.

What are you?

Chapter 19

Vengeance Becomes Her

Cady

M Y CHEEKS FLUSHED AS red as the neon lights outside the windowless building in front of us. We drove forty-five minutes out of Port O'Henry to a club across from an adult video store and a truck stop. A van with the word "churro" spray painted on the side was parked on the street in front of Eli's truck but by the look of the people inside, they weren't selling dessert.

Eli dropped me back at my house earlier this afternoon. He didn't kiss me at the door or ask for a second date. Which was good because the moment I got home I remembered the stakes. I couldn't afford to get distracted yet.

Sure, great excuse, Cady.

The reality was that I wasn't just falling for him, I was tumbling head over heels faster than I could handle. To say I didn't trust Eli would be a lie. Yet, there was this wall between us, this barrier of secrets I could feel myself bumping into every time I inched closer.

Honesty was a dealbreaker for me. He'd been clear since the beginning that there were things he wouldn't tell me, and that wasn't going to work. My heart had no room for betrayal and even a lie by omission was a lie.

So, here we were. Teetering on the edge of this *something* between us, drowning in sexual tension, and also standing in front of a strip club.

"Um, darlin'," Eli cleared his throat, trying not to laugh. "You sure this is the right place?"

"Yes," I choked, curling my fingers around my stack of post-it notes I found in Barlow's stuff.

This was the clue that made the most sense to pursue. If Barlow was involved in the increasing drug market in Port O'Henry then he wouldn't want to be obvious about it. A bunch of addresses that pointed to the outskirts of Port Tortuga, where most respectable people would avoid, seemed promising. I'd been picturing dive bars like the one by the motel in Port O'Henry. Dark and dusty places with shadowy alcoves for nefarious men to hide.

This place probably had shadowy alcoves. All kinds of alcoves.

The smile in Eli's voice made my face even hotter. "You still want to go in?"

"I have to. Maybe someone in there knows something." But my confidence sounded fake, even to me.

Still, I slid out of the truck and crossed the street, walking up to the door and nervously eyeing the giant man standing out front. The doorman's gaze jumped from me to Eli, and he scowled. Whatever he saw on Eli's face made his brow fall even deeper over his beady eyes.

Eli handed him a crisp fifty dollars and he muttered something about keeping our hands off before waving us in. I didn't know you had to pay to get into a strip club and now I wasn't sure if I wanted to know why Eli did.

I was not prepared for what was on the other side of the door. Almost-naked women were everywhere, their exposed breasts bouncing about as they carried trays of drinks and gyrated across the laps of mesmerized men. Several patrons seated at a bar in the back of the room studied me curiously as I stood there in a state of mortification and uncertainty.

"This was a bad idea." I said it to myself because there was no way Eli heard me over the music.

It was a vibrating pulse more than a sound, rattling my bones as I made my way to the bar. Two steps in Eli wrapped my fingers in his, tugging me back until I was beside him. It was a relief when he led the way, making room for me to approach the bar and draw the bartender's attention.

"Excuse me!" I must've said it four or five times before a buxom blonde in a bikini approached me with an amused smile.

"This your first time, sweetheart?" She dropped the heavy weight of her breasts onto the bar as she leaned toward us. "Diamond loves couples, if you're looking for a private show." She pointed with her angular chin to a dancer swinging around a pole in the corner.

"Yes—I mean no." I tapped my hands awkwardly, uncomfortably aware of Eli behind me. Wondering where his gaze was and wishing I hadn't asked him to come. "I'm wondering if you've seen someone here."

The blonde shuttered her expression. "We take our customers' privacy very seriously."

"It's my boss. He died recently and—"

"I don't care if it's your mama, doll. Our clients like to be left alone."

Two hours later I chucked my wadded-up pile of notes on the dash and moaned, "*Three* strip clubs? I worked for that man for almost two years, and I feel like I didn't know him at all."

"It's a good place to go if you're trying to stay under the radar," Eli suggested. "They've got plenty of folks coming and going that don't want people to know what they're up to."

He had one hand on the steering wheel, the other resting on the center console between us. It should have been the picture of relaxation, but we'd just walked out of our third strip club, and it was clear he was growing impatient.

"Eli, I'm sorry. We can go home. I've wasted half your night."

A hint of that charming smile danced across his lips. "Darlin', you can have my whole night."

He went quiet again, hand flexing over the steering wheel. I stared at the last address on my list, considering throwing in the towel and wondering how much a ticket to Seattle cost.

"You haven't been outside of Port O'Henry much, have you?"

"Why?"

"You got the street smarts of a lost kitten."

"I think I should be offended." I pulled my legs up into the seat and snaked my arms across them.

"We drove through the worst parts of Tortuga, walking past junkies and thieves and you haven't even looked over your shoulder." More hand flexing. "Don't know if I can go into another place like that with you."

"Well, I'm not going to wait in the car."

"That's not what I'm saying." Eli ground his teeth. Under his breath he said, "I don't like the looks you're getting in there. You're giving people the wrong impression."

For a second I didn't understand, glaring down at my jeans and fuzzy pink sweater. It was low cut, I supposed, and tight enough to show off my figure. After seeing the women in those clubs—more than I ever wanted to see—I was pretty sure my non-existent hips and B-cups were nothing special to look at. But it wasn't the clothes, it was the implication of my presence in a strip club.

The defeat that had been rooting in my chest bloomed. "I don't know what else to do, Eli."

He stared at the road. "There are options."

"Let's go home. I'm sure you could use some sleep after last night."

"Nope. We'll see this through." The engine roared to life, and he shifted the truck into drive. "But if it's another strip club, we're finding a twenty-four-hour place and grabbing burgers instead."

I punched the last address into my GPS app, and we drove west through Port Tortuga. Soon strip malls gave way to trucks

stops and restaurants that looked like even the health department wouldn't step foot inside. It was only when Eli turned
into a desolate concrete lot that I spotted the bar tucked
behind a boarded-up warehouse.

Music pounded from the bar as patrons spilled through
the doorway, shouting, and drinking, and revving motorcycle
engines. The name "*Wolfy's*" was illuminated in red over the
door.

This was much more aligned with my expectations. I was
almost excited.

"It's not a strip club." I turned to him with a pleased smile
only for it to slip.

Eli could have been carved from stone. Eyes hard, jaw rigid,
entire body stiffened in protest. He didn't have to say a single
word for me to know what was going through his head.

"I know you're more of a fresh air kind of guy. You can wait
in the truck."

"Like hell am I going to let you walk in there." Not let me
walk in there *alone*. Just let me at all.

I mirrored his stony posture. "I'm sorry, 'let me' go in there?
I don't need your permission."

Eli twisted the key and started the truck back up. I unbuck-
led my seatbelt. He punched the locks on the door. I tugged
the handle on the passenger side uselessly. Damn child locks.

"Elijah Barbeaux let me out of your truck right the hell
now!"

"You have no idea what you're getting yourself into. I hu-
mored you with those clubs, but this is too much."

"Unless you're planning to kidnap me back to my house, I'm
going in there. I have my gun," I hefted my purse onto my lap
to demonstrate. "I want to ask the bartenders if they recognize
Dustin or his daddy. That's all."

"And what if they do? I'm not understanding where this
leads."

"Then I find out who Barlow was meeting with here and confront them."

Eli laughed, dry and humorless. "You are the most ridiculous, stubborn lunatic I have ever met."

"You like it that way." I stole his words from earlier.

He rubbed his mouth, trying to hide a hint of a smile. "Damn woman is half as big as a minute, dressed like a Disney princess, over here trying to confront drug lords." Even as he grumbled, he was adjusting the gun he kept concealed along his lower back and shutting the truck off. "You're going to do this without me if I refuse, aren't you?"

"Yes."

Eli made a great point. There was no real plan after I figured out who wanted this money bad enough to drop bodies. Maybe I would kill them before they could kill me. This new, reckless version of me didn't need a plan. I needed vengeance, or something equally badass and furious.

"Let me take you home. I'll come back tomorrow and see what I can find."

"Nope."

He pinched the bridge of his nose with a sigh. "You don't talk to the patrons, don't lose sight of me, and don't pull your gun unless you're looking death in the face."

I rolled my eyes. "Yes, sir."

"It's not a game, Cady."

"I'm not playing. They tried to *kill* me."

I was about to shove the door open when Eli gripped my forearm. "We go in there and ask your questions, then that's it. This is over."

"What do you mean?"

"No more playing detective. No more burned houses and dead bodies. You get what answers you can tonight and then you let me handle it."

"You know I can't agree to that, Eli."

"You will," he muttered darkly, stepping out of the truck, and coming to open my door for me.

Agitation coiled around Eli as he pressed a hand to the small of my back and propelled me to the open door. Dozens of motorcycles were parked out front, some of them occupied by grisly looking men wearing black leather and puffing on cigarettes. I gave them peripheral glances as we passed, trying not to let their attention activate my nerves.

Eli paid them no mind. Despite the tension I could feel strumming through his fingertips as they pressed into me, he carried himself with that casual confidence, swaggering like he owned the whole damn world. We walked by scantily clad women, big biker dudes, and people that looked like they knifed old ladies for fun. There wasn't so much as a tick in his jaw.

The message was clear. He wasn't intimidated by any of them.

Outside the October air was damp and cool. Inside the dampness swallowed up the body heat until there was a visible cloud of booze-y sweat. Smoke mingled with the moisture, making the entire room hazy. Music filled every corner and it combined with the din of drinking and laughing. Despite that, half the room seemed to glance up from where they sat or stood.

I was suddenly uncomfortably aware of my clean pink sweater and the matching scrunch holding my hair in a neat ponytail. The only reason I kept walking toward the crowded bar was the heavy presence behind me, Eli serving as a shield against anyone that dared approach me. It made me feel more confident than I should be.

It took two full minutes to grab the bartender's attention. He didn't look pleased to see me.

"I need to know if these men have been in here recently." I presented a picture of Barlow and his son to the bartender. Barlow was standing on his boat, holding a red snapper on a line with Dustin at his side. The image was borrowed from the newspaper website and printed on regular paper with Nana's old printer. It was the best I could do.

"Not my job to keep track of every gringo that wants a walk on the wild side." Even as he said it, the man glanced over his shoulder to where a wall sectioned off pool tables and booths.

He recognized Barlow. There was nothing subtle about the nervous tic of his eyes. I pieced together the first lie that came to mind. "That's my father. He's got a bit of a drinking problem and we haven't seen him in days. Some friends said we might find him here."

The bartender crossed his arms dismissively. "We don't see guys like that around here." Then he left to help another patron.

Eli shrugged his shoulders, as if to say, "That's the end of it." But he knew as well as I did that the bartender was lying.

"Dance with me." I took him by the hand, not giving him a chance to refuse.

He followed stiffly to the dance floor, his stunned awkwardness almost comical. There were a million sets of beady eyes on us, oversized rats wondering if we were food. I didn't care. I didn't give a shit what they thought about the sweater that I purposely matched with my favorite lip gloss or if they saw me as an easy target.

I was angry. That anger liberated me, crawled up from the place where my heart had been sitting like a stone in my stomach for weeks and whispered to me that I was invincible.

Eli's hands rested possessively on my hips, and I believed it. I had all the brutal mystery of a Barbeaux wrapped around me. Nothing could touch me so long as Eli was mine.

Arrogant confidence emboldened me, and I shimmied by hips in a tight circle, grinding into Eli and laughing when he stood statue still behind me. "Do you know how to dance to this kind of music?"

He was taken aback. "Do you?"

"I used to be fun, y'know." I turned in his arms, taking his hands and returning them to their place on my hips. "Before my Nana got sick. And all this mess."

Eli made a surprised noise when I circled my hips again, pressed tightly against him and letting him feel *everything*. I grinned at the lust and conflict in those spectacular eyes, urging him to move with me. It took two songs but eventually he loosened up, gripping my waist as we followed the booming beat.

For a moment I forgot our audience. The bar melted away and I was lost in the music, addicted to the way Eli's fingertips dug into me. His chest was hard at my back as I whirled, and I could think of a dozen other ways I wanted to feel him.

There was something alive between us. Not just the tense energy in the air or the mutual attraction we shared. This was deeper, a yearning ache I felt every time Eli smiled at me as if he knew a secret that he wanted to share with me.

Even here, amid complete chaos, on terrain I had never tread, it was so easy to lose myself in him. Too easy.

Then I remembered why were here and my focus zipped to the bartender just in time to see him slip out from behind the bar, scurrying to a booth in the far corner and whispering to a man veiled by a shroud of smoke. I couldn't see much, only the way he spread himself confidently across the booth cushions. His posture and the dark aura around him oozed drug lord vibes.

Suddenly all the embarrassment from tonight seemed worth it.

The man nodded impatiently at the bartender, shooing him off with a wave. He was staring right at us.

And he was smiling.

I dropped out of Eli's hold mid dance and made a beeline for that corner booth, only to be twirled hastily back onto the dance floor. Eli wrapped me in his embrace, swaying as if we were at a high school dance and not the grungiest bar in East Texas.

His mouth dipped to my ear in a sensual caress of a whisper, and I struggled to hold back a moan. "Slow down, darlin'."

I exhaled through pinched lips, trying to calm my heart. Was it going mad because of his closeness or our closeness to a real answer?

"Do you think he knows Barlow?"

Eli watched the man in his peripherals as he stroked the side of my face. "Hard to say."

"Bullshit, Eli." My nerves were alight, burning from the way Eli's lips hovered above mine and from the unbearable need to storm my way through the crowd and confront the asshole in the booth.

"We're outsiders here and it's obvious." He gave my sweater a pointed look. "We need to be strategic about this."

"I don't want to be strategic." It came out whinier than I wanted, and I reeled it in. If I was going to use Eli like a shield, then I owed him the respect of considering his plan before I completely ignored it. "But tell me what you want to do."

The copper embers in his eyes blazed and it was only then that I realized that strange, sharp appearance was overtaking his face, making him look like he was on the cusp of becoming unhinged. There was a wild, vicious quality to his smile, a predatory tilt to his gaze. Last night I hadn't understood it and it scared me. Now it sent jagged thrill straight between my legs.

This wasn't the mild, gentle Eli that sprawled on the beach with me this afternoon. This was the Eli that killed two men. The Eli that stood dripping with blood, headlights bleaching his warm complexion and making him into a haunting vision of death.

I should have been horrified.

I should have taken him by the hand and made him leave before we triggered a dangerous chain of events that might cost me my life.

But I didn't because I liked *this* Eli. I wanted him, bloodshed and all, and it didn't scare me anymore.

Chapter 20

Hook, Line, and Sinker

Eli

THINGS WERE SPIRALING OUT of control far faster than I could fix them. The music was too loud, the cloying scent of sweat and booze too strong. Every instinct in my body was going haywire, the beast on high alert as threat after threat was detected. And Cady was in the middle of it, drawing far too attention much to herself.

She wasn't supposed to be here. This was meant to be my task. Over and over, I tried to divert her, to take this from her and *finish it.*

But there was no stopping this woman as she barreled forward on a suicide mission and all I could do was try to protect her. Right now, I wasn't sure I would be enough.

I scented the first werewolf as we stepped through the door. His was faint, mingling with the night air and telling me that he was outside. That should have been enough to turn tail and form a new plan. A Barbeaux didn't turn tail though, and these mutts needed to know it.

I was also walking the line with Cady, caught between my urgent need to keep her safe and knowing that if I over-stepped, it might end us before we ever really started. She couldn't be controlled, and right now she was all burning fury.

Over the stink of tobacco and sweat was another scent. Two. There were at least two of my kind here and I didn't doubt that they were aware of me. Maybe even expecting me. Someone had been watching us since we visited the Cray homestead. Earlier than that, if my suspicions were correct, and they knew that Cady and I were on their trail.

A carefully laid trail with too many breadcrumbs to be a coincidence.

To Cady it appeared a trampled mess, nothing that pointed in any obvious direction. It was some twisted fate that she found those scraps of paper that led us here. Otherwise, she was running in circles with no real results. My job was to keep it that way. To give her just enough closure to walk away and let me do the rest.

A shitty plan with shitty results because here we were, in the territory of unidentified werewolves that were establishing a pack right under Saul's nose. Days from the full moon, when all that violence and lust was rising to a peak.

This was a trap and I walked Cady right into it. No doubt they knew she was still alive and by now, they probably knew why. If I had only kept my distance—found these fuckers first before she ever got wind of them—she might be safe right now. This could be over.

There was no going back. It was time to be my true self and show this pack just who they were encroaching on. There wasn't a mutt in the world that didn't know who the Barbeaux family was. They were born from us, their diluted blood sourced from the very first of our kind.

We were still across the bar from my target, angled so my back wasn't quite to him. I could feel those steely wolf eyes burning into me, feel that feral thrill at the prospect of a fight. It wouldn't be a fair fight—mutts were weaker than the original blood—but where there were two, there could be more.

It wasn't concern over my ability to take on a pack that iced my veins. Cady wouldn't stand a chance against them if they got me distracted with a brawl and separated us.

So, I changed tactics. Cady was perched on her tip toes, arms around my neck in a moment of feigned intimacy, waiting for me to tell her my plan. Time to show her.

I leaned down, nuzzling into her neck, and nipped up to the lobe of her ear. She made a startled noise at my sudden affection, lips parting. Her gaze had been locked on the shadowed booth where our friend was watching us but now, she was staring up at me, pupils wide, expression questioning.

I dipped my head and kissed the question from her lips. She was luscious, sugary bliss, and she enflamed my senses. My instincts were on fire, reaching out with that invisible web of awareness to ensure we weren't ambushed. The contrast was maddening, drowning in the heady sweetness of our sealed lips and also frantically aware that we were in immediate danger. This wasn't what I envisioned when I planned to kiss her for the first time.

I wasn't behind the steering wheel though, not really. This was all beast, staking a very obvious claim for any other monster here to witness. Making it clear that messing with Cady was messing with me.

The werewolf equivalent of writing, "Property of Eli Barbeaux" across her forehead.

Cady panted when I broke away to kiss every inch of her throat. There was a sliver of confusion, dwarfed by the potent desire pulsing between us. She couldn't feel the bond. It was born of magic, and she had none. Not until I gave it to her. And yet, I almost believed she felt the magnetism of it, my insatiable need to touch her, because she had completely lost focus of her quarry.

Or so I thought until Cady was rocketing out of my arms and marching right up to the man lounging casually in the red leather booth at the back of the bar.

Except he wasn't a man at all.

Cady was walking fast, that stubborn chin held high. Her lips were as pink as her cheeks, eyes sedated from our kiss, and I hated that anyone but me got to see her like that. I hated it more that she escaped before I had my fill.

She was so out of place in this cesspool, pink sweater hugging her petite curves. I caught her in three long strides, wrapping my arm around her waist and stilling her. My palm splayed over her stomach in a completely possessive move, my gaze clashing with a pair of yellow-brown eyes.

White teeth gleamed from the shadowed corner booth and the other wolf leaned forward with a deceivingly friendly gesture.

"What are you doing?" Cady hissed, moving feverishly.

I dropped my hand to the back of her neck. Werewolves were all about posture. Couldn't explain that to her here.

We passed two more booths and a pool table with six tattooed men leaned up against it. They were watching our approach rather than playing and I noted each of their weaknesses in case they were a threat. They wouldn't know who or what they were working for any more than they would know what I was.

Death. That's what I would be if they didn't keep their distance.

"What a lovely surprise." The other wolf clasped his hands together as Cady sidled up to the glossy tabletop that had long since lost its sheen. "A Barbeaux graces us with his presence." That Cheshire grin went even wider. "And the bookkeeper. Weren't you supposed to be dead?"

I vaulted forward, letting the beast shine in my eyes. "Someone died on that bayou."

"Do you two know each other?" Cady stepped in front of me, glaring at both of us like enemies.

"We've never formally met. I'm Louis." His dark irises had a preternatural glint to them that he wasn't bothering to hide. Reckless asshole. His beast was goading mine. A deadly game, except he knew how careful my brothers and I played it. I wouldn't expose myself in a crowded bar unless he forced my hand.

And here I was, delivering exactly the leverage he needed for that. Goddamn.

"But you know who he is?" She pointed at me.

"I guessed. The family resemblance is uncanny." He turned his teeth on Cady, voice a purr as he asked, "You have no idea what you've walked into, do you, sweetheart?"

The tension from the night finally snapped, spilling out into the room. I pounded a fist on the table and let out an unrestrained growl, pleased when I saw apprehension flicker across the lesser wolf's face. "She has questions for you. You're going to answer them."

"Am I?"

"You are." Cady's smile was all southern charm and sweetness. Made me want to eat her.

"Ooh, good cop, bad cop. I like it." Louis echoed Cady's question. "Do you two know each other?"

"We do," her smiled persisted. "He's the one that killed the guys you sent to kidnap me." It was a bold statement, made with pride. Damn if that wasn't the most twisted, romantic thing I'd ever heard.

Once or twice, I questioned why I was bonded to Cady of all people and now I had my answer. This woman was insane in the very best way, and it made her perfect for me. So unbelievably perfect.

"Kidnap you? I would *never*." Louis gasped mockingly. "Why don't you ask Mister Barbeaux? He knows." The taunt worked. Cady looked askance at me, her composure cracking. Worse, I didn't school my face in time to hide the truth.

I did know—kind of. My original suspicion was Jacques. When Saul admitted Jacques wasn't coming back, I knew it had to be another of our kind. Now here he was, eyes wild with thrill as he watched his dart hit the mark.

"What does he mean, Eli?"

"Yeah, *Eli*, what do you have to say for yourself?" Louis prodded.

"Listen Louis," I bared my teeth, letting him see just how close I was to losing my humanity. The beast had no reservations about removing this wolf's head from his body and laying it at Cady's feet. She might find it romantic after all. "That money you're after? You're not getting it. As for whatever game you're playing in *my* town, on *my* bayou, with *my* girl, it's over. I don't know what you think you know about Barbeauxs, but we do not tolerate competition."

"I know a good deal about Barbeauxs, actually."

"Then you know the smart thing to do is get gone." The beast was eager to kill this intruder and his whole pack just for trespassing, but I wasn't keen to break the vow I made to my brothers and go into a mindless rage. Saul wouldn't want me to do anything without his approval.

"Be reasonable. There's enough space for all of us. Didn't your mama teach you to share?" The lecherous grin he turned on Cady was another goad and now I was half an inch away from a mistake I couldn't come back from.

We needed to leave. *Immediately*.

Louis stood, pressing his fingertips into the table. "We're having a big get together in a few days. Bunch'a guys howling at the moon. You should join us. Your girl too. Everyone would get a real kick out of her."

"I gave you a warning. You won't get a second one." I took Cady by the arm, twisting at an awkward angle so I wasn't giving my back to that prick as we made an abrupt exit.

We were almost out of earshot when he shouted, "Oh, Elijah! Your cousin sends his regards."

I froze. I froze until I realized I was squeezing Cady's forearm and she was trying to break my hold, her anger and panic making her frantic.

"I wasn't finished! Eli?" She shrieked over the noise. "Listen to me!"

I shoved through bodies until I created a path to the door. All the while I glanced over my shoulder, checking every direction for that other wolf.

Cady was yelling at me, trying to yank her arm free. I was gentle but insistent, dragging her back to my truck. Two yellow moons shone from the darkest corner around the bar, following our steady path across the lot. Then a snout pushed free of the shadows, black nose twitching, and I saw him.

A demon in the dark, a beast on the prowl. He wasn't as big as my beast but that didn't mean he was *small*. With all the chiseled muscle of a man but the inhuman features of a wolf on two legs, he made up the image of nightmares.

He wanted me to run. I felt his excitement, his complete lack of caution. There were a hundred people in that bar, at least, and more outside. Those bikers liked to play tough, but they would piss their pants if they knew what was only a dozen feet from them.

I picked up my pace, but I wouldn't give him the chase he was after. When Cady continued to resist, I lifted her over my shoulder, banding an arm around her and hauling her with me. All her flailing and kicking stopped suddenly and she went utterly still. Every muscle stiffened, the sour scent of fear pouring off her like a bad perfume.

"Eli?" My name was a hoarse whisper from her lips. She saw him, prowling after us in the shadows, and she couldn't fathom what she was witnessing.

"Get in, now!" I flung the driver door open and shoved her in and over the center console.

Cady was pale, eyes white, as she hunkered down in the passenger seat. "I thought I saw..."

"Seatbelt," I snarled, slamming down the locks, and whipping out of the parking lot.

Something heavy hit the tail of the truck with a thump and a metal screech that almost doubled me over. Rubber burned with my sharp turn out of the lot. A hulking shape raced into the shelter of shadows along the narrow road. I couldn't judge if he was retreating or following the truck. I gunned it, not willing to take the chance we were pursued.

"What the hell just happened?" Cady demanded, twisting furiously in her seat. At least she wasn't scared anymore.

"I made a mistake." I smacked the wheel with the heel of my palm, trying to calm myself down. It wouldn't help anything if I shifted in the cab of the truck while Cady was fuming at me. "Fuck! I made a huge mistake, and this just got a whole lot worse."

The wariness in her expression caused me physical pain. "What did you do?"

"I brought you here!" I threw my hands toward the vanishing bar. "I walked you right up to those bastards."

Composure. Find composure.

"You have a lot of explaining to do."

"Cady—"

"Now! Or you can let me out here and I'll walk home. I don't like liars, Eli."

And I didn't like lying, but I had my reasons. Question was, were they good enough to justify the web of secrets she was unknowingly trapped in?

"Give me a minute." I pleaded. "Let me put some distance between us and them."

Flashes of fur weaved in and out of the streetlights behind us and I had no doubt that we were being tailed. He was on foot, but he had supernatural speed and I was not taking another stupid risk tonight.

I drove twenty miles over the speed limit, not stopping until we were out of Port Tortuga and driving along the intracoastal waterway. Those rain clouds we were promised had rolled in, blocking out the moon and making the water churn black.

A gravel pull-off appeared on my right, and I turned into it, shifting the truck in park, and twisting the keys. The first of many rain drops pattered delicately on the windshield. Under better circumstances this could be the perfect place to pick up that kiss where we left off.

"Explain, Eli." Her voice was tight with hostility. "Explain everything that happened back there."

"You know the rumors about my family. There is some truth to them."

"Is that what you meant by 'competition?' Are you and your brothers selling drugs?" She covered her face with her hands. Then before I could answer she flung the door open and stormed out into the rain.

I jumped out after her, coming around the truck and standing as close as I dared. "I haven't always been a good man, Cady."

"You are, aren't you?"

"Selling drugs? No."

She let out a shuddering breath. "Then what's happening?"

"When my father died, we learned that he'd sold the bulk of the homestead without telling us. All that family property, all those years of hard work, it was just gone." I speared fingers through my hair, taking an agitated step to the side. "The money was gone with it. There were some members of my family that were stuck in the past. My father was manipulated into giving up his legacy for them and it left us with nothing."

Cady crossed her arms and leaned against the hood of the truck, unperturbed by the cold droplets splashing into her hair and wetting her clothes.

"The properties we own today, it's all that's left of the Barbeaux homestead. My brothers and I scrounged up every penny we had and worked hard for any extra cent we could get just to keep the few dozen acres that weren't sold off. I spent seventeen months driving back and forth to an oil rig in Carlsbad. Isaac took work in construction. But Saul is a lot like my father. He was raised in the old ways."

"What are the old ways?"

"Family first. Crush anyone that gets in the way of that. Anyone that threatens the Barbeaux line." I closed his eyes, shutting out memories that were better left untouched. "Anything to keep the family secrets."

"Like the secret bayou mafia you're running?"

"My cousin Jacques grew up on the homestead with my brothers and me. But his father wasn't like ours. He was always bitter about being the second born and he took it out on his son. There's poison in the Barbeaux blood and Jacques let it spread." Unexpected emotion welled in my chest. Despite everything he'd done, Jacques was family. Once, we were like brothers.

But we were all born with monsters and Jacques let his win.

If he was alive after Saul tried to kill him...I didn't know what to make of it. He would want retribution, I knew that much. Jacques would want blood for blood. It explained all the carefully placed hints, drawing me into his waiting jaws. This might only be the beginning.

"Jacques couldn't handle the bayou life. He wanted power and influence, and he didn't find them by any legal means." I scratched the stubble on my jaw and looked up at the clouds. "We moved some product for my cousin. Literally moved it from a boat to a warehouse. Never hurt anyone, not directly. We were going to lose everything, and Saul got desperate. Isaac and I couldn't let him handle that mess by himself." I dipped my chin, staring beseechingly at Cady. "That's all over now. You have to believe me, I've worked hard to make amends."

"*You didn't hurt anyone?* It doesn't matter if you were delivering them or putting them right in the hands of a junkie! You hurt family and friends. You hurt little girls locked in bedroom closets, waiting for strung-out mamas to come home and remember to feed them!"

I'd completely forgotten about Cady's mother and now I felt sick. The rain came harder, battering us and almost disguising the tears streaking her cheeks.

"I never meant to hurt anyone," I murmured. "I was young and selfish. I only cared about my brothers and me."

"And what do you care about now?" She whispered back.

I took her hands, drawing them up to my mouth and grazing her knuckles with my lips. "Not letting anyone else pay for my mistakes."

"This feels too coincidental, Eli."

"Only coincidence was that you and I ended up on the bayou on the same night."

Cady was shaking as she slipped her hands free of mine. "So, that Louis guy back there is working for your cousin? He's the one Barlow stole money from?"

"My cousin was supposed to be dead. Maybe he still is and everything Louis said was meant to rattle me." My gut told me that was wrong, though. All along I thought this was Jacques and I was right.

"What did you mean about competition then? If you're not selling drugs..."

"My brothers and I—how do I explain this without sounding scary?" Now was my chance to come clean. To get it all off my chest. But I couldn't stop picturing the horrified look when she caught a glimpse of that other wolf. Her logical brain was already working out some kind of excuse; a trick of the light, a shadow warped by the wind.

I couldn't bear it if she looked at me that way.

"We keep the bayou safe."

Gears turned in her head. "Is that why you were out there the night I was kidnapped?"

"Yes. There's a lot of nasty stuff brewing in Port O'Henry these days. We used to keep it from spreading but we were supposed to be laying low." It was true, just not in the vigilante sense she would assume. Saul tried to put a stop to it over the years, claiming the risk of exposure was too high to be worth the reward of protecting our territory. Didn't mean Isaac and I always heeded him.

"And are you," she swallowed tightly, "killing people to keep the bayou safe?"

"Usually, our presence is a good enough deterrent." For criminals and half-mad werewolves thinking they won a prize if they took out *the first of the first*. Not for vengeful cousins come back from the dead.

Those blue eyes welled with fresh tears, staring holes into me as she sifted through this new information. "Why didn't you tell me the truth before?"

"You couldn't trust me? Well, I wasn't sure I could trust you, Cady. I didn't know what you were going to do if you found out who took you and I couldn't implicate my brothers. They're everything I've got."

"Did you know who took me? Is that why you didn't want me to go tonight?"

"It looked like my cousin's handiwork. But he was dead, so I assumed it was someone taking his place. I don't know Louis or anyone else in that bar." I crowded her against the hood of the truck, dropping a hand on either side of her until she was trapped between my body and the cooling metal. "I didn't want you to go because there isn't a clean or easy ending to this and I'm trying to protect you. You're not making it easy, darlin'."

"You don't have to protect me."

"*Yes, I do.*" I hoped she heard the real confession in those words. That I was going crazy over her. That she was now included on that short list of people I counted as *everything.*

Cady wrapped her arms around my waist, burying her face against my chest. I scooped her up, dropping her hips onto the hood and holding her close. "Thank you for being honest. I don't have brothers, but I know I would do terrible things to protect the people I love."

I nodded, my nose to her scalp, inhaling deeply. By now we were both soaked, soon we would be freezing, but I wasn't interrupting this. She didn't hate me for admitting my worst deeds. She wasn't shaken by the notion that the same hands curled around her were hands that killed people.

"I think I'm ready to consider some of those options you talked about."

"Even though you didn't get your answers?"

She sighed sadly. "I thought if I looked him in the face—the man responsible for my kidnapping—I would get back my courage. Like if I could just demand an explanation, I wouldn't feel like such a coward."

"Darlin', *you* are not a coward. You just walked into a biker bar like a big pink cupcake and snarled at a man that would kill his granny without blinking. It was stupid but it took guts."

She tilted her head up to mine, eyeing my lips. "Are we going to talk about the other thing?"

"What other thing?"

"You kissing me."

"We could talk about how badly I've wanted to kiss you since the day you rolled up on my driveway with a box of cookies."

"Really? That long?" Her fingers walked up my chest until they reached my neck, wrapping around it and lifting herself up so her mouth was almost touching mine. "What are you waiting for?"

Our lips met, barely. Soft enough that some might not consider it a kiss. But that finite contact was the spark on the incendiary tension between us and the world ignited.

Cady's fingers delved into my hair. My arms tightened around her, and I lifted, carrying us to the truck and sliding into the front seat. She swung her legs over my lap, grinding her hips against mine. With one hand I started the truck back up, turning the heat to full blast.

Despite the cool wind and my drenched clothes, I wasn't cold. The car was too hot. I was too hot. My insides were going to ignite if I didn't release this savage need soon. Her hands were under my shirt. With a circling motion she rubbed herself over the seam of my jeans, and I couldn't hold back my groan.

"Cady." I forced myself to pull away. "We need to slow it down."

"No," she panted, moving back in to kiss me. Then she hesitated, asking, "Do you want me to slow down?"

"The things I want to do to you can't be done in the backseat of my truck."

Cady sat up, nipping my lip between her teeth and murmuring, "So, take me home, Eli."

Chapter 21

Trust Fall

Cady

I WAS RUNNING. My legs carried me up the stairs two at a time, Eli hot on my heel. When I reached the door I fumbled with the keys, hands shaking too hard to get the right one in the lock.

I almost lost my mind in the twenty minutes it took us to get home. The rain became torrential, the road difficult to see in the dark, and I knew I needed to let Eli focus on driving, but I couldn't keep my hands off him. And every time he scolded my wandering touch, cursing under his breath and sending me back into my seat, my body temperature rose another degree. The waiting increased the thrill tenfold when he finally whipped into the parking space under my house.

"You better get that door open unless you want to give your neighbors a show." Eli breathed down my neck, hands roving everywhere. His calloused palms scraped across the skin on my lower belly, and I whimpered, twisting the key, and flinging the door open.

Eli slammed the door behind us, taking me by the hips and lifting me against it. My legs locked tight around his waist, fingers diving into his hair as I kissed him. With every swipe of his tongue Eli ground into me, drawing all the blood between my legs. As if my pulse wasn't already throbbing for him there.

Somehow my sweater went over my head. His too, then my bra. Clothing dropped in damp piles all around us. The night air was bitter, but his skin was scorching, and I melted into him. Lightning flashed through the blinds, followed by a booming thunder that I felt in my bones. It drummed on my skin, building inside of me until I was a storm of my own.

Eli had to press a hand to my sternum and hold me back to break our kiss. "I don't think I can go slow, darlin'. Not right now."

I took advantage of his angle, letting my gaze wander across all his naked skin. His biceps flexed as they held me, veins popping all the way down to his wrists. He was broad, so broad, and the muscles lining his chest were each carefully defined. Down my eyes travelled to the trail of fine hair lining his stomach. He was sun darkened everywhere, not a tan line in sight.

I swallowed involuntarily when I got to his cock, wedged between my legs, each thick blue vein popping in contrast to my hot pink panties. I hadn't been with someone since I was in high school, but I found myself wondering if they were all that big and I'd just forgotten? I hadn't considered how our size difference would translate here.

"Don't go slow, Eli."

My head snapped back against the door as his mouth crashed into mine. Teeth were digging into my bottom lip. Hips bucked to drag his cock up and down my core through the thin fabric separating us. I squeezed him tighter, desperate for more pressure. His fingertips dug into the flesh of my thighs, pulling me closer. The length of him rubbed me with every teasing stroke, such delicious friction but not hard enough.

"So impatient," he murmured, slipping his lips from mine to nibble at my ear. "Maybe I *should* go slow. Take my time and draw this out. I think I promised some begging."

With two fingers I spread the fabric of my panties aside, arching with his next thrust and letting the tip of him slide into me. Eli clenched his teeth, his muscles shaking as he held himself still.

"If you don't get inside of me right now, I'm going to make you watch while I get myself off."

Quick as a whip Eli had my hands pinned over my head. He held me with only one arm, filling me with an aching slowness until he was fully sheathed. I wasn't sure if I could have breath in my lungs and him inside me at the same time.

"Careful, darlin'." The low rumble of his voice vibrated down to my core and I quivered. "I've waited a long time for this. I can wait another hour while I bring you right up to that edge." He punctuated his point with a half thrust. "Why don't you ask nicely this time?"

I yielded instantly. "Please, Eli."

"Please what?"

Our eyes met, his whiskey bright and scorching with that intensity that was all Eli. "Please fuck me until I don't remember anything but your name."

"Good girl."

Eli dropped me long enough to wrench my panties off. Then I was lifted again, back thumping into the door as he filled me with no overture. Thunder crashed and I wasn't sure if it was the storm outside or the raw power of our bodies finally coming together.

We started at the front door, rattling it with our frantic movement. Then Eli carried me into the hall, stopping at each wall between doorways and kissing me with an edge of brutality.

I wanted to tell him how often I fantasized about this. To spill every secret way I'd dreamed of him taking me but I couldn't form the words. This was the most untamed I'd ever been, and my voice was held captive by the rapture I was chasing.

We made it to the linen closet before I completely fell apart. Eli circled his hips with every pounding thrust, the base of his cock stroked me in just the right way to make lightning zing through my veins. I cried out, arching, weaving my limbs tightly around him.

My muscles slackened as the seconds stretched on. Even my heart became gooey with molten pleasure, ceasing to beat for long, panting breaths. Eli eased his pace, running a thumb across my lower lip and whispering, "Beautiful."

The world spun and suddenly I was on my back. The mattress squeaked and swayed when Eli covered my body with his. He bracketed my chest with his arms, the weight of him holding me in place. I was still on the quivering end of orgasm when he bucked into me again and the fullness of him spiraled me into bliss for a second time.

The storm continued, thunder drumming between my legs, fast and intense, and I wasn't sure it was ever going to end. I wasn't sure I wanted it to. Eli wore a downright wicked smile, watching me unravel in his arms and loving every moment of it. His movement became frenzied and erratic, the noise in his throat rising into something deep and animal. He stiffened, collapsing onto my chest with a drawn-out groan.

For many breathless moments we stayed like that. Sweat dripped from Eli's forehead to collect along my neck, his arms tight around me. My limbs were twined around him, anchoring myself to him. Otherwise, I felt as if I might float right off the bed, gravity having no hold over me anymore.

I wiggled free when his weight became too much, flopping onto my pillow with a breathy sigh. "You really are something else, Mister Barbeaux."

Eli propped himself up on his arm, palm absently rubbing circles over his heart. He was watching me a little too intently, concentrating more than I was capable of after sex. For a second I thought he was planning his escape but then his brow furrowed, and he asked, "Do you feel...different?"

"What do you mean?"

He pressed two fingers to my chest. "Here. Does anything feel, um, changed?"

There was a softness in his voice, vulnerability I'd never seen him wear before. "I don't hook up, if that's what you're asking."

That added to the confusion in his expression. "I only vaguely know what that means."

"I do feel *different*. About you."

His scowled deepened and he tapped that place on his chest again, almost seeming disappointed. I pecked his bottom lip, hoping to distract from whatever he was thinking much too hard about.

He returned the kiss, longer and more indulgent. "I want this to be something, Cady."

"You mean us?"

"Yes. I feel like maybe you were meant to be mine."

I shifted, drawing a circle over his heart where his hand had been. "You make everything seem less scary. Like I could be safe in the middle of a hurricane." His eyes closed when I whispered, "I feel like maybe I want to be yours."

He clasped my hand in his. Was he shaking? His lashes lifted and I almost thought I could feel what he was feeling. Soul-deep longing, a loneliness that stretched beyond time. Eli wasn't a stoic man, but I hadn't anticipated this emotional response.

Over *me*.

"I've waited a long time for you." He'd said it to me before and I got the feeling he meant much longer than the scattered weeks we'd known each other.

A memory surfaced at those words, and I sat up, taking the sheets with me. The storm had sharp, wintery teeth and the air around us was beginning to bite. "Eli?" I tucked my legs against him. "You weren't actually sleepwalking that night you were on my porch, were you?"

He dropped his hands behind his head, making eye contact with the ceiling fan instead of me. "I don't sleepwalk like other people."

"You mean most people don't walk six miles barefoot from their home and try to seduce random women in view of all the neighbors while they're dead asleep?"

"You weren't a random woman." He glanced at me. "That was the first time I ever left the bayou."

"Holy shit, you're serious. I thought it was a dumb excuse." I covered my mouth, not sure if I should laugh or be concerned. "Your eyes were open! And you were very—ahem—coherent."

He grabbed for me, hauling me on top of him and murmuring, "I wanted you so bad it was all I could think about. Every waking moment was spent obsessing over you and when I slept you haunted my dreams."

I swallowed my nerves. "What does it mean to be yours?"

"Means no one is going to hurt you anymore. You got a problem? I handle it."

As a girl raised by my grandparents, loving but limited in their capacity to nurture and protect, I spent a lot of time cultivating my "strong, independent woman" persona. I had to. No one was coming to save me but me.

Until that night on the bayou when Eli risked everything to save me.

That independent version of myself wanted to object at the idea of him *handling* things for me, as if I was some whimpering girl that *needed* rescuing.

But I did, didn't I? More than once in the last three weeks. The outcome of my adventure tonight would have been much different if Eli wasn't there with me.

And honestly, I was exhausted. For years I helped Papa carry the burden of Nana's illness. Then Barlow died and my life spiraled even more. My five-year adrenaline rush was burning out.

Here he was, offering to take that burden off my shoulders. Not to carry it for me but with me. Eli could have completely shut me out of this ridiculous investigation, and he didn't. He let me drag him along, tangling him further into this mess and putting him on the line, and he didn't complain.

"Well, no one is going to hurt you either. I carry a pistol in my purse, and I know how to use it."

He laughed. "My enemies are shaking in their boots."

F OLLOWING A LONG NIGHT of adrenaline—for varying reasons—I was wired in that exhausting sort of way and thoroughly regretting not hitting a drive thru on the way home. I glanced at Eli dozing naked beside me, his hard stomach rising with languid breaths, and I amended my thoughts. *Zero regrets.* I would just have to be satisfied with whatever was left in the fridge.

I slipped into a baggy sweater and the first pair of panties I could find, tiptoeing into the living room and gathering the damp clothes scattered by the door. Burning little butterflies fluttered around my lower belly as I replayed every earth-shattering second with Eli. My growling stomach reminded me why I wasn't going back to the bedroom to wake him up for round two.

After hanging our clothes in the bathroom to dry I rounded the corner into the kitchen and shrieked. The massive shadow waiting next to the fridge winced and I recognized the hands that clapped over his ears.

"Why didn't you turn the light on if the dark was going to spook you?" Eli bent to run his nose along my neck, breathing me in with a gruff breath.

My skin sparked with a now-familiar heat. Damn, even his *breathing* was sexy. "I was trying not to wake you."

"Oh, I'm awake." He jerked his hips against me to demonstrate.

I drew lines down his torso, memorizing the curve of each muscle. "Food first."

"Food first," he agreed, propping himself on the granite counter and crossing his arms to watch me.

Suddenly self-conscious being half-naked in the white kitchen light, I hurried to pull eggs, bagels, and whatever random jams I could find out of the fridge. It was just about empty except for breakfast food—thanks to Eli—and I made a mental note to take a trip to Port Tortuga for real food. I hadn't done a proper grocery run since September.

Egg shells clattered in the kitchen sink and the toaster clicked as I pushed a bagel in. I was about to reach for a spatula when hard muscle pushed me into the counter. Eli ran his hands up my hips, under the hem of my sweater, turning it inside out as he tugged it over my head. Apparently, he changed his mind about food first.

Calloused fingers scraped up my chest and plucked at my nipples. I arched into him, letting the heat of him engulf me. Okay, we were on the same page. Food second.

I barely noticed when he tugged my panties down, leaving them tangled around one ankle as he pushed my legs open. Even the slightest contact between our bare skin had my brain misfiring. I forgot everything around me, lost track of any nerve that wasn't touching him. Like my only biological purpose was to be consumed by him.

The veins in his cock were pumping so furiously that I felt him pulse against my back. He moved up and down, that silky skin torturously soft over his steely length. I wiggled impatiently, already soaked with the thought of him filling me.

Eli splayed his hand over my lower belly, dipping his fingers into my folds and groaning his approval. "You're dripping for me."

His hand retreated, both of them coming down to the tops of my thighs to squeeze. Thank goodness he held me in place like that because the first thrust was hard and sudden, and I almost slammed into the edge of granite. Eli didn't take his time building up and I liked it that way. He pumped his hips fast, each thrust so forceful I almost came right off my feet.

Heat coiled in my middle, pooling where we were connected until I felt that muscle melting climax rising fast. Then a loud pop startled me from my pleasure trance, and I cursed.

"Shit! I'm going to burn the eggs."

Eli shifted his pace, all the force but slower, steady. "Keep cooking. I'm perfectly comfortable where I am."

With a desperate little whimper, I tried to focus on the stove beside me. I grabbed for a spatula, breasts bouncing onto the counter each time he pounded me. He reached across my chest and took a nipple between his fingers, pulling it away from my breast until I hissed with the hint of pain. That zing combined with his endless, rhythmic thrusts had my legs shaking.

Somehow, I managed to flip each egg and push the pan away from the heat. I didn't dare reach across the stove and turn it off while Eli's cock was trying to cause an internal earthquake.

He stopped abruptly, breathing down my neck. "Impressive, but I'm doing this wrong if you still have that much focus."

We whirled and before I could catch my breath I was on my back, legs dangling off the edge of the parallel counter. This one was a bar top, just wide enough that my head didn't fall over the side. I gasped at the cold stone on my back, then double gasped when Eli took my clit between his lips and started drawing circles across it with his tongue.

He got exactly what he wanted. My mind blanked out and my body picked up where it left off, shooting me weightless into space as I climaxed with a scream.

I almost screamed again, losing all sense of gravity when Eli hooked his hands on the back of my knees and pulled me to the very edge of the counter. He plunged into me, returning to that merciless speed, and I wrapped all my limbs around him in a desperate attempt to keep from falling.

"Trust me?" he asked softly.

I didn't hesitate. "Yes."

"Put your hands behind you. Relax your legs. I've got you, darlin'."

I did as he asked, propping my palms beside my hips, and slackening my legs. His fingers locked around my thighs, my calves dangling. Every thrust had me teetering, my stomach doing flips as I felt myself slipping. Eli's hips caught me, balancing me perfectly on that fine edge. The fear became a tense thrill, making my core clench with echoes of another orgasm.

Eli gave me the slightest smile, a wicked twist to that normally sweet expression. His eyes gleamed like polished copper, neck taut with his own building release. I watched those tendons flex, watched the muscles in his stomach work, and I saw the moment he lost himself to ecstasy.

He wasn't going alone. He pinched my clit between his thumb and middle finger, using the index to stroke up and down. At the same time, he sank his teeth into the fleshy base of my neck. It wasn't a gentle bite, not that tiny jolt from earlier. I clawed at his back, writhing away from him, but he didn't let up.

Then I was moaning his name as a sharp, electric orgasm shook me—literally—and the pain swelled into a maddening wave of pleasure. Deep inside me I felt him explode with liquid heat and my core squeezed tighter around him.

I was gasping, eyes wide, hand pressed to the bite on my neck. Eli scooted me further onto the counter and disappeared, returning seconds later to slide my panties back up my legs. He tugged my sweater over my head, kissed my forehead, and murmured, "I need to feed you."

It was well past three when I brushed bagel crumbs from the bed and cuddled under the blankets. Twice I tried to speak and twice my words were swallowed by a yawn. Eli curled his arm around my waist, drawing me to his bare chest and letting out a contented sigh.

I stared up at him with bleary vision. His features wavered as my eyes focused and unfocused. I lifted my hand to touch one cheek, letting his stubble prickle my skin and assuring myself this was real.

People didn't meet like this. Under better circumstances they didn't meet and just *work*. I never believed in love at first sight—not that I was declaring this love—or even in *the one*, as if only one right person existed for someone in a world so vast. What if my *one* was across the globe?

What if he's been across town this whole time?

Eli was leading me to believe a lot of strange things that I once thought were fiction. I still hadn't figured him out, not entirely, but I intended to. Eventually I would find my way to all his secrets. I would earn them just like he earned my trust.

He was holding back to protect his brothers. To protect himself. What he didn't realize was that I meant it when I said I would protect him too.

Nothing Eli could tell me now would frighten me away.

Eli

I hated myself. Hated my very being and everything I was.

Because the monster inside of me was the reason I found Cady and it would be the reason I lost her.

I was lying to her. It came easily to me, too. Most parts of my life were a lie. To everyone but my brothers, I was a stranger.

Until Cady.

Now things were so complicated, and I didn't know how to untangle the web I'd weaved. Every day I spent with a Cady made it harder. I was falling in love with her, fast, but my loyalty to my brothers was fierce. I couldn't put them at risk because of my personal feelings. Not now that hellfire was about to rain down on all of us.

So, I lied to Cady. I lied to her about one of the biggest parts of my life. And about my true role in all of this.

If she found out—when she found it—that would be the end of this. Cady was honest and she valued honesty. Earning her faith tonight was a miracle. I wasn't foolish enough to believe I would regain it twice.

For now, she was huddled against me, seeking the heat from my body and the safety of my arms and I was going to relish that. Her hair was mussed, and she smelled like sex—and me.

The bond was the same as it had been before tonight. Tightly wound, thrumming, a living creature that wanted me to cling to Cady as madly as I could for as long as I could.

Somehow, it was supposed to become hers too. I had a feeling that wouldn't happen so long as I wasn't giving her the full truth. The real me, beast and all.

So how in the world did you tell the woman of your dreams that you were a werewolf?

Chapter 22

Rumor Has It

Eli

CADY HAD A SCAR on her right shoulder blade. A mole on her hip on the same side. They were just some of the many details I was memorizing about her body as the sun peeked through the blinds, dappling her naked skin in golden light.

Twice I woke with her pressed against me, cock so hard it hurt, and twice she welcomed me when I slid into her. Cady's back was to my chest, her leg hooked over my hip. One hand trailed down her stomach, fingers seeking out her clit and stroking as I thrust into her. The muscles in her thighs jumped, soft climax washing over her.

Each time she came, Cady whispered my name. Her hands twined in my hair, head turning over her shoulder to kiss me sweetly. Then she would fall back to sleep, and I would lie there, too wired to rest. Sex alone did not complete a bond, it would seem, but making love to the woman I was bonded to was unlike any pleasure I'd felt in my life.

Now, as she lay naked on top of the sheets with me hovering over her in my careful study, I felt hollow. Each moment I wasn't inside her I was missing an essential component of what I was.

I traced her spine, feeling every ridge and the soft skin that encased it. My fingertips drew circles over the dimples on her back, moving lower to massage her ass. Cady was petite in every way, short stature, lean figure with narrow hips and small breasts. But her ass was perfectly rounded, tempting me to sink my teeth in until she woke with a squeal.

Instead, I moved lower, fingers dancing up and down the inside of her thighs. A hitched breath told me that she was awake and when there was no resistance, I continued. Every time my sweeping caresses moved closer to her core, she shuddered. Her hips slowly began to lift from the mattress, chasing my touch. An impatient noise left her throat and I chuckled, drawing one finger slowly through her folds.

She was wet—*so wet.* The remnants of our lovemaking mingled with fresh excitement, and I purred at the sight. With thumb and finger, I pinched her clit and she jolted, gasping.

"Eli, you're torturing me."

"Darlin', I want to give you what you want." I lifted up onto my knees, rubbing my cock through her wetness. "But you're filthy."

She sat up, scowling at me. Before she could grumble, I added, "I need to get you in the shower," and her lips tilted up in a sultry curve.

The water was scalding, and it only added to the torment of slick hands on even slicker skin. We soaped and scrubbed each other everywhere, teasing with gentle touches until both of us were breathless. Cady lost the battle with her willpower first, fisting her hand around the base of my cock and pumping.

I pressed her into the cold tile wall, propping one hand over her head and taking her waist with the other. I leaned into her touch, letting her stroke me almost to the point of breaking. I stilled her with a squeeze to her wrist, dropping to my knees and spreading her thighs for a taste. She was screaming my name by the time I lifted her around my hips and fit myself inside her.

Steam curled around us, water dripping from my hair to collect on her cheeks. This time when I came, I was gentle, lowering my mouth to kiss her reverently.

"I can't believe it," I whispered.

"Believe what?"

"How beautiful you are."

An hour later we were in her kitchen, hair damp and fingers pruned from a rather distracted shower. I would have kept her in there longer, but her ancient water heater decided we needed to cool off.

"Bacon?" I held up the package of meat in question.

Cady nodded from her perch on the kitchen counter. "You know it."

"I've never met a woman that doesn't eat vegetables."

"I eat vegetables," She protested. "Ketchup is made from tomatoes. Those are vegetables."

"Technically, they're fruits."

"French fries are vegetables."

I smiled at her, shaking my head. This felt habitual, like this was the life I'd been living forever. Going back to the bayou would be jarring. In the back of my mind, I was already having imaginary conversations with my brothers, trying to determine the best way to make them understand my predicament.

The bacon sizzled on the skillet beside the eggs. My focus on breakfast was only second to the attention directed toward Cady, which was why I didn't realize someone was at the door until they knocked.

Cady was halfway to the front door, eyeing it warily, before I caught her. "Uh-uh. Where's your gun?"

"It's daytime, Eli! It could be a neighbor."

"Sunlight doesn't mean shit. We're not dealing with vampires, remember?" I turned her around and marched her in the direction of her purse.

"At least let me check the peephole before I start a shootout," she said. "You're burning the bacon!"

Cady

I was unclear if Eli was paranoid, or I was too relaxed. Hard not to be relaxed after last night. In fact, I was beginning to wonder if this whole thing was blown out of proportion. Someone kidnapped me. So what? They might not even come back.

Wow, apparently it was possible to fuck someone senseless because I was not thinking straight. But as I stood on my toes to peer through the peephole on the door, I felt justified in my calm demeanor. The face on the other side was a familiar one. I hadn't seen my childhood friend in a few weeks, but it was no fault of his own. I'd been preoccupied.

"Brandon?" I pulled the door open, only then realizing I was wearing booty shorts and a sweater with no bra. The air was crisp and the breeze mild but immediately my nipples responded to the temperature change. I crossed my arms over my chest and asked, "What are you doing here?"

"I think what you're supposed to say is, 'Good morning—'" Brandon's pleasant smile faltered, and his gaze moved up over my shoulder. I didn't have to turn around to know Eli was leaning on the door frame behind me, shirtless and looming in a way that didn't convey friendliness. "Ah, you have company. I wondered whose truck that was."

"Um, yeah. Brandon, this is Eli Barbeaux."

"We've met." Both men said in unison, gazes locked in a staring contest.

"You have?" Even as I asked it, I remembered seeing Eli at the sporting goods store that Brandon's family owned. "Right. Small town."

I fidgeted with the hem of my sweater, glancing over my shoulder to see that Eli was about to whip out his ruler for a dick measuring contest. It wasn't as if Brandon was competition. The last time I thought anything remotely romantic about him was in the ninth grade.

"So, what brings you by?"

"I came to check on you. Did you hear about the fire? At Barlow's?" Brandon forced his attention back to me.

"Yeah, I heard."

More unbearable, awkward silence.

"Can I talk to you? *Alone*?"

The noise that came from Eli almost sounded like a growl and it startled Brandon, causing him to look up in alarm. Yes, up. I hadn't registered just how tall Eli was in comparison to other men. Every man is tall when you barely pass five feet. I turned again, shooting reproach over my shoulder as another weird grunt made his feelings clear.

Anything I was going to say to him died in my throat. Unfriendly was too kind a word for the malice darkening his features. That *wrongness* ebbed into his eyes, the color too bright. Shadows made every angle on his face sharper.

Threads of thought twisted around in my mind, trying to tie themselves together. Desperate to make sense of what I was sure I saw.

What I did know was that Eli was dangerous and he was looking at Brandon as if they were two animals about to fight over a kill.

Then he met my eyes, sipping from his steaming coffee cup and flashing his most dashing smile. The adoration when he looked at me wasn't a show for Brandon. "I'll be in the kitchen if you need me, darlin'. Don't want to burn the bacon."

I smiled back, reassuring whatever unexpected, jealous part of him that was making an appearance. Though, when I closed the front door and shuffled to the edge of the deck to watch the waves churn, I had to wonder. Was it jealousy or mistrust?

I'd known Brandon all my life—even nursed a tiny crush on him during middle school when he was on the high school football team—and right now the dude was giving off weird vibes. He kept glancing between the front door, the stairs, and me, like he wasn't sure if he wanted to make an escape or not.

He hadn't spoken to me since the day I bought my gun. It wasn't like we hung out or texted regularly, but he only lived two blocks over and at the very least, I should have seen him out on his morning runs.

"What's up?" I was in my pajamas and hot breakfast was waiting for me with a hot chef to match. I was raised better than to be rude, but I also wasn't going to let someone spoil my first good morning in ages, even an old friend.

"That's one of the Barbeaux boys."

"Eli. You said you've met."

Brandon ducked his head, lowering his voice to a hiss. "I know *of* him. He and his brothers come to the shop a couple times a month to buy ammo and tackle."

"And what do you know *of* him?" One of the downsides to living in a town where everyone knew everyone was that everyone was also in everyone's business.

"You've heard the rumors about them, Cady."

"I've heard rumors that Mrs. Gonzalez eats canned dog food from the *Stop N' Shop* too. They're just rumors." I shifted impatiently on my feet.

"They're more than rumors. Trust me on this. That man is bad news. You need to be careful about the people you let into your home."

To his credit, Brandon wasn't wrong. Last night Eli admitted to a dirty past, and I'd seen firsthand what he was capable of. At the same time, this warning was oddly timed and out of character.

Brandon and I weren't close since Nana got sick, and our interests diverged with age, so we weren't in the habit of talking about dating. Once, Papa and his father were good friends and Brandon and I became friends by default. When you're the only kid in a room full of old people, it's easy to bond.

It didn't set us up for this pushy heart to heart.

"Is that why you're here? To tell me who I'm allowed to spend my time with?"

"No, Cady, no." Brandon put up placating hands. "I just came to check on you. Last I saw you, you were acting strange. Then Barlow's house burned down, and I've seen this truck parked in your driveway every day for weeks. As your friend, I felt obligated to make sure you weren't getting yourself in to trouble."

I am in trouble, and I didn't get myself there.

"The last year has been rough, but I'm managing." My eyes wandered to the front door, where I was pretty sure Eli was watching us through the peephole. "Eli's helped a lot."

"I don't trust him, Cady, and you shouldn't either."

"I do trust him, actually." I uncrossed my arms and motioned to the stairs. "Thanks for checking on me. I'm fine."

Eli was behind the door when I pushed it open, and I almost smacked him with it.

"Eavesdropping is impolite."

"So is showing up on your porch before breakfast and actin' all squirrelly."

I frowned through the crack in the blinds where I could see Brandon retreating down the stairs. He *was* acting squirrelly. Was it really just because of Eli?

"I've got some bad news, darlin'."

"You burned the bacon because you were snooping?"

His grin was adorably sheepish as he nodded.

"I bet you can find a way to make it up to me." I winked. "But first I need pants. It's cold."

"You won't need pants if I'm going to make it up to you!" He called after me.

I ignored him, padding down the hallway and pausing when I noticed a toppled frame on the floor. We were distracted last night, and I hadn't heard it fall. It was a print from a local photographer. Papa loved to support local business and this one always spoke to him.

The sun was setting across from the water, casting brilliant colors onto the horizon. Purples and pinks swirled with dark shades of orange, reaching down vibrant arms to encircle the day houses perched along sandy shores.

The day houses.

Holy shit.

"Eli!" I shouted. He was beside me in a heartbeat. "I think I know where the money is."

Chapter 23

Wild Goose Chase

Cady

OUR WINDBREAKERS DID LITTLE to protect us as Eli's boat left the intracoastal waterway and headed toward Cadalina island. The wind sliced into me so fiercely that I wanted to curl up into a ball. October was temperamental on the bay but even so, the cold was unusual.

This task was an impossible one and we could be on the water for hours. At least it was afternoon, and the sun was high enough to provide moderate warmth when the boat slowed to navigate around sand bars.

I spent the morning flipping through pictures on Facebook. Eli hovered on the couch beside me, his expression growing more perplexed with every minute. Unsurprisingly, he'd never used Facebook. By the way he looked at my computer, I was beginning to wonder if he'd used a laptop either.

"Barlow has a day house," I said in explanation when I hurried from the hallway, picture frame in hand. Eli was understandably alarmed when I started shouting and the concern clouding him didn't dissipate when I dusted off the laptop and pulled open a browser.

The legalities of day houses were unclear to me. There hadn't been anything in Barlow's paperwork that mentioned a second property and it seemed like most people were renting otherwise useless waterside land to build day houses.

Day houses became common when the town exploded in popularity almost fifteen years earlier. Wealthy vacationers decided that having an entire home on the beach with every amenity one could dream of wasn't enough; they also needed a second home on the water, somewhere to park their boats and relax for the day before heading to shore.

The houses that dotted the horizon like strange sculptures in the summer had no utilities. It was like the skeleton of a house, all the exterior structure with none of the stuffing. Barlow was always keeping up with the Jones', which was probably why he built his own.

I never would have remembered if not for the picture he kept on his desk: fifteen-year-old Dustin standing beside his father with a fishing pole in hand, grinning at the flounder on the hook. They stood on the deck of a day house, a rusted anchor hanging on the doorway behind them.

Barlow loved to talk about his son.

I used to think he told those stories because he regretted the distance between him and his son, but now I had no idea what their relationship was like. Maybe he regretted turning his son into a drug addict and a criminal.

"Still don't see the point," Eli grumbled for the tenth time as we approached the first line of houses. They jutted up from narrow sandbars, salt-licked and grey.

"Of day houses? I don't either. Why not just sit on the beach like a normal person."

"I mean the point of being here. Finding that money doesn't change anything."

I clenched my teeth to keep them from chattering. "For me, it could change everything. I can barely afford to turn the heat on and the chances of me finding a living income in Port O'Henry are zero. Maybe I'll take the money and live off it while I sit on the beach writing poetry collections."

It was true that I could use the money. Even a hundred bucks would go a long way. My grandparents left me everything they owned but Papa was so wrapped up in Nana's health during those final years that the house had fallen into disrepair. Coastal air wasn't kind to homes and the place needed a lot of maintenance. On top of that, cancer treatments were expensive, and the bulk of their estate was gone by the time Papa passed away.

I hadn't expected them to leave me a fortune—and if they did, I would trade it in a heartbeat to have them back—but I wasn't prepared to take on their house, either. Staying in Port O'Henry meant subsisting off whatever low paying jobs floated my way. Barlow paid me well enough, considering that I wasn't a real bookkeeper, but not so much that I could pay for forty thousand dollars' worth of home repairs.

When Nana got sick, my grandfather insisted that I leave for school in Chicago. Pride in her only granddaughter would help make her well. But I couldn't bear the thought of Nana passing while I was away. The doctors had given her months. No one expected her to live another five frail years.

Now I was realizing that all that waiting might have cost my future. It was a balloon caught in the wind, carried further and further over my head with each passing day. So many unfulfilled dreams. I might never get published. Never get married, have children, build a life of my own.

When I thought about it like that, taking off with a huge stack of cash and starting over didn't sound so bad.

"And just ignore the murdering assholes that want their money back?"

"I'll use it to disappear onto some tropical island and leave Port O'Henry forever."

Eli twisted his hands on the metal wheel. "I don't want you to leave."

"Come with me," I smiled teasingly.

He didn't return it. "I can't leave the bayou."

Somehow, I knew that. Eli would never willingly leave here. That was fine. I wasn't planning to leave either. My heart beat in rhythm with the rolling tide. I was born here, and I would die here. Hopefully in a very, very long time. I probably wouldn't use the money at all. I just needed to find it before

Louis and whoever else he worked with did. If only to lord it over him before he killed me.

And just like that my mind went morbid again. No matter the "other options" Eli offered me, I was pretty sure I wouldn't make it out of this situation alive. There was a missing piece to the puzzle and not seeing the whole picture was creating an enormous blind spot. A shadow that hid whatever monsters were lurking around me.

Cue anxiety.

"Just consider this another fun date on the water. Barlow could have tucked it into some untraceable account, and we'll never find it." But he was old fashioned—the kind of man to hide money under his mattress—and I had a gut feeling that if he had money he wanted to hide, it would be in cash.

"I can think of other ways we could be having fun right now." This man and his libido were going to be the death of me. I needed to start working out more if I was going to keep up with him. Every muscle in my body—even ones I hadn't known could get overworked—was tender.

I had no idea how to search for day houses and their property owners, so we opted for the extra hard method and hit the water in Eli's bay boat. I had a picture of Dustin and his father printed and tucked into my pocket.

Now we just had to approach every day house we could find and try to match it up to the picture. Easy.

More than an hour passed, and we didn't find anything. It was slow, starting and stopping the boat, holding up the picture and studying the deck and doorframe. That was about all we could do. Eli was not pleased with this wild goose chase and every time I shivered, he offered to head back.

"Come to the bayou with me." He cut through my darkening thoughts, shielding his eyes from the sun on the water.

"Right now? But we still haven't—"

"No, I mean pack your things and come stay with me."

I posed the same question from a week earlier. "If I'm not safe in my own home, why would I be safe in yours?"

"You would be safe on the bayou. I can promise you that."

"Even if I was, I can't spend the rest of my life hiding."

"You wouldn't have to hide." He gestured over the water. "We've been out here for hours. Your nose is getting sunburned. And even if we find a treasure chest full of gold, it's not going to make a difference." His hands found my hips and he steadied me as the boat shifted in the waves. "This is a waste of time, and you know it."

That gnawing in the pit of my stomach became more violent and I suddenly felt ill. Eli was right, of course. There was no true solution here and the last three weeks had been a coping tactic. I had no idea what I was doing or why. This was just some frantic last attempt to make sense of a situation I didn't understand, a drowning person grabbing for whatever was at the surface.

"What do I do, Eli?" I dropped my forehead to his chest and huffed out a trembling breath. His body seemed to absorb some of my anxiety, and I relaxed against him. "I don't know what else to do."

"Come to the bayou with me." He said it more firmly this time, a demand and not a request. "Give me some time to do this my way."

I froze, peeling myself off him and squinting up at his face. "Does your way involve death?"

"Do you care? These people want you dead. They almost killed you. And I can guarantee that you are not the first person they've taken out to that bayou. You're just the first one that walked out again."

I hurried away from him and leaned over the side of the boat. Breakfast threatened to climb back up my throat as I stared into the foaming water.

Murder. That was what Eli was suggesting. He was dead serious. Completely unflinching as he offered to *kill people* for me.

I found myself assessing him, wondering if I was putting my faith in a well disguised maniac. I thought back to Brandon's warning earlier that morning, to the rumors people spread about the wild men living bare on the bayou.

None of that bothered me. Most of the rumors were untrue, I knew. And the ones that were? About Eli and his brothers being criminals? Killers? That wasn't what bothered me either.

What crawled around my gut, churning up my insides, was the immediate relief I felt when he offered to handle it. To do things *his way.*

Yes, let Eli handle it. Hide away in his living room and watch cowboy movies while he goes out and murders people for me.

This was the point where red flags should have been waving in front of my eyes. What we were discussing was insane. So was what I felt for him. What I felt around him. Safe, sheltered from any storm.

And that was why I shook my head with a vehement, "No." Crossing the boat to look at him, I said, "I won't let you carry that burden for me, and I won't let you risk your life for mine."

Eli's fingers were shockingly warm on my cold face when he cupped it, drawing me up to him for a slow, delicious kiss. Some logical part of my brain was screaming, *You're kissing a guy that just suggested killing people in the same tone as when he offers to cook breakfast.*

Well, they started it. Eli was just offering to finish it.

"One more hour?" I pleaded. "Give me one more hour on the water. Then we can go home, and I'll pack a bag."

We didn't need another hour. I tugged excitedly at his arm, pointing to the next day house on our right. A briny sheen coated the wooden structure, dulling the color to match the sun-drenched shallows. The entire thing groaned as Eli climbed out of the boat and tied a rope to the narrow dock at the base of the stairs.

My heart was a throbbing lump in my throat as we climbed the stairs, stopping to compare the picture to the front of the house and confirm we weren't seeing things. A rusted anchor hung over the doorway and the banister lined up with the angle of the photograph.

"This is it," I whispered, not daring to let my hope rekindle yet.

There was a sturdy deadbolt holding the door closed, new compared to the rusted screws and supports holding the porch together. It seemed an odd addition to the place, more confirmation of my suspicions. I held my breath as Eli kicked at the door.

The wood splintered loudly, and the door swung inward, smacking into a stored Adirondack chair, and scooting it side-ways on the vinyl floor. Hazy, stale air greeted us inside. For a home without insulation, it was warm, heated by the afternoon sun. Lounge chairs and coolers littered the room, haphazardly stored like someone was in a hurry the last time they were here.

Eli moved in first, scanning the dim room before drawing open plastic curtains. The dust was even worse in the sunlight. Motes made halos around our heads and provoked a series of sneezes from me. I wiped my nose and stepped into the single room, determined to find what I was looking for.

Eli searched a standing bar on one side of the room, shuf-fling through liquor bottles and plastic cups. I took the other end, lifting the waterproof cushions on a built-in bench along one wall and checking for compartments. There was a hinge on the wood at the corner of the bench. I squeezed my fingers into the cracks and lifted. It squeaked as I leaned the wooden flap against the wall and peered inside.

Sun hats, towels, and half used bottles of sunscreen were piled lazily on top of each other. My enthusiasm was quickly ebbing. There weren't that many places to hide something in this house. Frustrated, I scooped the hats and towels out and dumped them on the floor. Then I froze, staring at the black duffel bag concealed at the bottom of the compartment.

"Eli..." The rest of my words were lost.

With shaking hands, I heaved the duffle bag onto the floor and pulled back the zipper. I felt Eli behind me, and I looked up at him to see if his face was as shocked as mine.

Bundles and bundles of hundred dollar bills were wrapped tight with rubber bands. Some of them were faded and a little crushed from being stuffed into the storage compartment but that didn't make them any less valuable.

"Well, you found your money," Eli murmured. "Now what?"

Chapter 24

MIA

Eli

I WAS OUT OF time.

There were still hours of daylight left but even now I felt the moon readying to prise me open. What was once a promise of ecstasy had me in a strangled panic. It was supposed to be a chance to be myself, to pause the endless battle between man and beast and become the hunter. Freedom incarnate. No rapture could compete with running on four legs.

Or so I thought.

There was one other pleasure like no other, one that burrowed into my soul and lingered there long after the moment had passed.

Cady.

All I could think about was Cady.

Cady alone while I drove back to the bayou to find my brothers. Cady's reaction if I told her the truth. Cady on my porch, listening to the unnatural howls that haunted the bayou for one night every month.

I couldn't bring her home tonight. There was no telling how Saul would react, and it wouldn't do to remove her from one danger only to put her in my brother's jaws. Not to mention her inevitable shock when I admitted what I was. Best case scenario was acceptance, but I wouldn't rule out the worst case.

I needed fresh clothes and a shower that wasn't going to distract me. I needed to make sure Isaac would be home safe tonight, and I needed to talk to Saul. No, I needed to argue with Saul. This wasn't his choice to make but he wouldn't agree with me.

Did it put all three of us at risk? Yes.

So did Isaac roaming the night in search of a new woman to entertain him. And so did Saul wandering the bayou, half-crazed as he seemed to be these days.

Cady opened my eyes to how we were living. While we were burying our heads in the sand, the others of our kind were closing ranks. Someone was forming a pack and if it wasn't Jacques, I would eat my hat. A pack was much more dangerous than a handful of gossiping locals getting suspicious about the Barbeaux family.

This would never have happened if we were still patrolling the bayou, protecting what was ours. I understood why Saul didn't want to anymore, after his confrontation with Jacques, but it wasn't a choice. Our way of life was threatened now more than ever, and it was because we checked out.

I wasn't numb anymore and I wouldn't let myself sink into the bayou and disappear like the rest of our legacy.

Now I had a plan. Not a great one—I was learning that planning wasn't one of my strengths—but hopefully it would get us all through the full moon.

I'd convinced Cady to move in with me—temporarily. Then my brothers and I would take care of the pack by whatever means necessary and make things safe for Cady again. By that point she would be so hopelessly in love with me that she would sell her house and stay here with me forever.

Only after my confrontation with Saul tonight, because I hadn't managed to pencil in a fight with my brother, admitting to Cady that I was a werewolf, and hiding stolen money all into a twenty-four-hour window.

My eyes danced to the bag sitting on the floorboard of the passenger seat. I considered digging a hole between two cypress trees behind the house and burying the money there but that was too long term. I had no intention of keeping it, so I needed it to be accessible.

The boat garage, then. Even my brothers didn't go in there much. The original Barbeaux barn was on Saul's portion of the homestead, and we stored the most used equipment there.

I didn't put it in the gun locker. That seemed too obvious. So did hiding it on the boat. In the end I opted for an old trash barrel, stuffed with decaying alfalfa. I quit keeping rabbits because Saul kept killing them in the middle of the night—another warning sign that hadn't seemed that serious before—and the hay would go to waste anyway.

Evening came fast, the time whizzing by as I worked. My house was relatively clean—hard to dirty it when I scarcely lived there for the last few weeks—but I wanted to make sure there would be no weird surprises. Decades as a bachelor made me blind to certain habits that might scare a woman off.

Next came the hard part. Rich, golden light poured through the trees as the sun came to rest on the horizon. Another hour and it would be dark. A handful more and the moon would be out. Still, Isaac was nowhere to be found.

His house sat empty and untouched as I rolled up on his driveway. The modern-looking monstrosity was sleek and square, it's massive floor to ceiling windows reflecting the sunset from the second floor. The bevel siding had a reddish tone that was as glossy as the first day Isaac finished the place.

There was maintaining your home so it was livable and then there was doing it like Isaac. My brother didn't just care about the inside being neat. He went to lengths most people would consider obsessive to keep his home spotless and fresh. I wasn't clear if he liked things to look expensive and new or if he was just that much of a control freak.

Which was why the smattering of dandelions sprouting along the concrete under the stilted house was concerning. When I opened the door to the utility room to grab the spare key for upstairs, I found clothing still in the dryer. Isaac didn't tolerate weeds or wrinkles.

He and Jacques were a lot alike, now that I thought about it. Isaac always hated farm chores and only went fishing when he wanted to eat fish, not because it was relaxing. He couldn't stand the suffocating atmosphere of a big city—our kind never could—but he wanted to live like city folks did. Nice clothes, fancy cars, expensive dinners.

Saul put the brakes on that lifestyle, where he could. No fancy cars because they called attention to us. No nice clothes when we were out and about in town. Isaac agreed, grudgingly. He knew Saul was right.

Ten years ago, the Barbeaux homestead almost ceased to be. We pulled ourselves up by our bootstraps like every other hardworking man in this town, but it wouldn't do to flaunt the wealth we accrued. Just another way to attract scrutiny.

Isaac's old fashioned answering machine flashed red on the black granite countertop. I wouldn't invade his privacy and play the messages, but it wasn't like him not to have checked them. The landline he kept was the only way for his real estate contacts to reach him and their calls were usually urgent.

I stepped through the living room, circling black leather couches and stepping down the hall. The office was empty, the curtains drawn. The beds were made in both the master and the guest room, not a wrinkle in sight. I couldn't quite see the dust collecting on the surfaces, but I felt it settling over me as I moved through the hauntingly empty space.

A stone sank in my stomach. Isaac spent a lot of time off the bayou these days, but he should be home by now. He knew the risk of being too far from home when the moon rose.

Saul was gone too when I drove down the road. I knew better than to let myself into his tiny one-bedroom cabin. If

Saul was awake, he wasn't inside. Instinctively I reached for the new cell phone in my drink holder, only to remember Cady's was the sole number in there. That would need to be remedied. Isaac wouldn't be able to disappear on us as easily if he was a phone call away.

Saul needed to keep in touch too.

After almost an hour of driving up and down the bayou, hunting for my big brother, I decided to call it quits and head home. Dusk was fading into darkness, and I didn't want to run over a deer because I was too eager to talk. Saul would call for me when the moon was up, and I would be compelled to answer. Talking would have to be saved for the morning.

It was probably better to speak with Saul after he had a chance to run off his aggression anyway.

I was just pulling back into the driveway when my cell phone rang. Goosebumps prickled up my arms and I reached for it too quickly, dropping it on the floorboard before snatching it back up and whipping it open. Only one person with my cell phone number and very few reasons for her to be calling now.

Shouldn't have left her alone.

"Cady?" I couldn't draw anymore words out of my tight throat.

"Eli?" My name was a choked sob. "I need your help."

Chapter 25

Ambush

Cady

THE LAST TIME I used this suitcase was when I took a trip to Chicago to tour the campus at my dream school. It was my first and only time traveling alone. Now here I was packing it again so I could move in with a man I met a month ago.

A man I met when he killed two people.

A man I was crazy about.

More than once I paused, folded clothes hovering over the suitcase as I questioned my situation. Was there some kind of Stockholm syndrome for rescuers? What if everything I felt for Eli was born from him saving me and it wasn't real?

And then I would ask myself, *what if this is how fate works?* Taking the very worst moments in my life and using them to stitch together the very best. Somehow, I knew future moments with Eli would be the ones I treasured forever.

So yeah, I was crazy about him and also just plain crazy.

A gentle knock echoed from the front door, and I stilled with a half-folded sweater in my hands. Yesterday, I would have smiled privately, thinking Eli had come to back with disgusting sandwiches from the *Stop N' Shop*. Today I knew he wouldn't knock because I dropped a key in his palm before kissing him goodbye.

He'd been vague about when he would be back, mumbling about preparing his brothers for company—even though they each owned their own home—and telling me not to leave my gun out of reach.

My hands shook as I reached for the gun tucked safely in a holster at the small of my back. Concealed carrying my SIG was Eli's idea and I was suddenly immensely grateful to know it was right there. My fingers wrapped around the warm metal, but I didn't draw. Opening the front door with a gun in my hand wasn't necessarily a wise idea.

I clicked off the bedroom light and started down the hallway. I was halfway there when the deadbolt shifted from its locked position. There was a scraping sound on the other side of the door, not a key being inserted but similar. My stomach curdled with fear, and I dove for the corner table by the couch, tucking my knees to my chest and watching as my front door creaked open.

A set of heavy black boots stepped into view. Whoever it was made an attempt at stealth, but their choice of shoe combined with their size was making it difficult. I ducked my head as low as I could manage, trying to peer up at the intruder.

Long legs in denim. The hem of a black shirt. A gun holstered on a hip.

A gun.

Though my heart was beating wildly in my ears, I forced myself to think.

Okay, the gun was holstered so whoever it was didn't intend to shoot me. Not immediately, anyway. Were they here to kidnap me again? I craned my neck, trying to judge if it could be Louis from the bar. If he knew I didn't have the money, then the only reason he would show up was to kill me.

"Cady? You in here?" A familiar timbre but not familiar enough that I immediately recognized it. The blood rushing in my ears distorted it too much.

"C'mon bitch, I saw your light on." Ricky Holt. It had to be.

Ricky? What was he—

Everything happened at lightning speed. Hands gripped my shoulders and yanked me out from under the table, scraping my back against it until I cried out. My right hand reached behind me even as Ricky dragged me, fingers fumbling for my gun.

At the last minute, I changed directions, grabbing instead for the baseball bat I kept by the couch. The handle almost slipped through my grasp as it clunked clumsily under the table, but I managed to haul it up with my body.

In one motion I wrenched my torso free and swung. My full strength was behind the bat as it came around to catch Ricky in the side of the head. His body seemed to move in slow motion. His eyes fluttered and knees buckled, a marionette with snapped strings. I stared wide-eyed and frozen at the crumpled man on my floor.

Crumpled Sheriff's deputy. Shit. This was not good.

I waited far too long, expecting Ricky to spring back up like a cartoon villain. He didn't move and then I was squinting at his chest and trying to judge if he was breathing.

Calm down, Cady. Calm down.

I was not calming down.

In a panicked flurry I rushed to the front door and twisted the dead bolt, hoping whatever Ricky did to it wouldn't render it useless. Then I fumbled for my phone and dialed. I didn't have to think, didn't even question the choice. I just punched in the newly programmed number and immediately felt a hint of relief knowing I could reach him.

It barely had a chance to ring. The gruff concern on the line broke the last of my composure and tears burned down my cheeks.

"Eli," I sobbed. "I need your help."

I DIDN'T DARE MOVE from my post in the living room where Holt's body was heaped on the floor. I also didn't stoop to adjust his legs even though they were bent horribly. He wasn't dead. I was pretty sure, anyway. But I had no idea how badly someone was injured if they didn't wake up from a blow to the head.

His brain could be bleeding and a quick call to 911 would save his life.

Why was he breaking into my house, though? Not dressed as a deputy and certainly not acting like one. I chewed my lip to the point of soreness, replaying my encounter with Holt when I tried to report my kidnapping. At the time, the shocked look on his face seemed fitting. A small town like Port O'Henry didn't get many middle-of-the-night reports of *anything* except drinking and driving.

Now I had to wonder if he looked so shocked because he expected me to be dead.

Ricky made a noise and I jumped, raising the bat in preparation to whack him again if he sat up. The only thing keeping me from completely flipping out was the knowledge that Eli would be here any minute.

"I'm coming. Get your gun and wait for me." He promised over the roar of his truck engine. "I'm coming."

He was there when I needed him.

No questions.

No hesitation.

Whatever happened after this, I picked him. Despite his past and every dark thing he'd done, I would be there for him too.

"Cady?" A scream caught in my throat when Eli flung the door open.

Hand over my heart, I gasped out, "I'm so sorry. I didn't know who else to call. I didn't know what to do."

Eli eyed Ricky as he stepped carelessly over his body and engulfed me in the warmest hug. He turned so that his gaze stayed on Holt, running a soothing hand down my back. "I shouldn't have left you alone. Not for a minute."

"You didn't know this would happen."

He dropped his arms to my shoulders, running eyes and hands all over me. "He touch you?" Then his eyes widened, and he asked, "Did you shoot him?"

"No and no." I resisted the urge to huddle back in his arms. There was an unconscious man on the floor, and we needed to deal with him.

"Why the hell not?" Eli demanded, patting my back for my gun, and scowling when he found it holstered there.

"Because he's a deputy!" I flung my arm in Holt's direction. "And I'm positive the Sheriff is in on this too." I rubbed my forearms, trying to calm down before I started shaking like a chihuahua. "Plus, I was worried that if I shot him and somehow our whole under the table investigation came into question, they might find out what you did on the bayou."

The surprise was evident on his face, but he nodded as if that was the answer he'd been hoping for. "Good girl. That was smart." He cupped my cheek, drawing a thumb over my chin and murmuring, "You okay, darlin'?"

"I think so." I let my eyes flutter closed, breathing deeply as his warm fingertips grounded me.

"I'm sorry I wasn't here."

"You have your own life outside of me."

"I should have seen this coming. He was obviously watching your house and waiting to see me leave."

My insides felt cold and clammy. Eli hadn't left since before our trip to the bar, where we met Louis. Did he have someone watching us that whole time?

"What do we do now?"

"Now you let me handle it."

Chapter 26

Against the Clock

Eli

"**Y**OU CAN'T KILL HIM."

I almost bared my teeth at Cady. My instincts were already humming from the approaching moonlight and the adrenal spike from her panicked phone call wasn't helping. Now she wanted me to spare the asshole that meant to take her or worse? Yeah, the beast wasn't going to go for that.

"Then what do you suggest I do?"

My tone made her flinch and I wanted to reach out, using touch to soothe her, but I knew better than to give in. I was too hot, my skin prickling with the inevitable change, and the only thing I wanted to taste more than blood was the honey between her legs. Monsters didn't care about inappropriate timing when it came to desire.

Outside the stars were emerging, the moon rising high with her full girth on display. Tension had my muscles jumping and twitching. The wolf wanted out and he wanted out soon. All the feral energy that was usually pumping through my veins on the full moon increased tenfold when Cady was close.

"I don't know," she mumbled, huddling in on herself as I moved erratically around the room.

A few laps of pacing bought me a plan. This had better be the last fucking plan I had to come up with for a decade.

"Get me that bottle of gin from the pantry."

Twenty minutes later I was hauling a disarmed and disgusting Holt down the stairs. His feet dragged against every step.

My hope was that anyone witnessing the scene would assume Holt was drunk. The half-gallon of gin poured down the front of his shirt would help if someone approached.

It was a quiet Tuesday evening in Port O'Henry and most of the houses had the blue buzz of TV light visible through the window, if there were lights inside at all. No cars passed as I hoisted Holt into the passenger side of my car and buckled him in.

When I searched the man, I found handcuffs in his pockets. That almost provoked me to snap Holt's neck then and there. I resisted because it was another nightmare Cady didn't need to have. If—when—I killed this bastard, it would be out on the bayou where no one would ever find him.

"Where are you going to take him?" Cady worried her lip as I climbed behind the wheel of the truck. Time was not on my side, and I was struggling to be patient with her fussing. I wanted to just toss the man in the river and let him become gator chow.

"The bayou." When her eyes rounded, I added, "To the boat garage. Just until we can come up with a better plan and get you safe."

"Now you're the kidnapper."

"Darlin'." I infused as much calm into my voice as I could, knowing it was bordering on a growl. "These are desperate times. I'm going to do whatever it takes to protect you." I gripped the front of her sweater and pulled her against the door of the truck for a quick, hard kiss. "Go upstairs and lock the door. Keep your gun on you. If anyone but me comes to that door, shoot them. Don't worry about the consequences for me. Just pull that trigger."

The moment Cady closed her front door I peeled out and booked it back to the bayou. This was a disaster. I had no idea what the hell I was going to say if I ran into Saul while I was hauling an unconscious man into the boat garage. As if Saul wouldn't notice his scent the moment we stepped onto my property.

I would just have to corral him toward his house tonight.

My brothers being MIA was beginning to seem like a blessing. The bayou was quiet as I parked on my driveway for the second time, all the usual players in the midnight orchestra hiding from the snapping cold.

I wasn't gentle with Holt when I dragged him to my garage. If he woke up with bruised knees and scraped up arms, it was the least he deserved. I dropped his limp body unceremoniously on the concrete while I gathered my supplies. Two minutes later he had a boat chain around his ankles, multiple combination locks holding it in place. The other end of the chain was looped around the metal worktable. Sucker was heavy and even if Holt woke and managed to move it, he couldn't get past the boat trailers. As a finishing touch I locked his wrists in his own handcuffs.

Even though he wasn't awake to see me, I let the first hints of change roll over my face, peeling my lips back in a vicious snarl. He would only live through tonight because he might have answers for me.

Jacques liked to use humans to do his dirty work. I still wasn't clear if my cousin was alive so I would assume this was Louis, having learned all of Jacques' worst habits. If Cady was right and both the Sheriff and his deputies were involved, I might have a lot more humans to worry about. Killing an off-duty deputy after he broke into Cady's house was one thing. Disappearing the Sheriff came with more complications than I could handle on my own.

For now, I was only making a list. Holt was number one and he would tell me every other name to put on it until not a single rat in this town was safe from me. Cady wasn't going to be happy, but the only real solution was killing the guy. And anyone that thought they could get their hands on her.

A growl rose in my chest, violent and full of rage.

Even though the threat was at my feet, I couldn't shake the feeling that Cady was still in immediate danger. The moon was calling to me, but her silvery song wasn't nearly as strong as the call to protect my mate.

Leaving the bayou and going back to her now was risky. Too risky.

I was trapped. I couldn't bring her here to witness what would happen tonight. I couldn't leave her to fend for herself while I was unreachable. I couldn't go back to her and stay, knowing I would be an unstoppable force of violence, a caged animal finally freed, in a mere hour or less.

I would never hurt her, I knew that down to my bones, but I understood I could do damage that wasn't physical. No matter how infatuated Cady was with me, the shock of seeing me change would terrify her without preparation.

And the hunter needed to run. To spill blood. It wouldn't do for me to bust through Cady's window and haunt the town with my presence.

I told myself that, even as I twisted the key in the ignition and kicked the parking brake off the truck.

FEAR. THE ENTIRE LIVING room was clouded with the heady scent. Even as it ignited my vicious urge to protect *mine*, it also excited my predatory senses. Cady was a new kind of prey, and I would thoroughly enjoy chasing her down.

The moon was tugging me inside out like another wave in the tide. I wasn't myself and the moment Cady looked up from where she stood sentinel in her living room, gun in hand, she knew it. Her eyes glistened, deep and blue as the midnight bay, questioning.

"I didn't think you were coming back tonight. What happened? Where's Holt?"

The part of me that was rogue and feral didn't grasp that Cady wasn't in on the secret. She couldn't possibly understand what was happening. In that way, I failed her. Deceived her.

That deception was the reason she was almost taken from me tonight. She should be safe in my bed, waiting for me to crawl under the sheets in the early hours of the morning to sate the last of my wolfish appetite with my mouth on her skin.

Mouth on her skin. That sounded like an excellent idea.

I prowled across the living room, my feet carrying me without my command. They were my own and yet not. The beast reigned on this night, the twisted, trapped spirit of the hunter ravenous for freedom. Most days he pounded against my skin in futility, my will over him like a steel cage. There were moments where I slipped—when I was threatened or when I slept—but never enough to do any real damage.

That was because there was never anything he wanted enough. Not until Cady.

"Eli? What are you doing?"

Cady was speaking but I couldn't hear her over the rambling madness of the beast in my head. Her expression was timid and searching as I took the gun from her hand and pulled her to me roughly.

"Your face..." She scanned my features, trying to understand what she was seeing. She wouldn't. Not until she knew the full truth. The shift hadn't taken hold of me, not in any definable way, but my eyes were bright. I could feel them burning with moon fire.

"Tomorrow," I promised her in a husky whisper. "All of your answers. Tomorrow."

That was enough for her. She dipped her chin, allowing me to draw her closer. When my lips nibbled at her jaw she sighed, the fear and tension in her muscles evaporating under my touch.

My skin tingled. My neck flushed with the heat of need. I didn't know much about bonds, but it was clear that Cady was becoming an addiction. Each taste left me hungrier, needing more.

And every time she touched me it felt better than the last. Already I was overcome with desire, a panting animal ready to drop down onto my knees and worship her.

The same hungry longing reflected on her face when she whispered, "I don't understand this. How you make me feel."

It's the bond, I almost told her. *You're mine and you can feel it.*

But I couldn't form the words. There was no time left. I shouldn't be here. The first tendrils of change were coiled in my muscles, the beast straining for his release. All that came was, "You're mine."

She rose on her toes and drew my bottom lip into her mouth, suckling gently and tracing back and forth with her tongue. "I know."

I had no control over myself and still, I was gentle with her. Careful as I carried her to the bedroom and wordlessly undressed her.

This is how a bond is made whole, I thought. My hands climbed up her legs, gripping her calf and bringing her ankle up to my lips. Her breasts rose with every rapid breath, and she bared herself to me as I climbed onto the bed. Another kiss for her ankle and then I was moving upward, trailing my way across her delicious skin until I found her core. The scent of her arousal sent me into a frenzy.

I dropped my head between her legs and inhaled deeply, a vibrating growl in my chest as my tongue darted out to taste her. That one draw of my tongue was enough to send her hips off the bed, a cry on her lips. She gripped the bed sheets, and

I growled harder, lapping at her wetness. Cady writhed under my attention until she was begging me.

"So close, Eli. Please," she panted. "Please."

My mouth closed over her clit with a possessive graze of my teeth, and she moaned long and low. I indulged her, nibbling and sucking until Cady's hips danced beneath my mouth, thighs caging my face. When I added to the sensation, slipping a finger inside of her, a whimper told me exactly how close she was to climax. Her thighs gave one final squeeze around my head and then her limbs went soft, dropping limply beside her.

Supple fingers smoothed through my hair, and I was tempted to purr. The sated look on her face was my favorite expression that she wore and if not for the other need that was humming in my chest, I would have stayed there all night, devouring her.

I circled my hands around her thighs and tugged her to me. At the same time Cady shifted down the bed. We met in the middle, my cock gliding through her juices and into her with no resistance. Utter perfection. There would never be another for me. This was it. Cady was all I would crave for as long as I lived.

"Cady," I snarled.

She lifted her head, an impatient frown furrowing her brow. "What's wrong?"

My thumb made teasing, light circles over her clit and she huffed. "Tell me."

"Tell you what?"

"That you're mine."

Indecision flickered in her blue eyes as she blinked at me. Then her teeth grazed her bottom lip and she smiled at me so wickedly, it was like she knew she had my heart in her hands. "I'm yours, Eli."

With a victorious rumble I pounded into her. "Again."

She moaned it this time, reaching for me in a desperate bid for more. "I'm yours."

I gave her more. "You are *mine*."

"I am," she gasped.

My hips pumped faster. Too fast. I wasn't going to last but I couldn't stop myself. The moon whispered to me. I was out of time, and I had to have her.

"Cady," I snarled her name as I tipped over the edge of maddening pleasure, marking her.

Claiming her.

Cady clamped around me as she followed on a second wave of ecstasy, drawing a shudder from me. Her heart raced at a rabbit pace, and I listened raptly. This was the rhythm that would lead every step I took from now until forever. I burrowed my face between her breasts. I would make a home here if I could.

"You came," Cady murmured, her fingers gliding through my damp hair.

"That's kind of the point, isn't it, darlin'?"

She slapped my arm with a scoff. Then that quavering, fearful note returned to her voice. "When I needed you. I called and you came."

I freed myself from between her legs and took her into my arms, stroking the side of her cheek. "You're mine, Cady. I take care of what's mine."

"I wasn't sure you meant it."

I dragged an unconscious man to my garage and locked him up for interrogation and she wasn't sure I meant it? I found her eyes in the dim room. "You call and I'll come running."

"Does that make you mine, too?"

"Completely." Indelibly. Irrevocably. Even if tomorrow, she decided this wasn't for her after all.

Cady kissed me, soft and at ease for the first time since she called earlier tonight. The kiss ended with a sigh, the last noise she made before she was dozing. As much as I wanted to lie there and watch over her, I couldn't last another minute. Fur prickled along my skin and pressure began to build in my chest. It would be a miracle if I made it to the bayou.

I dressed as quietly as I could. I hated leaving Cady. Felt sick to my stomach locking her door and sneaking down the stairs to my truck. But I hadn't planned this right. I didn't give myself long enough to figure out what to say to Cady or my brothers.

So, I ran away. Faster than was safe or legal, I bumped onto the bayou road for the third time since that afternoon. My hands ached on the steering wheel and my spine burned. The agony of the change was momentary.

If I didn't fight it.

In that moment I was fighting it with everything I had, teeth gnashing to keep from shifting behind the wheel. I was almost on the snaking gravel driveway when I lost the fight.

The trucked jolted as I slammed into park and threw myself from the driver's side. I hunched forward and clothing ripped along the seams, my body transforming under the pearlescent light flowing down from directly overhead.

Then Eli was gone, the hunter in his place, and he flooded the night with his battle cry.

Chapter 27

Hunter's Moon

Eli

A HOWL SLICED THE stillness of midnight, and I raised my head to answer it. My brother summoned me.

I obeyed, leaping over tree roots, and crossing rivulets that ran to the bay. Saul waited in the moonlight, a shadow come to life. He was as black as pitch and his eyes glittered the same color as the moon overhead. Together we ran, calling and calling for Isaac.

Saul and I covered the bayou. We slunk near the homes scattered about the perimeter, watching for any signs of life. The rights to this property didn't belong to us any longer. Didn't matter. This town would always be Barbeaux territory. We would die here before we gave it up.

Hunting on the bayou was harder now than it had ever been. Generations of deer had come to know the unique dangers the Barbeaux wolves posed, and they were skittish. During some moon runs we resorted to catching smaller prey—nutria and possums and whatever else wasn't fast enough. Once Saul had even taken on a gator during a particularly aggressive night.

Tonight, Saul ignored game trails and fresh spoor. His pace was almost punishing as we ran the border of our territory, marking it and checking for trespassers. It was only when we neared my property line that I tasted blood in the air.

The light over the door to my utility room glowed yellow, illuminating the concrete beneath the stilts of the house. There was nothing obviously amiss, but I couldn't shake the sick feeling in my gut.

Saul was unreadable as he found his place in the shadows of my porch and quietly shifted back into his tall, sturdy frame. Whatever emotion he was experiencing was cold—so frigid I shivered as he fixed his sights on me.

White fire burned in his eyes. "Where were you?"

I arched my back, stretching the pain of my own shift from my muscles. "Running."

"Don't lie to me, Elijah!" He boomed. "Were you with her when you changed? *Does she know?*"

"You know I wouldn't tell her without talking to you. I came to see you this afternoon and you were gone."

"You're not going to see this woman again."

I stormed my brother with a snarl. "I bonded to her, Saul! She's mine."

Horror flickered across his face. "No, you didn't." He stomped around the side of the house, grabbing something heavy and dumping at it my feet. It was Holt's body, bloody and mauled to pieces. "What kind of trouble are you in, Eli? You going to die for this woman?"

I came nose to nose with Saul, chest out and teeth bared. That was a threat if I'd ever heard one. "If that's what it takes."

"So be it."

Saul's shift was fluid, his body gliding from man to wolf in a matter of seconds. I reacted quick but Saul was quicker. My brother caught me by the nape and wrenched backward. My legs splayed out beneath me, wobbly as they transformed. When I finally got to my feet Saul was there, fangs gleaming with deadly intent.

So, this was how it would be. Brother against brother. Saul so fixated on guarding our way of life that he would sooner kill me than allow me to bond.

It wasn't a fair fight. Saul was the first born; the Barbeaux alpha. Even if he would never claim that title, he was stronger, faster, and more vicious than any other of his kind.

In other words, if he wanted to kill me, he could.

And as we clashed over Holt's broken body, jaws snapping and teeth tearing into hunks of flesh, I began to think Saul *did* want to kill me. We fought on occasion and sometimes it turned violent. Never like this.

Saul was out for blood.

I ducked, twisted, pivoted, and dodged. The blows I landed were surface level. Didn't matter how deeply Saul sank his teeth into my flank. I wouldn't retaliate. This was wrong and I could only hope my brother would snap out of it.

With a shove Saul knocked me back. My hind legs skidded on the gravel, and I lost my footing. In an instant he was there, maw locked around my throat in a finishing move. I panted up at those familiar eyes, like thunder clouds over the water, dark and ominous and endless. There was so much rage in those eyes. Rage and agony.

How did I miss it? Saul was in pain, a deep wound that was eating at his soul. The years had hollowed him out and now he was a ghost of the brother I knew.

I'm sorry, brother. I'm sorry I didn't see it sooner.

A figure crashed into Saul, sending both of us sliding across the gravel. I leapt to my feet and prepared for another blow. What I wasn't expecting was the blow to be in the form of a fist.

"What the fuck is going on here?"

I sprawled flat on my back, fur receding as the moonlight faded and the hunter slithered from my skin. My own face stared down at me. The reflection was distorted, jaw too narrow, cheek bones sharper, tan skin clean shaven and smooth, and I realized it wasn't my face at all.

Isaac glared, his usually sleek hair out of place and dangling over his forehead. He was naked as the day we were born, his face filthy. Saul crouched behind him, a snarl still lifting his lip. Recognition gleamed in his eyes and the snarl died. Saul collapsed under the force of the hunter leaving him.

Unlike us, Saul could become the hunter at will, not dependent on the draw of the moon. The disadvantage was that his changes were excruciating, and they took an enormous amount of energy. The day after the full moon he would disappear into his cabin and sleep until the next sunset.

Hopefully, that meant he was too tired to keep murdering me.

"I leave you assholes alone for one full moon and you try to kill each other?" Isaac reached into the utility room and grabbed a handful of denim from the basket of spares I kept on top of the washer, tossing jeans at each brother before tugging on his own.

"Where have you been?" Saul snapped. "Both of you! This is unacceptable."

"Sorry, daddy, I didn't mean to break curfew." Isaac rolled his eyes. "I think you're the one that has some explaining to do, Kujo."

"Here's the cliff notes: I bonded, and Saul took that personally, so he decided to kill me. But only after killing this asshole!" I jabbed an accusing finger at Saul. "This asshole who's a Sheriff's deputy, by the way. He had information I needed."

"Yeesh, I didn't notice the dead guy." Isaac kicked a bloody hand with his bare foot. "Maybe we should call a truce and grab a beer. Sounds like we have a lot to talk about."

Saul's jaw dropped. "Are you fucking crazy? You had a Sheriff's deputy chained up in your garage? He was moaning for help. I heard him clear across the bayou."

Isaac made a disgusted face and sidestepped the body. "Christ, remind me never to ask you for *help*, Saul."

"There's nothing else to talk about. Body goes in the bayou. Eli cuts this woman off. That's the end of it."

Both Isaac and I gaped at him. "Did you mishear? Eli *bond-ed*. You know what happens when you *cut it off*."

"I'm not going to argue—"

"No, you're not, because Cady is non-negotiable. She's on the radar of a pack modeled after Jacques' and she has no idea what she's up against. I'm going to get her right now and I'm telling her everything." I pointed at the dozen bleeding wounds across my chest and neck. "Unless you want to finish what you started."

"What makes you think there's a new pack?" Saul was as stubborn as stone. "This is probably just about drugs. Same as it's always been."

"Au contraire, big brother. Eli's right and I have proof." Isaac put a hand up to cut Saul off before he could disagree. "Jacques is in Texas again."

I cocked a brow at Saul. "I thought you said Jacques was dead."

"Dead?" Isaac looked genuinely shocked. "He can't be dead. I spoke to him today.

Chapter 28

Old Friends

Cady

A SHAPE MOVED IN the shadow of the bedroom, and I bolted upright. "Eli?"

It was unusually dark, and my eyes were struggling to focus. A shiver had me tugging the sheets tighter around me. Eli was so warm, and I wished he would come back to bed.

The figure moved again, and I called out, "Eli, you're scaring me."

Feet clacked on the wood floor and the hulking shape moved closer to the bed. The familiar dusted copper of Eli's eyes shone through the darkness but there was something off about them. The angles of his face were all wrong and he was hovering too tall over the bed.

Then he sprang up onto the mattress and pinned me. Those eyes were his eyes, but the face was animal, a monstrous wolf on the shoulders of a man. I'd seen this creature before. A walking nightmare that stalked the bayou.

His mouth was inches from me, breath hot. I peered up at him, a feeling of recognition coming over me.

"Cady."

I startled awake, yanking the covers up to my breasts and expecting to find Eli beside me. But it wasn't Eli's voice speaking into the quiet of my bedroom.

"I'm sorry, Cady. It's not personal."

The first thing I noticed was the barrel of a gun gleaming in the silver rays of moonlight that spilled through the blinds.

From there I travelled up to the terrible, familiar face that was glaring down at me.

Suddenly I was remembering bike rides along the beach, following the cracked asphalt to the jetty and back. There was a troop of us, mostly boys and most a few years older than me. Riding bikes was one of the only safe activities we had in a town this small.

Brandon was older so my grandparents let me go out with him and his friends, trusting him to be the responsible chaperone. I was eleven, maybe twelve, when I became too childish, and his friends complained about me following them like a duckling. Ricky Holt was one of those friends. I saw him clearly, making duck lips at me and shooing me away.

They were always close, weren't they? Even after the party incident, Brandon and Ricky were thick as thieves. It made sense that Brandon was here to kill me, then. If Ricky was going to rope someone into this, it would be Brandon.

"You never could resist peer pressure," I chided.

My false bravado wouldn't save my life, but it felt better. I was so sick and tired of being afraid. I had no plan to leave this earth cowering.

I didn't have to check the other side of the bed to know Eli was gone.

I was going to die alone.

That should have sent me into a tailspin of anxiety. I fought so hard to live these last few weeks. I guess I was desensitized to it all now, my insides oddly numb. No fear tickled through my legs, no sadness pooling in my middle.

There was a quiet, cold kind of rage building there instead. Some fury that had been incubating since that night on the bayou, ready to hatch into a storm of violence.

I casually glanced to the nightstand in search of my gun.

"I took it," Brandon said helpfully. "You should get dressed."

"Does it matter at this point?"

He looked pained but it didn't carry to his voice when he snapped. "I'm not hauling you naked into my truck. Get dressed. I waited days for that Barbeaux asshole to leave and now I'm almost out of time."

So, I was being kidnapped again. Fan-fucking-tastic. "Where are you taking me?"

The gun barrel came level with my face. "Get your damn clothes on." Then to himself he muttered, "should have known Holt was too chicken shit for this."

I stood on sturdy legs, reaching for my sweater and leggings without taking my eyes off Brandon. "Actually, he's dead."

"What?"

"Yeah, Holt showed up here hours ago. Eli killed him." My eyes thinned to slits and I showed my teeth as I said, "Eli's going to kill you too, when he finds out what you did."

It wasn't a threat. It was a promise. Eli wouldn't be here to save me this time, but when I was gone, I knew without a doubt he would make everyone who hurt me pay. He was loyal like that.

"Eli Barbeaux is going to kill me?" His pitch rose. "He can get in line. I've got another Barbeaux ready to take my head off if I don't deliver you before sunrise."

I paused with one arm through my sweater sleeve. "Eli's cousin?" What was his name? "Jacques?"

"How do you know him?"

"He hired someone to feed me to alligators."

Brandon scowled. "Are you dealing for him too?"

"Do I look like a lowlife piece of trash?"

"Easy for you to say. You've always had everything, Cady. Got your grandparents house, got their money. What would you know about being desperate?"

I yanked the sweater down over my head. "I grew up here, same as you, Brandon. I know what it's like to fight for every penny. Difference between you and me is that I have a con-

science. I would never make a living off the suffering of others."

He laughed bitterly. "That's rich from someone that worked
for one of the most notorious drug smugglers in the county."

"I didn't know Barlow was a criminal!" I shouted. "Now get
this over with or give me my gun back so I can shoot you."

"It's not personal, bush cricket," he said quietly, handing me
a pair of handcuffs and gesturing for me to put them on.

"Shut up! This is *my life* we're talking about. That's pretty
fucking personal." I snapped the metal handcuffs over my
wrist, trying to make them as loose as possible. Pointless since
Brandon reached his gun-free hand out and tightened them
until I winced.

The entire time he was adjusting the cuffs and threatening
to gag me, I watched the front door. The hope that Eli would
come charging through and rescue me—again—died a little
more with each minute that ticked by.

Guess this time I would have to rescue myself.

In the end, Brandon did slap layers of duct tape over my
mouth. Smart, because I intended to start screaming as soon
as we stepped out the front door.

That plan was foiled, and my only option was to thrash
violently as soon as Brandon holstered his gun. I figured he
wasn't going to shoot me regardless since Louis or Jacques or
whoever wanted me alive, but I also didn't want to risk a bullet
to the chest. Once he was unarmed, I fought like a wildcat.

I jerked my cuffed arms away from him, kicking and shoving
with all my might. My foot smashed his knee and we both
went down. Brandon collapsed on top of me, knocking the
wind from me and making it nearly impossible to crawl across
the floor. He recovered quickly and before I knew it, I had my
ankles taped together. It was too tight and the adhesive tore
at my skin as I writhed. Brandon didn't care.

I did my best to look vicious as Brandon tossed me in the
backseat of his truck. I wanted him to feel pure terror, to

believe that I would rain hell down on him the moment I was free.

And if I didn't live to see the sunrise? Eli would do it for me.

The first time I was kidnapped all I could think about was survival. My mind was a panicked mess. Now the approaching situation wasn't so unknown, and I felt resigned to it. At the very least I would die defiant to these assholes.

A sliver of that delayed sadness cut through my rage. To die when I was only just beginning to live again was tragic. As crazy as it was, I saw a life with Eli. I imagined myself watching the sunset over the bayou, pen in hand as I scribbled out lines in my journal. He would come home from a day of chartering tourists around and smile at me with all that southern charm and life would be perfect.

Too perfect, it would seem.

Brandon dumped me in the backseat of his truck, then disappeared up the stairs and back into my house. If the plan was to steal any valuables on his way out, he had nothing but disappointment coming. The only true valuable still left in that house besides my six-year-old laptop and my Nana's wedding band was the house itself. Even the TV was gone after I pawned it for spare cash last month.

Minutes later he climbed behind the wheel, carrying a stink with him that I couldn't quite place with bitter adhesive right under my nose. He glanced at me in the rearview and I spewed curses at him. Even if the words were muffled, he knew what I was saying.

I half expected Brandon to drive us down one of the old bayou roads. Instead, we passed it, driving along the perimeter of the bay toward the oldest neighborhoods in Port O'Henry. This didn't look good for me. The last time I was in old town I found a dead man in an abandoned house. My breath seized in my lungs until we passed the Cray homestead and continued toward the old pier.

Dark buildings dotted barren concrete lots, remnants of the boat launches and businesses that were taken out by Hurricane Harriet in '53. Some of the properties were surrounded by barbed wire fences—purchased by hopeful investors that saw the swell of tourism as an opportunity to renew old Port O'Henry—but most were wide open.

Concrete buildings stared at me with eyes made of shattered windows. Their desolate faces were dark, and unwelcoming and I felt terror begin to churn in my belly like the black waves on the horizon.

An SUV waited where a dead end met a boat ramp. Wood from the crumbling pier was scattered about the road, carried back to land by the thrashing arms of an October storm. Two figures leaned on the side of the vehicle, their arms crossed and faces shadowed.

I promised myself two things as I was pulled ankle first from the backseat and dropped painfully onto the ground.

No matter how bad it got, I wouldn't beg this time.

And no matter what they did to me, I wasn't going to give them Eli or their Goddamned money.

Chapter 29

Blood Brothers

Eli

T HE STORM WAS OVER. A thunderous cloud clung heavily to Saul, but it was all shadow, no lightning. He was furious and he was exhausted. The latter would work in my favor. Unless he tried to kill me again in the next two minutes, I was going to get Cady and bring her home. Every second she was alone was a second she was in danger.

Isaac was mumbling some story to Saul about a girl and a phone call. A fresh wave of growls emanated from Saul, and I elbowed Isaac before he provoked the devil again.

"You can talk while I drive." I tugged a stray t-shirt over my head and waved toward the truck parked haphazardly at the end of my gravel driveway. The driver side door was still askew from when tumbled out mid-shift.

I wasn't keen on cramming Cady into a truck with three angry werewolves, but this Jacques business was important, and they would be on their best behavior once we left the bayou. Out on the water a real storm was brewing, and I wanted to return before the rain.

"What about the dead guy?" Isaac jerked a thumb at Holt.

"Dammit, Saul!"

"You put us all at risk by bringing him here. What would you have done if he escaped?" Saul's eyes flashed and he looked ready to fight again. It left him in a gusty breath, leaving nothing but an ancient weariness. "Get a tarp, Isaac. We'll put him in the water where that chunk of a gator has a nest. Bet she's hungry."

I couldn't help but wonder what Cady would think of this casual exchange as my brothers and I worked to discard a body. It was hard not to be blasé after decades of death. Under the right circumstances, it haunted me. Under the wrong ones, I almost enjoyed it.

Ricky Holt deserved to die. So did the men I killed on the bayou the night I met Cady. And so many more that wandered into this territory with ill intentions. They knew there were monsters on the bayou, and they showed up anyway, hungry for violence and chaos and a quick cash injection by any means necessary.

Picking off the weak ones was our job. Kept our home safe. Somewhere along the way we stopped doing that job and look at us now. Neck deep in shit because we hadn't been mucking it up.

As soon as Holt was dealt with, I hopped back in the truck, not bothering to check if his body sank. He could be discovered by some idiot kayaker that didn't think alligators would attack a boat and I didn't care. Clearly, he was mauled by an animal. Coroner would take one look at him, bloated with bayou water, and think he stumbled drunk into gator turf.

I had more important things to worry about.

"Get the fuck in the truck. Both of you!" I boomed at my dragging brothers. They were arguing under their breath and pointing at me. "Or I can leave you to walk home. I'm going to get my girl and I'm going now."

"You're seriously going to bring her here? And then what?" Saul crossed his arms.

"I tell her everything, ask her to stay, kill my asshole cousin, and live happily ever after."

"Works for me." Isaac clapped me on the back and shouted, "Shotgun!"

Saul took me by the arm before I could get behind the wheel. "You tell her about us, you might as well kill her yourself."

"Is that a threat?"

"No, Eli." I saw a crack in his ice wall then, a thin vein of sadness, burrowed deep. "She'll run. And if she doesn't, she won't survive a life like ours. We're *monsters*. We don't get to love precious things." That last earnest whisper was wrought with a heartbreak I didn't understand. There was so much I didn't understand about Saul anymore.

"Maybe that's how you see yourself, Saul, and I'm sorry for that." I gave his shoulder a quick squeeze. "I'm not a monster. I know that now."

How could I be when the most beautiful creature in all the world looked at me like I was a rising sun?

I did my best to explain what happened between Cady and me in the seven short minutes it took to reach her house. I could feel Saul seething more with every sentence, but I couldn't care less about my brother's bad mood. If he refused to make us a real pack and play alpha, he had no say over the mate I chose.

Hell, *I* didn't even have say over that, not really. When this anxious rage passed Saul would understand. Cady was going to make everything better for us.

I was getting to my explanation of the Holt situation when the words died in my throat. My hands dropped from the steering wheel and if Isaac hadn't grabbed it, the truck would have veered into a ditch.

The road to Cady's house was lit up in red and blue. Brighter still was the light coming from the fire roaring through her home, devouring it.

"No!" I flew from the truck and ran past the barrier created by emergency vehicles. I grabbed the first person I could find and demanded, "Is she in there?"

"Sir, you need to—"

"*Is she in there?*" I was shaking the man, a deputy, but I didn't care. Let them arrest me. Or whip their guns out and shoot me. It would be less painful than witnessing Cady's body turn to ash.

I studied every inch of the house with intent, ready to charge in there and find her, but the deck was already burning, and the top steps collapsed under the heat. No one was getting up there now.

I wasn't here. She needed me and I wasn't here.

"Take your hands off me!" The deputy ordered.

Saul and Isaac appeared, gripping me around the middle and hauling me back. More words were spraying from my lips, but I had no idea what I was saying anymore. My movements were violent as I fought against my brothers.

I left her. This is my fault.

I realized I was howling the words out loud, repeating to anyone that was listening, "This is my fault."

"Calm yourself and focus." Saul snarled in my ear. "You can't do this here."

Several uniformed men stood too close to me and my brothers, eyeing us with heavy suspicion. One was talking but I couldn't process any of it. Saul was speaking to me too, murmuring censure.

"That's his girlfriend's house," Isaac was explaining with his hands up in a peaceful gesture. "Give him a minute, please."

The deputy that I tackled didn't look pleased when he nodded, waving us back toward the Ford parked in the middle of the road. Saul pressed my back forcefully against the driver's door and I snarled. I was moments from going completely feral and tearing the world to pieces.

"She's not dead."

I pointed to the flames crackling angrily around the remains of Cady's house. "A human wouldn't survive that!" I dropped into a crouch and vomited between my feet. How could I leave her to die? I protected my secret instead of her.

"*Focus, Elijah.*" Saul commanded in an inhuman voice. "You're bonded. What do you feel?"

Grief. A fathomless black pit of grief.

I squeezed my eyes shut and obeyed Saul, swallowing my immediate pain and searching for that tether deep in my chest. At first, I felt only the erratic beat of my heart and the uncomfortable heat from the fire. A stormy wind was blowing in from the northeast and the icy teeth of that air shocked me back into my body enough to feel that strange second pulse I associated with Cady.

It scorched my insides, like the flames jumped from her house and into my chest. I hadn't realized I could sense her like this.

"She's alive." I barely dared to whisper it. "You're right. Cady's alive."

Saul didn't mirror my excitement. "So where is she?"

The momentary elation that floated me upright whipped out from under me and I would have stumbled if not for Isaac. My eyes instinctively scanned the crowd, expecting to see Cady standing among the onlookers.

Instead, I caught a flash of yellow eyes and a lupine grin. Louis waggled his fingers at me from an alcove under a neighboring house and climbed into a sleek black car, starting it up and pulling away before I could even process what I was seeing.

"Motherfucker!" I growled, hauling myself back into the truck and snapping for my brothers to do the same.

"Who is that?" Asked Saul.

"One of us."

"There are no other wolves in Port O'Henry."

Isaac looked like he was having a revelation in the passenger seat as I yanked the wheel and followed the vanishing headlights around another block. "Yes, there are. They've been right under our noses this whole time."

"That's what I've been trying to tell you." I shoved an accusing finger at Saul in the backseat. "While we've had our heads buried neck deep in the sand, Jacques has been organizing a new pack. Who knows how long they've been here, watching us and waiting for a chance to make a move."

Whatever they planned, it was personal. They took Cady because they wanted to hit me where it hurt most. Because I told them exactly who and what she was when I brought her to that bar.

Saul's steely eyes met mine in the rearview, his thoughts wandering to the same place. "You're going to lose him, Eli," he warned.

He was right but my truck couldn't take turns like the compact car in front of us and the bastard was weaving through neighborhoods, heading toward the main road out of Port O'Henry. When he found his exit, cutting past the liquor store and zooming through the gas station, Louis gunned it.

My booted foot slammed the accelerator at the same time, two wheels coming off the road as I twisted sharply to follow. A pitiful whine was coming from the engine when I pushed the old truck to its limit, but I didn't slow. Not as the road curved or a blinding pair of headlights zoomed past us.

Louis made a risky move and switched off his headlights, his black car almost invisible in the cloak of pre-dawn light. This was planned, a deliberate move to draw me out of Port O'Henry and further from Cady. She was back there somewhere. I couldn't scout the whole town looking for her. My only chance of finding her was disappearing like a phantom down a dark, rural road.

"Right! Eli, go right!" Isaac startled me with his sudden command, and I almost missed the gravel drive. Settling clouds of dust shone in the headlights, letting us know we were on the right trail. There was a game ranch somewhere around here and I was pretty sure this was one of the entrances. Which meant at this time of morning the gates would be locked up tight, Louis completely blocked in.

Sure enough, he was leaping from the car and bolting into a field of high grass when I threw the gear into park and jumped out after him. I could hear Saul and Isaac behind me, their breathing even, hearts thundering in tandem with mine. We were wolves on the hunt now, the hum of the moon still alive inside of us. Our prey was fast but not nearly as fast as Saul.

First of the First, his body speeding ahead with powerful strides. He tackled Louis with ease, crushing him to the ground and swiping down his back with claws. His arms were bursting from his shirt as they shifted, brown hair sprouting between the seams. Louis let out an agonized scream and I smiled. Let Saul rip his heart out.

Saul flipped the lesser wolf over and wrapped a massive, clawed hand around his throat. "Call Jacques."

"I ain't doing nothing for you." Louis spat. Fear glistened across his face in beads of sweat, the air pungent with it.

Saul's voice was even and calm. "Do you know who I am?"

Louis was so white he was almost translucent. "First of the First," he whispered with a mix of reverence and horror.

"Take out your phone and call Jacques."

Louis obeyed, fumbling in his pocket, and tugging out a cell phone. His hands shook as big fingers punched buttons. Saul ripped the phone from his hand and placed it against his ear.

"I have the money you're looking for. Barlow's cash."

Jacques tinny voice was heavily accented, a well-practiced tribute to our history. "Saul, how very unexpected to hear from you."

"Cady Barber, Barlow's bookkeeper. You give her to me, you get your money."

"Always so impersonal, Saul." Jacques chided. "If you have my money then the bookkeeper has no use anymore."

"Where is she!" I snarled, yanking the phone from Saul's hand, and nearly crushing it.

"Ah, so it's true. You've bonded to her."

"You have no idea what hell you've got coming your way."

"You're wrong there, Elijah." There was a long pause. "In fact, I'm intimately familiar with the feeling of having my throat ripped from my neck by another Barbeaux. Do you remember, Saul? When you left me to bleed out in the dirt like some stray dog?"

"I didn't want to hurt you," Saul rasped. "You gave me no choice."

"Because you couldn't handle not being obeyed! I had plans for this family and you were too selfish to see my brilliance." Jacques' voice crackled with his booming words. "What you bayou mutts never understood was that a mate is not the only bond you can have. Our kind is woven together by our magic, meant to be bonded to an alpha. When you turned on me, you broke that bond, Saul."

Saul flinched away from the accusation.

"There is no agony as painful as a broken bond. That emptiness will swallow you whole."

I didn't know if what he said was true. Didn't care to find out. "Where's Cady?"

"I'm looking at her right now." I heard a growl, distinctly werewolf, and a muffled scream. "Thought it was only fair she learns about the darker sides of the family before she commits."

"*Where the fuck is she?*"

"Settle down, Elijah. I don't remember you being such a hothead." Jacques tsked. "Louis is going to tell you where she is. Then we're going to see if you can get to her in time. Let me spoil the ending for you: You won't. You'll play the valiant hero but, sadly, before the sun rises, you'll feel the snap of that bond and your soul will die with her."

"You don't have to do this, Jacques." I tried to calm myself, to quiet the raging beast inside me. "I'm sorry for what happened—"

"*What happened?*" He laughed incredulously. "Saul left me for dead. It was a calculated move from a heartless *monster*. And even after that I might have left you out of it, Eli. I knew you and Isaac weren't responsible for the attempt on my life.

You don't have the stomach for it. Then you stole from me. Both of you."

I almost denied Isaac's involvement in any of this, but the guilty pallor of his face stopped me before I could speak. Clearly there was more he wasn't telling us about what happened in his absence.

"You took my money. He took my mate." Jacques let out a long-suffering sigh. "You three act so righteous but you're no better than the rest of us animals. Now you're going to suffer like us, too."

Louis began to chuckle, his confidence revived as if Jacques would save him. Poor fool had no idea how expendable he was. I swung my leg out and kicked his jaw. It crunched, blood spilling from his lips to coat his chin and chest. I bared my teeth as I warned, "You listen very carefully, Jacques. If there is a single hair out of place on her head, you're dead."

"No, I don't think I am." The call ended.

Louis was scrabbling backward through the grass, grasping the side of his jaw. Pain glazed his yellow eyes. He was just prey now, wounded prey that would do anything to avoid more pain. I stomped after him, kicking his hands out from under him and sending him flat on his back. My knee dropped onto his chest, and he wheezed.

"If you tell me where she is right now, I'll make your death clean," I promised. "Otherwise, I'll let Saul have his fun with you." To emphasize Saul stepped up behind me and flexed his hands. Blood was drying on his curved claws, and I saw the way Louis trembled. Peripherally I knew that Saul couldn't take this. More violence might send him over whatever edge he'd been precariously balancing on for years.

The words were slurred and hard to understand.. "They took her to the old pier. The platform."

"What's the platform?" I demanded.

"It's a floating dock. When someone makes Jacques angry, he leaves them out there until they drown."

Those were the last words Louis spoke. With both hands I gripped his neck, squeezing until his eyes rolled back and he went limp. I took no pleasure in killing one of my own kind, despite what he'd done. The world was cruel to lone werewolves. Mutts, my father used to call them.

I couldn't imagine what he'd been through to make him like this.

"We need to be strategic, Eli," Saul said in a chastising tone as I shifted into drive and whipped back onto the road. We were almost half an hour from the old pier and Cady could already be out on this "platform."

"Don't have time for strategy. We're going to the pier and we're going to get Cady."

"The wolves Jacques has out there will be armed. They'll shoot you before you even get her in your line of sight." Saul leaned between the front seats, his elbows resting on the center console. "Trust me. I understand how Jacques thinks. He's using your mate as bait."

"Well, it's working!" My eyes scanned the horizon, trying to judge if the impending storm was moving closer. Too hard to see much in the dark.

"Just focus on getting us home. I'll figure out the rest."

I studied Saul in the rearview mirror. He settled back into his seat, fingertips pressed to his lips in concentration. *This* was the Saul I remembered. Saul that could walk up to a hungry tiger with confidence of steel. Saul that took charge and handled shit.

This was the Saul I was glad to have on my side right now.

After a tense, drawn out silence Saul leaned forward again and said, "We're going to need a boat."

Chapter 30

Revelation

Cady

T HE TAPE OVER MY mouth muffled my scream, pushing it back into my throat until it burned. A ringing buzzed in my ears as the sick pop of Brandon's neck seemed to echo through the hollow space between concrete buildings and out onto the bay. His arms flailed at his sides but otherwise he was unmoving on the ground, the light already fading from his face as a lake of blood pooled beneath his head.

The two men from the SUV had already moved on, wrapping massive hands around my biceps. They were huge, one shaped like a hunched quarterback and the other more height than thickness.

They killed him. Just like that Brandon was dead and they didn't even give him a second glance.

Panic became a wild animal inside of me and I continued to scream, swinging my legs until the tape came loose from my ankles. I kicked one of my kidnappers in the shin. The furious sound that came from him was completely inhuman, a growl that should belong to a predator.

My eyes darted to his hard face, and I saw a familiarity there, not because I recognized him but because I recognized the way his eyes seemed to lighten, the lines of his face too pointed and otherworldly. It was that same indescribable wrongness I sometimes saw on Eli's face, as if there was something ravening and dark lurking beneath his skin.

That niggling feeling that said I was missing an important detail came alive, pecking at me to notice what I didn't want to see. *They're not human,* my first instinct said but it was too absurd to believe. I thought back to the photograph of Eli's ancestors, the original Barbeaux homesteaders, and how I accused him of being a vampire. How easily I dismissed it when he laughed at me.

And yet, there was something distinctly different about Eli. The way his touch was electric, not in some poetic way but *literally* giving me tingles from the barest contact. His constant need to make that contact, always brushing fingers through my hair, caressing my arms, meeting his hand with mine. It was more than affection. Territorial. Possessive. Like the way he couldn't help rubbing against me when Brandon came to the door.

The way he *knew*. Knew when the weather was changing, when someone was near the house, when someone was watching him.

Over the bay the horizon was an ominous grey, billowing storm clouds blocking out the coming dawn and moving in to devour the moon.

The full moon.

"I'll be back when the moon is full."

Eli had that same excited energy tonight when he came back after dealing with Holt. Like he was himself and he was *more*. Wild in a way that wasn't natural.

I noticed the man that growled was staring at me, his eyes golden the way Eli's could look. Glowing.

"What are you?" I tried to say through the tape.

"He didn't tell you. Such a pity." A Cheshire grin stretched his thin lips, revealing sharp canine teeth.

I shook my head, throwing my weight backwards and trying to break free. Their hands tightened, bruising grips nearly wrenching my arms out of their sockets. There was death reflected in those strange eyes and every instinct inside me was screaming for me to run. This was not the fear I felt that night on the bayou. It was the primal reaction of prey stalked by predator.

All this time I thought I felt like prey when Eli watched me. I was wrong. He was always so careful. I knew—*I knew*—he was never going to hurt me. I was safe.

Now that safety was a distant memory and I felt like my entire body would rattle to pieces from the adrenaline that was shooting through my limbs.

"At first you were just a loose end." The man went on, inhaling deeply and letting his grin stretch wider. As if he could smell my fear. "See, your boss screwed us over. Big time. We thought maybe you knew about it."

I shook my head again, like that was going to make him say, "Hey, wrong person. No hard feelings. Why don't you head home?"

"But then that Barbeaux bastard had to stick his nose in our business. Barbeauxs are always making trouble for the rest of us."

"Careful, Trey," his friend muttered, looking tense. He was the tall one and I realized he was so gangly because he was just a kid. His features were smooth, chin rounded and hairless. He couldn't be older than seventeen.

"He can't hear us out here." Trey laughed without humor. "Jacques! Fuck your mother!" His sudden shouting startled me, and I screamed. "Don't let that bastard make you so paranoid."

I was missing something here.

"You're not supposed to disrespect the alpha."

The alpha?

"My mother is a corpse. I knew your standards were disgusting Trey but not *that* disgusting." A new face came around the corner of a concrete building. His voice was velvety and accented—French maybe? Hell, if I knew fancy accents—but that wasn't what drew my attention.

The resemblance to Eli wasn't one I could clearly pin down. The cut of his jaw or the shape of his eyes.

This had to be Jacques.

"Alpha, you know I'm just talking shit."

"What was it you said to Louis the other day?" Jacques purred.

"Talk shit, get hit," the teenager mumbled, rubbing a faded bruise on his jaw. Now that I was looking at him, his face was covered in the outlines of old bruises.

Jacques's hand snapped out and Trey exploded backwards, his back slamming onto the concrete and skidding a dozen feet. "Your wayward tongue is going to be the death of you." Jacques brushed his knuckles on his clean black slacks, looking every bit the old school gangster. His hair was even slicked across the top of his head in a shiny curve.

"Now, let's see what has dear Eli so captivated," Jacques said to me, inspecting me like a horse at auction. He clicked his tongue, shaking his head. "No taste, that one."

A cell phone chimed in his breast pocket, and he smiled darkly. "Right on schedule. Trey, why don't you show our guest what kind of company she keeps. Make sure he doesn't get carried away, Leo." Then, into the phone, he crooned, "Saul, how very unexpected to hear from you."

Saul? Was Eli with him? Was he looking for me? I didn't dare let that spark of hope catch in my chest.

I tried to listen to the conversation over the wind, but my focus jerked sideways when a shadow passed over me. That animalistic growl started again, and I twisted to look up at the creature from my nightmares. Shoulders as wide as a semi, tawny fur bristling along impossibly thick arms, and the slobbering mouth of a wolf resting atop them. A Hollywood wolf-man come to life.

A scream erupted from my chest, choked out by the tape over my mouth. I was running before I registered my body moving, concrete scraping under my bare feet. The nearest building was hundreds of feet away. It was also hollowed out and desolate, not the ideal hiding place.

I turned sharply, my shoulder smashing into the side of the building and sending me sideways. My throat burned from the cold air, and I couldn't breathe deep enough with tape over my mouth. Black spots were forming in my vision, and I wasn't sure if it was the undiluted terror or the lack of oxygen.

I collapsed against the side of the building, fumbling with the edge of the duct tape, and ripping it off with a gasp. Any moment I was going to get slashed in half by a set of claws that should only exist in a horror movie. That image spurred my legs into action again.

I saw no movement behind me, but the sky was overcast, the moon vanished, and any hint of dawn was hidden by the oncoming storm. I was barreling through a concrete world painted grey.

A world that was suddenly spinning. I tumbled through the air for what felt like minutes, crashing painfully onto my crumpled shoulder when my cuffed hands couldn't catch me.

Droplets pattered onto the ground by my face as I tried to rise, and my first thought was that the rain was oddly warm for October. There was a reason I didn't want to waste my time thinking about rain, but it escaped me, my body frozen in some kind of slow-motion mode.

Blood. It was droplets of blood. Rivulets of red stained my sky-blue sleeve, and my skin began to burn. Yellow eyes glowed above me and I could feel the malicious intent of the demon stalking closer. He was so impossibly large, and I wanted this to be another nightmare—it was another nightmare, a waking one where all the agony and fear were real, and I was going to die.

For some reason I screamed Eli's name, as if he would hear it from miles away and appear at my side. Or maybe he was on the phone with Saul, and he could hear my need for him.

But he couldn't and I knew that so I did the only thing I could think to do—I jumped.

Over the side of the concrete wall separating the bay from the boat ramps I flew, dangling in the air for far too long. Dangling and dangling because someone had me by the back of the shirt, reeling me in.

It was the teenager, his smoky blue eyes so unexpectedly sad, the apology clear on his face. "Can't let you do that."

He was taller than me, sure, but I expected it to be easier to wriggle free from his grasp. Those spindly arms were a steel band around me as I kicked and screamed. I didn't care if he set me free and I landed right back in front of that monster. I would go for the water again. I would fight the damn thing. Anything to get away from the fate I felt waiting for me around the side of this building.

Jacques was standing at the edge of a boat ramp when we came around the corner, tapping his foot impatiently and glaring at a shiny watch on his wrist. A small fishing boat sloshed in the water beside him, and I had a horrible vision of being tied to a brick and dropped at the bottom of the bay.

"Let's get this over with. I'm low on time and I have another woman I need to deal with." Jacques winked at me. "Apologies, darling. I never could stick to just one."

"Why are you doing this? I thought Barbeauxs were all about family first. Eli is your family, and this will only hurt him."

"Eli is a traitorous bastard. I'm doing you a favor, really. Sooner or later, everyone close to a Barbeaux gets their throat ripped out." He tilted his chin to the sky, revealing shiny, jagged scars along his neck.

"Eli didn't do that. I don't believe it."

"He didn't stop it either. He could have stopped his brother years ago. He's second in line to the Barbeaux crown and he squanders his legacy on a swamp in a shitty, nowhere town." He scratched his fingers down his neck and his face warped into that same wrongness, features sharpened and eyes glowing. He was a nightmare too. "You probably don't deserve this and if I was a better man—like *Elijah*—I would care. But I'm not and my cousins made sure of that so I will enjoy watching his face when you die."

Jacques grinned fangs at me and snapped his fingers to the teenager. "Get her in the water and take up position."

More questions tumbled out of me, my refusal to make pleas turning into a furious word vomit that was completely ignored by both men. I put up another fight when Trey—no longer wearing fangs and fur—reappeared to help hoist me into their boat but it ended quickly when he threatened to break my legs. I didn't doubt that he could, and I had a feeling he might even enjoy doing it.

There was a shape floating in the water several hundred feet from the boat ramp. A square made of wood planks, bobbing back and forth with the waves. Trey called it "the platform" and that was literally what it was. A platform about the size of my entryway.

"Looks like this is your stop." Trey gave me a feral smile, picking me up roughly and tossing me onto the platform. It was damp from sea spray, and I almost slipped off the side, my hands barely finding purchase on the plastic frame that held the thing together.

I lay there on my stomach, sliding back and forth, watching as they turned back for the ramp. I wanted to say something terrible to them, make a threat or deal some checkmate statement. By the time any sound left my mouth they were already so far away I wasn't sure they would hear.

"Hey!" I shouted. "You're going to hell for this!"

"See you there!" Trey called back as they climbed out of the boat and dragged it up the ramp, disappearing inside the nearest concrete building and not coming back out. I couldn't make them out through the darkened windows, but I felt them watching me.

Jacques was out there somewhere too, using me as a pawn in some Barbeaux game I didn't understand.

My stomach sloshed as much as the water around me, and I almost vomited over the side. Numbness crawled up my limbs and I wasn't sure if it was the cold or shock. I should be calculating the distance to shore, judging if I was a strong enough swimmer to make it to the ramp. But then I would be hypothermic and within arm's length of a werewolf. A real life fucking werewolf.

Three of them.

Did that mean—yes. It did. I knew it did, but I didn't want my last thoughts of Eli to be a twisted image of him chasing me like that *thing*.

A vicious wind was picking up from the northeast, the first taste of the incoming storm hitting me full force. My legs were shaking, and I wobbled back and forth as I tried to stand. I didn't know it was possible to experience something worse than almost being fed to alligators one appendage at a time but here I was.

I considered diving off the platform and taking my chances in the water, going around the ramps and trying to find the bayou, but I was much further out in the surf than I initially thought, and my hands were still cuffed. I was a good swimmer but not high-tide-during-an-October-storm good.

In the end I balanced there, screaming until my lungs ached, knowing that no one could hear me. Eventually I fell silent, too exhausted to keep making noise. Balancing was taking all my muscle strength and focus.

Stronger and stronger the wind picked up until the platform was shifting nearly vertical with the violent crash of waves. The tide had to push through a narrow channel to reach me, but the wind whipped the water into white caps.

If I fell into the water now, I would drown in minutes. Even without cuffed hands these conditions were extremely dangerous. The wind stole my voice as I sobbed, zipping it through the concrete graveyard behind me. Another wave and my shaking muscle couldn't hold me steady anymore. The bay would swallow me up.

The storm became a roar, the last sound I heard before I stumbled backward and crashed into the water. I kicked my legs frantically, but the current was so strong. My head bobbed up above the waves just long enough to gasp a breath.

Then I was under again, twisting painfully as incoming swells collided with the ones receding. Somehow, I managed to surface a second time. Rain pelted down from the sky now, adding to my disorientation. I caught site of the concrete ledge to the boat ramp, closer now. If I could just swim with the incoming waves maybe I could hoist myself onto the ramp.

Or have my skull crushed by the force of the wave slamming me into the concrete.

It was an impossible plan and even as I thought of it, the current jerked me further out toward the bay. The violent churning of white foam was like a slavering maw, ready to crush me to bits and devour me.

My last breaths became prayers, desperate pleas to God to give me another chance. A little more time.

The roar became louder. Just before my exhausted legs gave out, dropping me beneath the water, I imagined it was a boat. I could almost hear Eli calling my name.

I yelled to him in return, choking when I went under.

Everything was quiet under the water. Nothing but a dull, gentle swish like a peaceful wind in the early morning. Above me the chaos of waves looked just like clouds, and I could almost pretend I was on solid ground if not for the way my body swirled in the current. I could pretend Eli was here too, swimming toward me with perfect form, grabbing my upper arms and heaving as his strong legs kicked up, up, up to the surface.

Water was forced from my throat in a gurgling cough as I was lifted into the air. I coughed again, gasping while firm hands held fast to me. I was salty and slippery, and the hands tightened painfully to keep me from being pulled back under the surf.

"I've got you. I've got you, darlin'."

Eli hovered there, leaning against the side of a boat. Another man shouted from aboard, but I couldn't make out what he said with the blood pounding in my ears. The boat lurched in the waves, water jumping up over the sides.

Then a crack split the air, too smooth and clear to be thunder. More shouting. More cracking, this time coming from the other side of the boat where another Eli stood with a gun raised at someone out of sight.

Was this some death vision? My mind conjuring a rescue fantasy as I sank to my grave?

Suddenly Eli jolted, losing his easy strength, and almost going under. Somehow, he kept his hold on me as we both plunged further into the waves.

"Put your arms around my neck," He demanded, pulling me hard against him.

I shook my head frantically. "You can't, Eli. You can't swim with my weight."

Eli ignored me, sliding his hands to my hips as he ducked below the water. A moment later he surfaced, his head coming between my handcuffed wrists. My arms collared his neck, our body's pressed so close I couldn't kick my legs.

Eli adjusted so I was draped over his back and began to swim awkwardly but swiftly to the concrete ledge of the boat ramp. As we neared it, he propped his arms and legs out, catching the side to guard my body from crashing into it. Pain shaped his face into a grimace, but he held fast, waiting until a wave receded just enough to hoist us both over the side. My numb legs scraped across the concrete, and I bit back a cry.

There wasn't a moment of rest when we were out of the water. Eli scooped me up and ran, zipping around the corner of the nearest concrete building. More gunshots rang out, but they were muffled by the wind and the building.

As soon as he was sure we were clear, Eli collapsed backward, his legs sliding out from beneath him. It was then that I noticed blood on his shirt.

"Eli? Eli, you're bleeding!"

He smiled. The man had a hole the size of a grape in his chest, and he smiled as if I was fretting about a splinter. "I'll be fine, darlin'."

"No, you need a doctor!" My voice was so shrill that my words were more air than sound.

"My brothers will come for us." He started to brush the wet hair from my face but dropped his hand with a wince.

Without warning Eli leapt up, lifting me with him and running. From my perspective we were headed straight toward the bay with no rescue in sight.

Eli jumped. For endless seconds we were flying over the water, hungry waves rising to lap at our feet. We landed hard in the boat, the air leaving both of us as I landed on top of Eli's chest. His pained grunt had me scrambling to get off him but the cuffs on my hands locked me around him.

"Hold on!" A man called from behind me as the boat temporarily lifted out of the water. The voice was familiar but not. An echo of Eli.

His twin. I almost forgot that Eli had a twin.

I twisted over my shoulder to see him hanging on to a safety bar in front of the steering wheel.

Isaac. That was his name. His hair was shorter than Eli's and his face more refined. When he smiled and waved at me his eyes crinkled in the same way that Eli's always did.

He was smiling. Waving like we were meeting at a family dinner. What was wrong with these men?

Right about now I didn't care, couldn't think about the crazy nonsense I saw back there. They saved my life and risked a lot to do it. That mattered.

Focused as ever, Saul shifted the wheel of the boat back and forth, dodging the worst of the waves and battling against the storm. His beard was thick, hair to his shoulders. The spitting image of the man from that old photograph.

"Eli's bleeding!" I yelled to his brothers. "He needs a doctor."

Isaac kept up his smile and nod routine, too blasé for the whole situation. Much too calm.

"I'll be okay, Cady. Really."

"You've been shot." I sobbed, the emotion drenching me more than the rain. More incoherent words were spilling from my lips, tearful mumbling that had him shaking his head.

He curled his arms around me and squeezed me tight. I was only peripherally aware of the cold until I felt how warm he was. Shit, we might still get hypothermia.

"They didn't hit anything essential."

"Should I apply pressure? I don't know what to do. Please tell me what to do!"

"Hold on tight. This ride ain't getting any gentler."

"Please be okay, Eli." It became a chant I repeated every few minutes.

Eli shushed me, promising it wasn't as bad as it seemed.

I didn't believe him.

Chapter 31

Paper Cut

Cady

T HE BOAT ALMOST CAPSIZED a dozen times and with each bump Eli looked more pained. Try as I might, I couldn't extricate myself from his lap. My weight definitely wasn't helping with the pain, but he wouldn't let me go.

I had no idea where we were or where we were going. Thankfully Saul did. It shouldn't have come as a surprise to me when we drove his boat right up onto the sand near Eli's dock, where the bayou met the bay.

I jumped up, disentangling my cuffed arms from around Eli's neck and standing. I was shivering from the cold and my muscles and joints felt like they were soldered together. That wasn't going to stop me from getting Eli the help he needed.

Stumbling and slipping on the wet deck, I rushed to Eli's brothers. "Eli needs a hospital!"

"No hospitals," Saul said sharply, stepping out of the boat. He was tugging it further up onto the sand, despite the weight of three people in it.

"What?" Surely, I misheard him. "This is an emergency! He's got a bullet wound!" Why weren't any of them acting like this was an emergency?

"Saul can get the bullet out just fine, miss Cady." Isaac assured as he lifted Eli by his good side and helped him off the boat. Saul was already walking away.

I gaped. "Saul can—no he cannot. Are you out of your mind?"

"C'mon Cady. We need to get you dry." Eli stood next to his brother, tone beseeching.

There it was. I could see by the pinched corners of his eyes that this was it. We were suddenly in the middle of the things Eli couldn't tell me and it was bad. Way worse than I imagined.

Everything I heard in the last twenty-four hours was true. The demons from my nightmares were real.

Still, I begged, "Eli, please let me take you to the hospital."

"I can't, darlin'." He climbed back into the boat, reaching for me with one arm. "Cops keep track of gunshot wounds."

Of course. That made sense. After a deputy broke into my house, we couldn't be too cautious around authorities.

But what if Eli bled to death because we were being cautious?

"It's worth the risk."

"You don't understand the full risk. You can't yet."

"You're serious."

"Come inside Cady. Let me get those cuffs off you."

He was approaching me like an injured animal. I felt like one. Tears streamed down my cheeks, so hot in contrast to my icy skin.

"What if you die?"

"I've been hurt worse. A little metal ain't going to kill me." Eli was trying to be reassuring but the look on his face was devastating me. Something terrible was coming. I could feel it.

Yellow eyes glowed evilly in my memory, and I shuddered. *"I'll be back when the moon is full."*

I shuffled next to Eli and Isaac all the way up to the porch. Every muscle in my body hurt and yet, I was numb. A painful sort of numb that tingled and burned.

When Isaac opened the front door, he almost collided with his brother. Saul was loading a shotgun, his gaze fixed on the dock where he parked the boat.

"You think they'll follow?" Isaac seemed surprised.

"Doubtful, but they know where to find us," Saul answered.

Both brothers were ignoring Eli, who was bleeding everywhere. And staring at me with the most forlorn look a man had ever worn.

"Eli needs help," I said to Saul.

"You know Jacques. He doesn't do subtle."

"He's different than you remember." Saul snapped the barrel to the shotgun closed and pumped it.

Saul and Isaac started to say something else, but I interrupted them with, "Jesus Christ your brother is bleeding to death and you're just standing there! Do something you psychos!" Tearfully I turned to Eli. "What's going on?"

Something was terribly, terribly wrong and I knew what, but I didn't want to believe it. Literally couldn't, like my trauma addled brain was unable to recall the memories of today as reality.

Saul looked meaningfully at Eli and said, "You need to tell her." Then he walked down the porch steps and disappeared into the trees.

"Cady, we need to talk."

At the same time Isaac said, "I'm going to find something to jimmy open those cuffs."

"About what, Eli?" I was shaking so hard I must have looked insane.

"I don't want to lose you." He moved closer, reaching for my hand but hesitating. It was clear by the way he carried himself that the pain was getting worse.

I covered my eyes and whispered, "I'm going to lose *you* because you won't go to the hospital."

"I'll be fine." His boots shifted on the wood boards. "This kind of wound can't kill me."

"Tell me, Eli. Just say it." *Please rip the bandage off because I can't take anymore more shock without permanently losing my mind.*

Eli hovered there, silently pleading with me to save him from this. To forget there was this shadow looming between us. The silence was killing me.

"If you're not going to tell me then I'm going to guess." The rain had lightened but we were soaked, and the wind was vicious. If we didn't get inside soon, we would freeze to death before Eli had the chance to bleed out. "You're not human. You're one of *them*."

I really just said that.

"The men that put me on that platform were like you. They looked like you when you're angry. Wrong." I waved my hands at his face. "Evil."

Eli flinched and I almost apologized but some angry part of me wanted him to hurt the way his secrets hurt me. No matter what insane truth he admitted, keeping it from me felt like a betrayal. Those secrets were the reason I was dragged from my home, chased by a monster, and tossed into the bay to drown.

But he told you there were secrets. He told you and you accepted that. Don't throw it in his face now, I chided myself. *The man took a bullet for you.*

"Not evil," I am amended. "But they scared the hell out of me. They chased me and I—"

"Chased you?" His eyes roamed over me, noticing the blood on my sleeve, and grinding his teeth. "Goddamn—" His mouth clacked shut, nostrils flaring, eyelids shuttered.

Eli might have already frozen over from the cold because he just stood there. He was a man of action, confident and quick. This weird, paralyzed silence was messing with my head.

"Your cousin was there. They said so many things I don't understand." The ridges of his jaw bounced like he was chewing on the words he wouldn't speak. "Just say something, Eli!"

Instead, he did the last thing I expected. Eli started opening his flannel. It was clumsy with his injured shoulder, and it only got worse when he tried to drop his shirt off his arms. It slid from his biceps with a wince. He was half naked, soaked in blood and salt water, and I was about to have a mental breakdown.

"This doesn't change anything, Cady. It doesn't change who I am." With a palm over his open wound, he pleaded, "Don't run. Please."

Then he changed faster than I could blink. Denim clung to his contorting frame. It stretched to the point of tearing as he grew taller and wider than should have been possible.

He was one of them. A demon.

A werewolf.

He towered over me with those pointed ears and that long wolf snout. The perfect blend between man and animal, an entirely new creature. Something that shouldn't exist. I couldn't wrap my head around it, but the proof was right here. Close enough that if he swiped out one of those clawed hands, he could gut me.

And I knew with certainty that he wouldn't. Even as I clapped a hand over my mouth, fresh tears brimming, my gaze fused with the copper eyes glaring down at me, I saw Eli. Beneath it all, he was still in there, waiting for me to flee. To hate him. He expected me to.

Maybe I should have tried to, but something clacked onto the porch and rolled my way, denying any chance that I could. A dented chunk of metal. The bullet that Eli took when he was saving my life. *Again.*

But the free-flowing terror that pumped through me still carried an active charge, a muscle memory of the monster that chased me only an hour before. When Eli advanced across the deck, eating up those precious few feet between us, I almost forgot his request and let myself flee.

He came close enough for that hulking body to touch mine and I flinched, curling in on myself and huddling against the railing as if it would offer any protection from this supernatural creature.

If Eli was tall, the beast he became was a mountain. With him as near as he was, I could barely see his face, would have lost sight of those searching eyes had he not stooped to breathe me in.

Heat tumbled off him, rushing at me in soft pants as he dipped his head to snuffle at the gouges on my bicep. I startled when he lapped at the wound, expecting him to suddenly lose his awareness to some kind of bloodlust and eat my arm like it was a roasted chicken leg.

What happened instead was a terrible inhuman sound, a single word that rang with the promise of death. "Who?"

Who hurt me. He was cataloging my injuries the way he had my bruises that day on his boat, making note of what happened and who he needed to punish for it—if he hadn't already.

"Trey." I rasped the name, my pulse spiking at the memory of his yellow eyes. "His name was Trey."

Obsidian claws curled over my cheeks, carefully brushing along my skin. Every move he made was careful, treating me delicately. The contrast to my earlier experience was so jarring that I loosed a choked laugh, one gasping note to release the insane tension holding me together.

The beast took one final, deep inhale of me and then suddenly Eli was Eli once more. His clothes were wet, lopsided, and mostly shredded, and it was clearly hurting him to move the way he was.

With a step back, he rumbled, "Please believe me when I tell you I hated every moment I kept it from you. You have to understand, Cady." He swallowed, glancing at the door where his brother had disappeared, "It wasn't just my secret."

I followed his gaze. "Isaac too?"

"All of us. We were born this way. I can tell you everything. Please give me a chance." His throat bobbed and he repeated, "This doesn't change who I am."

But it did. He knew it and I knew it.

I stared at him, at a face that had become as familiar as home. It was foolish to let myself fall in love with someone like him. Somehow, he found his way under my skin and even if I ran from this town and never looked back, I wouldn't be the same. I would always feel him out there, that missing piece I'd been puzzling over all this time.

He didn't get to have that knowledge yet. Not until I had the full story. Not until I knew I was safe here. Eli was the reason I was on that platform. It wasn't his fault, but his presence in my life put a target on my back. If I'd known what I was up against, I could have been more prepared.

"Do whatever you need to do to make that bleeding stop. I can't look at it anymore." My nerves were making my tongue sharp, and it came out harsh. I just needed a moment. Some space to think. A chance to catch my breath.

I turned on my heel and stepped inside, leaving Eli out there in the wind.

Chapter 32

Unbreakable

Eli

I WAS SILENT AS Saul bandaged my shoulder. It hurt like hell, but I wasn't about to moan over it. Cady was disturbed enough. My gaze hadn't left her since I came in.

Her head was down as Isaac worked on the cuffs, eyes unfocused. She was going to give up on me. For good reason, too. Indirect as it was, I ruined her life. She was homeless and traumatized. There was no coming back from this.

And she knew our secret. I knew by the expression on Saul's face that he was trying to hold his tongue about that.

My brother was never very good about holding his tongue.

"This is why I told you it couldn't happen," He murmured, snipping the stitching, and tying it off. "No good ever comes of bonding. Better to just leave it alone."

"I don't believe that for a moment." I grit my teeth when Saul slapped a bandage on my chest. "Damn, your bedside manner is worse than your regular manners."

Saul lifted an eyebrow. "You're welcome."

"Saul." I touched his forearm. "Cady needs some things. Clothes, shampoo, the essentials."

That caught Cady's attention. "I have those at home."

All three of us went silent. She frowned at Saul, refusing to even look at me. "Am I a prisoner now?"

Fuck. Should've just told her when I admitted the rest. I was trying to find a way to say it gently, but Saul beat me to it.

"You don't have a home anymore."

Her complexion went even whiter. "What?"

"There was a fire," I answered, rising from the couch. I needed to be as close as she would allow. "Intentional."

"At my house?"

It didn't seem to be clicking. Saul was blunt when he explained, "Whoever took you burned your house down. On Jacques's orders, most likely. Trying to make it look like you died in a fire."

"Brandon," Cady spit. "Brandon burned my house down?" Whatever emotion she was experiencing over that revelation was unreadable. "What happened to Ricky?" Her head shot up and she offered me a three second stare.

"He's—"

"Disposed of," Saul cut me off, crossing his arms and leaning his hip against the kitchen island. Too close to Cady. Too menacing. If I didn't know any better, I'd say he was trying to intimidate her.

"You killed him?" She wouldn't look at me when she asked.

"I did," Saul answered, watching.

I shuffled to the kitchen, trying to step between them. Saul didn't budge. Cady didn't take her eyes off him.

"Why?"

"He was a threat to my family."

"Is that why you tried to kill Jacques too?"

The question caught him off guard, cracking the ice wall and softening him with sadness. "He was a threat to everyone."

Cady nodded, like that made sense to her. "He's real pissed about that. Called you all traitors."

"I reckon he did."

"What are you going to do with him now?"

"Don't know yet."

"He's bribing the Sheriff. Or threatening him—who knows. But the whole department is turning a blind eye."

Isaac cursed. "How deep does this poison run?"

"All the way to the heart." I caught Cady's eyes for a heart-beat before she looked back to her hands. "Jacques has been up to this for a while now."

"And we had no idea." Isaac whistled as something in the cuff clicked and they dropped from Cady's wrists. Immediately she pulled her arms up, rubbing them tenderly.

"Because we're hiding out here." I directed it at Saul. "We can't afford to be this removed from everything." I yelped as I gestured with my right arm. "Had to be the dominant arm. Goddamn."

"Sit down, Eli." Cady surprised me with the force of her order. "You're going to rip your stitches." I did what she asked, propping myself on the couch if it kept her from ignoring me.

"Jacques was going to make trouble either way." Saul was already retreating into himself again.

"That doesn't mean we get to check out," I growled. I need-ed him to be the unflinching man that drove a boat across the bay while bullets were flying, not this vacant ghost of a brother. "He took Cady because he knew what she is to me! You think it's going to stop there? Who knows how many wolves he's got waiting in the shadows."

"Eli's right." Isaac leaned his forearms on the kitchen island. "This is going to get ugly if we don't handle it fast. If he was a threat before then he's a nuclear bomb now."

Cady looked ready to bolt from the room, but she still raised her voice to ask, "How many of you are there? And why do they all seem to hate you so much?"

Saul scowled at her. Cady scowled back so Saul redirected his look to me. "You didn't tell her enough."

"He went for the, 'show-don't-tell' approach." Isaac smirked.

"You're an idiot," Saul said flatly. "No wonder she's scared."

"I'm not—" Cady shuttered the defensive comment and crossed her arms. She cringed, uncrossing them when her raw wrists rubbed the fabric of her shirt.

Her still wet shirt. She was damp and freezing and covered in cuts and bruises. For once, Saul was right. I was an idiot.

"Can I put something on that?" I gestured to her wrists, thankfully with my left hand. "Get you something dry to wear too."

"I'll make a run to the *Stop N' Shop.*" Isaac offered, grabbing the truck keys off the hook by the front door.

"Better head to Port Tortuga. She'll need a weeks' worth of clothes, at least. Grab extra food, too. Eli's not going anywhere anytime soon." Saul eyed Cady thoughtfully. "What else do we need? To make you comfortable?"

Both Isaac and I gaped at him. It was the politest he'd ever been to an outsider.

"Cell phones," she suggested. "We all need cell phones. You're too hard to reach out here." Cady perched on one of the bar stools and chewed her lip. "I want another gun. Brandon took mine." She stuck her pointer finger out and started counting, "Ammo, buckshot, bear mace. Oh, flares! And flashlights. Don't forget batteries for the flashlights."

A rare half-smile kicked up the corner of Saul's mouth. "I was thinking tampons and shampoo."

"I like Pantene," Cady told Isaac as an afterthought.

I watched quietly from the couch as Cady helped Isaac and Saul make a list. A furrow was forming on Isaac's brow, and he was beginning to look concerned, not because Cady asked him to buy tampons. The woman was planning for the apocalypse.

Saul was encouraging it.

"Can you shoot a .22? Eli keeps a rifle in his closet, but he can't use it in his condition. Probably ought to avoid shooting entirely if he can."

"I've shot that one," Cady nodded.

Both my brothers turned to me with surprised expressions.

Cady wasn't the only one I'd been keeping secrets from. Even if it was all on the table now, they were still caught off guard by how deeply entangled I was with a woman they'd never met before.

"You ghosted me," I jabbed a finger at Isaac, "and you tried to fucking kill me," and another at Saul. "Of course, I didn't tell you about her."

They ignored me.

"I'll be around but I can't be everywhere." Saul tapped the counter. "You make whatever noise you need to if someone comes. Get my attention and you'll have backup." He turned to me. "I don't think they're coming. Jacques is too smart for that. But you even think you've got company, you need to be the beast."

I nodded, noticing a change in Cady's demeanor when Saul mentioned shifting. Almost like she'd already forgotten what took place on the porch and the reminder had her reconsidering the wisdom of staying here.

Saul was heading for the door without so much as a goodbye when he said to Cady, "Whether you wanted to be or not, you're in this now. Don't get skittish, Barber."

Cady nodded seriously. None of this was going anything like I envisioned.

The silence that moved in when both brothers were gone had sharp little teeth. I wanted to get up from the couch and pace just to get away from it. Cady beat me to it, circling the coffee table in laps. A minute or two passed before she dropped into the recliner, sitting carefully on the edge so she could flee if she needed to.

Her chin rose slowly, bringing her gaze up with it until she was looking at me. Though her eyes travelled over my face she still refused to meet mine.

"I'm sorry," I said quietly. "For keeping things from you."

"I knew there was more." She pursed her lips. "I didn't know *what* you were, but I knew you were...*different*."

"Cady—"

"Just, let me talk this out. Please?"

I nodded and she continued. "You knew what was going on and you didn't tell me. All that investigating and you knew your cousin was still alive, didn't you?"

"I suspected."

"And you knew it was other—what do you call yourself? Werewolf?" She huffed a hysterical little laugh. "I can't believe I just said that out loud."

"Werewolf is a fine term."

"Louis is a werewolf. And you knew that." She wasn't asking anymore. "You knew there were more. That's why you freaked when we went to that bar."

"Yes," I admitted quietly.

"I was terrified—losing my mind! And you didn't tell me."

"I knew I could protect you."

"Until last night!" Cady accused. "I don't know if it would have made a difference in what happened. But I deserved the truth."

I started to apologize again but she lifted a hand to stop me.

"I understand your loyalty to your brothers. Who am I compared to them? The girl you're sleeping with?"

"Stop right there, Cady. You're more than that and you know it."

"Then why did you keep so much of yourself from me?" The tension in her body was growing tighter as her mind whirred. Any second now she was going to snap right in half.

"Because I knew how fucking crazy it sounded! If I told you half the shit that was going on you would have run from me. There's a whole world you don't know about, Cady." I shifted on the couch, inching forward. "Can I touch you?"

This time she was the one caught off guard. "Touch me?"

"Please. I'm going crazy being this close to you and not touching you."

She stood, taking a half step toward me. "Are you still you when you're like that? *Transformed?*"

"Mostly. There are times where one side loses to the other. Took a lot of years to find balance. You threw it all out of whack."

"Would you hurt me?"

I closed my eyes and puffed out a furious breath. "Never. I'll kill anyone that touches you."

Which meant Jacques was at the top of my list.

"Do you realize how insane that sounds? You and your brothers just...*killing* people." She covered her face with her hands, holding in a little sob. "I don't want any more killing right now. I've seen more than I ever needed to see. I think I need a minute."

She disappeared down the hall before I could stop her, the bathroom door clicking quietly as she twisted the lock. All I could do was sit on that couch and pray she saw past the violence.

Cady

I stared at myself in Eli's bathroom mirror, not recognizing the pale, haunted face in front of me. Memories snapped across my mind in horrible flashing images. Brandon crumpling, Trey chasing me, Jacques smiling like the devil. Eli—

Eli. He was like a beacon in the dark and even as I hid from him, trying to compose myself, my hands shook with a need to be near him. Maybe it was the shock from the rest of the morning, but it wasn't the talk of magic and murder that had me rattled.

I didn't feel fazed. Traumatized as hell by Jacques and what he did, but it wasn't the same when Eli said it.

I wanted him to kill the people that hurt me. *Like a psychopath.*

I was unfamiliar with this vengeful, angry person and I wasn't sure I liked her. Wasn't sure I wanted to be her.

But I couldn't avoid this right now. Jacques knew where Eli lived—knew *everything* about the Barbeaux brothers—and he could show up any minute to finish what he started. I needed to be prepared.

I counted to ten, took a deep breath, and stepped back into the living.

I barely made it around the couch before Eli said, "If I could go back to that night on the bayou—no, before. Before you were ever wrapped up in that Barlow mess, I would. If I could take it all back and protect you from what happened, I would do it in a heartbeat."

"We probably wouldn't have met," I said softly. "With no job and no family, I might have left Port O'Henry and never looked back."

"I know," Eli said with jaw clenched. "And you would be better off that way. We got you involved in this. It's my fault."

I watched him squeeze his hands into fists, face crestfallen as he waited for me to agree with him. To blame him. Maybe some part of me did blame him, but I wouldn't say it anymore than I would stick a pocketknife in his wound.

I watched him and I remembered his face as he tumbled through the surf with me. His determination. He was so damn determined to get me out of that water. Bullets sprayed across the bay—and hit him—but that didn't even slow him down.

There was a version of Eli I didn't know yet.

I wanted to learn that version of him, to listen to every one of his whispered secrets and memorize them. Right now, my heart was still in those waves, waterlogged and sinking. And Eli was following me right down to the ocean floor. I didn't ask him to, didn't expect it of him. That didn't matter to him.

I sank into the bay, and he dove in after me.

"I don't care," I blurted. "If you could turn back time, I would beg you not to change a thing if it meant this never happened," I gestured between us. "Not if it meant you never happened to me."

My heartbeat stuttered. Only once but I felt it skip, jolting in place as lightning zapped into me. The bolt left heat in its wake, immense and blooming. It was the most amazing sensation, so sublime that I almost giggled. My eyes wandered questioningly to Eli and my amusement stopped dead.

Copper irises smoldered in my direction, his jaw set in a way I was coming to know well. I stepped closer without thinking and he stood. It felt like Eli was pointing a tractor beam at me.

"What's happening to me?" I murmured, hand gliding up the uninjured side of his chest and climbing his nape. "What are you doing to me, Eli?"

"Not me," he growled. "Bond."

I'd never wanted anything as much as I wanted Eli Barbeaux. His touch tingled like a whisky buzz, warming, and softening me. I was love drunk, inhibitions tossed into the wind.

All my life I was careful. Followed the rules. I lived the quiet small-town life my grandparents wanted for me. Never ventured too far from shore. Never took any risks. Now suddenly Eli was crashing into me, a seven-foot wave barreling down on me, a storm sweeping me further into the unknown, and I felt so alive. Like maybe this was the first moment I was truly living. Sensation pelted me like the raindrops pounding the windows and I was drowning in the very best way.

This dangerous, mysterious man was under my skin. He was flowing through my veins. I couldn't figure out how he got there, didn't understand how expertly he sidled his way into my life, but I wasn't afraid to let him in. He had my trust.

He had my heart.

"Bond?" The word seemed foreign and at the same time some primal part of me understood. An inborn knowing that answered me with a flurry of sensation. I could feel it between us now, this pulsing awareness of him, like he was inside of me. The ache in my core reminded me that he could be *more* inside me.

"I bonded to you the night we met."

"And this is—" I kissed his bare chest, unable to resist putting my lips on him. "—something that happens to your...people?"

He shuddered, wrapping his hands around my hips, and digging his fingers in. "Werewolf. You can say it."

"Bonding happens because you're a werewolf?" I peppered more kisses along his pec.

"Yes."

My other hand slid down his belly and I cupped him through his jeans. I couldn't stop myself if I tried. The word *need* didn't even begin to describe what I was experiencing. "Did I bond to you?"

His growled "no" was accented with a rough hand on my chin, tilting it up to kiss him.

I put two fingers between our lips. I wanted Eli more than I had ever wanted anything, but I also needed an explanation for this compulsion to climb him like a tree. He was irresistible under normal circumstances, but he was also sporting a gunshot wound and I was bruised and raw from battering waves. Neither of us should have been thinking about sex.

"Explain. Please."

That wrongness settled into his features, eyes glowing, face too angular. But as I studied him in the lamp light, I realized it wasn't *wrong*. It was *otherworldly*. My brain hadn't been able to grasp what I was seeing because it was so far outside of the reality that I knew.

"Say please again," he demanded.

"Please, Eli."

Our lips crashed into each other, two universes colliding in a cataclysmic explosion. My life as I knew it was destroyed with that kiss, my entire being breaking open, my soul bared.

It was abruptly interrupted with a pained hiss, and I wrenched away, freeing my hands from him before I could hurt him further. He grabbed for me, and I dodged, gently pressing him back with my body until he settled onto the couch.

"We need to stop," I panted. "I don't want to hurt you."

Eli pulled me onto his lap, lifting his hips to grind into me. "Every second that I'm not inside you hurts, Cady."

I slung my shirt over my head. It hit the floor with a wet slap. I was still soaked with salt water, tender and bruised. But Eli was right; the empty ache in my core was growing to a point of pain. I needed him inside me more than I needed air.

With one finger Eli tugged my bra low and my nipples tightened in the cold. He leaned down and circled his tongue around one. When I moaned, he moved more insistently, biting, and nibbling across my chest to the other one. I climbed off him long enough to shuck the rest of my damp clothes. Undoing his jeans, I grabbed the denim and yanked them off him too.

Then I climbed back onto his lap, sliding my core along his length. My hand tickled up his thigh, dipping beneath him to squeeze his balls. Eli bared his teeth, jerking his hips up again. I circled them with my pointer finger, watching the first taste of ecstasy soften the hard lines of his face.

We hadn't even started yet, and we were both moments from shattering.

"Cady," Eli growled my name, beseeching and warning all at once. It made so much sense now—that bestial way he claimed me with his body. How he sounded almost animal as he came into me. There was the Eli I saw and then there was more. That more crackled in an aura around him, feral energy that snapped at my skin.

I tightened my hold on his balls and tugged gently. Testing. Teasing. "What happens if you bite me?"

His teeth grazed the side of my jaw in answer. "I'll come before I get a chance to properly fuck you."

I wriggled myself over the tip of his cock, but I lifted when he tried to pump into me. Not yet. Not until I knew what I was getting into.

"So, I won't become like you?"

His voice was tortured. "It doesn't work that way."

With his good shoulder Eli shifted his arm around me, pressing a hand between my legs and sliding his finger along the seam of my core. "So wet for me. Let me take you, Cady. Let me make you mine."

Not yet. "And when you were on my porch that night? You weren't sleepwalking. You were *the other you.*"

"Yes. I couldn't help myself." His finger dipped inside, and his thumb pressed lightly against my clit. "Couldn't resist."

I gulped a desperate breath. A few more seconds and I was going to come undone. Eli was a lit match, and I was combustible. Deep, vibrating pride purred from his chest because he knew it, too.

"I had to have a taste of you."

"Is this what it felt like for you the whole time?"

"Like I might die if I'm not breathing the same air as you? Like the only sustenance that will keep me alive is *here*?" He tapped his thumb against my clit.

"Like that, yeah."

"Yes," he hummed.

"Damn." Then I was riding his hand, coming so hard my toes curled. "Damn, damn, damn."

There was something I was supposed to ask him, but my mind struggled to focus on anything besides Eli. His touch, his skin on mine, the way his cock flexed when I fisted it and began gliding my hand up and down.

"What—" I swallowed, trying to catch my breath. "What does it mean to be bonded?"

"Means you're mine." He nipped my neck, sucking the skin between his teeth. "Forever."

Forever.

Forever was a long time. A very long time with a man I'd known all of a month.

A month where I almost lost my life *twice.* And both times Eli was there to save me. He was a man worth taking a risk for.

I grabbed his wrist, bringing his hand up to cup my breast as I sank down onto him.

"Forever," I whispered against his lips.

Eli thrust up to meet me, filling me so deeply that I felt as if I had to choose between breathing or taking him into me. I chose him, inhaling raggedly as I rose up and sank down again. I tried to angle my body away from his injured shoulder, keeping pressure off his right side and holding back.

Eli didn't allow that for long. He snaked both arms around my waist, crushing me to him and lifting me. Then he dropped me down as he thrust up to meet me, taking control and moving so fast I could do nothing but hold on. I was flying toward that second orgasm fast, my legs quaking, breath hitching, eyes rolling shut.

"Let me see you." The tendons in his neck pulled taut as he neared the edge of his control. I knew by the husky tone of his voice that he was a heartbeat away from finishing.

I swept my gaze to his, captivated by the force of his presence. He took up so much space, filling the room with this unyielding power. It penetrated my skin, boring into my marrow and becoming a part of me. A ripple turned into a wave, and I was screaming his name as I cinched tight around him.

Another of those guttural noises left his throat, almost a roar, and he buried himself so deeply in me that we were no longer two moving parts, just one. One being, one existence all tangled up together. He inhaled my breath as we landed, coming back down one gasp at a time.

When my lips slanted over his it was languorous, heady, and sweet. The look on his face was akin to awe and I could feel him adoring me, not just in his expression but in the hollow of my chest. A tingle under my sternum.

"Is this what you meant?" I touched his chest where I felt that butterfly flutter of emotion.

His big palm settled between my breasts. "I didn't know it would feel like this. Until that night on the bayou, I didn't even know I could bond."

I wanted to know more. I had seven thousand questions to ask him about all of this. But the endorphins were fading, giving way to an aching stiffness that settled into my bones. The skin on my wrists throbbed and I didn't even want to think about the rest. There was too much to process. So much grief that would need to be sorted through.

It was much too heavy a burden to carry today. Today I wanted to cocoon myself in whatever this buzzing magic was that Eli put inside me.

I probably needed a shower first, though.

And belatedly I realized that we were naked in his living room and his brothers could walk back in at any moment. Gathering my tenuous energy, I climbed from his lap. I considered redressing, just to have cover in case another Barbeaux came barging in, but my clothes were too wet to bother with.

"Where are you going?" He caught my hand, reeling me back in.

I wiggled nervously. "To find dry clothes before one of your brothers walks in on us."

Thunder clouds darkened his eyes. "Better get to it before I have to punch Isaac with my weak side." He rolled his shoulder and tossed a left hook to demonstrate.

I tried for a smile, but I was suddenly exhausted down to my soul. "Don't do anything to rip those stitches."

I turned to head down the hall. I knew where the bathroom was, but I'd never actually been in there until today. The living room was the only room in Eli's house that I'd seen. And just last night I was packing a bag to come stay here indefinitely, sight unseen. Guess that was still happening.

Eli followed on my heel, but I stopped him, picking up his jeans and handing them to him. "Eli, you need to get back on that couch and rest."

"I can't."

I glared at him. "You can and you will."

"Cady—"

"I need a moment alone." He gave in to that, as I knew he would.

I dragged my body into his bathroom, and I wished I could appreciate the tawny granite counters, stone floor, and rustic wood accents. There was no tub, but the shower was the most luxurious I'd ever used. Water streamed delicately from a massive square showerhead. The spray covered most of the open space, preventing the cold from claiming the gap between the shower wall and me. It was the perfect pressure, like a summer rainstorm.

I was practically sleep walking as I hauled my towel clad body to Eli's bedroom, but I roused when I stepped through the door. For a bachelor, he kept his space unexpectedly neat. The bed was made, king sized with a blue quilt that managed to look masculine and cozy all at once. No laundry littered the floor, and the walls were decorated with colorful paintings of boats out on the bay.

The vaulted ceiling and exposed wood beams made me feel like I was in an A frame cabin in the woods. Combined with the howling wind and frigid temperature I could almost pretend we were tucked away in some distant mountains and all the rest was just a nightmare.

Was it overstepping to open Eli's dresser and dig through his clothes? He hadn't given me any restrictions, but we were miles away from being a couple without personal boundaries. I almost laughed then because Eli didn't know what personal boundaries were. The man was always in my business and my personal space.

I pulled on a massive sweatshirt and a pair of sweatpants that I had to double knot at the waist to keep from sliding. Then I sat on the edge of the bed, hugging my arms around myself as tears quietly tracked down my cheeks.

It didn't matter if I had boundaries over my personal stuff because I didn't have stuff. My grandparent's house, their pictures, all their memories—gone. My poetry. My favorite t-shirts.

Brandon robbed me of it and that made me so furious that I was almost glad he was dead. More tears flooded my face. What a horrible, terrible thing to think.

Deep in my lungs there were sobs that needed to escape. One of those violent cries that only grief can provoke. I was too weary for that now.

The last of my energy was expended trudging back into the living room. I dropped onto the couch next to Eli, wordlessly curling up against him and resting my head on his chest. His arm came around me, heavy and warm. Lips left a tender kiss on my forehead, and I closed my eyes.

"When my Nana died, I prayed for a new life." I sighed. "This isn't at all what I expected."

"It's going to be okay, darlin'."

I wanted to believe that so badly. "But we're still not safe. This isn't over."

"As long as I'm here, you're safe." He made the same promise before and so far, he kept it.

I nuzzled his neck. "I know."

I heard the smile in his voice when he told me to get some rest.

Chapter 33

Normal

Eli

I PRESSED A FINGER to my lip, hissing as my shoulder burned. Cady was curled around my left side, her toes tucked under my thigh, head nestled against my neck. My arm coiled around her, palm beneath the fabric of her borrowed sweatshirt to rest on her lower back. The hole in my chest burned and my body was stiff from holding this position for hours, but I would eat hornets before I moved and woke her. She felt fragile and small right now and I was going to handle her with all the delicacy a man like me had.

Isaac flicked hazel eyes across the living room, noticing Cady and dipping his chin in silent acknowledgment. His arms strained as he hefted handfuls of overflowing shopping bags. Halfway from the door he froze, nostrils flaring.

"Seriously?" He scowled at me. "You've got a bullet wound and you still can't keep it in your pants?"

It was impossible not to grin. "Couldn't help it. We bonded."

Isaac dumped his load on the kitchen island and stared at me. We were twins and the resemblance was clear—same chin, same nose, same smile. But that was where the commonalities ended.

It wasn't just the angular cut to his cheek bones or the sleek hairstyle that made it impossible for him to blend with the locals. Isaac was cocky, a little arrogant, and so devoid of sentimentality that he would burn family photos if I let him. Bonding was about as appealing as a rattlesnake to him.

Yet, there was a green glint in his eyes I almost wanted to call envy.

The only sound in the house was the shuffling of plastic bags and Cady's gentle breath. Now that my brother was here, I should follow her lead and get some rest. I was dog tired, hadn't slept in at least twenty-four hours. I might never sleep again, knowing that my cousin could show up at any moment.

Isaac was stacking boxes of 9mm ammo on the island when he casually asked, "What's it like to be bonded?"

My brother didn't ask casual questions, though. Not after so many years.

I knew he could feel my eyes on his back when I responded. "Well at first I thought I was going mad, and the beast wanted to kill her." I quieted, thinking back to those first days with Cady. "Feels like coming home. Like waking up to hot coffee and breakfast on a Sunday morning and the whole world is just right."

Isaac scoffed. "That's corny as shit."

"By the way," I murmured. "What did Jacques mean about you taking his mate? Didn't think he was the settling down type." Isaac's shoulders hiked up to his ears and he didn't say anything.

"You told us you were with a girl that knew him. What happened to her? Do you think we ought to reach out and see if she needs help? Can't imagine Jacques would be very forgiving if she rejected him."

"She wasn't his mate." My brother turned with a snap, his complexion oddly pale. "She was just some—" A war was waging on his face as his lips tried to form the rest of the words.

"Where have you been all month? We were worried about you."

He relaxed his shoulders, dipping his hands into the pockets of his jeans and leaning back against the counter. "Getting my dick wet."

"You know it was secrets that got us into this mess."

Isaac deflated, sinking onto one of the bar stools and dropping his elbows onto his knees. "Her name is Tara." I waited. Finally, he whispered, "What are the chances, Eli? For both of us to—it wasn't supposed to be possible."

"Saul lied." I shook my head. "Hey, don't look so surprised. He lied about Jacques too. Would have let us go on believing he was alive out there."

"Asshole. Why does he do that?"

"He thinks he's protecting us. Plus, I think lying sort of runs in the family. It's got to stop now."

"Which is your way of asking me to tell you everything."

I nodded.

"Tara was Jacques's girlfriend. She doesn't know about us, not until she accidentally saw him shift, but she doesn't believe it really happened. She didn't even know his real name. I don't—fuck, Eli, I don't know what to do. She *lived* with him. And she's from out of town, planning to leave any day. But now I've involved her in this war and she's going to get hurt."

"She's going to get killed."

He stopped himself mid-snarl. "Don't say shit like that."

"It's the truth. You saw what Jacques did to Cady. You gotta find this girl and be honest."

Isaac shook his head madly. "Bad idea."

"It's your only option."

"I'm not like you, Eli! I haven't been some heroic gentleman this whole time. I'm a piece of shit and she knows it."

"Who's a piece of shit?" Cady murmured, blinking blearily.

"You look like one," Isaac teased, glad to have an out from our conversation.

"Some things never change." The front door clicked shut and Saul slipped into the kitchen.

Isaac whipped around, posed like he was ready to karate chop the intruder. "Dammit Saul, I hate that."

"You would hear me coming if you paid attention to anything other than your hair."

Isaac ran a self-conscious hand through his hair and lifted his middle finger at Saul. He ignored Isaac, strolling into the kitchen and setting the shotgun on the counter. He reached for a beer bottle in the open fridge and popped the top.

"We won't have any unwanted visitors. Not until the Winter Solstice." Saul sank into the recliner and propped his feet on the coffee table.

"That's awfully specific." Cady yawned, stretching her legs across my lap like a happy cat.

"I took care of it."

Isaac had the sense to look alarmed. "What was the price to take care of it?"

"That's between me and Celine. You'll be safe from here to Isaac's woodpile. No guarantees once you leave the bayou."

"What about your house?" I prodded. "You going to stay with Isaac?"

Isaac opened his mouth to protest, his eyes rounding. It shouldn't be a problem for Saul to stay there. Isaac had two massive bedrooms and it wasn't like Saul was a slob. As far as roommates went, he was a great one.

Always quiet, didn't have a lot of stuff, ate outside, lived outside, sometimes even slept outside.

Cady perked up, cutting off whatever Isaac meant to say. "Celine? Like Madame Celine?"

I twisted to stare at her, the hairs on the back of my neck prickling. "You know her?" Everyone in Port O'Henry knew *of* Celine but Cady sounded more familiar than that.

"Well," she reddened, "I went to see her. When all this started."

Saul leaned his elbows on his knees. "What did she want from you?"

"Nothing. She said the first reading was free. Gave me a bunch of vague warnings." Cady's eyes widened. "But what she said to me about you...it was the reason I accepted your help."

Suspicion burned my throat. "What did she say about me?"

"That you were dangerous. And that I would probably die without you." Quieter, she added, "She said you would need me too."

"Sounds about right." Isaac was taking things out of the overstuffed freezer. "Who wants pizza?"

Now that the initial shock had worn off, Cady was curious. I wasn't surprised that she had a million questions. I *was* surprised that Saul answered them with zero hostility. He sounded like a professor, telling her about werewolves and curses as if it was a matter of historical fact that wasn't completely blowing her mind.

For the most part, I was quiet. Cady and my brothers were deep in conversation, her eyes alight. She was enthralled by the Barbeaux story, and I was enthralled with her. After everything we'd been through in the last two days, I couldn't believe we were all together in my living room, eating frozen pizza and relaxing like this was a normal family gathering.

It could be, I realized with a delicate spark of hope. Make a truce with Jacques—or kill him again—and push Isaac in the right direction with this girl and we might live downright normal lives.

"You're how old?" Cady raised her eyebrows at me. "I think I'm too young for you." She chewed her lip. "Wait, am I going to get old and die and you'll be young forever?"

Thank God that wasn't the case. "Our lifetimes are bound."

"Please tell me that doesn't mean I'm going to live forever too." She licked grease from her finger and even now my blood burned with want at the sight of her tongue.

"If you're lucky, you'll have another sixty years together." Saul tipped his bottle and downed the last of his beer, standing and brushing crumbs from his lap. He met my eyes, his like summer moonlight. "I hope you're lucky, brother."

Then Saul disappeared, but I wasn't worried.

Suddenly, the future didn't look so grim for the Barbeaux boys.

Chapter 34

Priceless

Cady

W HEN I FINALLY COLLAPSED into Eli's bed long before sunset, I fell into a deep, dreamless sleep. I don't know how long I slept, only that twice Eli woke me and insisted I drink some water. Once I stirred enough to find him beside me in bed, the glow of some western movie hitting my eyelids in shades of golden light.

Exhaustion was a stone in my middle and sleep was the bay. The weight of it dragged me down, down until I was lost in quiet, blissful nothing.

Eventually that nothing faded and strange flickers of wolf-men and crashing waves chased my weary mind. My eyes cracked open to see a light shining underneath the bedroom door. Eli was gone but I could hear the low timbre of his voice in the living room, probably talking to his brothers.

I didn't know what they planned to do next and at that moment, I didn't care. I was safe, wrapped in the coziest quilt, sprawled in a pile of pillows that smelled like Eli, and I wanted to stay there forever.

Until I noticed the other smell in bed with me. Saltwater and sweat clung to my skin. My hair was a matted, crusty mess and I was sure my breath could knock someone unconscious.

Grabbing a random handful of clothes from the selection Isaac bought the day before—or maybe days—and a bottle of cherry scented soap, I snuck down the hallway and into the bathroom. It was still strange being in Eli's house and I wasn't interested in letting his brothers see me in my disheveled state. I wasn't quite a guest, but this wasn't home either.

Eli wanted it to be. He had zero reservations about moving me in and playing house. I would have warmed up to the idea a lot more if I had a choice. I hadn't processed any of it yet and I intended to wash the grief bubbling up through my skin down the shower drain.

Thirty minutes later I stepped out of the water to find Eli leaning on the door frame, wearing nothing but a pair of jeans and a seductive smile. He held a cup of coffee with his left hand, favoring the right one. The bullet wound was still an angry pink color, but the stitches were gone.

My eyes widened. "How long was I asleep?"

"Long enough that I was tempted to find some smelling salts." He pointed at this chest. "Told you it couldn't kill me."

"No kidding."

We stared at each other, me clutching the towel tight around me as if he hadn't seen everything already. His gaze was molten, and I felt that tug in my chest, like Eli had a rope tied around me and he was reeling me in. I dropped the towel when I was a foot away, my insides warming as his eyes raked over me. I took the coffee from his hand, sipping and licking my lips.

Eli took it back, his movement so careful and precise as he set it down on the bathroom counter that I was almost afraid. Not a true fear but that thrilling adrenaline that spiked when he prowled toward me.

My breath left me in a rush and suddenly I was perched on the bathroom counter, my ass nearly falling into the sink. Before I could regain my breath Eli had his pants undone and was pulling me forward until I slipped from the edge of the counter and down onto his cock. Gravity rocked him in to the hilt, then he caught me, holding me against him and shuddering.

His voice had dropped several octaves when he murmured, "You are perfection."

I expected another intense, hanging-on-to-him-for-dear-life thrust. Instead, Eli was tender, building this slow burning tension until my core was fluttering desperately on the brink of that delicious sensation. That was the point I became impatient, nipping at his chest and urging him on with a wiggle of my hips.

Grinning, he obliged me, pumping fast and hard. I was clawing and screaming as I orgasmed, uncaring if his brothers were still here to hear us. Making love to Eli was a cathartic release, my mind temporarily fracturing too much to feel anything but pleasure. Nothing should feel this good, this freeing, but I hoped it never stopped feeling like this.

When we finished Eli lowered me carefully from the counter, retrieving my discarded towel and drying my hair. He pumped a handful of lotion from some sweet, scented bottle he must have grabbed from my stuff and massaged it into my legs. The final touch was a languid kiss that left stars sparkling in my eyes.

Now that I wasn't so distracted by all those hormones, I realized there was a weird scent layered under the floral fragrance from the lotion. And Eli had black smudges across his face.

"Why do you smell like an ashtray?" I sniffed him.

He smiled so bright I almost shaded my eyes. "Saul and I went on an adventure this morning. Get dressed and meet me downstairs."

Even with the wind blowing salty air off the bay, the ashtray smell was stronger downstairs. Eli was still shirtless, almost skipping as he dragged me under the house and onto the covered driveway. Saul was in the shadow of the house, arms crossed, and shoulder wedged into the wood. The only greeting I got in exchange for my wave was a flicker in his steely eyes.

I turned, noticing a small collection of cardboard boxes. They were covered in black handprints and reeked of smoke.

"Probably ought to leave it all in the garage for now. I haven't figured out how to get rid of the smell." Eli waved at the boxes of soot like he was a game show host. "It was hell getting up there with no stairs and Saul put his foot through the living room floor, but your bedroom was mostly untouched by the fire. Not a lot was salvageable, but I took everything that wasn't melted."

"My—my bedroom? You were in my house?"

My stuff. This was my stuff. I reached for a filthy black and white photograph of my grandparents on their wedding day, hugging it to my chest. The glass was broken but the picture was mostly intact. I didn't realize I was crying until Eli wiped a tear from my chin with his thumb.

I became frantic, carefully taking every item from the boxes and laying them on the concrete. There were framed pictures, a photo album, and my Nana's favorite teacup. Items that really had no worth but to me were priceless. My laptop was crushed, and I doubted it would turn on but maybe a tech shop could get the data off for me.

At the bottom of the last box was a leather-bound journal. The chestnut color of the leather was faded, and the edges of the pages were dusty and rumpled. When I flipped the journal open though, every handwritten word was there. Years of my work, the most precious belonging I had.

"Thank you," I whispered to Eli. I turned to Saul, who looked thoroughly uncomfortable with my emotional display. "Thank you."

Saul gave a slight nod before tucking his hands in his pockets and walking off. His figure melded with the shadows of trees and then he was gone. Saul was strange and brusque, but I had a feeling there was a good man under all that hair and brooding.

"I know you didn't get to choose this, but I want you to feel at home all the same." Eli rubbed his jaw, nerves making him twitch his bottom lip. "And I hope that even if it's not your first choice, I can make you happy out here on the bayou."

"You seriously scaled a burned building just to bring me a bunch of keepsakes?"

"Darlin', I took a bullet for you. This was nothing."

"I don't understand." Theoretically I understood the bond, but I just couldn't fathom all of this. Everything Eli did. Constantly trying to make me happy.

"It's the Barbeaux way." He shrugged, trying to come across casual when he added, "We take care of the people we love."

I wrapped my arms around his neck, kissing him all over his face as he laughed. "I might not have chosen it today, but even if all the circumstances were different and we met while reaching for the same container of night crawlers at *Rocky's*, I would choose this."

I kissed him hard on the mouth just for good measure. "You are my first and only choice, Eli Barbeaux."

Chapter 35

Sacrifice

Saul

A SWEET LITTLE BELL chimed when I shoved the door open, and I winced. I hated this place with all my being.

It wasn't anything against Celine. My brothers believed she was the devil incarnate but I knew better. Witches could cause all manner of chaos and it was never without consequence.

Magic had a price and the wielder always paid first. We were living evidence of that.

I wasn't sure what part of this little shop bothered me most. Maybe it was as simple as my animal instinct not to get cornered in small spaces. Or maybe it was the sparkling rocks and hippie music and disgusting cloud of incense. My skin itched and I had the urge to pace while I waited for Celine to finish with whatever gullible fool was mumbling tearfully on the other side of the wall.

I forced myself to move slowly, letting my feet guide me to the corner where Celine kept framed pictures from early Port O'Henry. My brothers and I were front and center, me a statue next to their beaming faces. I still remembered that day, Isaac teasing in an attempt to make us laugh, Eli prodding me in the side when I refused to smile.

They were happy then and I was pleased to see Eli happy now, even if it did go against everything my father taught me. In one night, Eli had broken every Barbeaux rule, taken an enormous risk—and won. The battle, not the war, of course, but he saved the day, got the girl. All the things my brother deserved.

So why did I feel gutted every time he smiled at Cady?

I knew why and the moment I let my thoughts wander too close to that terrain my limbs started to shake. *Not now, not here.*

That God awful bell dinged again, and an older woman bumbled out to the parking lot, leaving a trail of perfume in her wake.

Celine stood in the doorway to her reading room, too graceful and poised for a woman her age. I was pretty sure she could make herself look younger if she wanted to, but I supposed she was keeping up an image as much as the rest of us.

Being old was easier. After a certain age people stopped questioning your presence, just believed you were on your way to death as quickly as they were.

"Bingo!" Celine clapped her hands, smiling in that wicked way that revealed what she really was.

"Excuse me?"

"I've just won at Barbeaux bingo. All three brothers under my roof in one month. There must be something in the air." She waved me into that dreaded back room, humming cheerily to herself.

The statues in this room terrified me as a child. Ironic since several of them depicted my kind. Even after all these years, a hint of that fear lingered. Was it the statues or was it accompanying my father during his dealings with Celine? I could almost hear his impatient voice, barking orders for me to pay attention.

"First of the First. You must know everyone's weaknesses and how to use them to your advantage."

That was why he brought me with him. I was meant to study Celine, to find her soft spots and learn to exploit them. I never found any, and I took a beating for my worthlessness more than once.

"Sweet Saul." her smile turned saccharine as she dropped into her fluffy green chair. "Do tell me what you need."

Celine played a character, and I never could tell which one was the honest version of her. Maybe they all were, and her extended life made her as bat shit crazy as me.

"Wards."

I knew she could do it. Her shop, which doubled as her home, was warded from anyone meaning harm. A man with ill intention would walk right by the place, seeing only a vacant building. There were also wards that could make a location impossible to find.

That was what I needed; Jacques's men driving aimlessly through the bayou for hours, never able to make the conscious choice to turn down our driveways.

Her smile dropped. "That's no simple task. There will be a significant price."

"I'll pay it. I need wards to deter anyone and everyone that means harm."

"I wasn't aware you had that many enemies."

I propped myself on the arm of the chair opposite hers, knowing better than to sit. Sitting put me at a disadvantage, made it harder to attack quickly.

"Jacques is alive, which I'm sure you already know."

She pursed her lips, and I felt the lie when she said, "I didn't know he was dead."

"Would'a done me some good to get a heads up about him," I chided. "Now Eli's got a bullet hole in him, and his mate nearly drowned."

"Mate?" Celine's eyes sparkled, momentarily going red. "So, he figured things out with Cady. How sweet."

I narrowed my eyes at her. "Thought you didn't get specifics?"

Celine swore she got only brief, vague images. It was up to her as the clairvoyant to put the pieces together.

Then it dawned on me. "Eli came to see you about Cady."

"Both of your brothers have come calling."

Shit, I forgot all about Isaac and this woman he was with. "What did Isaac want?"

"Ask him yourself. I'm not your mother."

I crossed my arms, hardening myself into the version of Saul that everyone expected to see. This camaraderie between us was false and I needed to watch my step. I liked Celine but I never had found her weaknesses and that made me leery.

"I need wards. Can you do them or not?"

"Yes, but they won't last forever. Only until the Winter Solstice. You'll need to renew them then." She didn't beat around the bush. "And I'll need your blood."

If I had any other option, I would have walked out that door without another word. Blood from my kind was powerful stuff and I shuddered to think what she would use it for. I had no doubt my brothers and I could take Jacques and a pack on our own. It would be a bloody, violent war but we could do it.

That was before we had a human in the mix, maybe two since Isaac had inadvertently involved this woman that Jacques claimed was his mate.

Fucking Isaac. Couldn't keep it in your damn pants?

Eli could believe what he wanted about me. I didn't wish harm on Cady, and I hadn't lied to him about bonds to hurt him. Even the night of the full moon, when I lost it to my rage, I knew I wouldn't have killed my brother. Probably did more damage than I should have but I only meant to beat it into his stupid head that this wasn't a good idea.

Barbeauxs ruined people and I didn't want to watch him lose everything when this woman walked away from him.

Now that I'd seen them together, I was willing to admit that I was wrong. Eli didn't ruin people. Eli was the best of us—kind, selfless, reluctantly violent. Even Isaac could be considerate, if he felt like it.

It was me who ruined people. Me who had no right to bond. I let that cloud my judgment.

I wanted the best for my brothers. I would do anything for them. And I had, over and over, from the time they were children. I took the wrath of our father, bore the burden of firstborn without complaint.

Now it was my turn to bear the burden again. To sacrifice for the only people I truly cared about. Even if they would never know what I was willing to give up for them.

I took a piece of paper and pen from one of the cluttered bookshelves surrounding the table, scribbling out three addresses and sliding the paper Celine's way.

She scanned the words, stopping on the last one and arching a brow at me. "This address isn't on the bayou. Who lives here?"

I thought about lying to her and saying it was one of Isaac's rentals, but I knew there was no use. She would see right through me.

"Doesn't matter. Can you do it or not?"

Celine turned to a glass cabinet tucked behind her chair and rummaged around, turning back with a half-pint amber jar and a small dagger.

I took both, holding my wrist over the jar with the knife positioned at the veins near the surface of my skin. "What happened here tonight doesn't leave this room. I want your word."

Her eyes dipped to the paper again, a quick flick at the last address. I knew if she was curious enough, she would figure it out.

"No one else will know. You have my word."

I nodded, dragging the blade across my wrist, and watching as rivulets of blood trickled into the bottom of the glass. With a growl I shuttered my eyes, willing the beast inside. He never did like the sight of his own blood.

But with my eyes closed I couldn't stop the visions of dark, flowing hair and irises like warm coffee. They bombarded me, one after another, until I could almost hear her voice, feel it like summer rain speckling my skin and soothing that constant, simmering fury.

I ruin people, I reminded myself as my head swam, my blood overflowing the jar and spilling ominously across the table.

Thank you for reading Shroud of Exile! Want to see more from Eli? Join my newsletter and I'll send you some bonus chapters from his perspective.

Gulf Coast Homesick

Gulf Coast Homesick by Cady Barber

Sometimes I wonder how a place
with water poisoned by manmade detritus
and grating gravelly sand and gargantuan burs
and seething snakes and eager alligators
hungry for hapless geriatrics on kayaks,
can also have sunsets like orange sherbet,
decadent swirls the color of citrus sweet,
and seagulls singing merrily on sandbars,
and plump neighbors with cherry faces,
waving and honking and welcoming you
like grandmother waiting on the porch
with rum on her breath and chocolate on her hands,
smiling like you've finally come home.

A Note from the Author

There are several thousand people that I have to thank for this book. Some of them are reading this now, some of them will never know this story existed. Those hardy Texas strangers that inspired the Barbeaux history will always have a piece of my heart.

The first whispers of Shroud of Exile came to me years ago, when I was just a girl standing on a rotten pier in who-the-hell-cares, Texas. It was a nothing town with a garbage beach and the air reeked of fish and diesel.

I loved it.

I have a strange affinity for the places less traveled. Destinations so off the beaten path that it feels like I'm an explorer discovering a new culture for the very first time. That's the type of town Port O'Henry was meant to be. A tiny, foreign place right smack in the middle of the state that brags about it's bigness.

I'm eager to revisit it in the next book, and I hope you are too!

With love,
Moira

Also By Moira Kane

Silver Bullet Security

Relentless

Dragon Brides Series

Blood Feud
Black Heart
Midnight Ruin
Forgotten Daughters
Birthright

Beasts of Barbeaux Bayou

Shroud of Exile
Haven of Shadows

About the Author

Moira Kane is a paranormal romance author addicted to creating happy endings with a little magic and mayhem sprinkled in. She enjoys writing ferocious, shape-shifting, arrogant men and the bold and clever women who love them.

When she's not writing, Moira can be found nose-deep in a romance novel or searching the woods for her reclusive husband. Some of her other titles include baker, tree-hugger, dog whisperer, mushroom enthusiast, and weird homeschool mom.

NEVER MISS A THING!

 tiktok.com/@moirawritesromance

 instagram.com/moirawritesromance